Beyond Destination
A Collection of Short Stories

Book One

Charlie Triano

Fiction

Beyond Destination
A Collection of Short Stories
Copyright © 2017/2018 Charles Triano
All rights reserved

Cover Art / Photograph © C Triano

The Library of Congress © 2017 / 2018

ISBN-10: 0-9987396-0-X

ISBN-13: 978-0-9987396-0-1

About the Author

Mr. Triano went to the State University of New York at Albany while still attending high school, where, as a senior he taught a semester of music theory and graduated with accolades in creative writing; though his major interest at the time was art. Shortly after commencement ceremonies Mr. Triano relocated to California and went to UC Berkeley. While there he was generously offered, and accepted, an honorary, if not exemplary degree of windowpane acid, which helped enlighten him to the elusive, if not discouraging realization that what he had essentially been participating in were the remnants of an abandoned revolution. Several well-lived, and well-loved years later, Mr. Triano journeyed to France where he continued his studies while residing in Paris. It was while at the Sorbonne that he was introduced to a misguided cast of expats who overindulged in cheap red wine and French cigarettes while in search of dead writers, though not at Pere Lachaise as one would think. When that ill-fated pursuit was inevitably met with disenchantment, as one would expect, their literary survival was challenged yet again when confronted with overpriced and overcrowded, and what were certainly now theatrically staged cafes. Upon his return to California, specifically The Bay Area, Mr. Triano dedicated the following decade to instructing himself at the piano. But it was the immeasurable accumulation of life experiences that eventually brought him back to writing. Mr. Triano feels obliged at this point to state that it wasn't his sole intention to mislead, or for that matter, to misinform the reader with spurious particulars concerning his academic accomplishments, which may give reason to reassess or even doubt his carefully chosen words. Mr. Triano wishes to be implicitly, if not earnestly candid, if for no other reason than to assure the reader that it wasn't his prime objective to be deliberately deceptive, as he also hoped to be entertaining as well. Additionally, he'd like not to be judged by degree, or lack thereof, which is often socially and academically the case. So, to reestablish the reader's trust, Mr. Triano would like to affirm that he never actually matriculated, or attempted to matriculate, at any of the aforementioned-universities. The confirmable truth is, Mr. Triano merely visited these institutions with a variety of motives in mind; some dubious, some innocently misdirected by hormonal or sophomoric curiosity. The fact of the matter is, Mr. Triano did go to SUNY, if only on occasion to play guitar under a shady tree on campus in hopes of dating above his station; just as his time at Berkeley was solely, if not romantically, spent protesting what was the popular war of that era. And if forced to further clarify his misconstrued and vague wording, it was on an extended youthful sojourn abroad that Mr. Triano succumbed, or rather resigned to, the obligatory lifestyle of cheap red wine and French cigarettes while in Paris, and not necessarily for frugal reasons alone; while reading The Tropic of Cancer, in now historic and costly cafes. But for now, Mr. Triano has chosen not to expand on those tales in this tome of short stories in fear of possibly spoiling what remains of those cherished, if not questionable, though certainly heart-felt recollections. Perhaps when they're less discernible to memory, which they are no doubt destined to eventually become, and in need of resuscitation; he may choose at that time to attempt to re-inflate them again in fiction. Until then, Mr. Triano recommends, this, his critically ignored collection of short stories entitled, Beyond Destination.

Also by Charlie Triano

Après L'Amour – One Hundred One Poems ©

Forthcoming-

Glimpses of Life & Its Brush with Celebrity
...Not Quite a Memoir ©

The Day Before Tomorrow ©
A Collection of Short Stories - Book Two

Bar Stories ©

For the many friends, no longer here to live their tales
or share the ones we had together…
And my sister June, who shared so many of mine.

"The hero looked a lot like you, and his lover looked a lot like me."

'Fantasy' – Leon & Mary Russell

Acknowledgments

Special Thanks To

Sharon Risedorph for proofing this collection of stories, not once, but multiple times, and still retaining a genuine interest in them. And of course, for over forty years of loving friendship.

Mike Phillips: our Zulu dancer in the sky.

Contact info:
Charlie Triano
PO Box 543
Sausalito, CA
94966

beyond-destination@charlietriano.com
www.charlietriano.com

Table of Contents

Familiar Rooms - 1
Bedding - 7
With Your Heart On - 13
Scenes from The Road - 21
Neighbors - 45
The Old Man - 51
Caught in A Doorway - 57
The Attack - 69
About the Room - 75
Special Needs - 93
Stalemate - 99
Merci - 111
From Carlton To Carton - 123
Routine Questioning - 129
Beyond Destination - 135
Hardy Hughes Makes His Move - 153
Loving Daughter - 157
Winners & Losers - 165
Raising the Bar - 171
The Interviews - 185
Making the Cut - 193
Scenes from The Island -197

Beyond Destination

Familiar Rooms

Claire was the last person that Jake expected to see at his door that morning, though he shouldn't have been that surprised after what happened to Bess. But he knew Claire was also curious by nature and would have taken any opportunity to drop by and see him. It was a quality he had once found endearing, though not as much now, as he was certain the true reason she'd come was to see how the last few years had been for him; wondering if he'd married and divorced as she had, and to see if life had been as disappointing as it had been for her; and if he'd also regretted not holding onto what they'd had as she did now.

She walked in as if she still had a visceral investment in him and the place. He once admired her tenacity, but he found it a bit forward now, if not intrusive.

"I see that you're still single," she said, offering a slight smile as she glanced around the room.

"Not really," Jake said.

"What I mean is, you're still living alone, as I can see the place lacks a woman's touch." Then added as she turned away from him, "That sacrifice was never easy for you, was it Jake? It seems not much has changed."

Claire appeared visibly satisfied as she toured and touched and teased the remains, in search of memories, perhaps even remembering a dream.

"The place hasn't changed," he agreed. "It's pretty much the same. But I've changed some."

"You look the same Jake," she said, unmistakably flirting now. "You'll never change."

He recognized the familiar tone. It was one he'd once held dear.

Claire was still an attractive woman. Her strong, lovely, Jewess features were smooth and delicate, almost ageless. He couldn't deny a part of him still wanted her, still loved her. The years hadn't lessened his desire for her skin or for the taste of it on his parted lips. But he'd chose to live without it, however reluctantly at first. But he would always have those memories to cherish.

Jake found her more aggressive, more cynical now. Pain has a way of doing that to people. As she spoke, her words made her seem less attractive. In fact, her tone began to eat away at the image he'd had of her, the very one that he chose to hold onto even after their breakup, as he attempted to find comfort in other women. He'd held that image so tightly that it often felt as if he were cheating on her.

"I'm very sorry to hear about Bess," he said with an earnest measure of compassion. "She was a beautiful woman."

Claire studied his face, searching for something that she knew probably wasn't there, though had suspected had been for years.

"I know you were close," she said watching for his reaction.

"We were, at least back then," he said.

Claire kept her eye on him.

"Close enough," she said, brushing it off as a joke now, "that I thought there was something going on between the two of you."

"Were you that jealous of Bess?"

"I was jealous of her qualities; jealous that she was able to hold onto them even with all the pain she went through."

"If it's any comfort, we only shared a few laughs," he said.

She let that truth settle where it had always been, though perhaps still not fully convinced.

"Funny," she said attempting a smile, "I can still hear her laugh."

"It certainly was adhesive. She lived life to the fullest."

"I envied that as well," she confessed as she continued to walk around the familiar room.

Jake watched as she continued to evaluate it, though he hoped her visit would be less confrontational than the last time they saw each other; but he knew it would eventually come to that if for no other reason than it always did.

It was a large space divided by partitions, separating the sleeping area from the main room, and another from the office and the kitchen. There were tall narrow windows on one wall that allowed the morning light in.

Claire passed through the bright beams of sunlight as she went across the familiar space.

"I see you still have this," she whispered as she lightly traced her finger along the circular top of a slender glass vase. "I gave you this shortly after we met." She smiled. "I'm surprised you still have it."

Before Jake could share in the sentiment, she was onto something else. It was obvious that she'd come with a purpose, one she'd gradually reveal, as if seductively slipping out of transparent lingerie; another image that he'd held onto after their breakup.

Jake was hypnotized by her every move as he'd always been. He could feel it tighten in his loins. He could almost taste it on his lips, but he knew he couldn't give into it.

"You've become so neat and organized. Even your clothes are carefully arranged. It seems you finally grew up, Jake." Claire offered another smile. Then added, "And four suits? You must be doing well. I never knew you to have more than two."

Claire continued her tour without need of a docent to help clarify things as she went. It was obvious she still knew her way. He silently observed her as she circled the room, her intent clearly sexual now. In fact, every move she made was familiar in that respect, as she playfully toyed with various props as she went, as if teasing them, and him. But he knew her touch and its tempting grasp, and its undeniable capabilities; even from a distance he could feel it.

In a low deep voice, Jake whispered her name.

"Claire?" he said gently as if trying to reach out to someone in a trance, or a deep sleep.

She failed to respond.

"Claire?" he said again, this time a bit louder.

It was obvious she wasn't listening.

She continued her sojourn, as if searching for a part of her past, perhaps hoping to find something that she'd lost along the way; not unlike opening a book to where she left off, or having marked a favorite passage, in hopes of continuing a cherished, if not delayed storyline.

She moved gracefully about the room like a retired dancer hoping to recapture an audience she'd lost.

She finally volunteered in a soft voice, "What Jake? What is it?"

She anticipated his words, no doubt expecting the same ones that he'd passionately repeated over and over to her as he'd held her in his arms when they were together.

Her back was to him now.

"I need to tell you something, Claire."

"I need to tell you something as well," she said.

"This is important."

"This is just as important." She turned to look back at him briefly over her shoulder.

"There's something you need to know," he said.

"I already know," she whispered. "I can see it in your eyes."

He came closer. "Claire, I …."

Just then a key went into the distant lock and the loft door swung open.

"Hello?" a voice echoed cheerfully, shattering the room and the mood along with it. In that moment, it was as if an hourglass had been smashed to the floor and time along with it.

"Am I interrupting?"

"No, of course not," Jake said as he quickly stepped away from Claire, acknowledging now what had obviously been a bad idea.

"Are you sure?"

"No, I'm glad you're here. I was just going to tell Claire about you."

Claire stared blankly into what was now a forgotten distance. It wasn't the view that she'd expected, and certainly not the one she came to see. Her shoulders involuntarily slumped like a waning marionette at the close of a performance. The magnetic spell that she had gradually weaved through the room disappeared; and in that same moment, the stardust evaporated as the sunlight slipped from the window, leaving the room in matted tones and shadows, which revealed its truer nature to her now. It had entirely escaped her as she'd danced around it, cleverly scrutinizing it for traces of another woman; that a man with a similar build and taste in clothing, had also lived there. As Claire looked around, she wondered how she'd missed it now, for it was there if she'd wanted to see it.

"This is Winston," Jake said cautiously.

Claire was unable to formulate the words to respond. It was as if she'd forgotten the lines to a well-rehearsed play. In fact, in that moment, she was incapable of even improvising. She felt exposed and betrayed now, though more by herself than by him as she stood in the middle of the room with nowhere to turn.

"Claire?" Jake tried again.

"How did I get it so wrong?" she finally said.

"Don't Claire."

Without acknowledging Winston or the fact that he was in Jake's life now, she added, "Was it always wrong?"

"It was never wrong," he insisted.

"No?" she asked, as if questioning herself now.

"It was never wrong," Jake said in an echoed whisper.

"The truth?"

"The truth, Claire? I loved you more than anything."

"And now?"

"It's different now."

"Would you have loved me again?"

"If the time were right. But a part of me will always love you."

Her empty palm softly stroked the air as if it were intended for his face.

"You haven't changed, Jake," she said in a low voice. "But I have. I'm not the same woman I once was."

"Don't doubt yourself, Claire," he said hoping to comfort her. "You're going through a lot and I know you're hurting. Why don't you have a seat?"

She ignored the suggestion as she continued to balance herself.

"I never truly considered it a possibility, regardless of our having talked about it. I certainly never visualized it," she said. "And I never expected you to fall in love with someone else, mostly because we were perfect together. At least, I thought we were. But how conceited of me to think you wouldn't fall in love again, be it with a man or another woman. How vain of me to think that I was the only one you'd ever love, or that I'd had that big of an effect on you."

Claire gathered her thoughts, hoping to hold onto what was obviously disappearing in front of her eyes; her past, and any promise she might have

4

had for a future with him.

"You were my entire life at one time," Jake said.

She wasn't listening.

"But now it has a face," she continued, as if she were looking up from a hospital bed. "And a nice face too," she added, acknowledging Winston for the first time.

She was obviously at odds with herself.

"I shouldn't have come," she said. "In fact, I should go."

"No, please stay. I'm glad you came. I only wish that it had been under better circumstances, and not about Bess."

Claire repeated the name as if she'd forgotten her mother had recently passed-away.

"It wasn't about Bess. Well, maybe at first. But I needed something or someone familiar to help take away the pain; failing that, someone to at least help lessen it."

Jake could see that it was no longer about Bess now.

"I certainly haven't helped with that."

"No, I'm okay. But I should go."

"Stay. I was about to offer you a glass of wine before Winston arrived."

"Wine would be good," she said, knowing that she needed something to calm her nerves. "Yes, wine would be very good. Thank you."

"You two relax, I'll get it," Winston said.

Claire finally sat and leaned fully back into the couch, and as she did, it seemed as if every muscle in her body had atrophied. But that was because she felt helpless in that moment, and no longer in control. Claire was also forced to reflect on what initially motivated her to come in the first place, if not the outcome as well, which made her feel like a fool now. That truth was indisputable. And even as she reluctantly resigned to it, she wasn't the kind of woman who was accustomed to being defeated, certainly not for a second time. But she knew Jake's world would be inaccessible to her now, and that she would never be able to acclimate to it, regardless of the love she still had for him.

While caught in that solitary and ambiguous moment, the room she had once lovingly embraced seemed to vanish before her, and along with it, the memories she cherished; as even the light appeared rearranged and strangely unfamiliar now.

When Winston returned, he carefully handed Claire a large glass of red wine, which she anxiously took and proceeded to empty in one swift gulp.

Winston gave Jake a worried look. "That can't be good," he whispered.

"It's not," Jake said, bracing himself as he recalled a similar occurrence years earlier.

A moment later, Claire skillfully lobbed the empty glass of wine across the familiar room with near practiced precision.

Bedding

A petite young woman came to see about buying the mattress he had for sale, though she seemed to be equally attracted to the room and perhaps even the man who slept in it. Maybe it was the way the sun captured the coral painted walls and white trim, or the drawings that hung on them; or even the piano that seemed to fit so well in the bay window.

It was a charming and inviting room.

He said hoping to get her attention as she danced about, "Just so you know, it has no history." Vance couldn't be certain, but by the look on her face, she seemed offended by that fact. "What I'm trying to say," he said hoping to clarify exactly what he'd meant, "is that it's still virgin, if you know what I mean."

As sad and true as that fact was, Vance thought it a good selling point. He'd always been suspicious of what sexually transpired on the mattresses that he'd slept on in motels; or even in the finer, more elegant hotels, as he suspected that money tended to align itself with kinkier activity. Of course, any remnant of that insipid imagery was invisible to the naked eye; as it had been camouflaged and professionally staged to appear immaculate, and any trace of its unsavory history cleverly eradicated and intentionally topped off with a delicately positioned piece of gold-foiled chocolate on a freshly cased pillow.

She attempted a smile, but it was more a sad one, as if that fact had diminished the possibility of taking that part of him with her if she decided to buy it.

An assortment of colorful people came to inquire about the mattress that afternoon. A large man with an even larger wife came by, who laughed loudly as she settled deeper and deeper into the memory foam until she finally had to fight her way back out of it.

"It's very nice," the woman offered once she'd recovered from her struggle out of the abyss. Then as she straightened her clothes, she added, "But I don't think it's for us."

That fact was obvious to everyone else in the room, especially the two young girls who patiently waited their turn. And when they finally did climb on, they kept a discreet distance between them, as if hoping to conceal their apparent lifestyle.

At one point a short queue formed, which made Vance think of it as an amusement park ride.

After patiently waiting their turn, an older couple cautiously mounted the mattress, curious, if not fearful of the memory foam.

"It's like sleeping on the moon," the man said with gleeful surprise as his wife fell into a catatonic, if not dreamlike state, as if drifting off into a celestial orbit.

It had never occurred to Vance that buying a mattress could be such a romantic adventure. But as he watched several couples try it out, he realized given enough time, some lost a measure of their inhibition, even under the watchful eye of others, as they exposed a sexual side of their relationship.

All the while the petite woman stood in the middle of the room like a student in a museum watching others come and go. She had the figure of a ballerina and an accent that he thought may have been Romanian; one that he imagined leaned more toward The Bolshoi than Balanchine.

She stood erect in a low-cut gray leotard and a short matching skirt; a single-braid ran down her slender muscular back, posed as if absorbing the room as well as his life. Though the longer Vance watched her, it seemed as if she were absorbing applause after a triumphant performance; her delicate, strong frame, balanced and perfectly still as if waiting to take a deserved bow. Her well-toned arms were draped elegantly by her side like quarter notes anticipating the next musical phrase, ready to articulate a movement as a seasoned dancer might. But Vance couldn't help but notice a cool sadness about her as well.

"Eleven hundred," he restated, though she hadn't asked this time.

He couldn't help but acknowledge a measure of flirtation in her body as she swirled around ready to do battle with the price. But just then a nervous voice broke the air.

"Honey, are you going to buy it, or should I put more money in the meter?"

Vance could tell by the fragile and cracked tone in his voice that it wouldn't necessarily be his to sleep on if she did buy it. It was more a voice that hoped to, as his involvement in her life was no doubt limited, as was their history. Because it was obviously too early in their relationship for him to offer his opinion, as he seemed to exist mainly in her peripherals; just as he was positioned now, off to the side at the top of the stairs in the doorway. There was a strict and undeniable strength in her silence that Vance knew had probably emasculated him on more than one occasion.

Proving that point, she chose not to respond to his inquiry.

Vance thought it odd that she hadn't tested the mattress as others had, but in doing so she'd have made herself seem vulnerable, and he knew she wasn't about to reveal that side of herself; a side that would also expose her horizontal charms, or lack of, which he suspected might be less practiced. But she had that classic and alluring look most men would find attractive, though few would be able to bridle, as she insisted on being in control. It wasn't so much her words but her exquisite beauty that would undoubtedly steer and direct every step of her relationship.

As Vance watched her analyze the room, he was convinced that she had expected her undeniable charisma to hypnotize him just as easily. The look was unmistakable. Vance had come across it on numerous occasions, so he came prepared. It was a look that he thought was best viewed as a piece of art; a sculptured figurine, though in this case not as fragile. Perhaps more a cherished season ticket to be admired and discussed during intermission.

Vance patiently waited for her counter offer, though he wasn't going to compromise on the price.

Finally, she said, her trained body taking a practiced twirl, "I will offer you eight hundred, no more."

He'd give her kudos for her performance, but he wasn't going to give on the price.

"It's a brand new Tempur-Pedic. I've only had it a couple of weeks. I can't possibly go less than eleven-hundred."

He could tell that his words offended her, as she obviously wasn't used to being challenged, or denied her way. But she seemed even more attracted to him now because of it.

"I will give you a thousand," she said in a lilting voice, her lips slightly pursed as if making a runway turn.

He sensed her spirit break as he held firm to his price. He wasn't going to let her pull him willingly into her pas de deux; or give up the lead if he did.

Failing to win him over with her well-rehearsed charms, she appeared deflated, but even more determined now.

Her timid friend was still balanced in the doorway, uncertain of what to do or say, clueless of the fact that he'd no doubt have his hands full later that evening, even if he didn't end up carrying the playing field down to the car. Because Vance was certain her passion would be just as intense as her rage. He also knew the poor guy was in way over his head, and unaware that he was already drowning in the shallow end.

As the challenging beauty circled the bed like a bird hunting her prey, an elegant young woman slipped into the room, a set of pearls gracing her smooth and delicate neck.

"Do you mind if I sit on it?" she asked demurely.

"No, of course not," Vance said.

The young woman guardedly perched herself on the edge of the foam mattress, barely balancing against what he suspected were her social ethics, no doubt preferring to have been chaperoned under the circumstances.

"It's not for me," she said in a reserved whisper, offering an innocent smile. She kept her shoulders straight as she gently glided her gloved hand over the surface of the mattress. "I thought to get it for my cat."

Vance watched the ballerina, as he thought of her now, measure the challenge of her competition, as he was sure she was ready to strike.

"You can't be serious?" the ballerina shouted bombastically, her hands firmly cupped on her slender hips. "An eleven-hundred-dollar bed for your cat? What did your daddy buy you, a Bengal tiger?"

The young woman was obviously defenseless, and discreetly offended. Vance thought to intervene on her behalf, but she vanished as quietly and gracefully as she'd appeared. Wouldn't it be ironic, he thought, if her family was in fact a benefactor of the ballet? He'd have loved to be within earshot of that conversation during the intermission of her performance.

"Can you believe that?" the ballerina said. "A bed for her cat!"

Her frail and accommodating boyfriend was still leaning partially in the doorway shaking his head in agreement like a trained puppy.

Vance had never sold anything before. He'd either left things behind or gave them to friends. But the mattress had come at considerable expense, being a medicinal purchase for a herniated disc. But after trying it out for a couple of weeks it failed to remedy his discomfort. But it made him realize that buying a mattress was more like choosing a musical instrument, as he'd be equally intimate with it, not unlike a loving and long-term relationship. But in the end, it proved unsuitable to his needs.

Another young woman came to see the mattress, a working-girl with a hemline as high as her waist. But before she had a chance to even get near it, the ballerina performed a near-perfect grand jeté, or so Vance imagined, and defiantly said, "Sorry, it's sold!"

The woman disappeared just as quickly as the last.

"Okay, eleven hundred," the ballerina said with more resignation than she wished to share.

Vance had been pleasantly entertained for most of the afternoon, so he was disappointed to see it come to an end. But he was glad to have finally sold the mattress without losing much on it.

The ballerina's companion comically fumbled with it as he went down the stairs as she followed close behind, repeatedly scolding him in a parental tone to be careful with it.

When they finally reached the street, the ballerina glanced up at Vance with a seductive look as if to say, 'Aren't you coming?' It would seem she expected more for her money than she got.

"Sweet dreams," he said.

Having regained the power that she'd relinquished while negotiating, she lifted her chin and confidently said, "Just so you know, I'm usually the dream." With that she closed the door behind her, the world hers again for the taking. Humored by that remark, Vance shook his head as he went down to lock the door. Just as he was about to head back upstairs the bell rang. He couldn't imagine what she could possibly add after that.

"Ah, the dream," he said, opening the door.

"Excuse me?"

"Never mind. How are you?"

"Fine. I see you sold the mattress."

"And it's been quite a day doing it."

"I'm sure she'll be happy with it."

"I doubt she'll ever be happy," Vance said catching a last glimpse of the couple as he closed the door.

"The guy looked happy enough. Like a little puppy in fact."

"That's what I thought. But that's because he'll probably get more bang for her buck than she will."

"Sorry you never got to break it in."

"Funny thing is, it might have sold for more if I had."

"Really? How odd."

"I know, right?"

"That doesn't make sense."

"I think she wished it had more history. A memory, if you will."

"A memory mattress with an actual memory?"

"For fantasy purposes, I imagine."

"Sounds more like sleeping with a ghost if you ask me."

They reached the top of the stairs.

"It would seem you lost out all around."

"It would seem so," he playfully conceded.

"And now you don't have a mattress even if you wanted to."

Vance looked at the empty bed frame in the middle of the room.

"I've waited this long, I guess I can wait a while longer."

She took him by the front of his shirt and pulled him close.

"It'll be more memorable without one, I promise," she said kissing him.

With Your Heart On

Every Friday Wes felt the pulse of the city calling to him. After a hard week at work, he'd shower, pull on a tight tee shirt and jeans, then take the shallow stairs two at a time from his one-bedroom apartment down to the ready street. It was a routine he welcomed. And its purpose was two-fold; to get pleasantly intoxicated, and hopefully righteously laid. Though he always hoped he'd find something more, something special.

That night, Wes met Madison, as he had a hundred other guys out on a Friday night. And with any luck, after a few rounds and some laughs, he'd be set for the evening. Nights like this were reminiscent of the boyish behavior he experienced in college. It was that camaraderie that made him feel it was something more substantial, something more promising than just a body to have sex with. He welcomed that kind of intimacy even more than the sex at times. That, and the smell of a man's warm skin.

Bar conversations rarely start with introductions. It could take an entire evening before he got around to exchanging names with the guy next to him. And that was the case in the hours in which they talked themselves to the bottom of countless cocktails. Because it wasn't until they were out on the dark closing street that they finally and laughingly, introduced themselves. With that done, they knew pretty much everything they needed to about one another. Wes was convinced that Madison wasn't a serial killer, at least not a practicing one. Anything else could wait until morning.

They playfully helped balance each other as they went.

Once in his apartment, Wes blindly kicked the door closed behind him with his foot, then immediately pulled Madison close to him. For Wes, the first kiss was usually the most important, if not the most interpretive. It was where he initially downloaded the more intimate and intrinsic information about someone, as it often revealed everything he needed to know. So, he was surprised to find that they were heartfelt kisses; lengthy and gentle, and they grew more intense as they grew closer. In fact, he found them sincere and almost familiar, if not genuine. He certainly hadn't anticipated them, but he knew they were exactly what he needed.

He lowered Madison's body onto the bed and slowly went down on him. As he silently separated fabric from skin, he ran his mouth lightly along his smooth tight stomach, tasting the soft fuzz as it rolled against his upper lip. After partially lowering Madison's jeans, Wes grasped his buttock firmly in his strong hands and nestled his face into the top of his musky blonde pubic hair.

Wes recalled the first time he'd ever been hit. He was just a kid. It was on the chin, and it had slightly chipped his front tooth. He remembered it well, because like a kiss, first times are usually the most memorable. But the pain startled and confused his senses. It was the first time he'd felt anything like it; till then, the only real contact he'd had, had been limited to his mother's kisses and the comfort of her soft turquoise terrycloth robe on his smooth young cheek. His father had abandoned them when he was very young, and with him went the threat of an angered hand against him. He hadn't quite fallen on his face yet. Not in those days. Those days, he thought.

Wes recalled the first time that he'd smelt the unmistakable scent of another boy, as well as the first time that he'd felt another boy's penis, so different from his own, yet so similar. Perhaps it was the angle, the way it turned toward him and not away from him as his own obviously did. He found it intriguingly curious, though he mostly found it desirable. He felt a similar difference now with Madison. His own now fully erect penis pressed eagerly against his tight jeans, buckling against the fabric, hoping for that moment to break free. But it would seem his excitement apparently had less of an impression on Madison, as his cock hadn't reacted in the same way yet. Perhaps it was the alcohol, Wes thought. Still, he wasn't one to show disappointment in a guy's lack of response or even his endowment, for that matter. He would never slow his passion or his pace because of it. He may purposely retrace an area again with his lips in anticipation, but he was certain it wouldn't be misconstrued or perceived as hesitation or even doubt. He hadn't sensed the slightest twitch of a muscle or a variation in Madison's pulse, or a change in his breathing for that matter to indicate that Madison considered his actions as anything other than being attentive and caring.

Wes continued without expectation with the same zest with which he'd started, never breaking his cadence. He also never gave it a second thought, or at least he never let it seem so.

When he finally made his move, his mouth failed to find what he had expected. It was as if he couldn't find the words he'd wanted, as his mouth was equally empty, which caused Wes to lose his train of thought, certainly his direction. His mind collapsed as his hemispheres started to converge like astrological bodies doomed to collide; a transition where Mars went into Venus in a rundown cottage on a beach somewhere in Maine one scorching young summer years earlier; his head in a cloud, so to speak.

Wes slowly parted his lips, as if gasping for air, then he gently pressed them against it, immediately knowing his way around again, however long it had been since the last time; however distant the texture; however faraway the taste. Of course, he knew where he was, and it was no less a satisfying sensation. His mind drifted as he recalled that day in Maine when Claudia walked out slamming the screen door behind her, as she slowly became little more than a fading mirage that shimmered into an abstract blur like an erased pencil sketch in the afternoon heat, a heat that never truly dissipated for him. He could smell her now. He could even taste her on his lips again.

Wes hadn't had sex with a woman since then. He consciously let one world slip away while fully embracing another, though one equally familiar, however distant in his past. And he fully embraced that other world without looking back with more than an occasional glance, as if looking in from time to time on a sleeping memory. He had never fully abandoned one for the other until then. Because Wes had always followed his passion; he just didn't frequently initiate it. If someone relatively attractive showed an interest in him, he usually went with it. Now here he was some ten years later gently gliding down the body of a woman that he'd thought all night was a man, however boyish, though one he thought masculine enough, if not equally well endowed. He couldn't deny the strange irony he faced in that moment, because it was there between her gentle legs that he'd met up again with his past.

In those ten years, Wes had never truly found quite the same love that he had that summer in Maine with Claudia. He called her Cloud, because that's where he usually found his head while with her. And with Madison beneath him now, he realized just how emotionally lost he'd felt since then, and how that one decision had failed to fulfill his needs. Because physically, being with a man was exceptional, but it usually left him feeling intrinsically empty. He had failed to establish the same connection with a man that he had with a woman; as he had with Cloud. Sexually, he was more attracted to men, though women tended to find him more desirable. And in that sad fact, Wes found a pain, an ache he couldn't quite remedy; one he certainly failed to resolve. It was a cruel and constant dichotomy; one that made him feel as if he had gone into room for something he'd forgotten, only to realize what he wanted was right there in front of him all along, right there on his bed where he had left it all those years ago.

All those years ago, he thought. All those years.

Well, sort of.

Wes had never been attracted to androgyny, in men or women, for that matter. But there'd been times when he watched that world from a distance and found it artistically fascinating. But he found himself leaning into that world now as close as humanly possible. And in a moment, he'd be deeply inside it, which only added to the confusion. With his face passionately, if not comfortably nestled in Madison's warm pelvis, it occurred to him that in her mind they were two guys making love, which would help explain the impression he got at the bar earlier. It was apparent now that Madison had found her masculine identity, and Wes would need to quickly adapt to it.

Only then did Madison sense Wes' hesitation.

She whispered in a voice that was faintly audible, as if caught in a long-awaited dream, "Are you okay?"

"Of course," he whispered into the darkness.

A strong closeness passed between them when he penetrated her. It was as if their bodies melted together and their organs mysteriously interchanged in that singular motion they shared. Because there were moments when Wes couldn't be sure who was actually being penetrated, as it felt at times as if Madison were entering him, especially when their pelvises were tightly pressed against one another, as if lost to one another, which made him feel as if they were connected, even conjoined. It was an odd, though pleasurable sensation, if not an unfamiliar illusion for him. But strangely enough, it seemed to bring his mind and body together, and he found a comfort there; a peaceful comfort in fact that he'd never felt with a man before, or even with Cloud for that matter.

After they climaxed together, she pulled him close and whispered again in his ear, "Are you okay?"

Wes felt the breath come out of her like a warm breeze as she said it. He knew she'd expected a scene, and being spared that, had made it all that more incredible for her. He could sense it in her touch. He was no stranger to these parts, he just hadn't stopped by in a while. Though he had forgotten what a sweet drive it was getting there, as he felt her heart pounding inside her. It had obviously been more than just sex for Madison as well, because she seemed to cross from panic to pride, accomplishing something she'd no doubt thought inaccessible; finding that blossoming boy buried inside her, one she had apparently been searching for her entire life.

As he held her, he realized he was also embracing another boy's world as well as his own; however adolescent it may have been for her. He could tell that Madison had just experienced the very same sensation he had with a boy when he was twelve; when the sweet taste of taboo raced, and tingled, as it journeyed through his body.

"Of course," he finally whispered.

It made Wes recall a night some years earlier when he'd chatted with a tough little lesbian in a bar South of Market. They had a few good laughs together. And after just as many drinks she turned to him and said, "I wouldn't mind taking you home and fucking you."

Wes had heard her correctly, but he challenged her words over the loud dance beat to give himself enough time to run it through his inebriated head again, perhaps not entirely sure what he wanted.

"What's that?" he shouted back against the music.

She opened her black leather jacket and exposed a rather large strap-on. The waist belt dangled playfully from the inside pocket as a preview.

"I said, I wouldn't mind fucking you," she shouted back.

Of course, the image seemed more hilarious than probable to him, as it was one fantasy that he'd failed to fabricate.

"I'm flattered, but I'm not really designed that way," he said.

Wes was usually open to most anything, but he doubted being pounded by such an impressive piece of plastic was one of them. Though perhaps he'd be more adaptable to the idea now if Madison had made him the same offer, because the passion they shared was undeniable

The mind can be a magnificent place, if you get it right.

It was all still whirling around in his head when Wes opened his eyes to the early morning sun. He could feel Madison curled up against him like any other guy on most any other Saturday morning.

A moment later, Madison yawned and stretched across the bed.

"Good morning."

The voice was familiar, though he hadn't truly heard it, at least not at full volume since they'd ascended from the street to his apartment. But it seemed just as boyish as he remembered it, though he couldn't help but acknowledge a certain tonal difference now. Otherwise, it was like any other morning with any other guy, with one exception, he might actually like this one, even if he did turn out to be a woman. The image of Cloud came back to him, which made him wonder if he'd screw things up again like he had before. He could only hope not to be the catalyst this time.

"Is there coffee?" Madison asked.

"We can go out for some, if you want."

"That'd be great."

Madison pulled the covers off and headed to the toilet. Wes stole a glance as he usually did the next morning, curious to see what he'd brought home in the light of day. But he was amused to find that from the rear she looked the same as any other young guy heading off to take a piss. Nice body. Nice ass.

"So, are we okay?" Madison asked when she came out of the bathroom.

"Of course. Why?" he said feigning a measure of innocence.

"Well, I'm sure it wasn't quite what you expected."

"I keep an open mind." He smiled.

"You were quite the stud last night," she added, giving him the kudos, she undoubtedly thought he deserved.

Wes hadn't expected to get into it so soon. As far as he was concerned they could have let it go for a while. But isn't it just like a woman to want to talk things out, he thought humorously.

"There aren't many surprises in life," he said. "And when you come across one, you should embrace it. Life's all about embracing its surprises."

"You know you're my hero, right? I expected you to freak out."

"It took me a moment to find my way, but sex is pretty much the same regardless of the equipment."

"That's why you're my hero," she repeated.

"I'll admit it's been years since I slept with a woman, if you don't mind my calling you that. But I've usually had closer relationships with women."

"I've felt like a girl my entire life, even back when my dad dragged me to Little League. Though that was more for him than me. But I'm still not used to being called one," she admitted.

A shiver ran through him that he couldn't visually shake.

With a disconcerting look he said, "I'm not sure what you mean."

"The reassignment," she said.

Wes felt his body tense as he struggled to respond.

Only then did Madison realize what was happening.

"Where are you going with this?" he asked as if needing directions to a place beyond an intended destination.

In that moment, they both feared the truth in front of them.

"What did you think?" Madison asked with the same concern that had caused her heart to beat so frantically when he first went down on her, when with every breath and touch, she'd anticipated his outrage.

"I'm not sure now," he said as he felt his throat close-up on him.

"Does it matter? Like you said, sex is pretty much the same regardless of the equipment."

The room grew cinematically dark, and almost dangerous.

"Of course, it fucking matters!" he yelled.

"Well, it didn't seem to matter a moment ago," Madison said hoping to appease what was clearly an increasingly serious situation.

"A moment ago, I didn't know you'd had your dick chopped off!" he screamed. "A moment ago, I was under the impression that I ate pussy last night!"

"You did, and you were amazing," she shot back, determined to hold her ground.

"Don't get smart!"

"What did you think?" she asked again defensively.

"What do you think I thought?" he said, his rage building. "I thought you were a guy. At least that's what I thought I brought home with me. Then to my not so unpleasant surprise you turned out to be a woman, albeit one I eventually thought felt like a boy inside. And no wonder, since you're actually a boy who'd had his fucking dick lobed off! So, what the fuck am I supposed to think?"

"Let me get this straight. When we met you thought I was a boy? Then later in bed you discovered that I was a woman, and that was okay. Then while having sex you sensed I had boyish desires or a masculine impulse? Now who's confused?"

"There seems to be plenty of it to go around," he screamed back.

His words though, had unexpectedly forced Madison to reassess what she believed would come naturally to her as a woman. She had never once considered that any remnant of the boy she left behind would still be buried inside her. But it would seem now that his essence still lingered, however dormant at times. But the last thing she would allow him, or even Wes for that matter, to do now, was give her cause to doubt herself. But she knew she would eventually have to come to terms with whatever remained of that boy, regardless of how she'd altered herself physically. But she also knew it was inherent in people to share both characteristics; male and female. So, Madison saw no reason to fight it, or even hide it now, as she had for years. Her journey was complete, she was sure of that, and of herself.

Wes sat on the bed so as not to do anything stupid.

In the troubling silence, Madison threw a pack of cigarettes at him. He tore the pack apart and pulled one out and lit it. When he finally exhaled, she could feel the room gradually become less hostile.

"I'll ask again. Are we okay?"

Wes appeared calmer, but Madison couldn't be sure.

Finally, he said, his voice lower and more balanced now, "I don't know what to think." Then he whispered, "I thought I did."

"We had an amazing night together," she said in a gentler tone. "One I got the impression worked out nicely for both of us."

He stared at her through the smoke, searching for the spark that caused the fire. Then as if in a trance he said, "Halfway around the world there are trannies with incredible breasts, the kind that kiss the sky. The kind you may want yourself one day. But they still have their dicks. They walk the beach all made up with big hair and lipstick, their tits glistening in the sun, with their dicks swinging back and forth like pendulums. Guys love that shit over there. They love to suck dick and play with tits at the same time. It's quite something to see."

"What are you saying?" she asked cautiously.

"I'm saying you're like them, only in reverse. You have a pussy and a boy's chest. Though somehow I doubt you'd be as popular."

"I was pretty popular last night," she replied.

Wes stared at her from across the room as he put his cigarette out.

"I should probably get dressed and go," she said, nervously picking her jeans up off the floor. He watched her slim, boyish body step into them as they snuggly fit against her tight ass. It seemed a perfect image. It was only then that he realized that he was still naked, and that he had a hard-on.

"Maybe that knows what it wants better than you do," Madison said, acknowledging his erection.

Wes got up and slowly started across the room.

Madison didn't know what to expect, or how it was about to go down. Half-naked, and with her jeans only partially zipped, she readied herself for either consequence.

Scenes from The Road

1
At the Light

"All right, now how many fingers do I have?" he asked.

She looked at him with a curious squint in her eye.

"Let's see. One. Two. Three."

Her voice faded as she continued counting under her breath, at which time she turned her attention to the road in front of them as if attempting to recall each one. It took her a couple of minutes. Finally, she said, "That makes twenty-two."

"Are you sure?" he asked, questioning her accuracy.

"Positive. Though I think you intentionally piss people off," she said, suspicious now that he'd stacked the deck in his favor.

"I promise, each gesture was unsolicited. But I will admit that I do tend to piss people off rather easily, especially on the road. Anyway, I said fifty people would flip me off before we got there, and we still have a way to go yet."

"I still don't trust you, especially now that we're in a congested area again. It'll be easy for you to rack up at least ten."

"No need to flatter me. Anyway, I always win."

"As I'm sure you're also used to eating your words. Tell me, do you chew them well or hold your nose and swallow them quickly to avoid the sour taste in your mouth?"

"It depends on the words," he said smiling. "Some are tough like steak with bits of grizzle and fat; while others are smooth like a puree, allowing them go down easily."

"I'm sure some get stuck in your teeth like spinach and that has to be pointed out to you on a regular basis."

"It's a look I've learned to live with," he said checking his teeth in the rearview mirror.

They'd been on the road for several days and had crossed several states. Trish wasn't quite sure where they were, though that was mostly because the landscape and skyline seldom changed. Certainly, nothing like Dresden after the war, or Vegas in the past thirty years.

It was then she turned her focus to the other cars on the road, imagining their destinations; even creating dialogue for them.

"That couple look suspicious," she said pointing to a black compact. "In fact, they look like Boris and Natasha."

"It's a rental, but I wouldn't be surprised if it's stolen," Crane said.

"Should we call it in?" Trish said in an authoritative tone.

"Probably not a good idea since I wouldn't be all that surprised if we weren't wanted somewhere for something ourselves by now."

Trish failed to offer the witty retort he expected. Instead she confessed, "Personally, I'm not feeling all that wanted right now."

Crane glanced over at her without saying anything. Having just come from a bad breakup, he knew she was emotionally vulnerable.

Trish closed her eyes and immediately fell asleep.

She woke as the car reduced speed.

"This looks familiar," she said stretching.

"It all looks the same to me," he said.

"Don't tell the natives that, they think it's paradise."

"It must be. The sign coming into town said it was."

"To some it is, but whatever you do, don't alienate the locals."

"That sounds familiar."

She ignored the association. Instead she asked, "How long did I sleep?"

"About three hours. More than I have in three days."

As they waited at a light she scrutinized the guy in the car next to them. "Is he smelling his finger or just trying to look pensive?"

The man had his hand cupped over his mouth with his forefinger curled under his nose. His thumb was firmly braced below his chin.

"He's probably trying to figure out where he's going like the rest of us. But if I was playing your little game, I'd say he's rehearsing the excuse he's going to give his wife when he gets home, because he looks guilty as hell."

"It doesn't matter what he tells her, she'll still smell the sex on him. Woman have an instinct for that," she said having recently gone through a similar experience. Then pushing her finger under his nose, she added. "You can still smell it almost a week later."

"That smells suspiciously young," he said, turning his head away as if offended by it. "What have you been into?"

"It ages well too, don't you think?"

He glanced at her, then back at the intersection and the road ahead; not sure which was going to be more of a challenge.

Trish looked back at the guy in the car.

"Look at those hands. I'm sure they more than get the job done." She pressed her lips against the window, which got his attention. The guy looked confused. Then she made a V with two fingers and she stuck her tongue out and licked the glass between them.

"It's all in the technique," Trish said, retrieving her tongue. "The first thing I do is tease that vertically amused smile until it widens and offers a thankful grin." She paused for a moment, as if picturing it. "Then I whisper it a secret. Something, entre nous." She paused again, but this time to fully appreciate the image. "Then I take its breath away." She held hers captive to prove her point. "Then I playfully resuscitate it," she said exhaling, her lips pursed perfectly.

She couldn't help but notice that Crane was slightly aroused.

"I hope that's not for me. It'd just go to waste."

He adjusted himself as best he could.

"I'll admit I miss it at times," he confessed. "Until I'm back in it. Then I realize I'm in the wrong place again. As if I'd entered the wrong room."

"You must admit, it can be a very sweet room. It even comes heated. And it's the only place that I feel at home. And there's no place like home, right?"

"Is that why we're driving away from it at eighty miles an hour?"

His words hung frozen in the air between them.

Finally, she said, "I wasn't there long enough to call it home."

Trish stared out the window, focusing on the world in front of her.

Conversations tend to be less demanding and often intermittent while on the road, so after a considerable silence Trish said, "I did put my heart into it. I tried." She glanced back at the guy in the car. She'd unknowingly had his full attention now. "It looks as if I have a stalker," she said with concern in her voice. "The cheating husband has locked his sights on me."

Crane offered the guy a warm smile. "Perhaps the pheromones on his finger have dissipated. Maybe he'd like to take another dip."

"You mean the sweet nectar of the goddess," she said correcting him.

"I'm sure you have some to spare," he said, nodding at her cut-offs. "I can pull over."

"Not funny. How long is this light, anyway? We've been here forever."

"It won't get any greener than you look right now when it changes," he said jokingly. "I thought you were tougher than that."

"I can still kick your ass. But he's giving me the creeps."

"You've let your little game get the best of you. Lock your door just in case, though." He smiled.

"Screw you," she said, then locked the door when he wasn't looking.

He smiled when he heard the click.

"Can you just run the light?" she said.

"What?"

"At least stop looking at him."

"Okay, okay."

"What's he doing?"

"I'm not looking at him, remember?"

"Good."

When the light finally did change, Crane waited a couple of seconds to put some distance between them. But as it did, the guy sped off.

"Let's not play this game anymore," she said.

"He's probably just an innocent guy."

"No one's innocent out here. You're either road kill or a killer on the road. And if you're lucky, you survive long enough to keep on running."

He knew what Trish was running from was still running right alongside her. It wasn't lagging or fading behind, as she'd hoped. The emptiness she felt was still there, and no distance was going to change that.

2
Miles from Somewhere

"Don't take this the wrong way, but you're not a very good driver."

"Are you kidding?"

"No really. In fact, you're a rather bad driver."

"You waited fifteen hundred miles to tell me that?"

"I had to be sure. I had to let you go the distance."

"That was nice of you."

"I wanted to give you the benefit of the doubt."

"That was very charitable of you."

"And just so you know, it's been a very nervous fifteen hundred miles, especially under the circumstances."

Joan knew he'd never change the way he drove. And the truth was, she didn't want him to, because it was that same unpredictability and dangerous characteristic that excited her when they made love. She'd grown fond of his reckless nature and she knew he wouldn't be the same person without it.

"You can tell a lot about a person by how they drive," she added. "They tend to show their true personality on the road."

"Really?"

Darren didn't feel particularly enlightened by her words.

"You get to see their generosity, as well as their selfishness."

He waited for her to play out her theory before he responded.

"You can also tell how they'll be in bed."

"Are you saying, I'm bad in bed?" he asked, though more confident than upset. Still, he didn't like what he was hearing.

"I'm not saying that." Joan noticed a change in his mood. "You're just as dangerous on the road as you are in bed. But that's a good thing. I'm sure it'd also be the best place to die."

She feigned a laugh, not sure why she'd mentioned that.

"I'll keep that in mind," Darren said, though he seemed more offended by her crack about his driving than anything else.

Hoping to offer him kudos, she added, "I'm sure you've driven me at least fifteen hundred miles, and I should thank you for that. It's always been a good ride."

Joan could still feel it in her groin like a fond memory even now.

"You're welcome," he said. But he couldn't help but wonder just how much it had cost him per mile; just as it was still costing him now. But he'd had worse, he thought.

A stillness settled between them. It was a silence that seemed ready to break as if on schedule.

"Should I turn on the radio?"

"It's too early." Darren took his eyes off the road for a moment to look at her. "Be patient."

It was only then that he took notice.

"Weren't you wearing a scarf earlier? Where's your scarf?"

Joan felt her neck, and then her lap, and then the floor in front of her.

"I'm sure it's here somewhere."

She unbuckled her seatbelt and reached around into the backseat.

"Find it!" he shouted angrily now.

She nervously searched everywhere.

"Did you leave it in the other car?" he asked impatiently.

She pulled herself forward, nervously settling into her seat again.

"I may have," she confessed. "I'm not sure."

"How stupid of you!" he screamed.

"It's just a scarf."

"Just a scarf? Something as simple as that is traceable."

"It probably fell on the road. They won't think anything of it."

"Don't be an idiot! Forensics will go through it thoroughly. And on the road, is even worse. At least in the car there's a chance that it'll burn in the blast. We didn't drive all this way to fuck up!"

She sat in silence.

The heat which radiated from his anger was undeniable.

"Turn on the radio," he said. "Let's see just how bad it gets.

3
On the Radio

'Breaking news. We're getting a report about a school shooting. Stay tuned for more information as it comes in.'

As he waited for an update he leaned his arm against the window of the car door. He put his hand to his face, his forefinger slightly curled above his upper lip, and his thumb set firmly below his chin, letting the weight of the situation rest there until he knew more. He could only pray now.

As he waited at the light, the woman in the car next to him caught his eye. She was licking the car window with her tongue, no doubt attempting to be sexy. He prayed that his daughter would never do anything so senseless and vile. But he was praying right now that it wasn't her school that was under attack by some crazed gunman. He stared blankly, praying to God that he'd be able to see her on her wedding day, and hopefully wearing white.

He prayed that his prayers would be answered.

The voice on the radio came back.

'We're getting more information on that school shooting.'

The announcement snapped him out of it.

It was only then that he realized that he'd been staring at the woman in the car next to him all this time, which apparently upset her. He was about to roll down his window to apologize when the voice on the radio confirmed his worst nightmare.

'There's been a shooting at The Good Shepherd School.'

Just then the light turned green, and he accelerated as fast as he could. Not only did he nearly lose control of the car when he did, but he also lost his peripheral vision. So much so, that he couldn't be certain if he hadn't clipped a guy standing on the curb when he made a sharp turn. He didn't have time to stop but he prayed that someone else would.

'This just in. There's been an explosion reported downtown. Seems to be a busy day folks. Be careful out there.'

4
The Kiss Goodbye

The night air was thick and densely humid. There was a trace of what smelt like heavy dung in the air. Something had died somewhere, and there was no mistaking that people were out for blood. Tucker could feel it. He expected it to get brutal, even messy out on the road. It was one of those nights when humanity would be tested. He'd be surprised if a higher number than usual didn't end up as road kill. To help prove that point, they came upon several accidents, mostly fender benders. But it was still early.

"Does it feel crazy out here tonight or is it just me?" she asked.

"You feel it too?"

"Yes, so be careful. Who knows what'll happen out here tonight."

They didn't see the blast, but they heard it. Strangely, it coincided with the distant and fading sunset, and the glow from it only added to the reality of the situation. But the air remained oddly still, almost surreal. Less than a mile down the road they'd thought they'd come upon it, but instead what they found was a lone body in the middle of the street. There was no sign of an explosion.

Tucker instinctively jumped out of the car.

"Where are you going?" Connie asked frightened.

If he'd heard her, he let her voice fade in his head as he had many times before.

"Are you all right buddy?" he asked as he attempted to comfort the man lying on the ground.

The man just looked up at him.

"Don't worry, you'll be fine," Tucker said.

The man whispered, "I can feel the life draining from me."

"No, you'll be all right."

Only then did Tucker see the true extent of the man's injuries. He saw the life in him dissipate as it slowly evaporated into nothingness. His body had been badly torn up. His legs were twisted, and his mid-section had been partly crushed. Tucker was surprised there wasn't more bruising or blood on his face. In fact, his face seemed oddly peaceful.

"You'll be fine," Tucker lied this time.

"That's nice of you to say, but there's no mistaking the feeling," the man said, his voice fading.

His broken body was sprawled out on the cold and cracked concrete, waiting his imminent demise. It wasn't how he'd pictured going in the end, but at least he wasn't alone, he thought. Thankfully there was someone with him, even if it was a stranger. He was grateful that it was someone who'd had enough compassion to stop and try and help. And for that reason, he knew he was in good company. Besides, he had a kind face.

Tucker knelt and gently lifted him up onto his lap, cradling his head in his arm to console him. He knew better than to move someone who had been seriously injured, but he knew the guy didn't have much life left in him either way, so he might as well make him comfortable.

The man spoke again, though this time his voice was barely audible, so Tucker leaned down in order to hear him better. There was no mistaking the words, as they were inherent to our very nature.

"This might sound crazy," he whispered, "but would you…would you mind kissing me goodbye?"

Tucker knew there was no time to debate the request, and he saw no alternative; not under the circumstances. Besides, he knew in his heart that a refusal would have been morally offensive, and it wasn't in his nature to spoil the essence of such a moment by even hesitating. So, he instinctively leaned down and kissed the man on the lips. Then as is the natural progression, if not the very nature of a kiss, their lips parted slightly, and they silently and gently slipped deeper into it, more figuratively than literally, though their tongues did share a muted dialogue. It was in that solitary adhesive moment that Tucker realized that he was no longer just an anonymous roadside Good Samaritan, but a proxy for whoever was absent as the man lay there dying, as the kiss gradually transitioned, and even localized, like an anesthetic helping to diminish the pain. There was no mistaking it. Tucker couldn't deny the connection as each exchange passed his lips. Strangely, he could almost see their faces, particularly their eyes. And at the end of the kiss when he had said his last goodbyes to those that mattered, and it was just the two of them again; while their lips were still conjoined in one last shared breath, he offered Tucker a parting and thankful one that he unassumingly accepted.

When their lips finally did part, Tucker felt as if he'd peeled his own skin away from his body as one might do after too much sun. It was then that the man's head reclined lifelessly into the nook of Tucker's arm, where he gently held the full weight of it until the ambulance arrived. Only then did Tucker truly acknowledge the effect that the kiss had on him. He couldn't deny that his very core had been intrinsically enlightened by the soul-filled experience. Even his senses seemed sharper as he felt the world around him slowly evaporate, leaving just the essence of life in its emotional aftermath. The fact was, Tucker could still the feel the kiss on his mouth, as if refusing to let go. He had even expected to find the taste of blood on his lips, but instead he felt a lasting tingle of the man's existence still lingering there. He wouldn't deny its presence as it remained constant and undying. And when Tucker touched his tongue to them it only seemed to intensify the sensation.

It had been the quintessential kiss, one that Tucker was sure he'd never experience again. It was certainly one he'd never forget, and it was from a man. He had never kissed a man before and he was confident it would be the only time. It had been an innocent act that fulfilled a dying man's last wish, but he knew that his expectations in a kiss from that point on would change forever, and that he'd need something as close to it as possible in the future, as it would be the standard he'd compare all kisses to now; however unfair that would be to those who'd follow.

"Why would you do that?" Connie asked with concern after they took the man's body away. "Why would you kiss him? I don't understand. He was a total stranger, not to mention a man. Why would you kiss that man?"

He knew it was just another divide in their relationship, one of many. She would never allow herself to get past the social structure to see the true humanity of life. It was one of the unattractive flaws in her character.

Tucker paused to choose his words carefully, knowing they would no doubt define their future.

In a soft and quiet monotone, he finally said, "You may wake-up one day and put on your blouse just as you have a thousand times before, not realizing that after the sun went down someone else would be taking it off, and not as you might dream, with love and seduction. No, you'll look down and see a nurse pulling it off to save your life. You're alone, and all you truly want and need in that moment is to reach out and touch another human being, hopefully someone you know and love. Failing that, someone, even a stranger, to share that last moment with; and if you're lucky, a warm body to hold you. It's not sexual. It's more than that. It's an essential piece in the puzzle of humanity."

"But you don't have to kiss them," she said.

"I believe you should do what needs to be done in those last moments."

"So, if he'd asked you to pull on his prick and blow him before he died, you'd have done that too?"

The divide between them was obviously widening.

"Sadly, you're mistaking a sacred moment in the scheme of things for something perverse and obscene. This was not that."

"Have you kissed a man before?" she asked looking him straight in the eye. "I'd like a measure of assurance that you're not gay."

In that moment, he realized their relationship had never been a shared experience, and that each touch, each interaction between them, had been lost on her; and that nothing he'd ever done for her, or to her for that matter, had made its intended connection. It was obvious to him now that she didn't know him at all.

"No one would know the answer to that better than you," he said.

"The man I thought I knew wouldn't do what you did tonight."

"It would seem we know different men, and how that escaped us both is the real question. Because you know he probably wasn't gay either, right? This wasn't about that."

"You don't know that for sure," she said.

"I know it wasn't me he was kissing. I was just a stand-in for someone who couldn't be there with him at the end."

Not wanting to complicate matters even further, Tucker decided not to mention the various dimensions of the kiss, especially the one intended for him at the end. He knew it would only make things worse; if they could get any worse that is.

"I watched you kiss him. It looked like a gay thing to me."

"It wasn't."

Tucker knew the true reason she was so upset was because he'd never kissed her like that, and probably never would.

"So, you've kissed enough men to know the difference?"

"No, though I imagine you have."

She didn't respond.

"How can you not be sympathetic to that man's situation?" he asked.

Connie didn't answer. Instead, she watched as an entire piece of her life vanished before her eyes, and some of its possibilities along with it.

She stared at him now as if he were a stranger.

"I think you should just drop me off," she finally said.

"At your house?"

"Anywhere. I just need to get off this road," she said.

There was no mistaking which road she meant.

It didn't matter where he stopped.

When he finally did, she got out and walked away without a kiss or last embrace. Not even a goodbye.

There was nothing left to say.

All that remained were shadows set deep in the darkness of what had obviously been a waste of time for them both.

5
The Short Ride

It was the third time in a week that Rita found herself perched on a barstool at The Corral. Before that, it had been six years since she celebrated going off to college there. And as often happens when you leave home, the experience had changed her enough that when she returned, the place, and even the town for that matter, no longer suited her lifestyle.

Regardless, there she was.

They bounced about as they rode along the narrow dirt road.

"It sure was something," the cowboy declared as he smiled over at her. "It handled like a wild animal. I could've had any girl with that car!"

It was a Saturday night and he was drunk, and all revved up.

"That car was so hot that even my sister would have put out!"

He laughed.

Rita wasn't sure if it was the ride or the image of the cowboy and his sister that made her stomach turn.

"How much further?" she asked.

"It's just a short ride, babe. We'll be there in no time."

There, there, she thought. Hang in there. It'll no doubt be a short ride just like he said.

He passed her the bottle. Rita accepted it with a measure of resignation. But she needed something to kill the pain, or at least help her get through it.

"Here we are, babe," the cowboy said, as he pulled his truck alongside a doublewide trailer. "Home sweet home!"

It was just as she pictured it.

The line he'd used to pick her up would have normally killed the deal if she weren't so desperate to see it through. He'd sidled up next to her at the bar, and with that ready and eager handsome cowboy grin he said, 'Babe, I just want to be sure I knew how you like your eggs in the morning.'

Rita wondered how many times that line had worked. Being a local, she knew the girls in town would normally respond with a giggle to that kind of flirtation. But however sophomoric Rita found it now, she needed someone, or something to take her mind off her broken life, if not help to reestablish her reputation, and he wasn't an entirely bad looking something.

She considered telling him she liked her eggs anyway but fertilized, but she didn't want to scare him off.

So, instead she said, "Surprise me, stud."

"I'm full of surprises, babe," the cowboy promised. But Rita knew they rarely were.

When he finally made his move, she pushed him away instinctively and said, "I'm not that kind of girl."

"They never are, babe," the cowboy grinned.

He was used to women playing that game, so he thought nothing of it. In fact, he expected girls to put up a fight, at least at first. If for no other reason than to try and save a semblance of their reputation. But deep-down Rita wasn't that kind of girl. Not anymore. Besides, she wasn't looking to keep her reputation. Quite the opposite in fact. So, when he tried to pull her close again, Rita didn't resist, because after all this was where she'd chose to be. So, she willingly resigned to that choice, especially since she knew Trish was probably halfway across the country by now and out of her life forever. She felt her heart being pulled like a bungee cord, and when it broke, the backlash was going to hurt, and hurt bad. She also knew when she woke in the morning with this strange, though handsome cowboy next to her, it would hit her, and hit her hard. But the truth was, Trish knew how she liked her eggs, and her coffee, and especially her sex.

Just as she'd anticipated, her cowboy plowed her with no regard for her sexual needs, employing the same absentmindedness he would his morning chores. And after that short and poorly tilled ride, Rita felt even lonelier than she had before she got on. But given the circumstances, she couldn't deny the irony of the situation, as she was forced to face the fact that she was caught, however voluntarily, in the same trap that she had successfully escaped nearly a decade earlier. Because it could have been any Saturday night back when she was eighteen, but for the simple fact that she was no longer content with the conquest of her flirtations as she might have been then. Rita was far less naïve now, though just as bone dry and unsatisfied. But for a split and unsettling second, it appeared as if nothing had changed in her life. It was as if she'd been taken back to a time before she discovered those dormant feelings inside her; a time before Trish. It was a sobering thought, and certainly one that deserved another drink.

As she lay in the dark with her eyes wide open, Rita knew she'd be forced to live with the residual effects of the pain she'd inflicted, not only on herself, but on Trish as well. By not committing to her openly and lovingly, she'd caused them unnecessary heartbreak. But she knew it'd be impossible in this small town, especially with her mother's failing health. There was no escaping it. And she couldn't fault Trish for leaving either, or for refusing to live a closeted life with her; certainly, not after their liberating time together at college.

Rita reluctantly resigned to the weight of the drunken cowboy passed out on top of her, who would undoubtedly forget her name. She'd been here before, though she'd hoped to have gotten out from under it, if not literally. But she had let herself back in of her own accord, and she'd have to make the best of it until she figured out how to get out again.

But for now, she even considered changing her name to Babe, because it wouldn't be her life she'd be living. Her heart was elsewhere, and it always would be. Though Rita couldn't help but humorously wonder as she closed her eyes, just how many women named Babe had gone through the exact same experience, and never got out.

6
Entre Nous

"There's still no answer. He's probably at work," Trish said.

"Shouldn't Kate be at the house?"

"She's probably also working now."

"Don't you remember the address?"

"No. But let's drive and see if we can find it."

There were two police cars in front of the house.

"I think this is it."

"It doesn't look good," Crane said.

Trish jumped out of the car while it was still moving.

The front door was wide open.

Kate was sitting at the dining room table. A policeman stood next to her taking notes. When she saw Trish, she ran to her.

"I'm so glad you're here." She hugged her tightly. "I wouldn't be able to get through this alone."

"What happened?"

"Chris has been killed. A hit and run."

They gathered around the dining room table after the police left.

"They said that he was probably in shock before he died. I'm thankful for that, at least." Kate cried.

"How long did it take before the ambulance arrived?" Trish asked, her eyes filled with tears.

"Not that long. But he was already dead when they got there. There was a couple on the scene who were with him when he died. At least he wasn't alone."

It had been five years since Trish had seen her brother at their wedding. She regretted not hitting the road earlier now.

"I would like to talk to the couple and see if he said anything before he died," she said.

"The police have their names. We should call and find out," Kate said.

"I'm on it." Crane got up and went to the phone.

Kate wanted to say they'd get through it, but she wasn't so sure.

When Crane hung up, Trish was right beside him.

"Did you get their name and number?"

"The police are going to call them and have them call us. Apparently, they're not at liberty to give out that information since they weren't actually involved in the accident."

"Accident isn't the word I'd use." Trish was obviously upset. "Children have accidents. Bedwetting is an accident. Killing someone with your car is more than an accident. Accident suggests an apology can make it better. But nothing can possibly make this better."

Trish found a comfort in her anger. It helped to balance her from what she knew would be her inevitable collapse. But she had to keep it together, at least for the time being, especially for Kate.

"I'm sorry to say the news doesn't get better. They think two cars were involved now. It appears that the first car probably just clipped him, and that the second one ran him over. But they're not sure how much time transpired between each incident."

"Un-fucking believable!" Trish screamed, as she pulled her hair back from her forehead with both hands. Then she angrily added, "Why are these fucking people even on the road?"

There didn't seem to be an answer to that.

"So, what they're saying is, Chris might still be alive if the first car stopped?" Kate cried.

"It looks that way. It would seem the second car killed him."

They hoped for a measure of closure when they got the opportunity to talk with the couple that was at the scene.

They hung out aimlessly while they waited.

Kate said, "With all that's happened I forgot to ask about Rita."

"Nothing went as planned. Shortly after we set up house she changed. While in town at the local bar one Saturday night, she started flirting with a cowboy. It was innocent enough at first. But we know those boys have only one thing on their mind, and they can only be teased up to a point; or it can get dangerous. A while later, Rita disappeared, so I went looking for her. I eventually found her in the parking lot making-out in some cowboy's truck, having sex. At least it looked that way to me. Though at first, I thought she was being raped, but that obviously wasn't the case. I didn't want to make a scene, but I was angry as hell. When we got home, Rita cried and said she was sorry and that she loved me more than anything. And that she was only trying to save her reputation, because people were beginning to talk."

"Things like that used to ruin a girl's reputation," Kate said.

"Not if they think you're a lesbian."

"Interesting."

"Small-town folk have small-town ways. They're not like us. I told her she shouldn't care what other people think. But of course, being from there, she did. Though she was more concerned with what her mother might think. But I'm sure the old gal knew and just didn't want to get into it. Which I can understand, considering her health. But Rita also wanted to stay in the good graces of her minister, who preaches about the evils of homosexuality. And as you expect, he pretty much runs the town."

"I know the type, and the town," Kate said.

"I was angry as hell. The image of that cowboy is still branded in my brain. Of course, I knew what she was going through. I even tried to see it through my love for her, but I still couldn't stick around."

"I never knew banging a cowboy out of wedlock on a Saturday night kept you in God's good graces. I might have lived my life differently if I'd known that." Kate attempted a weak smile. "But I was brought up to believe it was a sin. And there were consequences; the least of which was saying ten rosaries. The other was being called the town slut. I hope you guys work it out. But living with small-town expectations can be tough."

"It's tough here too," Trish cried.

She curled up on the couch hoping to put her world to sleep for a while.

The call finally came later that evening.

"My name's Tucker Down. I was at the scene of the hit and run?"

"Thank you for calling. I'm a friend of the family of the man who was killed earlier. They hoped to talk with you about it. Anything you can share would be greatly appreciated."

"Of course," Tucker said.

"They're sleeping now, and I'd hate to wake them. As you can imagine, it's hit them pretty hard."

"I completely understand," he said in a sympathetic tone. "I could come by tomorrow, if you think that'd be okay."

"That'd be great, thank you."

"Let me find a pen so I can get the address."

"Sure, I'll hold on."

The mood in the house still felt like a crime scene, especially when the morning sun broke through the living room window like a vandal smashing the plate glass. And sleep had only helped to embed the nightmare.

"The guy who was with Chris called. He should be here soon."

Trish tried to adjust to another day.

"I thought they said there was a couple on the scene?"

"I thought so too, but he didn't mention coming with anyone."

"I'd like to hear her side too," Trish said. "I want as much information as possible. Besides, women are more sensitive when it comes to this kind of thing. They understand the importance of emotional detail. I'm sure she'd have more insight into what happened."

"What's his name?" Kate asked.

"His name is Tucker Down."

"I like the name Tucker," Kate said.

"Tucker Down? Are you sure?" Trish asked.

"I couldn't make that up. Who'd ever name their kid Tucker Down?"

"Tucker's a nickname," she said.

A surprised look came over Crane's face. "You know him?"

"His real name is Peter."

"How do you get Tucker from Peter?" Kate asked.

"Apparently, having a big one can be just as embarrassing as having a small one. He tucked it down deep in his pants to hide his impressive bulge. He was very modest that way."

"That's not modest; not compared to the rest of us. Who in their right mind would do that?"

"I can't believe it," Trish said.

"Either can I. I'm sure it's just a rumor."

"It's not. I should know. We dated in high school. What I can't believe is that Tucker was with Chris when he died. How fortunate for us."

"You dated Tucker Down?"

"He was the last guy I slept with," she confessed.

"In an alternate universe."

"We could use an alternate universe right now," Kate offered.

"I'm sure you turned him off women," Crane said lightheartedly.

"I doubt that. And he wasn't designed to turn a girl lesbian either. My not marrying that impressive piece of equipment is proof that being gay is a part of nature, and not something nurtured."

Just then the doorbell rang.

"That must be the heavy equipment now," Crane said.

Trish found a smile where she hadn't expected one.

"Hi, I'm Tucker Down. I believe we talked on the phone."

"Yes, of course. Please come in."

"How have you been, Tucker?" Trish said when their eyes met.

"Trish?" He was equally surprised.

Their embrace seemed so familiar it appeared rehearsed. But being in her arms again brought back the best years of his life.

"This is Kate, my brother's wife. And this is my friend Crane."

Tucker offered a faint though concerned smile.

"Let's sit," Trish said. They sat on the couch together, while Kate and Crane took the chairs across from them.

"I only just learned that you were with Chris when he died. I'm so glad it was you. I feel better now knowing that."

"I'm sorry I didn't recognize him."

"I wouldn't think you would. He was younger than us."

"It's interesting. I thought of you when he was in my arms. It was the eyes. You have the same eyes."

Trish visualized her brother's eyes again and started to cry.

"I'm sorry," he said.

"No, it's okay," she said trying to regain her composure.

"You held Chris?" Kate asked hoping now for a better image than the one she'd been carrying in her head since she got the news.

"I did," he confessed.

"Did he go quickly?"

"No, he hung in there for a while."

"Was he conscious?"

"He was definitely aware of what was happening."

"Was he in a lot of pain?" Trish asked.

"No, I don't think so. Considering the circumstances, he seemed rather calm. His body was torn up badly, but his face was surprisingly peaceful. I told him to hang in there, and that help was on the way. And that everything would be all right."

"Did he say anything?"

"He knew he was dying. He said he felt the life draining from him."

"Was there anything else?"

"No, not really," Tucker said.

He sat quietly reliving the moment again in his mind.

They gave him time to reflect, hoping he'd offer something more.

He finally added with hesitation, "Well, there was one other thing."

"What was that?" Trish asked leaning toward him.

"I wouldn't mention this if it were anyone else."

Trish put her hand gently on his leg. "I understand."

In a soft voice Tucker said, "He asked me to kiss him."

A silence filled the room. It wasn't awkward or uncomfortable. It was more peaceful.

Kate leaned forward, resting her elbows on her knees.

"He asked you to kiss him?"

Tears filled her eyes. She had no intention of hiding her emotions or allowing vanity to intrude as it sometimes does. She even chose to wear her hair pulled back from her face since receiving the news, to better focus on what happened.

"It wasn't sexual," he quietly insisted, hoping to clarify the kiss.

"I wouldn't expect it was," she said calmly. "At least not toward you."

"I was afraid you'd take it the wrong way."

"There's no wrong way to take it," Kate said.

If Trish had forgotten why she'd loved Tucker, she remembered now.

"It was just about the kiss. It was the most important thing to him."

"Did he close his eyes?" Kate asked.

"I'm sure he did." Tucker only then realized that he'd closed his.

"What was it like?"

"It was as if he was saying goodbye to different people. I could tell by its varying degree of intensity. Don't get the wrong idea. It wasn't a make-out session. It was a single kiss filled with multiple levels of affection."

He paused.

"Is there anything more?" Kate asked softly.

"It might sound crazy, but I think there was one for me at the end."

"I'm sure that there was," she said, with a smile on her tear-filled face. "And I couldn't think of a better understudy for the part."

Trish wiped her eyes.

They sat in silence, until Kate finally broke the quiet.

"Thank you for helping Chris, and for kissing him goodbye for us. That means everything to me."

Tucker nodded his head. It made sense now. It all came together just as Chris had hoped.

"The police mentioned that a couple were at the scene. Were you with someone?" Trish asked.

"The woman I was with took offense to the kiss."

"I'm sorry to hear that."

"It was probably for the best."

They let the quiet set in again for a moment.

"Do they have any leads?" Tucker finally asked.

"There were no witnesses. Not unless someone grows a conscience and comes forward," Trish said.

"I imagine they have their hands full with that school shooting and the bombing at the government building downtown," Tucker said.

"We hadn't heard anything about that. The peripherals have been vague since Chris' death, as you'd expect."

"Of course. In fact, I should let you have some time alone."

"Thank you again for coming, and for sharing his last moments with us. You can't imagine how much it means," Kate said.

"And thank you for stopping," Trish added. "Few would have."

At the door Kate said, "Thank you again for being there for him, and me. I'm sure it wasn't easy."

"It was easier than I imagined," he said, assured now. "It was an oddly electric experience, as if we were all wired together in that one moment. That's how I see it now, at least."

"The universe works that way sometimes."

"I might not have understood that before, but I do now."

"Can I ask a favor?" Kate said, putting a hand on his arm.

"Of course, anything."

"Would you mind very much if I kissed you?"

"I wouldn't have left without one," Tucker said.

As Kate expected, the kiss was predictably familiar. In fact, she sensed a spiritual bond when their lips met, as if there were a transference of souls passing intrinsically between them. As they stood close together captured in that magical moment, neither seemed to notice Tucker's member discreetly unfold and press gently, if not ethereally, against Kate's inner thigh, as if stimulated involuntarily.

40

7
Loners

"Put your seatbelt on," he demanded.

"Dad I was…"

"Just put it on!"

Amy intended to put on her seatbelt, especially since her dad's driving had recently become more erratic than usual. It was as if he were allowing his emotions to determine his performance on the road now. But the truth was, she never felt safe with him behind the wheel anyway, and she was particularly concerned now since he appeared angrier and more distracted than usual. She wondered if one day he might snap and go on a rampage like the shooter at her school had; and what the life-changing consequences of that would be.

Since the shooting, her father drove her to school every day on his way to work and picked her up again on his way home, which meant she had to stay late in study hall until he left the office.

Like Amy, the shooter was a sophomore. But she barely knew him. She doubted anyone knew him. He was usually curled up in a corner by himself during lunch reading some obscure book. The police couldn't find out why he went on a rampage, but they figured it was the same as the last time there was a shooting, just as they probably would the next time. He was a loner. A quiet kid, who was forced to isolate himself from others. Someone who'd been bullied most of his life and whose main goal was to remain as invisible as possible, however unsuccessfully.

When calm was eventually restored at the school, nearly everyone had survived unscathed. The only loss of life was that of the shooter. The police concluded that his primary objective was suicide, and that his show of force had probably been a last attempt at getting a measure of respect. But they'd never know the truth for sure. His social media page offered little insight into his state of mind. And within a few weeks, there would be nothing left but the memory of spent cartridges scattered on the floor of several shattered classrooms.

"Did you hit something, dad?" Amy cautiously asked her father. "I see there's a new dent on the front fender."

"I hadn't noticed," he lied. He had hoped to avoid the subject. Failing that, he instinctively offered the conclusion he usually came to when things went wrong with the car. "Your brother no doubt got reckless again. I'm going to have to beat that boy blue."

Amy was sorry she'd brought it up now. The last thing she wanted was to get her brother in any more trouble than usual, or her father angrier than he already was.

She sat quietly for the next few miles until the strained silence began to suffocate her. She turned on the radio, but her father immediately instructed her to put the news on.

"I don't want to hear that noise you listen to. I'm not in the mood right now."

Amy pushed the worn button for his favorite station. It would seem stocks were down and that the temperature was going to get unbearably hot. The monotonous voice droned on about current events. But Amy found the soft cadence surprisingly soothing, as it helped to numb her mind against the world she was forced to live in.

The broadcast was suddenly interrupted.

'Breaking news. There's been a second car bombing. The police report charred remains of a woman in the automobile. We'll have more details as they come in.'

Amy continued to brace herself against the craziness.

8
Motor-Psycho Cop

He pulled the bike up in one fluid motion as the worn heel of his tall black boot set the kickstand. He stirred the dust on the road as he walked toward the vehicle.

"Good evening officer," the driver said.

"License and registration please."

"Certainly. Is there a problem, officer?"

Of course, there's a problem. Isn't there always? Everyone out here is a problem. But I always seem to find a workable solution.

He handed the officer his license and some papers.

"You were driving erratically, sir."

"I hadn't noticed."

"Have you been driving a while?"

"Not long."

"Are you here on business?" the officer asked in a cold and direct tone as he glanced at the out-of-town license. He also recognized the vehicle as a rental.

You don't want to be out here alone.

"I was here on business," he said attempting to be friendly.

I'm not sensing much truth here. I know you're not this nice.

"May I ask what business you're in, sir?" the officer asked.

"Bombshells," he said jokingly. "Of the blonde variety, if you catch my drift."

"I'm not sure what you mean, sir," the officer replied showing no sign of wanting to share in his humor.

"I'm a talent agent. And as you'd imagine, I usually have my hands full of beautiful girls," he explained feigning a wide grin, hoping to connect with the camaraderie that men tend to share when they talk about women. But he failed to get the response he expected.

Bullshit. The only thing that you get your hand around is your dick. As usual this is going to be easy and so right. People will thank me.

"Let me run this and I'll be right back, sir," the officer said.

Must take him out. Can't chance it.

He took his sweaty hands off the steering wheel.

'204? 204 please respond.'

I was designed for this. It wasn't part of my training, but it's my MO now. It's in my fingers. It's an itch, and the scratch will be quick, I promise. It didn't look like a phone? No, it looked like a gun handle. I understand it turned out to be a black eye glass case. But I tell you, it looked like the butt of a gun in his hand when he started to pull it out. There's so much shit that happens out here on the road it'll just be another one for the books.

It was a clean shot, though he wished the scene was messier, something for the boys to talk about for a while. More to sift through.

It should have been more of a major event. More photos. But anything more than a single shot would have been overkill. There would have been more questions and not as many of the right answers to go along with them. Next time. Next time the barrel will get as hot as a branding iron.

He walked around the car.

It's important I go through everything. Can't leave anything to chance. Success is in the details. And each detail must be thought out and double-checked.

He went to put the black eyeglass case into the driver's inside pocket, but instead he found a .38 revolver in a holster tucked under his arm.

Well, well.

He removed the gun and balanced it in his hand.

You just made this a whole lot easier.

He put another bullet into the already dead body just for the hell of it. Then he ran his flashlight along the floor of the front seat. The carpet was immaculate. Not even a candy wrapper or an empty Styrofoam coffee cup. Strange, he thought. Then he opened the glove box. Empty, not even a map.

He must've known where he was going, and how to get there.

He shined his flashlight across the backseat.

No luggage. Not even a briefcase. It's all too clean. Suspiciously clean.

Then he walked around to the back of the black compact and opened the trunk, where he found a scarf.

And not even a nice one. Not the style the wife would like, that's for sure. It wasn't about that anyway. I can get a five-dollar scarf anywhere.

"This is 204," he finally responded.

'204. There's been an officer involved shooting. Do you copy?'

"Copy that," he said. A smile came over his hard, square jaw. It was the same smile the driver had hoped to initiate earlier but had failed to achieve.

"Copy that," he repeated.

Neighbors

Joe sat out on his back deck to smoke on most evenings. It was a space that he shared with the adjacent unit, which was occupied by an attractive woman who constantly complained about his use of tobacco. Then one day she seemed to vanish rather mysteriously, leaving her car behind. Of course, Joe welcomed her departure, though he still found it suspicious nonetheless. Then about a month later, two young men moved in. Joe was pleased to find them smoking on the long narrow deck in what he considered a mutual and solidarity space between them. Though he usually found it difficult to hear their conversation as they tended to talk in whispers, which Joe thought odd since they were at an age when they should be blasting music and having loud parties. Joe remained vigilant though. At one point, he even considered that they might be terrorists. But nearly everyone looked the part these days, he thought.

In truth, only one smoked, and he was usually out on the deck more often than the other. Night after night he'd give Joe a silent nod and a thin smile, as he swayed back and forth in the dark as a sea captain might on the bow of a boat as he watched the world unfold before him. But there wasn't much of a worldly view to be had. In fact, it was little more than a parking lot and a few trees, and the backs of other houses. Though one can dream.

On most nights, the two men huddled close together at the far end of the deck. Joe suspected they were probably gay since they rarely mentioned women in their conversation. Joe knew if guys didn't bring up the topic of women every ten minutes, they were more than likely gay. Though perhaps they were too preoccupied with fucking people over in the business world to have time for them, he thought. He'd met a lot of guys like that who were too busy strategizing and calculating their careers and futures to find time for women. But once successful and obscenely rich, they arrogantly screwed whomever they pleased, as many women are attracted to that kind of thing.

One evening Joe caught an endearing term across the distance of the deck, which in fact revealed they were brothers, who'd no doubt exhausted their conversations about women years earlier; unlike strangers who need to reinforce their sexual stature so as not to be misunderstood or questioned.

Several women did eventually make a brief appearance. Some as if cast for a theatrical production, as girls who are picked up in bars at closing time often seem; still auditioning for the part as they work their way drunkenly in high heels up and down the hardwood floors of the adjacent apartment into the wee hours of the morning. Joe lay in bed late one night wondering why they hadn't already been bedded, as they certainly couldn't have been that difficult to put down. He laughed as he thought, even wild animals go down easier. He wanted to suggest that they either needed stronger booze or better moves.

One night while he was on his end of the deck, a voice broke the quiet evening air.

"I never did get your name."

Joe was involuntarily forced out of his solitude.

With what seemed like a genuine smile, the distant voice added, "I'm Bill."

The unexpected introduction took Joe by surprise. In fact, it was more like an answer to a question that hadn't been asked. Though he found it odd that Bill declined to change his position at his end of the deck to even come over and offer his hand. The exchange of names seemed sufficient, but only because the intent had been poorly initiated; one with no follow-through. And there didn't seem to be enough of a connection to expand on anything more than that at the time. Their names just dissipated into the quiet night air as if they'd never been shared. After Joe extinguished his cigarette, he said, "Goodnight then," as he went inside.

It wasn't until another week or so that his neighbor asked as if in an ongoing conversation, as a stranger might later in the evening at a party after encountering one another again, "So Joe, what do you do?"

Joe never welcomed that inquiry. In fact, he felt that information should be volunteered and not required, as many seem to believe. For that reason, he'd rehearsed several responses, some even humorous. But he never knew which would find its way out of his mouth at any given time. The question was relentless in social circles, so he could only hope for the best.

"You have my name and you know where I live. I'm sure that's more than sufficient for now. We probably shouldn't rush into this."

It might have seemed somewhat defensive at first, even rude, but Joe felt the question was equally so. He could tell it caught Bill off-guard, but he didn't appear offended. In fact, he seemed to appreciate the odd reply, as if it were appropriate for the distance between them in that moment. Or perhaps he accepted it as antidotal. But Joe's tone was also slightly flirtatious, if not off-putting as well; not unlike how a woman might reply when playfully bullied into a goodnight kiss.

Joe had withdrawn from making excuses for himself, or for that matter, apologizing for things he'd said. But there was a time when he would have felt obligated to explain his words. Now he let them remain where they fell, crash and burn, he didn't care.

So, Joe was surprised then when his neighbor made his way across the deck with his arm outstretched.

"We never did actually meet," Bill said putting his hand in Joe's. Joe didn't quite remember extending or even offering his hand, but there it was being comfortably cradled for a moment in the other man's firm grip, which didn't attempt to impress or dominate as Joe might have expected. It also didn't linger longer than socially acceptable, as he felt the cool air quickly rush in as it vacated his palm.

Bill was tall and full-shouldered. Joe was sure that he'd played football in college. In fact, he looked as if he might still have the voice of his coach in his head; one that sometimes continues to echo loudly even years later. Joe had anticipated hearing that same demanding tone, but instead, his voice was gentle and barely audible. It had a whispering characteristic to it, just like the one he'd heard from a distance on most nights out on the deck.

"Would you like a beer?" Bill asked.

"I could do with a beer," Joe replied as he followed him back across the length of the open deck. He decided it was also a good time to ask, "What happened to the woman who used to live here? She disappeared overnight." Joe was still curious because her car remained parked in the designated spot for Bill's flat.

Without responding, he handed Joe a beer, glancing momentarily over the railing through the dark of the night at the dusty car below.

"Where'd you bury the body? I only ask so as not to bury one of my own in the same spot. Because that would be awkward."

With a trace of a smile Bill said, "I wouldn't worry too much, it's a fairly deep grave."

Joe knew he was getting his in return for having responded as he had about what he did for a living.

"Actually, she's my ex. She's in Europe working right now."

"I've seen the women you guys have brought home, but they're nothing compared to the ones she had around. They all looked like models."

"That's because they were. That's what she does."

Joe studied Bill's face for shavings of a lie, but his expression remained unchanged.

"Not many women around these days," Bill offered, almost confirming Joe's suspicions. Then he added matter-of-factly, "My brother is separated. And until that's resolved, he's steering clear of women. If he ever goes back to them, that is."

Joe was surprised how easily Bill had volunteered that information.

"I would think he'd be out with a different woman every night."

"He's not that kind of guy," Bill said.

Joe didn't respond. He just waited for the words he expected to hear.

"He was studying to be a priest when he met his wife. But he gave it up for her. He sacrificed his vocation for her. And he'll probably go back to the church; not as a priest, of course. But if they get divorced then he'll be left with nothing. Because as you know those Roman Cats frown on that kind of thing."

Joe was caught off-guard. He hadn't expected the church to be part of the equation. Mostly because he'd struggled to free himself from it when he was younger.

"You probably thought he was gay," Bill added into the darkness.

"It crossed my mind. It seemed the logical conclusion."

"Have you ever slept with a man?" Bill asked.

The question was straightforward, but it didn't judge or seem to bait. In fact, it was more curious than anything else, as if Bill were looking for a way through the darkness they shared. Joe anticipated the conversation, but he hadn't expected it to be so direct, at least not so soon. It had somehow quickly advanced from what Joe did for a living to who he slept with. But before Joe had a chance to answer, Bill added in an even quieter voice, as if fondly recalling a part of his past that had slipped away, "I did once."

Joe recalled the nervous and exciting sensation that he felt when he first touched another boy. Or was touched by another boy. They were twelve. His stomach and groin tightened as they embraced what was taboo at the time. And it had been as much a mental adventure as it was a physical one. In that moment, he'd discovered his true nature, and had held onto it regardless of the detours he chose to take through life. He knew that Bill was recalling a similar experience now. .

"I'll admit though, it meant a lot to me," he added.

Maybe they had buried those bodies in the same place after all, Joe thought; however, a decade or so apart.

"I guess I'm just confused right now. I'm sure you understand."

Joe understood. He'd gone through it himself. He also understood that he didn't expect an answer.

"Can I ask about the images in your head?"

"I'm not sure what you mean."

Joe knew what he'd meant, but wanted confirmation nonetheless, as the conversation proved to be full of surprises.

"Sexual images. I'm sure you have them."

"They tend to vary from person to person," Joe admitted honestly. "I'm sure we get just as tired of our fantasies as we do some of our relationships."

"I would think fantasies were more resilient than that."

"I find even fantasies have flaws," Joe confessed.

"I probably have more faith in mine."

"You don't find that they change?"

"They seem to grow, more than change."

"Mine tend to morph into something else."

"So, you can be jerking off to a pretty girl in one moment, and in the next, what, you're jerking off to me?"

Bill remained facing the darkness in the distance, one hand firmly on the railing in front of him, the other tightly around his beer.

"I might not make that exact transition," Joe responded truthfully.

"So, you have thought about me when you jerk-off?"

Joe was humored that he'd assumed the transition involved him and not another girl. He also thought it presumptuous, if not conceited. Regardless, it did present the opportunity he'd hoped. Because Joe had to admit the nods across the mysterious silence on that late-night deck had sexually stimulated his imagination on many occasions.

Bill took a long swig from his beer. Maybe it was the vacant night air that seemed to help free him from his structured demeanor, because in that moment he offered a measure of vulnerability.

Without looking at Joe he added, "If you did, I wouldn't mind. In fact, I'd probably be flattered. But I'd rather not know."

But he was sure he did. Joe could see it in his face and in the thin smile he wore. Bill wanted him to share those stimulating images, if for no other reason than to verify that they'd been impressive and had done the trick, as it were. Not unlike asking a woman after sex if he'd been a skillful lover; a question that he suspected Bill had asked on more than one embarrassing occasion. Reassurance was important to Bill, that was obvious. Just as it was evident that Bill felt safe in another man's fantasy; preferably one similar, to his own. But however virtual and lonely that reality sometimes proved to be, it was an ideal place for Bill to embrace those desires without fear of social repercussion; like a long-distance relationship, though with barely a wall between them. But Joe knew it was an unhealthy compromise.

The erotic thoughts that he had of Bill began to diminish, proving that the fantasy he'd imagined had been better than the man. The illusion had worked up until then. But Bill lacked the finesse he had expected. Instead, what he discovered was a shattered man sadly out of sorts with himself. And whatever likeness had held that image firm in his mind on those late nights had evaporated in the dark in that moment. What had once been a promising figure, had become broken and vain, as he attempted to solicit a boost to his ego.

Fantasies change. In fact, some even die a quick death.

Joe wondered now about the women in high heels who had paced the hardwood floors in those early morning hours. Maybe they hadn't played hard to get after all and weren't teasingly resisting his charms, but had in fact, grown impatient as they waited for him to make his move, leaving them with no option but to parade their wilting wares up and down the hallway in hopes of recapturing his interest while he questioned his loss of appetite.

The fantasy had waned for Joe, and with it the character next to him as well. He no longer found Bill interesting, or even attractive for that matter. Joe knew he would never be able to place himself in the arms of someone who barely had a grip on them self, even in a fantasy. It was obvious now that the fantasy he created was no longer desirable. In fact, it disappeared. And when he finished his beer, he would as well.

Joe replied with neither flirtation nor encouragement.

"No, you're right, you really don't want to know."

Bill seemed disappointed as if another world, and another fantasy, had dissipated in front of his eyes.

Joe knew he'd be unable to compromise even in the abstract. He also wouldn't be responsible for leading Bill in that direction. They would be his steps to take, and his alone. He'd leave Bill exactly where he found him, on that deck, incapable of allowing anything more than a fantasy into his life; one that would quietly lay naked on the other side of a mutually shared wall, caught in the same unfulfilled illusion. But Joe wouldn't allow himself to be trapped behind a wall, not again.

It was apparent now that Bill's sexual ambivalence had been reason for his brother's concern. And that he had no doubt attempted to pull Bill back into the faith as they talked for hours at the other end of the deck on those late nights, hoping to guide him, if not reunite him again with his ex-wife; perhaps even praying to correct a curse, as it were, with God's help. Joe would even speculate that his brother's efforts to salvage Bill's marriage had more to do with his own failed and irretrievable one.

After that evening, he rarely saw Bill out on the deck again. On the rare occasion that he did, Bill no longer offered that once familiar nod, not even a knowing one. It was as if they never shared a beer that evening.

A month later, Bill's ex-wife returned from Europe and moved in with him; reaffirming Joe's theory that most bodies are buried shallower than the truth.

The Old Man

Jesse assumed that the old man sitting on the curb was enjoying a quiet moment in the sun while waiting for someone to pick him up. In fact, he reminded him of the old men in his neighborhood where he grew up, who sat in their wife-beaters on the front stoop of their buildings in the summer heat. But the old man was properly dressed, as some men of his generation continued to do. He wore a dark suit and tie, and a black hat that covered his freshly trimmed white hair. He appeared to be a tall, thin man, with a faded but still noticeable twinkle in his eye. But then Jesse watched as the old man struggled to get up, swaying back and forth until he finally fell gently back onto the curb again.

Jesse walked over.

"Are you, all right? Can I give you a hand?"

The old man didn't respond. Instead, he appeared to have resigned to his situation. It was then that Jesse noticed the bag of groceries scattered next to the parked car beside him.

Retrieving the items, Jesse said, "It looks like we lost the eggs, but the apples will be okay if you give them a good wash."

The old man looked disoriented.

"Did you fall?" he asked as he gently helped him up by the hand.

The old man nodded.

He set him upright.

"Are you Irish, by chance?"

Still somewhat at odds, he nodded again. But this time he found his voice, and frailly said, "Part Irish."

"I ask because the Irish are notorious for taking some pretty nasty falls after a few drinks, and living to tell about them," Jesse said offering a smile.

The old man smiled back at him.

"Do you live nearby?"

The old man pointed to the building across the street.

After gathering up the groceries, Jesse helped him cross the road. Every few steps, the old man nearly lost his balance, and each time Jesse helped to steady him.

When they reached the other side, Jesse asked, pointing optimistically to the ground floor apartment, "Is this you here?"

"I'm at the top," the old man replied, his voice still thin and broken.

Jesse looked at the exterior stairs that led up to the top floor. Of course, it would be, he thought.

Each step was a challenge for the old man. But Jesse helped to balance him with a steadying hand to his back until they eventually maneuvered the three flights to the top landing. There were a couple of times when Jesse thought he might lose him. He'd have certainly taken a tumble if he hadn't been there to guide him along.

"This is me here," the old man said pointing a trembling finger to the door on the left. Then bracing himself with one hand against the wall, he attempted to steady the other enough to put the key into the lock. He fussed with it for a moment until the door finally opened.

"Are you going to be okay? Can I call someone?" Jesse asked.

"No, I'll be all right," the old man said in a stronger voice now, having no doubt reached his comfort zone. "Thank you for your help," he added as he slowly closed the door behind him. But a moment later it opened again slightly, only to close once more as if he were having trouble shutting it. Just as Jesse took the stairs the door opened again, though this time nearly halfway, as if it had swung open on its own.

Jesse retraced his steps up to the landing.

He stuck his head into the doorway.

"Are you, all right?"

There was no answer.

Jesse called out again, but this time he stood fully in the doorway.

"Sir, are you okay?"

There was still no answer. Fearing the worse, Jesse entered the dimly lit apartment. It was only then that he saw the old man sitting in an armchair. It was undoubtedly where he'd spent most of his time. When he saw Jesse, he waved him over with a loose hand.

"Are you okay? Can I get you something?" he asked.

The old man just waved at him to come closer, until Jesse stood within arm's reach. Then he just sat motionless as he stared straight ahead without saying a word. Jesse thought that perhaps he'd had a stroke. But there was still that noticeable twinkle in his eyes. And he could see now that he'd been a handsome man in his day.

Then as if in a hypnotic trance the old man nervously extended his arm. And with an open hand he gently placed it fully on Jesse's crotch, just as he might a bible or a gravestone; as it was almost spiritual. But it was also as if he were recalling a memory. Jesse couldn't help but feel sorry for the old man. The truth was, he often saw himself as old and lonely one day as well. And it wouldn't be the first time that he'd offered himself in a charitable way.

The old man continued to rest his hand on Jesse's crotch as if searching for a heartbeat. He was no doubt waiting for affirmation. Which didn't take long, as Jesse immediately began to get hard. It was only then that the old man proceeded to slowly unzip Jesse's pants; and as he did, his hand shook slightly. Jesse wasn't sure if it was from age or anticipation. But a moment later his full erection was carefully balanced in the old man's palm, where he held it pensively, as if weighing it in comparison to his own or others. Then he slowly leaned forward and took it into his mouth delicately, as if it were something rare or fragile. Jesse was surprised to find that it wasn't much different from a younger man's mouth. But he wouldn't deny the old man his moment by closing his eyes and trying to imagine a fresher face with a more attractive pair of lips. Instead, he appreciatively watched as he tenderly, if not awkwardly, attempted to swallow it; though never taking it in entirely. The old man took it more as a baby would a pacifier. But less than a minute later, he gently removed it from between his thin lips and let it dangle freely in front of him. Then without averting his eyes, he silently watched as it pulsated and gradually diminished in size; lowering itself, not unlike a conductor's baton fluidly bringing a movement to its final cadence, until it eventually came to rest and was flaccid again.

The old man looked up at Jesse and said with the same gratitude he had earlier, "Thank you." Then leaning back into his chair, he took a long deep breath, and added apologetically, "Sorry, it's not quite what I expected."

Jesse couldn't help but be offended; hurt in fact, that the old man had been dissatisfied with his appendage, not to mention his generous nature. Of course, it wasn't as sacred as some, but it certainly wasn't a burnt offering either. But then the familiar words came back to Jesse like lyrics to an old song, recapturing a moment some years earlier. Those exact words in fact.

Tom put his fork down and politely pushed the plate away from him. "Sorry, it's not quite what I expected," he said.

"You mean to tell me you've never had lobster before?"

"No, this is my first."

Lobster was out of season and fishing for it was banned on the island to allow for recruitment. But Jesse made special arrangements with the owner of the restaurant to catch two especially for them that night.

"Do you know what lobster costs, not to mention out of season? That's an eighty-dollar lobster," Jesse said.

"I know, and it looks lovely. Really it does."

"You don't order lobster if you haven't had it before. You try it first to see if you like it. It's not hamburger."

"Actually, I wouldn't mind a hamburger. Do you think they have them here?" Tom asked demurely.

Only then did Jesse realize that the old man didn't have an acquired taste for what he'd just put in his mouth. But that it was more likely just an item on his bucket list. In fact, Jesse suspected it was probably the last item on it. It made sense now.

After tucking himself neatly back into his pants, slightly amused, Jesse said, "I'm guessing that was your first time."

"Oh yes, absolutely," the old man said innocently.

Jesse thought to ask him how it was, but he didn't want to sound like a waiter asking about the steak he'd ordered. At least he hadn't asked with his mouth full as many waiters often do.

"I suspected it wasn't for me," the old man said. "Maybe I should have tried it earlier on. Maybe it's just a younger man's game. But the truth is, I always loved my wife and her pretty places far too much to have had a desire to venture from them."

Jesse smiled, envious of his dedication.

"If I could reach my own I might have tried that instead," the old man added with a smile. "It would've saved us both an embarrassing situation."

"That's usually part of the experience. At least at first," Jesse said. "But you have nothing to be embarrassed about."

"That's kind of you to say."

"It took guts to do what you did, though."

"When you get to be my age you don't care what people think."

"Can I ask you something?"

"After that, I think you can ask me anything."

Jesse smiled.

"How did you know I wouldn't bash your head in? This isn't exactly a gay neighborhood."

"I knew almost from the start," the old man said.

"How?" Jesse was curious.

"You were just too kind."

"I didn't know that was possible."

"If you'd helped me up and left me there I wouldn't have taken the chance. But unlike the others, you saw me to my door and made sure I was okay. But it was when you placed your hand on my back to guide me up the stairs; there was just something intimate in your touch."

"The others?" Jesse asked, realizing now that the entire thing had been staged.

"I couldn't have approached just anyone," the old man confessed.

"You could have rented an escort."

"That would've been illegal, if not dangerous," the old man said. "And on my limited income it would have been a waste of money if I didn't like it. And as you see, I didn't. No offense."

"None taken. And the eggs? Did you sacrifice them for effect?"

"I hadn't planned on losing the eggs," the old man said in a frugal tone. "That was an unexpected casualty. I also hadn't expected to get so dizzy."

Jesse felt less like a casualty himself now.

"I can get more eggs if you'd like?"

"I've put you out enough already," the old man said.

"The putting out was my pleasure," Jesse said jokingly. "But let me do that for you. And while I'm gone you might want to call a doctor."

The old man shook his head.

"He'll just tell me to stay in bed and tuck my dreams in with me."

"I understand. I'll get the eggs and be right back then."

When Jesse got to the door, the old man sincerely said, "I'll say this. If I ever thought to venture in that direction, I would have hoped to have met someone like you."

"That's very kind of you to say," Jesse said with an appreciative smile. As he went out he added, "I'll keep the door ajar, so you won't have to get up to let me back in."

The old man offered a friendly though fragile wave.

Then leaning deeper into his armchair, he closed his eyes and dreamt of his pretty wife and her pretty parts, and an even prettier place now; as he fell into a peaceful and endless sleep that he hoped would bring them together again.

Caught in A Doorway

After putting his cigarette out, Duncan poured himself a second cup of coffee as he waited for his overnight guest to wake up. He felt captive in his own house as he moved about quietly trying not to make too much noise, though perhaps just enough to stir him out of his deep slumber.

Duncan took his coffee out onto the deck into the bright sunlight, which made his hangover feel even worse. But it was then that he noticed that one of the tall deck chairs had cast a curious shadow on the side of the house. He thought he was seeing things, so he approached the likeness cautiously, just as he had as a child. Then lifting his sunglasses, he studied it, not certain if his eyes were playing tricks on him. But there was no mistaking the image. It was of a holy figure. He moved the chair into the shade just in case the paperboy or a neighbor came by. He wasn't constitutionally prepared for visions or visitations, even on Sunday.

Then pushing his shades back against his face, he lit another cigarette and went back to sit in the sun.

When Duncan got out of bed that morning, all he wanted was to crawl back into it again and sleep. But the muscular figure he'd tangled with the night before was sprawled diagonally across his queen-size mattress, and he was in no condition to reignite those same desires. At least not then. And as mornings like these usually went, for the life of him he couldn't remember the guy's name.

As he took another sip of coffee the telephone rang. Duncan welcomed the diversion.

"Whatever it is, please say it quietly," he pleaded, his broken and raspy baritone reverberating into the receiver.

"I guess phone sex is out of the question then," the voice teased.

"Sex is the cause for my current state," he responded.

"How young was he this time?" Veronica inquired jokingly.

"This isn't a crime scene," Duncan replied.

"I'm guessing the victim's still there then."

"I'm the victim," he grunted. "It's been a cruel morning. My bed's been taken hostage. And I had a visit from the Virgin Mary."

"She still comes around?"

"It's a side-effect of being brainwashed as a child."

"And just so you know darling, morning's over."

"Then why do I still feel so miserable?"

"Probably because you're going to cancel our date for brunch."

He squinted painfully behind his dark glasses.

"I completely forgot. But the truth is, you wouldn't enjoy eating while sitting across from me. Not with how I look and feel."

"I was counting on just those dietary benefits," Veronica said.

"You already look like Kate Fucking Moss."

"It's a never-ending process."

"Well, you'll have to be content with being a zero for now, because as soon as Adonis leaves I'm going back to sleep."

"How's next weekend?"

"Better."

"Okay. Bye."

The quiet settled in again.

The trees below the deck swayed gently in the warm breeze. Duncan was about to turn away from the sun when a tall figure came out of the bedroom. He watched the strong silhouette move behind the partial glare of the sliding glass door as he tucked his white tee shirt into his faded blue denims. Duncan watched as he ran his fingers through his black hair, pulling his bangs back away from his eyes. When he eventually came out onto the deck, Duncan felt his jeans tighten as the image began to arouse him again. But he was still too drained and isolated in his own head to think about sex.

"Good morning."

"I was just informed it's no longer morning." Duncan forced a smile.

"I hope I haven't kept you from anything."

"Nothing I can't put off till later."

"I'm sorry if I did," he said apologetically.

"It wasn't important. I made my bed, so to speak." He joked.

"Well, actually, I just did," he said gesturing toward the house.

"You didn't have to do that."

"It's the least I could do."

"Can I get you some coffee?"

"No thanks. I should get going. But if you have a pen, I'll give you my number." He smiled into the warmth of the sun.

Duncan never cared for the morning after routine. In fact, if the roles were reversed he'd have likely tried to slip out before daylight.

As he leaned down to write his number Duncan watched as his hair fell onto his brow again like the dark lining of a rogue wave. He closed his eyes, recalling how it lashed softly across his face in the close darkness; the sweet smell of his sweat like a driving mist against his surrendering skin. With his jeans unzipped and low on his strong hips, he pushed into Duncan with unbridled passion. He recalled that his sensuous lips offered kisses filled with unexpected desire, as the force of his firm upward cock pressed into his groin. He remembered being barely able to hold on, though he resisted, as Duncan wasn't ready to resign to it. It was something he regretted later. In fact, that regret came as soon as he'd put a match to his cigarette after they eventually pulled themselves apart. It remained a visceral vignette across the screen of his closed eyes, like a heavily intoxicating and romantic foreign film; one filled with ambiance and undeniable direction. The heat between them had been so intense in fact, that Duncan felt the bulb burn through the celluloid right up the middle of him.

He put the pen down.

Duncan studied the fine script.

"Give me a call," Matthew said, offering a smile that revealed a slightly chipped tooth in an otherwise perfect mouth. Then he threw his black leather jacket over his shoulder and let it hang by his thumb. Duncan thought him wickedly sexy again. Then Matthew added, "I had a great time. We should get together again soon. Maybe even have dinner."

When Duncan closed the door, he immediately realized the excessive caffeine and countless cigarettes had only intensified his painful hangover. Welcoming the quiet of the empty house again, he dragged his merciless body back to bed. As he went, he instinctively tossed the piece of paper into the trash, if for no other reason than to free him from the sheer weight of it.

* * *

The late morning sounds of the bustling city continued to brew as they sat outside on the patio of the restaurant.

Veronica was sure Duncan wasn't listening.

"I heard on the news recently that ninety percent of parents say they'd rather their kids told them they were gay than have them move back home again."

She waited for a response.

Upping the volume, she said, "Did you hear about that?"

"Are you serious?"

"Of course not. But with the economy the way it is, I wouldn't be at all surprised."

He surrendered.

"Okay, you have my full attention."

"Good. Now tell me about your date. The one that forced you to cancel on me last week."

"It wasn't a date," he said dryly. "Who goes on dates anymore?"

"Girls do."

"Exactly."

"So, what do you call it then?"

"A night out. Hooking up. Taking someone home."

"So how was your night out then?"

"Nothing special," he lied unconvincingly.

The truth was, it had been more than that. And that fact had distracted him just moments ago.

"You live such a crazy life," she said.

"We both live crazy lives," he corrected her.

"We do, don't we?" she agreed. Then added in a serious tone, "You know, I thought you would have found love by now working at the bar."

"That's the last place I expect to find it," he said truthfully. "But it's served its purpose in other ways."

"But once you get it out of your system, what are you left with?"

He let her words go without responding.

"Enough about me. What's been happening with you? Have you slept at any of the finer houses in the city recently?" he asked.

"No," she said matter-of-factly.

"You never stay over, do you? Why's that?"

"Because I don't want to be treated the way you treat your guests," she said teasingly, as she leaned back taking a sip of wine.

Veronica kept her world at a preferred distance, one that made her feel safe. She would rather be the one to reach out to it than have it reach out to her. Perhaps they were alike in that way, she thought.

"But it's not my house you're staying at," he said.

"I'm too old to sleep over. There's too much I need to do before I go to bed. Too many things to put on, and just as many to take off."

She intended her words to be humorous, but they proved to be more revealing. Veronica was an undisclosed number of years older than Duncan, though still an attractive woman. Her long red hair and ivory skin perfectly framed her hazel green eyes and full lips, in stark contrast to his darker and more European tones.

The idea of the process frightened Duncan.

"I won't ask what that means. But I know how you are."

"Okay smart guy, if you know me so well, what's my favorite color?"

Sensing a trap, he said, "You don't have one. You're color-blind."

"Lucky guess. Okay, then tell me why I always end up with a guy who has an average sized dick?"

"You get what you ask for."

"That's not what I mean when I say I want to meet an average guy."

Just then the waiter arrived with their salmon crepes with capers.

"Is there anything else I can get for you?" he asked politely.

Recognizing a familiar look in Veronica's eyes, Duncan replied, "No, I think we're fine. Thank you."

"Enjoy," the waiter said, as he walked away.

"You're no fun."

"He's just another average guy," he said as he cut into his crepe.

"I doubt that he's average," she said confident in her estimation. "Did you see those hands?"

"Those tells are tall tales. Never trust them."

But he knew she'd never abandon them.

"Speaking of commitment, are you any closer to the concept?"

"I'm fine with things as they are," he said. "I just like to know more is there if I need it."

He listened dubiously to his own words.

"So why beat yourself up over it?"

He hesitated. Then said, "Because I'm closer." He feigned a smile.

She hadn't considered it a matter of logistics, but she saw it now. She could tell that he was struggling with something, but she decided to let it go. The last thing she wanted to do was add to the beating.

"Love isn't always as obvious as we think. It can be right there in our hands, fully embraced, and we don't realize it."

"I'm sure it's slipped out of mine more than once," he confessed. "But only when they're empty again do I realize it."

"Some people find true love, the kind that will last forever, even after the other dies. Then there are others who think they're in love. They marry and have children. But they're never satisfied. Because it wasn't really love at all. It was just something that took its place when all other options were exhausted." She took a long sip of her wine. "Then there are those that never find love and see it for what it is; a situation they have no control over."

"That sounds more like me."

"I think you just need to recognize it and let it into your life."

"I'm afraid I won't recognize it though."

His mind drifted back to his earlier thoughts again.

"We don't always realize what we have when we have it," she said.

"I doubt we'll ever get it right," he said. "What would it be like if we did?"

"Boring. Not to mention, probably a sobering experience."

"Exactly."

Veronica pulled her hair back and tied it up behind her head in one fluid motion.

"The way you're going, you might as well charge for it. If it's not love, then you're just giving it away."

"I like to think of it as a gift."

"You're not that charitable. What you are, is chicken."

He pushed a piece of fish onto his fork.

"When we're young, we're called chicken and beat up on. Later, we're called chicken again. But it's desirable, even advantageous. Especially with older men." He paused for effect. "Then we're beat-off on."

"Not exactly an appetizing image while eating. But that's not what I meant. Besides, you're too old to be considered chicken."

"But I still have a yellow streak when it comes to relationships."

"You need to learn to sacrifice a part of yourself in order to accept that part of someone else," she said.

"I doubt there's room for both," he said unconvincingly.

"You're such a liar."

"But it suits me."

"What, the lies?"

He smiled.

"It's a shame a penis doesn't grow when it lies. It would make the lies at least tolerable."

"Lie to me baby! Oh yeah, give me a big one, and make it original!"

She laughed.

"I already get that. But sadly, without the grow factor."

He poured more wine into their glasses.

"Maybe the Virgin can do something about that. I'll ask, the next time I see her. But tell me, how's your love life? And don't shut me out. Don't be like your mother."

"My mother still thinks oral sex is when someone sings romantically under her bedroom window. Believe me, I'm not my mother."

"Share then."

"Okay, how's this? I recently went out with a guy who didn't even bother to take me for a drink, no less dinner. He just pulled into a shady spot near the bridge expecting a blow-job."

"What did Veronica say to that?"

"She told him just because he drove an expensive car, that he shouldn't assume he was going to get his dick sucked. And if the salesman told him he'd get more pussy than a crazy cat-woman living in a shuttered old house if he bought the car, he should go back and drive it through the showroom window, because he wasn't going to get the pussy promised him. Not unless that pussy frequented the vet every week."

"You said that?"

"Damn right I did."

Veronica was clearly offended by the experience.

They were different in that respect.

"I guess I'm usually more accommodating."

"Usually? That deserves an explanation."

Duncan hesitated.

"Fine. I met this guy, and when he pulled it out, I didn't know what to say, no less do."

"I can't imagine you speechless. But I always find it a surprise either way. So, what did Duncan say?"

"I said you don't expect me to put my laughing gear around that thing, do you?"

"Did you?"

"Of course not."

"Was it too big, or too small? Or was it just weird looking? I've seen those before." She made a face.

"I'm not saying." He coyly took a sip of wine.

"I've never known you to be chivalrous."

"Of course, I let him do me."

"That's my Duncan," she said. "And how was that?"

"It wasn't much of a blow-job. It was more like a head wind."

She lifted her glass.

"Any port in a storm. I guess that's what we should expect."

They clicked glasses.

"The thing is, I never know what to expect."

"Just the unexpected," she said, finishing the wine in her glass.

Duncan pulled the bottle out of the ice bucket.

"It's empty. And it's only noon!"

"Then we're way off our game," she said. "Waiter!"

* * *

When Duncan woke, the guy next to him said as if waiting to be cued, "When I was younger I got into bed for money. Now I'm forced to get out of it to make a living."

Duncan ignored him just as he had the night before. Instead of leaving after they had sex as he normally would, Duncan passed-out and fell into a peaceful and welcoming dream. Thankfully, the guy wasn't in it. But it was the last place he expected to have that kind of a dream, because the sex had been bad, almost as bad as the guy's breath. But that may have had more to do with the words that came out of his mouth. Regardless, he found the guy boring and self-obsessed.

He had come into the bar on several occasions asking for coffee.

"You know every other door knob in this city is a Starbucks, right?" Duncan said in a tone not quite as off-putting as it was meant.

The guy just smiled.

"Why pull on this one? It's obvious we're a bar."

The guy remained unfazed. In fact, he seemed amused.

Oddly, Duncan found his determination attractive, if not challenging.

"So how old is the coffee, then?" the guy asked.

"Old," Duncan said pouring him a cup.

He took a sip.

"It tastes better than the last time I was here."

"Interesting. Because I'm pretty sure it's the same pot."

The guy just smiled again.

There was something about him that Duncan couldn't quite put a finger on. But when he eventually did, that very first touch told him it was wrong. And the kisses were wrong too. In fact, the entire experience proved insipid. But Duncan pushed through anyway hoping it would end sooner than usual. But he knew his body. He knew the less he liked someone, the longer it took to release his passion. And he couldn't fake it. He couldn't pretend he was spent. Of course, he'd also be expected to get him off as well. But Duncan didn't always do what was expected.

He grabbed at images in his head like an old newsreel searching for the right story, the right face, the right fantasy. And when he finally found the image he was looking for, he shot his load like a bullet just as he had on that unforgettable night with Matthew. He couldn't deny the effectiveness of the image. Duncan didn't need to fake his moans or even his gasp for air, as his lungs pounded involuntarily. His muscles contracted, and his knees gave out, causing his body to collapse on the bed. Duncan had embraced the memory until his eyes were forced to face the truth in front of him again. He wished now he'd just given the guy a c-note not to get into bed with him, rather than risk spoiling the image he had of Matthew. But with the images juxtaposed, one obviously more real than the other, as it unfortunately remained next to him, the other felt more significant and real in comparison. Oddly, Duncan felt fulfilled and empty in the same moment. In his mind, it was a wonderful experience. But his body felt strangely unconscious, even defiled. Of all the doorways, he chose to pass through, he questioned why he chose this one. But there was one consolation; it was likely the guy wouldn't come around again.

Out in the bright morning street a young boy was clinging tightly to his mother's leg. Duncan could see the frightening world in his early and eager eyes. It doesn't get better the further you get from the ground, he wanted to tell him. You only have that much further to fall.

A girl in a summer dress was kicking a large ball with what looked like her younger sister. Duncan came up behind them as they were deep in play. The girl's face was suddenly filled with fear when she saw him. He could see that the world had stripped her of a considerable measure of innocence, as her eyes were ready to tear.

Duncan smiled.

"Excuse me, ladies," he said as he passed around them to get to his car.

How easily someone could just take her, he thought.

As he closed the car door he said, "You be careful out here."

The girl forced a smile to her face as she held her hand up to block the sun as he drove off.

Later that morning he telephoned Veronica.

He could no longer deny how he felt about that evening with Matthew.

"I always knew I wanted to get divorced," she said. "But I was never sure I wanted to get married."

"You know you can't do one without the other, right?"

"Sadly," she said.

"You're probably the wrong person to have called about this."

"Then call your mother," she offered jokingly.

"There's still no service in purgatory."

Veronica acknowledged the desperation in his tone.

"So, he got away. Accept it and move on. Now at least you'll recognize it the next time. Because there will be a next time."

"That's comforting."

"I'm being serious."

"I am too," he admitted soberly.

"Good," she said, catching the proper cadence.

"But if you find me messing up again, tell me."

"I look forward to it."

"Me too."

Veronica knew to choose her words carefully to ensure what she said wouldn't be misconstrued.

"Forget the past. Clear your mind of it before it drives you crazy. And do it before you go to sleep tonight. Then you can wake up a new man and hopefully move on and look toward the future."

Later that evening Duncan tried to clear his head. But the more he tried, the more congested it seemed to become. In fact, he found himself reflecting on the negative events in his life. In that emptiness, he sought, he also found the emptiness he'd lived. While staring into that crowded darkness, Duncan hoped to free his mind of his cynicism about love and help purge it of the meaningless encounters he'd had, if not offer him a new start. He also hoped to cleanse his tortured soul. Instead, he spent most of those sleepless hours retracing his past. Though few recollections were truly sustainable, as most made him feel emotionally barren. He realized that somewhere along the way he'd lost focus of what he was truly looking for; and instead had found himself in a shallow routine of pulling someone in late at night, and pushing them out again the next morning, without ever considering the possibilities.

Duncan ran through the images quickly. Mostly because he knew if he hadn't there'd be little time for sleep. It was somewhere near the end of that long and somewhat painful list that Matthew's face came into focus again. In that heavy darkness with his eyes closed, he could see his image clearly. It was so close in fact, that he could reach out and touch it. And for a brief second, he could feel his skin against his again as if he were there with him, just as he had when the same image had rescued him from the insipid coffee guy. Duncan embraced the image again as he had before, allowing it to seep into his consciousness as he fell off into a comforting, if not deceptive sleep.

Duncan stood in the entranceway of the cafe waiting for a break in the torrential downpour. Just then, a man jumped in out of the rain next to him.

"Damn it's coming down," he said angrily. Duncan didn't respond.

The man silently brushed himself off and went into the café.

A few moments later, another man jumped into the doorway out of the heavy rain with a newspaper over his head. He bent over and shook himself like a puppy, tossing beads of moisture from side to side with his hair as he wiped both arms simultaneously. Then he dried his face with the underside of his scarf.

Duncan silently acknowledged their shared situation with a nod.

It was only then that he recognized him.

"Well, hi!" the voice said genuinely surprised.

His familiarity nearly startled him.

"How have you been?"

"Fine," Duncan lied, as he turned to allow someone else to pass on their way out of the café.

"I was just thinking of you the other day," Matthew said, exposing that slightly chipped tooth behind his wicked smile. "I was wondering why you never called."

Duncan knew the piece of paper he'd written his number on was little more than illegible pulp buried somewhere at the bottom of a heap of trash now. When he finally regretted throwing it away it was too late.

"I think that house burned down," Duncan offered humorously, though he was also noticeably embarrassed.

Just then a couple came in out of the rain.

"Excuse us," one of the women said.

"I haven't seen rain like this in years," her friend offered as they went by. "I think the drought is over," she added with a smile.

A quiet took the air again as the café door closed behind them.

"I thought we'd made a connection that night," Matthew offered as he challenged the silence now.

"It was a fun night," Duncan replied. But the truth was, he didn't know what else to say. He'd regretted not following through. He knew it now, and he knew it then, he finally confessed to himself.

"I thought it was more than that. More than just the sex."

Matthew's words felt like a knife in Duncan's chest, right there where he'd once rested his chin and embraced him so passionately. He felt his heart in his throat. If he ever questioned where it was, there was no doubt now. He immediately felt close to him again. In fact, even closer than he had before. He felt his step advance toward Matthew, though he didn't recall changing his footing. It was as if his body reacted involuntarily to the dream in front of him. He hoped the tears that ran down his cheeks would be thought of as rain, as the wind continued to kick up a measure of moisture into the open doorway. The downpour was like a heavy curtain dividing their tiny shelter from the distant storm now, cutting them off from the outside world. On one side the gray, steel-like sheet of rain; on the other, the crowded café filled with people living their silent lives, little more than stories behind a pane of glass.

Duncan couldn't be sure, as the untamed mist drifted into the doorway, but he thought he also saw tears in Matthew's eyes. His thick black hair was matted against his damp forehead, exactly as Duncan remembered it during those heated hours that passed between them some months earlier. A night that Duncan was ready to recapture now and never let go of.

As they seemed to lean into one another and take hold of destiny again, a slender figure broke through the rain into the doorway. Duncan felt their sanctuary had been invaded. He politely moved aside to allow the young man to get by, anxious now to be alone with Matthew. He wanted to reach out and touch him. He wanted his face in his hands again. He wanted to push his wet hair from his forehead and kiss him. He wanted to pull him close, and in doing so, close a long-endured gap in his life; a vacancy he'd occupied as a lone boarder for far too long. Because in that moment, Duncan knew he'd be able to allow Matthew into his life and keep him there forever.

The young man remained in the doorway trying to catch his breath.

"Man, it's really coming down," he said. Then he smiled at Duncan, who attempted to return the look, but it felt forced, so he let it go.

Instead, Duncan said, "Sorry man, you want to get by?"

"Thanks," the young man said bashfully. "I'm okay. Just soaking wet." Then he attempted to dry himself, but he seemed overly animated doing it, as if trying to be playful.

"Sorry," he said as if apologizing now for the intrusion.

His presence began to annoy Duncan.

The rain grew louder as Duncan listened for Matthew's voice across the doorway. He hoped he'd ignore the intrusion and finish what he was about to say. Duncan impatiently watched his lips waiting for the words he needed to hear, the ones he'd denied himself when he foolishly tossed his number into the trash that morning.

To his unpleasant surprise the words that broke the quiet weren't what Duncan had expected.

"It took me fifteen minutes to find a space," the young man said. Then he kissed Matthew on the lips, which responded without hesitation.

Duncan felt his heart die again right where he'd rediscovered it.

"We should've come together," Matthew said after their embrace.

"Who knew it was going to rain like this?" the young man said. "They never get it right. But we should probably get out of this weather."

"First I want you to meet Duncan. He's an old acquaintance."

Duncan failed to lift his arm to take his hand, as his body felt too heavy now. But to his surprise he found it extended in front of him anyway, as he mindlessly went through the motions.

"Nice to meet you," the young man said.

"You're right though, we should go," Matthew said. "It was good to see you again, Duncan. Take care of yourself."

Duncan was unable to focus. It was as if he were trying to make out his image in a shattered mirror.

"Bye," the young man said with a friendly and innocent wave.

Duncan reluctantly echoed the sentiment as he watched the single word fall from of his mouth and onto its face, then disappear.

As Matthew opened the door, he said with a noticeable measure of regret, "Try not to burn down any more homes, Duncan."

As the café door closed behind him, a stream of warm air escaped from inside that gently brushed past his face as if teasing and challenging his very existence. But it dissipated just as quickly into the unsettled air as he stood alone in the doorway trying to focus on the shattered remnants of his life.

As his heartbeat gradually returned to normal again, an odd feeling ran through him. It was then that Duncan looked toward the thick wall of rain, which was more a solid metallic sheet now, and caught a faint trace of his own reflection. Though in truth, it was more a distorted shadow. But still, he sensed an intrinsic change in it, perhaps even a recognizable one. Duncan couldn't deny he felt abandoned, especially since he was unable to go back into the café now with Matthew inside. But he also knew that he couldn't journey back out into the storm again either.

As he looked past it now toward a distance that appeared closer than it had before, Duncan envisioned a new direction; one that he voluntarily embraced.

The Attack

Detective: Have a seat. I have a few questions. First, state your name and the date.

Jerry: Jerry Marks. February 13, 2004.

Detective: And your friends name?

Jerry: Danny Klarsfeld.

Detective: Okay Mr. Marks, tell me exactly what happened.

Jerry: There's not much to tell. I was driving along, and I saw my friend Danny getting gay-bashed.

Detective: Go on.

Jerry: He'd been gay-bashed once before.

Detective: I read the file.

Jerry: That attack traumatized him. He couldn't even leave the house to go to work. It nearly ruined him financially.

Detective: I guess it's sort of like rape.

Jerry: What?

Detective: Like rape. I imagine it's like being raped.

Jerry: It's nothing like being raped. Where're you going with this anyway?

Detective: Nowhere. Why?

Jerry: You always attack our sexuality as if it were to blame for everything.

Detective: It seems to be the cause of most of your problems.

Jerry: What's that supposed to mean?

Detective: It means, it wasn't a hate crime.

Jerry: I saw the whole thing.

Detective: You saw what you think you saw.

Jeremy: What does that mean?

Detective: It means it was a robbery plain and simple.

Jerry: So, he also robbed Danny. But it was still a hate crime.

Detective: It wasn't.

Jerry: It looked a lot like a gay-bashing to me.

Detective: But it wasn't.

Jerry: Okay, so I helped him fend off a robber.

Detective: No Mr. Marks. It was your friend doing the robbing.

Jerry: No way!

Detective: You helped beat-up a guy who was just trying to defend himself. What you did was, interfere in his self-defense.

Jerry: But when I drove by---

Detective: When you drove by you just assumed your friend was being assaulted. When in fact, he was robbing that gentleman. But he got the better of your friend.

Jerry: That can't be right. I know what I saw.

Detective: Did you see him hit your friend?

Jerry: Of course, he was pounding on him.

Detective: Perhaps when you got there. But I have two witnesses who saw the entire thing.

Jerry: But the guy was beating up Danny.

Detective: In self-defense.

Jerry: That's not how it happened.

Detective: Like you said, he had financial problems.

Jerry: But he wouldn't rob someone.

Detective: Not just anyone. But a guy who looked a lot like the one your friend had a problem with a few months back.

Jerry: So, it was the same guy.

Detective: No, it wasn't.

Jerry: That can't be right.

Detective: He only looked like the guy who beat him up.

Jerry: You mean gay-bashed. You can't say it, can you?

Detective: The fact is, you helped assault an innocent man.

Jerry: But Danny was getting the crap kicked out of him.

Detective: And maybe he deserved it. But that guy didn't deserve the beating you helped give him.

Jerry: I only hit him once.

Detective: That's irrelevant.

Jerry: When I pulled him off Danny he took a swing at me, and I hit him once.

Detective: You're lucky you're not facing aggravated assault.

Jerry: What?

Detective: Where did you go when you left the scene?

Jerry: We went for a drink. Danny wanted to buy me a beer. But I knew he needed it more than I did.

Detective: Had he been drinking before the attack?

Jerry: I don't know. Like I said, I'd only just gotten there.

Detective: Did he seem intoxicated?

Jerry: I can't say for sure. He'd been drinking a lot though since he was gay-bashed.

Detective: We haven't quite determined that fact.

Jerry: You might if you'd put as much time into finding out who bashed him as you are with this.

Detective: Relax.

Jerry: It doesn't matter because it's some fag, right?
Detective: Calm down.
Jerry: You're no better than the guys who bash us.
Detective: Choose your words carefully, kid.
Jerry: I can see how carefully things are done around here.
Detective: Let's stay on track. What did your friend say?
Jerry: He said he was ready for the guy this time.
Detective: Ready? Or waiting?
Jerry: He said he was ready for him.
Detective: And you just happened to be driving by?
Jerry: That's right.
Detective: Where were you coming from?
Jerry: The bar.
Detective: So, you were drinking as well.
Jerry: No, and we don't know if he'd been drinking either.
Detective: But you had.
Jerry: I just told you no.
Detective: But you said …
Jerry: I work in a bar.
Detective: And you don't drink? I find that hard to believe.
Jerry: I never drink at work. You get put off the stuff when you
see what it does to people after a while.
Detective: Like what it's done to your friend?
Jerry: It's not quite the same.
Detective: Isn't it?
Jerry: No. Because we don't know the facts.
Detective: Don't we? Admit you got it wrong.
Jerry: I'm not so sure I did.
Detective: Maybe you were part of it, but you just got there late.
Jerry: Fuck you.
Detective: Calm down.
Jerry: Maybe I should call a lawyer.
Detective: You're not enjoying our little conversation?
Jerry: Not if you start steering it away from the truth.
Detective: That's what I'm trying to get at.
Jerry: It seems selective to me.
Detective: Sometimes there are multiple truths.
Jerry: Like I said.
Detective: Like your friend supposedly getting beat-up.
Jerry: Supposedly?
Detective: Sure, he was beat-up. But the question is why?
Jerry: He was gay-bashed.
Detective: Or maybe he just hit on the wrong guy.

Jerry: That's an over-played defense, and you know it.

Detective: Maybe. But you guys don't always know when to stay on your side of the fence.

Jerry: And maybe some of you guys get drunk and fall off that fence into some guy's bed. Has that happened to you, detective?

Detective: Be careful, kid.

Jerry: Be careful that shit doesn't get out.

Detective: Be careful or I'll throw your ass in jail.

Jerry: All you have is a case of mistaken identity.

Detective: You think so?

Jerry: But maybe not so much mistaken as confused.

Detective: The guy's married.

Jerry: You're joking, right?

Detective: And he's got kids.

Jerry: You can't be that naive. I get married guys in the bar all the time. Some even have kids. It's sad to see them live that way.

Detective: No one's forcing anyone to live that way.

Jerry: Except guys like you.

Detective: I'll have you know I'm a fairly liberal guy.

Jerry: Tell me detective, what would you do if your partner told you he was gay? I'm thinking he'd get it in the back.

Detective: He's also married with kids.

Jerry: That's a seal of approval for you, isn't it?

Detective: It's an institution.

Jerry: And a damn good one too. I wouldn't mind getting into that institution myself one day. Though I'm sure if that ever happens someone will only try to take it away again.

Detective: It's a respectable institution.

Jerry: With a fifty-percent divorce rate. As well as a substantial number that hope not to run into their wife's hairdresser in a gay bar.

Detective: You really get married men in there?

Jerry: Priests too.

Detective: All right, enough with that.

Jerry: What'd you expect when gay men are forced to live in the closet and marry women. And some even become priests.

Detective: Those are the perverts.

Jerry: I'm not talking about the priests who molest children. I'm talking about regular priests.

Detective: The church is a moral institution, just like marriage.

Jerry: That want priests who aren't attracted to women.

Detective: I imagine they wouldn't want men who'll run off with a pretty girl.

Jerry: But you see, they never asked if they were homosexual. At least not back then. I'm not sure what they do now. But the thing is, they wanted homosexuals. Not sexually active ones, of course. Just as they didn't want straight guys who were either. And they certainly didn't want child molesters. And contrary to conservative rhetoric, not all gay men are child molesters. Just as not all straight men are either. The fact is, the church wanted men who'd commit themselves to God, gay or straight.

Detective: Are you saying that all priests are homos?

Jerry: Nice choice of words, but no, I'm saying in the eyes of the church being gay isn't a sin. It's the act that is. But there's always going to be some fooling around.

Detective: Ah man, don't mess with my head. I was an altar boy.

Jerry: And I can see you got through it all right, just as I did.

Detective: You were an altar boy?

Jerry: Sure.

Detective: And you were molested, and that's why you're gay?

Jerry: That's not why I'm gay. And no one ever touched me.

Detective: Really?

Jerry: Really.

Detective: Things were better when they said mass in Latin with their backs to you. It seemed safer. Holier.

Jerry: Don't get spooked.

Detective: Now you got me wondering. The guy practically puts his hand in my mouth during communion. And I'm not so sure where that hand's been now. Or maybe I am, and it scares me.

Jerry: The same place your girl puts it, I would think. So, I don't see the difference.

Detective: I'd rather not think about it.

Jerry: Probably better that way.

Detective: About the charges. I see now that you were just trying to help your buddy. I'll overlook your misguided intentions since the guy swung at you first. But a jury will determine your friend's fate.

Jerry: I'm sure he could use the time to dry out anyway.

Detective: Probably so.

Jerry: Can I go?

Detective: You can go. But be more careful next time.

Jerry: Good advice.

Detective: All right, get out of here.

Jerry: Thanks, detective.

Detective: Yeah, yeah.

Jerry: See you in church.

Detective: (He waves him away) No need to say hi if you do.

About the Room

1

I telephoned about a room, a houseboat share, needing something for a couple of months before going off on an extended trip through Europe. I spoke with a woman named Jean several times during the week to try and schedule a day to drop by and see the place. She seemed overly cautious when we talked, mentioning that her previous tenant, a Dr. Strangelove, as she called him, was everything she didn't want in a roommate. She failed to offer details, so I couldn't be certain if the nickname was the result of having been romantically involved with him or not. I couldn't help but wonder though if the name might be the result of some odd sexual proclivity he'd perhaps suggested, or that she discovered he was gay, which would certainly make him unresponsive to her charms. I'm sure she would find that strange, if not off-putting, as some women obviously might. Either way, I assumed he was a doctor of some kind and had likely offended her in some way. I also found it odd that she chose to whisper when she spoke of him, as if he were still there, even though she'd mentioned he already moved out. I guess his spirit continued to haunt her, because she added, "That would explain the dishes left in the sink every morning, as I always do mine before I go to bed at night."

I imagined her a thin woman in her sixties with a short bob, probably white. She had a crisp British accent and mentioned that she was a retired crisis management councilor. She seemed clever enough as I've found Brits usually to be.

I telephoned from the car again after I'd parked at the appointed time, as she hadn't answered when I'd tried earlier.

"Hi Jean? This is Thomas. I'm just outside."

"Oh dear, I've just gotten in," she said as if in a panic. "Can you give me ten minutes to freshen up a bit?"

"Absolutely."

I wasn't sure what impression she had hoped to make, as she made it sound as if she were preparing for a blind date than showing a room to a potential tenant. It also made me wonder if she'd feel the need to freshen up each morning before seeing me in the kitchen. That should have been an indicator of what was in store for me.

I'd shared housing with several women in my life, with great success, so I expected this to work out just as well, at least for a short period.

Considering her age and her plea, I gave her fifteen minutes.

The woman who opened the door was mostly as I'd pictured her. Her hair was nearly all white with barely a trace of blonde surviving through it.

"Was that ten minutes?" she asked offering a thin smile, her eyes wide as if feigning surprise. Or perhaps I wasn't the knight she'd expected. Or worse, I was.

"Fifteen actually. I grew up with sisters, so I thought to give you a little extra time," I said attempting to lighten the exchange.

But Jean failed to react to my words or offer any feedback. I might as well have said nothing.

"The boots!" she immediately declared, expressing her concern, as she pointed to my feet. "You'll have to take off the boots. You never know what you'll drag in with them."

Then she backed away from me and the door as if wanting to avoid an advancing contagion, which I found interesting since the gray carpet that ran through the length of the room behind her was not only worn, but in need of a strict vacuuming.

"Clean is a must," she insisted. But I certainly couldn't tell that from what she'd presented so far. I knew in that moment that I wasn't going to take the room, but since I'd already removed my boots I decided to stay for what promised to be an odd, if not curious experience.

I wasn't disappointed.

She stood in the middle of the living room as if ready to conduct a well-rehearsed performance; however, one that failed to enthuse me. The place appeared comfortable enough, but it was cluttered with an odd assortment of pieces not unlike you'd find in an overstocked second-hand store. In fact, it was so congested and visually confusing that it felt unwelcoming.

It was then that she turned and pointed.

"Do you know what that is?"

I was puzzled since she'd gestured toward the general area of the open kitchen.

"I'm not quite sure."

"The kitchen," she said staring into the open space as if it offered more than the usual mechanics and culinary function. Just then a dusty black cat jumped onto the granite counter, perhaps searching for a way out. I thought to follow his lead as I was getting a bad feeling from the place, and her.

"Who's that?" I asked, hoping for a more fluid conversation.

"Who?" Her voice slowly dissipated into the air. It appeared I'd lost her for a second. So, it was like that, I thought. Clear and clever in one moment, and unsure of her very existence in the next.

After a few seconds, she came back into focus again.

"Tulip," she finally offered light-heartedly. I decided to give her the benefit of the doubt, thinking perhaps she'd just forgotten the cat's name. Then she oddly added, "I had a cat named Tulip once." But then she faded off again.

We'd had several conversations on the telephone that proved not only coherent, but that had given me the impression she was sharp, perhaps even invigorating, which I'd found not uncommon in women her age. But as she started to drift in and out again I was certain now that she regarded me more as a gentleman caller, not unlike a character out of a Tennessee Williams play, than a probable renter, as she seemed to somehow confuse the two in her head.

From the kitchen, we went through the adjacent hallway where several paintings hung on the wall, which I was confident were hers, as they seemed just as dark and troubling. One was of a small child falling from its mother's lap. Another of a young woman who seemed to be contemplating death. Perhaps they'd both lost their grip at one point, I thought.

Hoping for confirmation, I asked, "Are you the artist?"

The sun came in at an angle through the sliding glass window. I noticed several red blotches and broken veins on Jean's face, which I was sure were the result of alcohol abuse. It made me wonder just how rough it had been for her along the way.

Jean stared at the paintings as if they were blank canvases, ignoring my question. Perhaps she answered to another in her head instead. But then she cried out in a fearful voice, nearly startling me, "The socks!" It was as if she just remembered leaving a pair in the dryer. Then looking down at my feet, she added, "Are they clean?"

She seemed more concerned with them than she'd been about the boots earlier, which should have made me suspicious of her motives. At this rate, I remember thinking, I could very well be naked by the time she got around to showing me the room. But thankfully, she was easily distracted, because just then the boat listed, gently throwing us off balance for a moment.

"It's just a rogue wave," she said as she braced against it. "You learn to live with them or they'll take you down."

It was evident that she was fighting against something because I knew that it was more likely a passing skiff clearing the protected channel. It was equally apparent that something or someone was still haunting her.

At the bottom of the stairs there were two closed doors.

"This is the room where Tulip sleeps," she said opening the one on her left. Inside was a bed that barely fit the space. "It's a timeshare," she added, offering a theatrical smile. "I have it for eight hours, and she has it for the rest of the day. But she doesn't very often pay her share."

The other door went without mention.

She appeared cognizant again, however rehearsed it seemed. But I also knew I couldn't depend on her clarity to last.

Jean closed the door and led me down a long hallway. The dark wood paneling grew closer as it narrowed like a funnel. At the end, she turned, and without explanation or warning, opened a door and pushed me into it with surprising force. Then just as quickly she slammed the door closed behind me. Startled and disoriented, I found myself in a dark and compact space. Then a thin voice on the other side of the door said something, but the words were too muffled to understand. I felt imprisoned and somewhat confused, hoping it wasn't the room I'd come to rent. As my eyes adjusted, I realized that it was a small bathroom. I was about to try the knob when she suddenly appeared through another door on the other side, one that connected into a bedroom.

"Tulip is not allowed in here," she quietly whispered. Again, with the whispering, I thought. Who did she think was listening, certainly not Tulip?

We stood in what looked more like a storage room than a bedroom. There was a double bed and chest of drawers on one side, and a plaid couch that leaned on its end against the wall that nearly filled the room. There was also a row of bookshelves that lined the interior that were tightly jammed with paperbacks.

"Dr. Jekyll moved out a couple of days ago," she said, restating what she'd told me on the telephone, but at that time she'd referred to him as Dr. Strangelove.

The room was drab and lifeless, as even air seemed to have been denied a proper place in it. The walls were the same dark paneling as the hallway. There was a single small rectangular window close to the ceiling just above the waterline.

"You didn't mention the room was furnished." It was then I realized I'd lost her again, as she just stared ahead as if in a trance.

When she resurfaced, she extended her arm as if showing a contestant on a game show the prize he might win.

"As you can see the mattress is a Beauty Rest. Go to bed ugly, wake up beautiful!"

Her attempt at humor was that of a bad salesperson, which lacked even the honest cadence of spontaneity.

Along the far wall, there was a mysterious hump covered with a large white tarp that appeared to be stained with red paint. I didn't recall that red paint had been used anywhere on the houseboat. The outside was all wood shingles, which were well-weathered and in need of repair. The interior was mostly wood-panel, except for the kitchen, which was painted white enamel. So, it seemed odd that there'd be red paint. Maybe it wasn't paint at all, I thought, letting my imagination run wild. In fact, the contours of the object appeared to change as my mind began to perform a thorough, though virtual, autopsy of the suspicious shape.

"What's this?" I nervously asked.

A startled look came over her face, which caused her to nearly lose her balance. But after steadying herself, Jean said, with a casual wave, "That?

I'll move that later." But she still couldn't take her eyes off it, as if surprised to see that it was still there. It was obvious now that she'd forgotten to move it. In fact, she appeared confused now, as if searching for the story that she'd rehearsed, the one she'd apparently forgotten amongst the many lies she had undoubtedly practiced.

I was convinced that it was Dr. Strangelove, in what appeared to be even stranger pieces now. Of course, I didn't know the man to be certain of what shape he might assume even under the best of circumstances, but I began to formulate an idea.

I slowly headed toward the bathroom door that connected through to the hallway, where I nervously said, "It was my understanding that the room would be unfurnished." I moved as casually and slowly as I could, hoping to catch her in one of her catatonic moments as I went, but she instinctively adhered to my every move and design, growing closer and closer as she followed me back through the dark hallway. I was also sure that I felt her on me as I took the steps. Then something suddenly hit me, causing a chill to cross my face, which made my spine shiver.

In the cooler air of the living room she said, "Come and sit, so we can talk."

I'd assumed we were done, as I'd seen all I'd come to see, if not more. But I sat on the large couch across from her anyway.

"Don't sit there. I can't see your face with the sun," she said pointing vaguely to the window behind me that had barely a trace of light left in it now.

I slid down to the other end of the couch.

"I still can't see you," she insisted, holding a hand up against the fading light. "Come, sit here," she said, patting the area nearer to her.

She appeared a fatal, if not faded attraction, in that moment.

I sat.

"Like I said, I expected the room to be unfurnished."

"What could you possibly need?" she asked, more into the air around her than to me.

"As I mentioned on the phone, I have a desk and a large armoire. And of course, my own bed."

"I don't understand why you need all that," she said, as if talking about something else entirely, perhaps even another woman. As if to say, 'I don't understand why you even talk to her anymore.'

It was obvious there was more than one elephant in the room, as it was only then that I noticed a large white porcelain elephant next to the couch. And after glancing around, I realized there were others amongst the clutter. Some were used as bases for glass tabletops, others had been made into exotic lamps. And there were at least a dozen similar miniature figurines on a shelf against the wall, as well as an impressive figure of Ganesh behind the front door.

"Have you traveled to Asia?" I asked, hoping to capture her attention, though just enough to be able to break away.

"What?" she responded vaguely.

"Have you been to India?"

"Why would you ask that?"

I'd hoped not to have to point out the obvious, however fitting.

"Because of the elephants in the room," I said nearly failing to restrain a laugh.

The herd seemed to roar in their silence as well.

After an expected delay, she replied, as if hypnotized by an ongoing journey in her head, "Not for quite some time."

I couldn't be certain if it was a response to what I had asked, or just a vague answer in general to her very existence. She seemed to vanish within herself after that, as if going into a focal impaired awareness seizure.

My boots were now clearly in my vision near the door.

"I should be going," I said in a held breath.

I crossed toward the entrance.

"Thanks again for showing me the room. But as I mentioned, I didn't expect it to be furnished."

There was still no response. Just then her chin gradually began to sink down into her chest. She seemed deflated.

"Thank you," I repeated.

When I reached the door, I picked up my boots, and with them in hand, my departure was guaranteed.

She continued to sit limp and lifeless.

"I'll be going now," I said in a farewell tone. But as I opened the door she started to come around again.

"Hello?"

"Thank you again," I said.

In that moment, she came back to life as if I'd just arrived.

With my boots firmly grasped in hand, I walked cautiously across the parking lot in my socks. I even considered driving in them so as not to delay my departure.

When I finally found the courage to look back, I saw her standing in the doorway. She appeared rigid and lost, as if watching a son go off to war, or an abandoning husband escape in search of his sanity. As I hurriedly went, I suspected each step that I hastily and determinedly took had been previously tread by another just as desperate. Though of course, I couldn't be certain if they'd gotten out alive.

The next morning, I had a new voice message. The now familiar accent seemed fresh and clear again.

"Hi, this is Jean. Just checking to be sure we were still on this afternoon for you to see the room. And just so you know, Dr. Strangelove has moved out entirely. Ring me when you get a chance. Cheers!"

That last salutation was pretentiously emphasized and high in tone.

Concerning Dr. Strangelove, I couldn't be certain if she had meant the rest of him, or the rest of his things. Either way, I knew better not to go back just to satisfy my curiosity. What would be the point? I wasn't going to take the room. Besides, I was glad to have gotten out of there in one piece. Just the same though, I couldn't help but wonder about the room and about its questionable contents. I also found her odd behavior intriguing. I should also mention, that I'm known to be foolishly inquisitive by nature.

"Hi Jean? ...

2

When I returned at the arranged time the next day, I decided against calling as I had on my previous visit, hoping to catch her unprepared and perhaps even more at odds with herself than before.

"Is it that time already?" she asked, with the same surprised look on her face when she opened the door. She immediately added, "The boots! You'll have to take off the boots. You never know what you'll drag in."

I was fully prepared to surrender my footwear this time.

"Clean is a must," she said on cue. I'd anticipated the words. In fact, I expected the entire scenario to be presented unchanged, as if seeing a play, a second time with minor variations. I couldn't help but notice though that the carpet had been vacuumed. Maybe she'd hired a new set designer, I thought.

We stood in the exact same spot in the living room, but Jean failed to acknowledge that fact. The room was brighter in the noonday sun, which made it seem more spacious. In fact, the lack of shadow made it appear less congested. Even the herd of elephants seemed to have more room to roam on their quiet display.

"Do you know what that is?" she asked.

I was tempted to alter the scene and improvise by replying the obvious, that it was in fact the kitchen. Instead, I played along hoping for a different response from her this time, perhaps something more revealing.

"I'm not quite sure," I said, sticking to the script.

Being a quick study, I knew my lines.

"The kitchen," she said looking at it again as if it were more than that.

There's the woman I'd come to know. The one I'd come specifically to see, I thought. Though this time she seemed to stay with me, remaining cognitive of the situation. In fact, I hadn't lost her once since I'd arrived. Surprisingly, I was missing that side of her now.

There was also no sign of the cat.

"Do you have pets?" I asked, curious what she'd say about Tulip.

"No pets. They're dirty creatures. All they do is shed and poop."

I was somewhat confused, but I accepted things as she presented them, hoping for more answers as we went along. That was pretty much what I was after, though this time I was prepared for her to drift in and out and change moods at any moment.

The place looked the same, but somehow it felt different. There was also no mention of Dr. Strangelove this time around.

We passed the paintings without a word.

"The room is downstairs," she said leading the way.

When we reached the bottom of the stairs Jean walked past the two closed doors without mentioning the cat or timeshares. She seemed more clear-headed in fact. But sadly, she also lacked that clever edge that she'd shared on my previous tour. I became suspicious of the transformation. But I was certain that I couldn't depend on it for very long.

At the end of the hallway I braced myself instinctively, but this time she simply opened the door to the bedroom in front of us without any regard for the other that she'd pushed me through on my previous visit.

The room was entirely empty. Even the bookshelves were vacant. And the stale musty air that had almost suffocated me the day before was also gone. It was curiously fresh now.

"What do you think?" Jean asked cheerfully.

I think something's not quite right, is what I thought. The room was too pristine, as if it hid a crime scene now. I discreetly eyed the area where the tarp had been. That too was empty. And the carpet was also immaculate. In fact, there wasn't even a trace of an impression left of what had once existed there now.

"I think your desk and armoire would go nicely here," she said pointing to the now empty wall behind the door. "And your bed should fit under the window. Sadly, it doesn't get much natural light."

I didn't know what to say, especially since I hadn't come with the intention of taking the room this time, as I was merely playing amateur sleuth. I certainly hadn't expected to be soberly challenged by an adversary so articulate and energetic. I had come prepared for a loonier tune. It was obvious now though that she'd found her misplaced meds since I last saw her.

"It's not much. But you did say it was only for a few months. Think of it as your man cave."

She was eager to sell me on it now.

"I'm not sure it's exactly what I'm looking for," I finally said.

"I'm sure you expected something with big windows and a view of the bay," Jean said with a shared measure of disappointment. "I'm sorry to say most houseboats aren't that luxurious."

I suddenly felt appalled now for having entered her house under false pretenses. I realized now, I had probably just caught her on a bad day, and I should have given her the benefit of the doubt and not turned it into some kind of murder mystery for my own entertainment.

"I think I need something with more light," I lied, my words fighting against the truth, as well as hoping for an easy way out.

I followed her back upstairs.

"Should we sit and talk a bit?" she asked. "That is, if you have time."

"Sure, I'm not in a rush."

I'd come to satisfy a curiosity and I wasn't about to leave without some satisfaction. But I knew I was searching foolishly for things that just weren't there now.

"Would you care for something to drink?" she asked. "I usually have a glass of wine about this time of day."

"That would be great. Thank you."

She disappeared into the kitchen and returned with two glasses of white wine a few moments later, as if she had them ready for the occasion.

I sat across from her as I had previously. But this time my choice went unchallenged.

"I'm less active these days," she said. "I stay home most of the time. It would be nice to have company, even for a short while. Especially since my husband passed away."

"May I ask how your husband died?"

"Suddenly," she said in a matter of fact tone, without going into details. "We think doctors are invincible. But the truth is, they're just as human as the rest of us."

"Your husband was a doctor?" I asked, hoping to tie some of the loose ends together,

"More a doctor of the dead than the living." Then changing the subject, she said, "So what are your travel plans?"

I was thrown now by how coherent she was. I hadn't come prepared for a cognitive conversation. In fact, I expected the same woman I'd met during my last visit; one disoriented and disillusioned. And I'd lost the opportunity, at least for the moment, to question her further about her husband. But I knew if I pushed her, my inquiries would have been inappropriate, if not suspicious. I concluded he was probably a mortician or medical examiner of sorts. At least that's what I hoped. Though I still couldn't help but speculate on a darker curriculum vita.

"I'm hoping to travel for about a year or so," I said, happy to at least be truthful about something. "I have a couple of loose ends to tie-up first. Then everything goes into storage."

"How nice to have that freedom."

She'd finished her wine. I was nearly done as well.

"Can I get you another glass?" she asked.

My imagination continued its wild adventure as it briefly crossed my mind that she might have put something in my drink. But I said, "Sure, why not," figuring one more glass wouldn't kill me anymore than the first would. Besides, it helped to settle my nerves. And the more I relaxed, the more I realized that my suspicions about Jean, and about the room and its contents, were totally unfounded, if not immature. And that fact was only reaffirmed when she returned with the second glass of wine and had accidentally given me the one with a trace of her lipstick on it. But before I had the chance to point that out, she took a sip from the other, which made me realize just how absurd I'd been about it all.

"So, what are your plans?" she asked.

"Typically, most people start out in London. But I thought to fly into Amsterdam, and then head down to Paris. I don't have a set itinerary. I'm open to anything."

"That's very romantic," she said. "Let love be your guide. Let the love for someone or even a place be the deciding factor. I can't recall who said it, but someone once poetically wrote, 'A city becomes a world when one loves one of its inhabitants.' So, I suggest you keep an open heart."

The fact that she knew such an obscure quote, not only made me smile, but it endeared me even more to her. I began to see her in a different light now.

"I believe that was Lawrence Durrell," I said warmly.

"That's right. It was Durrell," she agreed with a smile. "I was sure it wasn't Henry Miller."

A look came over her face as if she remembered a person or place, perhaps having once felt that same connection.

"Miller was a bit crasser," I offered.

"Didn't he write more about sex?" she asked demurely, as one would expect an older, proper English woman to respond. But then she added with enthusiasm, "You should make your trip a literary adventure."

"I considered that. I thought perhaps to write the occasional travel piece to help sustain my time away."

"Exactly. Just like the writers did before and after the war."

I knew which war she meant. I suspected that she might have even lost family in it. She seemed just old enough to remember the London Blitz, but I wasn't about to stir those memories. I'd leave that to her if she chose to go there.

I began to reevaluate my criticism of Jean. I even contemplated taking the room, as it could prove interesting for a few months. Especially since we shared an interest in literature; specifically, Lawrence Durrell. And a good author is always a good start.

"I wish I'd been more adventurous when I was your age, to take on the world like that," she said with envy, her voice offering a measure of regret. "Instead, I opted for a traditional life. I married young and took care of my husband and our home. Sadly, we never did travel again after moving here. He was too much of a homebody. I should probably fault myself though for making such a good home for him; one that he never wanted to leave it."

At first, I thought it was just the strong sun coming in from the skylight above that had caused my eyes to begin to lose focus. But then I started to become less lucid, even my words became more difficult to form on my lips. Confused, I looked at the lipstick on the glass again.

"Yes, Thomas, the lipstick," she said with a satisfied smile. "I thought it a nice touch. Genius in fact. It's the first time I used that strategy. I was sure you wouldn't suspect anything once you saw the lipstick on the second glass of wine." Her voice was steady and reassured. "I put a mild sedative in both of our glasses earlier as I needed to calm my nerves a bit so as not to give myself away. But the second, well, that was all you dear. So just relax. It'll be a nice stay, I promise. It might not be quite the sojourn dear Durrell had in mind, but I assure you, you'll like the room. Many have. Sadly, you won't write about it since it'll just be our little world."

I could feel my body gradually lose strength as every muscle began to slowly atrophy. I even started to slur my words, unable now to barely form them on my lips. But I found enough strength to ask, "Why?"

"It's quite simple. I dislike being alone. Besides, I enjoy taking care of people. After my husband died, poor soul, I got very lonely. The only thing I truly regret is that he went so quickly. I kept him alive for as long as I could. But then again, I'm no doctor. Though my mother did teach me how to sew when I was a young girl, and that's come in quite handy over the years."

I was confused by the correlation between the two. Though I was sure I didn't want to know the connection.

"Dr. Strangelove?" I had to ask struggling on.

"No, Thomas. Oliver wasn't Dr. Strangelove. My husband was Dr. No. Because in all the years we were married the man barely touched me. Most of my advances were met with a negative response. No, Strangelove was my most recent boarder. He stayed for nearly eight years. And the time went so quickly. But toward the end he began to smell. Why is it that men smell so? I trust you won't smell like him, Thomas. But you're younger, so it should take years before you begin to smell. Who knows, by then I might very well be smelly myself, if not dead."

And I'll be trapped here when she dies, I thought.

"Let's not dwell on that right now. There's plenty of time before either of us starts to stink. We'll have many years together, Thomas."

A chill ran through me every time she said my name. She hadn't used it before, so now it made it all that more real and horrific.

"But Strangelove?" I forced myself to ask again, attempting to work the weakening muscles around my mouth before I lost them entirely.

"Why did I call him that? I'm a bit embarrassed to say now since we barely know each other." She hesitated. "No matter, I'm sure it won't spoil the surprise. It was because of the strange things I did to him. Sexual things. Sinful things, I'm sure. I must confess, I find sin to be rather addictive." She nearly blushed. "I won't say anymore. I won't spoil it for you."

I wanted to pull her words back out of my ears one by one to erase the horrendous image they'd created. Failing that, I continued my questioning as best I could in hopes of distancing myself from them, as well as trying to hold on for as long as possible.

"And Dr. Jekyll?"

"Jekyll was in the other room."

I was afraid to ask. Besides, any attempt to articulate was getting more difficult. But her whispering made sense now. I suspect that she'd neglected him, and likely starved him to death when she went off her meds.

She slowly and poetically finished her wine.

"I should probably prepare you something to eat," she said. "I'm sure you worked up an appetite." When she reached the kitchen, she stopped and added, "I knew you'd be back, Thomas. I knew you were curious by nature. You thought I didn't recognize you. Of course, I did, dear. I just couldn't let on, because I needed you to feel safe. I should apologize though for your earlier visit. I wasn't quite myself."

She was right, I was inquisitive. In fact, I was still curious about a few things, including the cat. But I was too afraid to ask.

"And when they look for you, which of course they will. They'll look anywhere but here; as I expect you told everyone about the crazy houseboat lady and how you'd never go back even if your life depended on it." She offered a thin smile. Then added, "They'll look overseas before they think to look here."

She was right. I'd told almost everyone exactly that.

She smiled, content that her plan had come to florisshen.

As I heard her fussing about in the kitchen, no doubt puréeing my food since I'd be unable to chew, I wondered again why she had asked if I knew what it was; not once, but a second time as well. I could only speculate now. But I feared I would find out soon enough.

She fed me as if I were an ailing patient or a small child. And as one, how she'd go about toilet training me was another frightening thought.

"I'll go prepare your room," she said, as she finished putting the plates into the dishwasher.

At the top of the stairs she turned and fondly said, "I think I'll call you Dr. Kildare." She smiled, amused at how clever she'd been. "That's fitting, don't you think?"

86

The humor wasn't lost on me.

"How nice!" she exclaimed. "There's a new doctor in the house!" She repeated the name as she descended the stairs, as if it tickled her tongue as she articulated it. A few moments later, I could hear her dragging what I assumed was the bed back into the room at the end of the hallway.

I thought about the room. I knew in time there'd be something about it that I'd like; however reluctantly. Perhaps it would be the dark paneled walls, or the small window perched near the ceiling. I didn't know which, but there'd be something about the room, something that I'd come to endear to sustain my existence in it. I tried not to think about who had inhabited it before me, and what they'd sacrificed to survive in it. I just hoped it would allow me a measure of freedom in the darkness of night, and that it might even offer me the opportunity to imagine a different world; one where the darkness could be filled with hope, not unlike a movie theater projecting my leftover dreams.

Jean came back up the stairs.

"Dr. Kildare, your room is ready!" she said, as a concierge would in a two-star hotel, as if I were patiently waiting in the lobby. This was going to be interesting, if nothing else. If only it was going to be nothing else but interesting, I thought.

I was rather impressed by the strength she demonstrated as she lifted me without much effort. But then, she'd been carrying her captives about for years, so I shouldn't have been all that surprised.

As we cornered the banister at the top of the stairs, there was a gentle knock on the door, which startled both of us. Though I was sure she was no stranger to the occasional intrusion since she casually dragged me back and laid me behind the door next to Ganesh. Then she calmly walked over to the hall mirror and adjusted her hair and clothing as if readying herself for another gentleman caller. She was confident that I was incapacitated enough not to speak since she'd undoubtedly bumped up the drugs when she fed me.

"Good evening," she said softly with a smile as she leaned against the open door. It was as if she were flirting.

"I've come to see about the room."

"The room?" she asked.

At this point my body was entirely numb, and I had no voice left now to even whisper. I had nothing. Well, almost nothing.

"I'm sorry. I'm confused," she said. "Who are you?"

"My name is Thomas," he said.

By the look on her face I could see that she was having some difficulty understanding what he meant. I could also tell that she wanted to steal a quick glance in my direction if only to reconfirm my whereabouts; perhaps even wondering now if I were the imposter. And if so, who was I?

"I don't quite understand," she said, in a voice that exposed a degree of vulnerability now.

"We spoke on the phone, Jean," the voice said. "Don't you recall?"

I could see she was questioning now exactly what had transpired, and with whom, during the recent sequence of events.

"But I thought you'd been to see the room. Wasn't it, yesterday?" She stuttered her words as she began to doubt herself.

"Yes. But on the telephone, we talked about my having a second look." She paused to think.

"Did we?" Then she added as if convinced of that fact, "We did, didn't we?"

By now, I was sure she forgot I was behind the door.

Ready to play her part again, she said on cue, "The boots! You'll have to take off the boots. You never know what you'll drag in."

Or hopefully drag out again, I thought.

I saw them through the narrow gap of the door. They were well-worn and dirty, not unlike my own, which were nowhere to be seen now.

"That won't be necessary," the voice said.

Jean apparently wasn't prepared for such impertinence. It was obvious that his defiance threw her off-script, as she appeared confused now.

Just then the boots pushed their way through the door, causing my limp body to press further into Ganesh.

"Where is he? What have you done with him?" the voice shouted.

"Who?" Jean appeared visibly shaken. "Strangelove?" A confused look came over her face. "He doesn't live here anymore."

"You know exactly who!" he shouted directly into her face.

"Your room is ready," she mumbled incoherently.

"What are you talking about?" the voice shouted.

In that moment, Jean shut down as if someone had pulled the plug on her. She started to sway against her own weight as if ready to fall. Just then he caught sight of me behind the door.

"What did she do?" he asked, pulling me up onto his kneeling lap.

I tried to speak but nothing came out. Every muscle was numb.

"I better call a doctor."

I needed one, but it wasn't the first thing that came to mind, especially under the circumstances. But it was somewhat comical nonetheless.

"And the police as well," he added.

I silently agreed.

Seeing his face up close helped put me at ease. I felt safe again. But I was even more thankful that he recognized the renewed fear in my eyes in time to avoid her attack; as he pulled us out of the way a split second before Ganesh smashed into the floor next to us.

Out of reflex he punched her out cold.

"Was that overkill?" he asked, almost embarrassed.

My eyes reassured him it wasn't.

When the paramedics finally arrived, they immediately administered an antidote as well as something to stimulate my compromised immune system, which gradually brought me out of whatever she gave me. But still, every move that I made felt as if I were pulling myself out of quicksand.

"Thanks, Robert," was the first thing I said when I was finally able to speak again. The second was, "How long were you going to sit in the car and wait?"

"I just assumed you needed time to get what you came for," he said. It was obvious he wasn't telling the truth.

"You fell asleep, didn't you?"

He tried to conceal his guilt; however, he reluctantly confessed, "It's so peaceful out here near the water."

"Out here maybe, but it wasn't in there."

"What did she do to you anyway?"

"It's what she wanted to do that scared the shit out of me. And I wasn't even sure what that was."

I closed my eyes to the thought of it, and to what she might have force-fed me.

"You're okay now."

"Thanks to you."

"It was your idea to have backup."

"But it was yours to confuse her and tell her you were me. That was genius. It definitely threw her off her game."

"After what you told me, I figured it would."

The cool night air embraced me as I welcomed the open space. But it wouldn't be enough, at least not for the moment, because just then an officer approached.

"That's quite a crime scene we have in there," he said. "I haven't seen anything like it in my twenty years on the force. You're one lucky man." He looked pale and nauseous, but it was obvious he was trying to push through it and put on a brave face.

"What did you find?" I asked, still curious to get as many answers as I could.

"I'm guessing quite a few missing persons. But I don't know how the coroner is going to sort it out." He paused to pull himself together, but he was well past trying to conceal his emotions now. It no doubt took a lot out of him. "What we have in there," he continued in a grim voice, "is a freezer filled with male genitalia. It's hard to say just how many until we thaw them out, because we don't want to take a chisel to them."

I was nearly as speechless as I'd been earlier. Robert of course, was a bit more articulate.

"Jesus! How will you ever determine who they are?"

"I have no idea. It's not as if their wives will be able to identify them in a line-up?" the officer said.

That struck me as a rather odd, if not comical scenario. Perhaps it was the drug still running through my tired and exhausted system. But I couldn't help but picture what that line-up would be like. I imagined a long narrow table, covered in a white cloth, with an assortment of appendages lined-up neatly in a straight row by size, as a frenzy of wives savagely rummaged through them as if at a bargain basement sale; searching not for their own husband's penis, the one that had pleasured and possibly even impregnated them over the years, but for a more impressive one, as if now given an opportunity to upgrade to a larger member, and in doing so, improve on their sex lives; however moot that proved to be. As the scene continued to play out in my head, I watched as they brutally battled it out in a tug-of-war; each hoping to be spared the humiliation and embarrassment of having married a less endowed man, leaving the poor dismembered and well-hung victim not only regrettably deceased, but posthumously accused of bigamy, as each claimed to be his wife.

In an unexpectedly resentful tone the officer added, "I'd be surprised if their wives ever got a good look at them anyway."

Evidently, that had been his personal experience. And normally I would have thought it an absurd generalization, if not judgmental. But I couldn't help but laugh, being hard pressed for one anyway under the circumstances. Robert gave me an irreverent look, but I knew he was struggling with the urge not to laugh as well. But I also knew I'd be forgiven my immature and inappropriate behavior, considering what I'd gone through.

After that short-lived levity, I felt obligated to mention another detail about Jean's handy work.

"It gets even worse," I said.

"How could it possibly get worse?" they both asked.

"From what she'd told me, I think she kept them alive long after she'd castrated them. She had mentioned being skilled with a needle and thread. I didn't understand what she'd meant at the time, but it makes sense now."

"None of this makes any sense," the officer said. "The question now is, where are the bodies that go with the frozen appendages?"

I had my suspicions that some of the remains were in my stomach, as it began to churn at the very thought of it. But I wasn't about to share that bit of insipid information with either Robert, or the police.

"You'll undoubtedly find remnants in the garbage disposal in the sink, and probably some evidence out in the bay. The cat too, I'm afraid."

"Consider yourself a lucky man," the officer reaffirmed as he walked away shaking his head. "A very lucky man."

"I doubt they'll ever find out who those guys are," Robert said.

"I knew there was something odd about that kitchen, the way she kept going on about it. Both times she had asked if I knew what it was, and both times I thought it peculiar. I never suspected it was actually a trophy room."

"Do you think she ever used them on herself?" he asked as his thighs instinctively tightened against his groin.

"I'd rather not think about it. But she did tell me that what she did was addictively sinful. It would appear it was all that and more. So, I wouldn't be surprised."

Then I mentioned to Robert the names she'd chosen for her captives.

"That's odd since she was the one wielding the scalpel. But I guess it's fitting then that she spends the rest of her life surrounded by them."

We quietly let that thought dissipate into the night air.

Jean sat motionless in the back of the patrol car, her face badly bruised from where Robert hit her. She also appeared catatonic and out of sorts, not unlike her hair. But I suspected she was fully aware of her situation, and of every detail that occurred.

In that moment of gradual recovery, I realized it would take more than a trip abroad to even begin to pixelate the images branded in my head, or to escape the phantom blade I felt against my groin. Under the circumstances, I felt an urgency to leave even sooner than originally planned. But I suspected the trial would delay my departure indefinitely. That fact would undoubtedly make Robert happy, though I'm sure he'd never let on if it did. That had been the initial reason for my wanting to leave, and perhaps the pretext for things to happen as they did. But I would never blame him for the decisions I made. They were mine alone. Though the truth is, it was his inability to be emotionally accessible that set things in motion. But perhaps things would be different now. Sometimes it takes a life-altering experience for people to change. This one had certainly changed me, and maybe it would change him as well.

Robert leaned into me.

"Can I ask a favor? Can I ask that you at least remember what my dick looks like, just in case?"

I was more than happy to add to the kudos he deserved.

"Don't worry, it's more than memorable, believe me. As I'm sure many can testify, if not eagerly pick out of a line-up."

"Perhaps, but you're the only one I can trust with it."

That was as close of a commitment that I was going to get from Robert. At least for now. And I was happy to have that. In fact, it was more than I expected. Maybe there was hope for us yet.

As we looked out over the dark bay toward the bright shimmering city, I couldn't deny that my love for it had been closely and intrinsically tied to my love for him. And if I was going to continue to follow my heart, I knew I wouldn't be able to leave either of them.

Special Needs

Most women have special needs, especially sexual ones, which most men can't seem to satisfy, no less find. Louise's ex-husband certainly never discovered them, and the truth was they weren't that difficult to locate. As far as her sex life usually went, those magical places were left dormant and untouched. And the sad fact was, they weren't being attended to in that moment either; though the circumstances were of course very different. However, the sex was just as mundane and unfulfilling. But she was having it for him now and not her, as she had long ago resigned to living without it as many women did at her age. But he was young, and he had a young man's appetite.

His body writhed savagely into her, constantly beating against hers as if searching instinctively for something deep inside of her, something that she was sure he wouldn't find or even understand if he did. Though she knew he was searching for something entirely different anyway, as it was a mindless act. But she endured it without judgment or criticism, accepting each thrust willingly, but always hoping the next one would be his last.

There had come a point when Louise was at a loss with what to do with him, especially when she found him ceaselessly rubbing himself against a table or bedpost. She initially thought to hire a sex worker. But the fact was, she was the only one he'd allow to touch him. And without an outlet for his frustration, or a natural release as it were, Louise felt obligated to share the burden of his torment, knowing he couldn't remedy the situation himself as most boys instinctively did at his age. So, she was essentially forced to make a life altering, and certainly life-changing decision. Though she continued to battle with the idea for some time before finally giving in to his innocent, but abrasive advances. The truth was, the boy was so filled with rage and raging hormones that he even came close to hitting her one evening.

At first Louise closed her mind to it completely as she lay under him, his full weight pressing against her. It wasn't easy to block out the guilt, but she certainly tried. She also knew what she did, what she had to do, what she sacrificed, was not only morally wrong, but also medicinal. She resigned reluctantly to the fact that her actions would bring a necessary calm to him; a satisfaction that nothing, or no one else could. Thankfully, he'd go days, and not hours, as a normal seventeen-year-old might, before he'd approach her again. And each time he did, Louise accepted it until it became routine; just as a wife might feel obligated to satisfy her husband's basic desires, she couldn't deny her son those same demands, not under the circumstances.

She understood that it was sinful, but she also knew it helped alleviate the chances of his hurting, or perhaps raping, another woman, or girl, if left on his own.

Bud was her only child, and she dedicated her life solely to him. There were times while out in public when he'd lay his head against her breast and fondle them, which usually caused a glaring reaction from those around her. That is, until they realized he was a special boy, with special needs, and the mind of a three-year-old. Then of course, she was viewed with empathy, and thought to be a caring and loving mother, in more respects than she wished to acknowledge even to herself.

Bud also had the sexual endowment and drive of a typical boy his age. Years earlier, when she went through menopause, Louise welcomed it. She was thankful she could no longer get pregnant. Thank God for that at least, she thought. But if she did, she'd have accepted the consequences as being justified; unlike her previous pregnancy, which resulted in giving birth to a disabled child without a reasonable explanation. Because she'd taken good care of herself and her baby through all three trimesters. Louise never smoked and had quit drinking once she realized she was pregnant, though she wasn't much of a drinker anyway. But regardless of her efforts, her son Bud was born mentally challenged, and all she could do was resign to the fate dealt her and accept it as an unfortunate act of nature.

From the outset, she took care of his every need, and labored to his every whim and desire. And now Louise found herself fulfilling a need she never anticipated, one that no book on child rearing could prepare her for. It was an entirely unexpected obligation, one only she could perform, and a sin that only she could partake in.

Unfortunately, the sex with Bud nearly broke her as badly as when she pushed him out almost two decades earlier. But now he was reentering her face to face, and his eyes were just as empty and blank as they were then.

If his father had been as well endowed, she thought, perhaps their life would have been better. Because it would have at least helped sustain their relationship through their many hardships. But that endowment only added to the pain she felt now as Bud tore into her. But there was one consolation; he had no concept of what he was doing or how morally wrong it was, and that innocence helped to blind her to her own offense.

Louise eventually acclimated as best she could to the situation. In fact, in time, their relationship seemed to change, however briefly. At least in her mind it had. Because there were occasions when she felt like a woman with him, and not a mother. And it was while lost in that welcoming deception that she could escape the reality of it. At times, she even felt like a young girl again, imagining that Bud was the seventeen-year-old boy who took her virginity when she was sixteen, when sex was new and more a mystery. Maybe it was the familiar fumbling and aimless probing of his unskilled and immature hands as they explored her unknown parts, unsure of what they found even when they discovered it. But Louise knew her son's touch would always remain naive and unresponsive, even crass. Unlike Willy Wagmore, who'd probably become an experienced and perhaps even thoughtful lover. But Willy was a clumsy boy back then, as most were. But unlike the other boys, he'd made her laugh, which helped make it less awkward. And unlike her son, Willy at least attempted to feign his expertise, if not comically, as he tried to reenact something he'd no doubt seen in a movie or had read in a dirty magazine. Though with little success, as Willy expectedly ejaculated shortly after entering her. Bud on the other hand, had phenomenal and fearless stamina, due to his being mentally liberated from questioning his performance since he had no idea or care of what was expected of him. He was driven by a basic instinct, which never considered what she thought or needed. But his endurance often wore her down, to the point of nearly passing out on one occasion. But Louise knew she had to hold on. If she hadn't, he would have thought her dead, and there was no telling what he would have done then.

One night, Bud forced himself into her dryness with such determination that it caused her to bleed. She was startled at first. Mostly because it made her recall her first period, as they were surprisingly similar. But that was one memory she would have preferred not to embrace again.

Of course, it would have been different if there'd been love behind his touch, and if the intercourse they shared had been morally correct and less criminal. But the truth was, Louise no longer saw the little boy that she held while praying to God in those years after he was born. That image gradually diminished after puberty. And when her prayers went unanswered, her belief in God diminished as well, leaving her entirely alone.

Louise often anticipated Bud's needs, knowing that once they were met he'd be satisfied. But there were nights when she found him hovering over her while she slept like a stranger intent on raping her; one equally unable to push away. Unlike her husband in the last years of their marriage who she could easily deny, Louise submitted to Bud's needs because he had no sense of rejection.

Unable to deal with his son's mental disability, Bud's father left five years after he was born. Her body had disappointed him just as it had her. A wife can blame her husband for many things, but she couldn't blame him for this. Louise only blamed herself for her son's condition.

One morning Bud's father casually mentioned that he was going out for eggs, and he never came back. No doubt in search of better eggs, in a better woman, she thought, with a serving of sanity on the side. He'd held Louise responsible for Bud's condition, convinced her eggs were not only rancid, but rotten. Only once did she go to the window to check the driveway to see if his car was there. But even then, it felt more as if she were checking the weather, because at least that was less predictable. She knew even then, he had no intention of returning. She could still hear it in the tone of his voice even now as he went out that day.

The intrinsic truth was, Louise wished she got out before him, and even more so now. Though she couldn't help but laugh hysterically at the thought of him being forced to take her place beneath their son, as she knew Bud wouldn't discriminate concerning his sexual needs. It was an image Louise hoped to hold onto instead of the one she had of her life now, which would last forever. It was an act that she would have happily done to him as well, if possible; if the roles were reversed. The thought of it made her laugh even harder, which was something she rarely did anymore. The very idea of it made her wet in the most impossible of places. Because she knew she'd have given it to him better than he'd ever given it to her. She would not only have found his secret place, but she would have discovered ones that even he didn't know existed. In fact, she'd have been so skilled that the thought of leaving her would never cross his mind, even under the circumstances. His car would not only still be in the driveway, but he'd have had no reason to ever leave the house, or her. It was all too much for her. She laughed so hard she felt a pain in her side; and it was there that the two pains eventually met, colliding into each other, the physical and the mental; until the pain in her side lost out to the one that inhabited her head, which only forced her to resign again to the reality that was her life.

Early on, Louise even considered having Bud chemically castrated. But she knew it would have destroyed her, and him, as it was all that Bud had. It was the one thing in life that allowed him to escape his repetitive and spastic existence, as nothing else stimulated him. Not like that. And without it, he might as well be dead.

Louise often thought, if Bud had been given a normal life; or a chance at a normal life, she was sure that he would have made some girl happy. Just as she was equally certain the girl would have adhered to him forever. If for no other reason than he'd have at least satisfied her sexually. Many women held on for less, as she may have done herself if given the chance. There were also times when she imagined them having an intelligent conversation. And others when she caught a brief glimpse of him being witty and clever, even capturing some girl's heart. Louise often pictured him as well-educated and confident, and full of prowess and finesse. He certainly had the face for it. His thick auburn hair fell nicely over his fine features. His shoulders were strong and wide and would have been stronger still if he'd carried himself correctly. Or given the opportunity to play sports. Especially football. Just as Louise was equally convinced that his firm mouth would have won every argument and been more than capable of persuading others out of their own opinion.

As the long years went by, some proved more complicated than others; though the others were a welcome and rare surprise. But even they came and went, until a new fear eventually presented itself. Louise realized she'd soon be faced with the inevitable problem of what to do with Bud upon her death. Who would take care of him? More importantly, who would take care of his special needs; the ones she'd secretly fulfilled for him? There was no doubt there would be that need for years to come; a need that only she was able to fulfill. Louise even envisioned Bud mounting her casket as he had her, and in doing so, reveal the immoral truth of their relationship. The consequence of her death would be nothing less than devastating.

In the end, there was only one obvious answer. Just as they'd been only one obvious remedy years earlier. The choices went hand and hand. There couldn't be one without the other she realized. And the closure would have to be simultaneous.

One final thought came to Louise as she stood over Bud's still body as it rested peacefully on the kitchen floor; perhaps she should have done this in the beginning and avoided the nightmare entirely. But there must be some good in what she had done, some proven justification; be it compassion or love, because where there's life there must also be some good, she thought. Not necessarily, she was forced to concede as she firmly pulled the trigger to the gun at her head. And with that, her body laid with Bud one final time.

Stalemate

"Can you guess who this is?" the endearing voice on the other end of the receiver teasingly asked, certain he would even after all these years.

He was pleased to hear her voice again. Not only was it familiar, it was distinctively so. It had an eloquent timbre that seemed just as innocent as it had years earlier. Though perhaps now there was a trace of pretense to it. He couldn't be certain. It'd been so long.

It was a voice that came from a distance further away than he imagined even the phone company could reach out and touch. Yet there it was, clear; even close. It had been more than two decades, but it was as if the voice had been there all along. It had dominated his last two years of high school, and even came to visit him while working a summer in Maine. He'd last heard it when she visited him in California before he moved to Paris. It was a voice that always seemed to soothe his soul, and now it was stirring his memory as well. It was one of the few voices in his life that could pick up right where it had left off, as if the conversation never ended, and was only momentarily interrupted. That was the nature of their friendship as well. And that was the voice that captured him now as he held the receiver.

"Of course!"

The years quickly raced through his head.

"I was going to call last year after you contacted me through the school web site. But things weren't going all that well at the time, and I didn't want to burden you with that while reconnecting."

"I'm still here for you, you know. We can still share our problems even now," he said.

Hearing Chloe's voice took him back to a freer time.

"Life is more complicated now. Certainly, more than when you met that rebellious girl in high school." She paused to reflect on the young girl she once was. "If only things were that simple now. If only it was as easy as running away from my problems. I'd welcome that liberty again. But I have four children now. All of them grown of course, but still dependent on me."

"Four?" Ryan knew of only one.

"I know, it's been quite a while, hasn't it?" she said lightheartedly. But she couldn't help but acknowledge the time that had escaped her as well.

"If there's one thing we weren't, was dependent on anyone."

Chloe ignored the comparison. She wanted to move on from the past in hopes of capturing something promising for the future.

"I thought I would have seen you by now."

Ryan sensed a frailness in her voice. They had taken turns over the years showing up unexpectedly at each other's door.

"I'd hoped to by now, but then we lost touch. I did try to locate you, but it was usually at four in the morning after a few drinks. At least the operator was happy to chat away about the weather."

"I'd moved several times over the years," Chloe admitted. "But the last I heard, you were in Paris. After that, I had no idea where you'd moved to."

"I don't quite recall myself. South, I think."

Ryan remembered, but the telling would have opened the conversation to questions he wasn't ready to answer just yet.

"Does that mean I might see you soon?"

"It does. But where the hell are you?"

"Buffalo," she confessed.

"Remind me to ask how that happened."

"I don't quite recall either," she offered humorously.

Of course, she did. But she'd rather forget the circumstances.

"I'm not exactly sure when I can get away."

"I have no plans. So, surprise me."

"All right." Ryan smiled at the ambiguity of it. "I'll surprise you."

The conversation on the telephone proved more fluid than the one they had in Buffalo after he arrived. In fact, Chloe's mood seemed to change with each episode she shared of her life. Ryan found it especially curious that it took her more than an hour to mention Aaron; and even then, it was just in passing, as she quickly scanned the years. But when she finally opened-up about her life with him, it was with mostly resignation and regret. But she also seemed pleased to point out that Aaron's disposition had changed, and he'd become cruel and almost violent after the birth of their son Jonathan. Though Ryan questioned her intentions, as he assumed they were those of a bitter ex-wife, and that her words were filled more with resentment than truth. For that reason, he listened with apprehension and a measure of doubt as she spoke of Aaron, trying to resist her attempt to shatter the memory of the boy he knew all those years ago. It was as if he'd come more for him now than her. Because as far as he was concerned, the three of them were still inseparable. At least in memory.

The truth was, he'd come to right the past. Or rather, her idea of it.

While driving through Albany on his way to see Chloe, Ryan stopped in the small town where they once lived west of i80.

He sat staring at the mountainous countryside, and an old house that was now partially hidden by thick foliage and tall pine trees.

"What are you looking at?" Leo asked.

"I'm watching two boys climb out an upper window," he said. "They're perched on the overhang waiting for an older couple to make their way from the car to the front door."

"I can't see anyone."

"I can barely see them myself now," Ryan said.

"Where? Through the trees in the distance?"

"A distance of more than twenty years," he added, failing to hold onto the image as he rubbed his eyes with the tips of his fingers.

"Are you okay?"

"I'm fine. But we should probably head back to the thruway."

Leo pulled away slowly as Ryan continued to watch as the house faded to just a memory again.

"I'm happy he doesn't look like Aaron," Chloe said of Jonathan. "That way I'm not constantly reminded of him." It was true, there wasn't a trace of Aaron in the photograph of the young boy. "I'm also glad he didn't inherit his bad temper. I'd hate to think he'd treat anyone the way he treated me."

It was obvious that Chloe wanted to erase any thought of Aaron. As she spoke now, she shook her head as if reflecting on having made the wrong choice years ago. He didn't have the heart now to tell her there really wasn't a choice, at least not as far as he was concerned. Ryan had come prepared to fill in that bit of history that she'd missed while living it. Of course, he loved Chloe, but he'd been in love with Aaron. But he was curious now if Aaron's behavior toward Chloe was the result of coping with his own sexuality, and perhaps even his feelings for him. Or if his violent nature had been inherent, just waiting to emerge regardless. He couldn't help but wonder if he'd been spared a similar fate if they'd been together. But Ryan chose to think his life with Aaron would have been different from the one he had with Chloe.

Ryan expected the words he came to say would come easily, and when he explained that truth to her, they'd laugh about it. But he could see that her dreams had been shattered several times, and the truth that he brought with him would only cause her more pain, so he decided to leave his words where they were, and everything she'd thought about him as well. Ryan had come to change history and present a certain truth. But he knew he couldn't now, even if it did go against what he felt was right. He didn't want to hide that part of himself from her. But it was clear that the wounds she carried would only grow deeper if he took away the power she thought she'd held for all those years; one that she still thought she held. Not to mention, the hope she now had for the future. Ryan knew it would be a delicate and heartbreaking moment when the time came. But he hoped that the geographical distance between them would be to his advantage. He would let her think she'd made the right choice all those years ago, regardless of how wrong she thought they were now, and leave it at that. At least for now.

Chloe had dedicated her life to be a doula; a choice that undoubtedly helped to resolve several issues, one of which was being nearly miscarried while her mother was pregnant; something she was constantly reminded of throughout her life. Nothing like the guilt of a mother's embryonic pain to emotionally harness a child. The other was simply her need to nurture. But Chloe wasn't completely selfless. She was also rather clever at manipulating people. And poor Aaron proved easy prey. Though his erupting hormones undoubtedly worked in her favor, that being part of their design.

On the other hand, Ryan seldom fell victim to her skilled calculations. Though that was mostly because his interests were elsewhere. In fact, Chloe misinterpreted his affection, but only because she was blinded by her own ego. So much so, that she failed to recognize his love for Aaron.

Time had been kind to Chloe. She still looked like the same girl he knew in high school. Her long dark hair was pulled back from her soft, round face, enabling her eyes to clearly focus on the journey in front of her. Ryan could still see traces of that girl who'd made him his first pot of herbal tea that late autumn morning; the house still dark with barely a stream of light breaking through the evergreens as the sun began its final angle toward winter in that small town in Upstate New York. It was also the first time he'd heard Joni Mitchell. He could still picture her slender fingers as they gently set the needle on the record. It was a memorable period in Ryan's life; one captured forever in time, and one that he still held close.

He had loved Chloe, but he never thought of her sexually.

As they drove, he continued to think about the two boys perched above the driveway.

It was in their senior year, while Chloe's parents were away, that she asked them to stay at the house with her. During that time, she would make her final decision about which of the them she loved more.

Ryan watched as Aaron made all the required moves; the ones expected of a seventeen-year-old boy interested in girls. But Chloe also found Ryan's unassuming and quiet disposition just as attractive. Though in the end, her rebellious and defiant nature chose Aaron. But that had more to do with his radical personality, as it was equally suited to disrupt the family institution that she fought so hard against at the time.

Chloe's bedroom was downstairs off the kitchen; Aaron and Ryan slept upstairs in her parent's room, which overlooked the driveway. Of course, Ryan had always wanted more than just an emotional bond with Aaron, but he happily took what was offered him.

"How did you sleep last night?" she asked one morning, as if teasingly inquiring how Ryan had slept without her.

"Aaron tosses and turns," he said, taking the tea she'd made him. "He's a restless sleeper."

Ryan could see Chloe wanted to take credit for that, but he was equally satisfied in thinking that Aaron had wrestled with a desire for the body next to him as he slept as well.

The days passed slowly as if in a transitional dream, until one morning a car unexpectedly pulled into the snow-covered driveway.

They woke to Chloe shouting up the stairs.

"It's my parents!"

The boys were huddled close together against the cold when they were suddenly forced out of bed into the late autumn chill. They hurriedly slipped back into whatever they slipped out of the night before, comically steadying each other as they tried to figure out what to do next. It was then that Aaron suggested they climb out the window.

Once they were carefully perched on the overhang above the doorway, they patiently waited for Chloe's parents to make their way from the car to the house. When the door finally closed behind them they bravely jumped into the soft mound of snow below.

Chloe mentioned divorcing Aaron less than a year after Jonathan was born; hinting that Ryan had missed an opportunity.

He asked after Aaron.

"Where's he now?"

"I'm not sure." But then she added without a trace of compassion, "It's possible he's still living on the streets in Boston."

Ryan acknowledged the bitterness and distain in her voice, which made him even more cognitive of what Aaron must have gone through toward the end of their relationship.

As their day together went on, they talked mostly about lives that went in opposite directions. Ryan was surprised that she hadn't been curious why he'd never married. But she appeared to accept it in her favor; perhaps even thinking his love for her the reason.

The cadence of their conversation seemed rushed at times, as if Chloe were trying to expedite the past in order to find the future, while waiting for him to reaffirm his love for her before the opportunity was lost again. Ryan consciously attempted to slow things down since he'd come for the moment and didn't want to hurry it. And he certainly didn't want to damage it either.

At one point, Chloe tested him, as if interviewing Ryan for a part in her life. She wanted to know what he considered his greatest achievement. She watched him closely. She watched his lips as they spoke, and his face as he looked at her. She watched with what appeared to be tears in her eyes when he told her he was proudest of the fact that he'd never hit anyone. It wasn't what she'd expected to hear. But it forced her to recall the battered life she'd experienced at the hand of her second husband. In fact, his words reminded her of the long list of bad choices she'd made. His words also made her wish even more now that she'd connected with him; if not early on, then certainly after Aaron left. In turn, Chloe searched her soul for her own achievements. She hesitated, then said, there had been nothing more wonderful in her life than having had her children. Ryan wouldn't deny her that fact, even though she seemed to resign to it. But he also knew life's greatest achievements and triumphs were often inevitable, if not unplanned. Just as life is often more interrupted, than guided. But he wouldn't deny her those accomplishments or the pains that no doubt went along with them.

One summer, when he was sixteen, Ryan worked at a seaside resort on the coast of Maine, painting an endless row of weathered cottages. He'd also dug a twenty-foot long seepage ditch, four feet deep, in order to drain the overflowing septic tanks beneath them; the proprietor being too frugal to hire a service that would've taken less than an hour, and not the three days he labored doing it. That under-paid summer job, which often felt more like an internment camp, required that he also answer late-night inquiries about accommodations.

On one of those evenings, Ryan expected to find the usual newlyweds, or the French-Canadian who'd already brought several wives, over several weeks that season since he typically arrived around midnight. And with each visit, he seemed more embarrassed than the last; just as each bride seemed equally shy, both obviously more Canadian than French, Ryan remembered thinking at the time.

So, he was surprised to see the slight silhouette of Chloe caught in the porch light through the ragged screen when he opened the door. It was one of the many sojourns that she'd made over the years to visit him in places he had either worked or lived, just as he'd often done to her. But he knew this particular visit had a purpose. Chloe had hitchhiked up the New York State Thruway, through Vermont and New Hampshire, in order to be certain that he hadn't lost interest in her; absence being what it is. Because it wouldn't be until later that fall when Chloe would make her choice and give her heart to Aaron.

Her visit lasted a few hours. Which meant they'd avoid the awkward question of where she'd sleep. But he was sure she'd planned it that way, as it was obvious she hadn't come to complicate matters. Just as he was certain she expected her presence to be tempting nonetheless.

They talked over fresh lobster omelets and straight black coffee until nearly noon; when Chloe decidedly threw her open thumb back to the road and headed south again.

Ryan could tell by the expression on Chloe's face that she wanted him to know she'd made the wrong choice all those years ago. He wanted to tell her that she hadn't, at least not as far as he was concerned. He wanted to tell her it would have never worked between them either; and that she should be satisfied with the children she had, regardless of the pain that the two men she married had caused her.

Still an attractive and radiant looking woman, he knew Chloe could easily find someone to fill the void in her life. But he suspected she doubted herself now, and her ability to make the right choices. Though she wished he had made the choice for her all those years ago. But it had always been

Aaron's face and body Ryan wanted. It was Aaron's lips he wanted pressed against his own. But she misunderstood the look on his face and thought to read it in her favor now. So, she decided to make her move.

"Drive as slowly as possible for the next few miles," Ryan said as they went along the narrow two-lane black top through the rolling countryside. "Just slow enough to keep the honking to a minimum."

Ryan watched the landscape closely, hoping to catch a glimpse of the past as they went. But it was the familiar smell of freshly cut grass that finally helped to recapture those memories.

The morning sun had barely cut a deep red hue across the horizon when Aaron woke Ryan from a deep sleep.

"Time to put that dream to canvas," he said in an enthusiastic whisper.

When he finally did get Ryan out of bed, Aaron had to practically push him into his clothes and then pour coffee into him to get him motivated.

"It's too early," Ryan pleaded repeatedly. "There won't be enough light to even see what I'm doing."

"At this rate, the sun will be setting by the time we get there."

As they headed out the door they were met by a brisk spring sky filled with broad white strokes, not unlike the remnants of snow that still covered the rolling hills. A wooden easel and blank canvas were strapped to Aaron's back, his blonde hair blowing briefly in the gentle breeze as they fought the summit. A heavy box of paints pulled at Ryan's arm as he walked ahead, his pace filled with promise, like the one he made when he first spotted the old structure in the distance on his way to school one day.

"It seemed a lot closer from the road," Aaron shouted.

"Don't worry, we're almost there," Ryan shouted back.

It wasn't until they passed through a thick group of low branches into a clearing that it finally came into view like a monolith unveiled before them. But disappointment quickly filled their young faces. The large washed-out red barn was still standing, but that once magical hayloft door that had hung down at an angle from a single hinge was now splintered into planks on the ground, and Ryan's dream shattered with it. The box of paints fell to his side as he squatted on the hard grass. He felt the cadence of life skip a beat as the loss continued to stare him in the face. It might seem insignificant to some, but it made Ryan realize in that moment that dreams could easily slip away, even while attempting to live them. Of course, he could easily paint it from memory since the image was just as vivid in his head as the day he first saw it. But there was a need at that time to portray life as it was lived, and not as it had died.

Aaron suggested he paint the barn as it was, with the door shattered on the dust-filled ground. But Ryan had come to capture its sustainability, and not its defeat. And with that sense of hope diminished, it seemed to Ryan as if death had been victorious. But he wasn't ready to surrender to it, at least not yet.

Aaron crouched down behind Ryan. And with his hand on his shoulder, he gently rested his head almost passionately against the side of his face. Then with his lips close to his ear, he whispered, "Just push on to the next dream."

The next dream, Ryan thought. Yes, the next dream.

As they drove, Ryan caught a partial glimpse of the barn in the distance through the heavy growth. From what he could make out it seemed just as he remembered it on that day with Aaron. He watched quietly until it finally disappeared. Maybe it was someone else's dream now, he thought.

Aaron's words echoed in his head now. Words he'd always held close. But why hadn't Aaron pushed on to the next dream? The thought made him feel empty inside. Why hadn't he found a future after his life with Chloe? In that moment, Ryan couldn't help but hold her responsible, knowing she had probably chipped away at him to his very core. He was also surprised Aaron hadn't also found the dream in Jonathan. It was only then he looked at the photograph on the table again. Chloe was right, the boy looked nothing like Aaron. It was just as clear to Ryan now as it must have been to Aaron then.

Before Chloe could make her move, she knew she'd have to take Aaron out of the picture. She would have to challenge the very the idea of him, by taking him out of the present, and leave him in the past where she felt he belonged. Even if that meant destroying the memory Ryan had of him. She would need to shatter the image he had of the three of them, and bring Ryan into the present with her, and only her.

"We eventually had to acknowledge the probability of mental illness in Aaron's family," Chloe said, offering her implied remedy. "In fact, it proved more prevalent than we first anticipated. Of course, we all knew about his grandfather, the mad Swede. But it hit closer to home with Aaron's brother. Though I didn't expect it to take Aaron out with it."

"Jason?" Ryan asked. "What happened to Jason?"

"He fell in love with a beautiful woman named Josey, who taught third grade. Shortly after, they moved to Oregon, where they had three beautiful children. But then a few years later, for whatever reason, Josey asked Jason for a divorce. But he said he'd never give her one. Then one spring day he called her at school and told her that one of the kids had a dangerously high fever. She immediately drove to the house. When she arrived, he handcuffed her to the fence at the bottom of their property. Then in a strangely casual tone, he told her he'd tied the children to their beds. She could hear them screaming from their room. Once he was satisfied with the pain on her face, he walked up to the house and set it on fire. The smell of gasoline quickly filled the air. When it was all lit up, he came back down and stood next to her as it burned to the ground. She screamed and cried and tore at the flesh on her wrist. Blood ran down her fingers as she listened to her children burn to death. When the flames subsided and there was nothing but simmering smoke and ash left, Jason said in a calm voice, as if in a trance, 'Now there's no reason for us to stay together.' Then he got in his truck and drove away, leaving Josey to die inside as she collapsed in the dirt."

Ryan's eyes were drowning in tears. He knew Aaron must have been shattered as well. He remembered Jason as little more than a quiet kid in the peripherals.

"Is that why Aaron's living on the street in Boston?" he asked.

"He was living on the street long before that," she admitted. "But I'm sure it helped keep him there."

Ryan eyes continued to water.

"It was only after I told him that he couldn't see Jonathan again unless he showered and wore clean clothes. But he never came around after that."

Ryan doubted there was much truth in her words, as he knew there was no reason for Aaron to come around again. Why would he want to stare into the eyes of another man's son? He knew it was Aaron's way of dealing with the pain, unlike Jason's.

"I'm grateful he didn't burn the house down with Jonathon in it," she added.

Ryan was overwhelmed by the horrific imagery, but he was also angry. Her words had not only offended his memory of Aaron, but also his feelings toward her. Something she hadn't anticipated.

Ryan changed the subject as she'd hoped, as there was nothing positive for him to say in that moment. Aaron's name became synonymous now with madness. She succeeded in destroying something, but it wasn't his love for Aaron; but whatever love he had for her. She got the result that she wanted, ending any conversation about Aaron, but she'd lost everything else with it.

Chloe could now talk about the two of them without referencing Aaron; and hopefully revive the love he still had for her. She hadn't said those exact words, not yet at least, but Ryan recognized their intent nonetheless. It was in the deceptive cadence of her voice, as each phrase she spoke exposed her passive aggressive agenda. Even her gestures seemed to whisper, 'I broke your heart all those years ago, but I'm here now.'

Ryan continued to fight the urge to share the truth he'd come to tell her, because he wanted to hurt her now; and he knew revealing that truth would have done just that. In fact, it would have crushed her and any hope that she had fashioned for the future. It would have made her powerless and stripped her of an important dimension in her life. It would have taken those choices that she once thought she had and left her with little more than the reality and pain which was her life. But Ryan wasn't capable of being that cruel or allowing himself to be the catalyst to such an emotional crime. He wasn't a vengeful person.

Chloe had suspected that Ryan's move to California was due mostly to her choosing Aaron over him, and that he needed distance to deal with the pain. But even if he leaned in that direction and physically wanted her, every underlying and insipid offense she had articulated or even insinuated, would have put him off her now; because all he felt in that moment, was the need to escape.

"It's seems our visits are always so short," he finally said.

"You're not leaving, are you? I thought you were staying a few days."

It wasn't the response she'd expected, or what she had planned.

"I wish I could. I need to get to Chicago for business. This was a nice, though narrowly timed detour."

Chloe couldn't hide her disappointment.

"I guess that's been our story; a moment here, a moment there."

"But it's always been a sweet moment," he forced himself to say. "Like lost letters that eventually find their destination."

"I'm sorry you didn't get to meet the kids."

Ryan knew it was probably better that he hadn't. It was too complicated as it was. There was no need to add to the mix.

"How long till the next time?" she asked, resigning to the fact that they weren't going to connect.

He said the words, but his heart wasn't in them.

"Surprise me." He forced a smile.

Ryan knew the only thing that could possibly save their friendship now, was the geographical distance between them, and he would leave what was left of it caught somewhere in that distance.

A substantial part of Ryan unexpectedly died during that visit. It not only proved disheartening but damaging as well. Whatever memories he'd cherished of that time in his life were now badly bruised. Not to mention the anguish he felt knowing Aaron was living on the streets somewhere. But Ryan also knew Aaron would never blame Chloe for the misfortunes or the madness he fought against. Though he was sure it left his soul intrinsically extinguished, without even a glow of hope to save him. And as far as Ryan was concerned, Chloe was not only responsible for her own pain, but also for Aaron's. It was clearly captured in the framed photograph of Jonathan; just as it was in nearly every vowel and consonant that Chloe had uttered during his visit. The voice that was once familiar and even endearing, now seemed more like white noise to Ryan. But what truly broke his spirit was what Aaron's brother Jason, had done. Images of that atrocity continued to haunt him, as they would for years. But for an illusionary and heartbreaking moment, it was Aaron he witnessed commit that unspeakable crime. It was Aaron who tied the children to their beds and torch the house with them in it. But that was only because he could no longer picture Jason's face, as it remained where it had always been, lost in the peripherals.

It frightened him.

It was then that Chloe's voice woke him from the nightmare.

"That's right, it'll be my turn."

Then for the briefest of seconds, it was Chloe that he saw handcuffed to that same fence. But perhaps that was merely a momentary consolation.

"It'll be my turn," she repeated, with a trace of hope in her voice.

Ryan knew the words he'd come to say, the one's he'd decided to hold onto for now, would have to pass his lips on that day.

At their hotel in Buffalo, Leo asked, "So how'd it go?"

"I'm not sure."

"That bad?"

"Maybe worse. Certainly, worse than expected."

"Are we staying?"

"No, let's drive back to Manhattan for a few days."

"Should we stop again along the way?"

"We'll drive straight through this time," he said, not wanting to chance another hinge in the dream giving out along the way.

Merci

"It's all set," he said. "I found a great apartment in the city. We'll be sharing with another couple. I think you'll like it."

She could sense his enthusiasm.

"Sounds wonderful. I can't wait. I should be there no later than Friday. The road turned out to be more distracting than I'd expected."

"What do you mean?" There was a trace of jealously in his voice.

"There's so much to see driving across country. I didn't expect it to be so interesting."

"I missed it flying out. So, you won't be here until Friday now?"

"Definitely by Friday. And I can't wait to see you baby."

"You'll be surprised how incredible it is here. You'll love it."

"I'm sure I will. And I love you too." She found comfort in just saying the words again. "I'll see you Friday."

"Okay, bye baby."

He let out a deep breath as he hung up. "She'll be here on Friday."

"Then relax. We have almost a week yet."

Merci knocked, though she thought it strange not having a key to her own apartment.

Bruce was naked with a firmly erect penis when he opened the door. It bounced about playfully, even proudly, as if it were greeting her.

Merci was surprised to find his body unfamiliar. Maybe it was just the angle of it, or its odd presentation. It had only been two months.

"I thought you were coming on Friday!" he said, startled to see her.

"You seemed disappointed on the phone. So, I decided to drive straight through. But it looks like you were expecting me."

She smiled, acknowledging his stimulated member.

"But I thought you wanted to see the sights," Bruce babbled nervously.

"We can always take a road trip. But I just couldn't wait to see you. And the city. What a spectacular place. And you. Look at you!"

"It's crazy beautiful, right?" he said, still distracted.

"Just as handsome as I remember it. But why are you naked? Is this a San Francisco thing? I don't think I'd get used to people answering the door like that."

She had always liked his body, and seeing it again made her realize just how much she'd missed it. Though it didn't seem to miss her as much, as his hard-on quickly diminished when a voice shouted up the stairs from behind her.

"They were out of regular condoms, Bruce. So, I got the mega size. But don't worry baby, we can use a rubber band to keep it on."

Just then a busty blonde in a tight pink tank top and crotch length cut-offs emerged at the top of the stairs, her enormous breasts leading the way. When she caught a glimpse of Merci, a quizzical look came over her face.

"Is it Friday already?" she asked.

Merci felt a wave of desperation sweep over her. But she refused to fall apart in front of him or his friend for that matter, or to even make a scene. Instead, she found the strength to say, "It would seem you're a small man in a big city, Bruce."

She wouldn't give him the rage that he no doubt expected. But that was mostly because her mind and body were still in motion, still moving with the road in front of her; still in a state of inner inertia. Luckily, she hadn't unpacked, she thought, which would have made it more difficult, and perhaps even delayed her escape. Instead, it seemed a natural transition.

Merci picked up her bags, turned around, and brushed past the busty blonde. As she descended the stairs she shouted, "And I'll need that money back, Bruce!"

Merci had traveled across country to San Francisco for love that early summer, lured by the promise of year-round sunshine and a life-changing future. Instead, she found a city blanketed in fog, and her boyfriend seduced by a dubious blonde with equally dubious boobs.

In comparison, Merci was petite, with the firm and structured figure of a practiced gymnast. Her shoulder-length hair complimented her fresh, eager face, which was enhanced by her hazel-green eyes.

After three failed and long-tortured pregnancies, her French-Canadian mother was blessed with a child she named Merci, as she was thankful every day to have her in her life. Her daughter on the other hand, had an abortion before she was even nineteen. But Merci never mentioned it to her mother, because she knew it would have broken her heart. Though maybe she would have welcomed her choice; avoiding the pain she'd gone through.

Merci found a job at a cafe in The Mission, but she was still financially forced to live in East Oakland and share a house that she found with two of her coworkers; her hopes of living in the city being short-lived.

The place needed major repair. In fact, when she first saw it, she thought it should have been condemned years earlier.

The house came partially furnished with the obligatory soiled and torn couch in the living room, as well as other odd pieces. There were also stacks of garbage piled high in the kitchen; likely remnants of the squatters who'd previously inhabited it.

The countless holes around the windows where wooden boards had once hung, looked more like bullets holes; if not for the fact that there were what appeared to be real bullets holes in the walls as well. Each morning the sun caught the dust through them like a beam from the scope of a rifle retracing its path.

There was also a broken-down car in the driveway.

She had expected to live in the city. At least that was the intent, though not necessarily the dream. That hadn't been defined yet. It remained silently unsorted and in pieces, and even more so now. But she was disheartened to come all this way only to be isolated outside of the city. Especially since she got a taste of it on the days that she worked there, which made it difficult for her to return to the East Bay in the evening. That, and the congested traffic she was forced to endure in both directions.

They settled into the house as best they could, considering. But a week later the broken-down car was still parked in the driveway. Merci figured it was likely abandoned, especially since the landlord didn't know whose car it was either. She thought to wait to tow it in case the previous occupant came for it. But her roommates argued that they'd appear weak if they didn't tow it. They insisted that a show of strength was crucial.

Even with the obvious condition of the house and the rundown look of the neighborhood, it never occurred to Merci that the area was a challenging one. That harsh realization gave her cause for concern. But against her better judgement, she agreed, and called the police to have the car towed. The next day a truck came and took it away. Merci had to admit, it felt more like their own place once it was gone.

When they woke the next morning, everything changed.

The house had been tagged with vulgar and threatening graffiti. A rock had also been thrown through the front window. She called the police again, but this time it took a couple of unsettling days for them to respond.

"I was beginning to think you guys weren't coming," she said, pleased to see the two officers when she opened the door.

"I'm sorry ma'am, but we're not here in response to a call."

"I called about the house being vandalized," she said. "You can see the graffiti, and that someone threw a rock through the front window."

"We'll make a note of it, ma'am," one of the officers said. "But we're here about the car that was towed from your driveway."

"The car?" she asked confused.

"Was it your car, ma'am?" the officer asked.

"No, that's why we had it towed. It was here when we moved in."

"I see. And you don't know whose car it was?"

"Obviously not."

"Do you think the vandalism is a response to having the car towed?"

"I had hoped it was a coincidence. But apparently, that's not the case."

"It would seem, they're related." He jotted down some notes. "Ma'am, we had hoped to have it towed back."

"Why on earth would you do that?" she asked.

"Ma'am..."

"My name's Merci. Merci Kay," she said.

"I'm Officer Tyler. This is Officer Peters," he said, acknowledging his partner with a nod in his direction. "The thing is, Miss Kay, we found drugs in the car and we had hoped to tow it back and monitor any activity around it. But it would seem whoever was using it, since it's in fact a stolen vehicle, probably won't be coming back now."

"What do you mean, like a couple of joints some kids left in the ashtray after a joyride?" she asked.

"No Miss Kay, it had several thousand dollars' worth of drugs in it. We suspect it was a drop-off point."

The officer watched for her reaction, but it was as he'd expected.

"Are you shitting me?" she nearly shouted.

"Please keep your voice down, miss. We'd like people to think we're here in response to your call about vandalism now that we have that to work with. Why don't you point out exactly what they did, just for show?"

She felt used and patronized. They hadn't come when she needed them. But now they needed her, and that fact irritated her. Though she went along with their charade, knowing she'd undoubtedly need their help again sooner than later, especially under the circumstances.

"And the bullet holes?" he asked. "Are they new?"

His indifference frightened her. The fact that he didn't know the history of them gave her cause for concern. It also made her wonder just how many bullets passed blindly through the night unnoticed, as he could have just as casually been asking about the paint job. She assumed they'd been there for years, and from a more violent time. But it would seem, that time was now.

"You make it sound like a daily occurrence," she said nervously.

"Apparently, you're new to the area."

"I just moved to California," she confessed.

"And you moved specifically to East Oakland?"

"It's a long story. I planned on living in San Francisco."

"People usually have a good idea where they're moving to."

"It didn't seem so bad during the day when we first looked at it."

"How long did you say you've been here?"

"A little over a week."

"This area is known as the Killing Zone, Miss Kay. I suggest you find a safer place to live since it's probably going to get even uglier around here. Someone's out a lot of drugs. And I'm sure they're not happy about it."

"Is it possible to leave a patrol car outside the house?"

"I'm sorry, but we just don't have the manpower. But we'll try to drive by as often as we can," he said.

"Thank you."

He walked her back to the front entrance before leaving.

"And keep your doors locked," he advised.

Merci knew she'd have to do more than that.

While sitting alone in the house that evening, someone threw a trashcan through the kitchen window, which shattered like an avalanche of stardust onto the linoleum floor.

She telephoned her roommates at work, who told her that they decided to move to LA. Fearing for her safety, Merci left the house, only to find the tires on her Honda Accord slashed.

She was forced to take a cab into the city.

With nowhere else to turn, and short on money, having used what she had on rent and an unreasonable security deposit, which she thought now an ironic misnomer, Merci reluctantly called Bruce.

It was a conversation she had prepared just in case, though one she had hoped never to have to use. But she was forced to resign to it now. She filled him in on recent events and asked if she could sleep on his couch for a few days; curious though, if he was still hanging with that blonde, as it certainly would make things awkward.

Unlike the last time he heard her voice, it was desperate and vulnerable, which he hoped would work in his favor. He said he'd help, mostly because he felt responsible for her predicament.

Bruce could almost taste her perfume over the phone, which made him want to curl up in her familiar places again. In fact, he made that very offer, but she insisted on sleeping on the couch.

After a week of crashing in the living room, his roommates told Bruce that he'd have to make other arrangements. So, Merci was forced to give in to his original proposition. But she slept fully clothed and kept her distance. Though there were those moments when she wanted to pull him close, as she needed someone to hold onto, however flawed. But she knew him better now, and knew he'd never change. She knew herself better as well, and knew she'd never let go again if she did, and that would prove even worse in the end.

About a month later his roommates told Bruce that Merci was welcome to stay but would have to pay her share if she did. But instead of sharing that news, Bruce lied, and told her that they wanted her to go. He'd decided if they weren't going to have sex, then he wasn't going to let her take up the space where he planned on having it, regardless of her situation. But before leaving, she asked for the money that she'd given him to set up house in San Francisco. Bruce reluctantly wrote her a check.

Merci immediately went to the bank where she was told the funds were unavailable. The following day, the funds were still unavailable. She knew if she called Bruce, he'd just tell her to cash it next week after he'd made a deposit. He'd tell her that until the check was no longer good.

But Merci was cleverer than that.

When the funds were still unavailable the next day, she stole a glance at the computer screen when the teller turned away for a moment. She knew Bruce had purposely kept the balance just short of the amount of the check, and probably would for quite some time. Merci wrote out a deposit slip for a dollar over the difference and deposited it into his account, then cashed the check. She wished she could have seen his face when he realized her brash maneuver.

Merci called about the house in East Oakland, but the police told her it wasn't safe for her to move back in. But they did offer her alternate housing, which proved nearly as bad. Most of the tenants were drug addicts. And her deviant landlord tried to molest her every time she came and went. If she got away with just a pat on the ass from Gus, she felt lucky.

Mercy

With nowhere else to turn, Merci knew she needed to establish a social life. Especially after her recent ordeal with Bruce, as she wouldn't be able to call him again. She was alone now, and it frightened her. At least work was busy. It was also a good venue to meet new people.

Bryan recently started to come into the cafe. He was a tall, good-looking guy, with a sense of humor. And if she needed anything in that moment, it was that. He eventually asked her out. Of course, she said yes. He'd joked that she was too skinny and in need of a decent meal. Only a foolish girl would be offended by a compliment like that; not to mention the offer of a good meal. Merci also felt a connection with him, something she hadn't felt with anyone in a long time. And she needed that connection now to survive.

After an expensively generous dinner, Bryan suggested they stop by a friend's place for a few drinks.

Her first impression of his boisterous buddies, Allen and Jerry, wasn't favorable. They certainly didn't seem like people Bryan would hang with; at least not the Bryan she got to know in their short time together. She couldn't put her finger on it. But without him there, she wouldn't have felt safe.

Though as the night went on, and the drinks went down, Merci became more relaxed. She eventually found herself at ease enough to laugh, which she hadn't done since she'd arrived in the city. She'd been forced to put a barrier around her world, and even more so now, to avoid the advances of her landlord on a daily basis. But it was only when she got a glimpse past that barrier that she realized she'd misjudged them.

After several more drinks, Bryan confessed he was probably too drunk to drive, and suggested they stay the night. Merci appreciated his concern. In fact, it made her feel protected; something that even Bruce had failed to do.

He said there was a spare room she could sleep in, and that he'd take the couch. The truth was, she hoped to end the night in his embrace, because she needed his strong arms around her to feel secure again. In fact, she decided earlier that evening, when the time came, she would playfully pull him into the spare bedroom with her.

It didn't take long for that to change, as it was soon obvious that Bryan had orchestrated a different event for the evening.

In one moment, Merci was having a wonderful time. In the next, an odd sensation came over her, and she was unable to stand. Then her very being gave-out, and she collapsed on the floor. She didn't know why her body had failed her. But when she woke the next morning, the sun coming in brightly through the window, she knew she'd been seriously violated.

Under different circumstances she'd have welcomed the room, as it was light and airy. But as glimpses of the previous evening came back to her in what proved to be cruel and vile vignettes, she could see their dark figures above her again in the dimly lit bedroom. Three faces, and three painfully separate entries; each forcing their way into her with brutal force; each one noticeably different; each more violent than the other. In fact, her body was so crippled and numb that she failed to feel the endless tears streaming down her face. Inside though, she felt everything. But she hadn't had the strength to fight them off, as her paralyzed body had been tossed about involuntarily; almost lifelessly.

When she woke alone and sore, every foul and insipid touch came back to her. She could still smell it on her. But in that moment, she was too afraid to challenge what they'd done. She would need to escape first.

She quietly dressed and pulled her hair back away from her face. It felt hard and sticky. She was sure her makeup was a mess, but she chose not to look in the mirror. Vanity had been devalued along with her self-esteem.

When she eventually found the courage to open the bedroom door, she cautiously entered the living room. Jerry was passed-out on the couch, Allen was asleep on the floor; their mouths wide-open like slaughtered animals. At least that's what she wished they were. Their faces were distorted. But their breathing was content; undoubtedly dreaming their evil deed again.

There was no sign of Bryan.

Still shattered to her core, Merci silently crossed the room. She knew she would never be the same again, at least not inside. But she had enough reserve left in her in that moment to fight if she had to, and she was ready. She was ready to battle it out, unable to do so the night before.

Instead, she slipped out unnoticed.

As expected, when she entered the building, her landlord Gus made his scheduled appearance. He tried his hands on her as usual, but this time she took him down with a single firm knee to the groin. Merci threw her entire being into it, along with every ounce of pain that she had accumulated since arriving in California. Gus screamed like a wounded beast. In fact, she could still hear his shrill cry echo through the halls when she got to her apartment, where she quickly locked the door behind her. What she'd done to Gus was out of character. But in that failed moment, she didn't mind sharing the pain.

After gathering her thoughts as best she could, she realized calling the police was no longer an option. Not now.

A single woman drinking alone with three men, with the intention of sleeping with one of them, would prove a poor defense. Not to mention, it would probably challenge or even negate any previously considered truths that she'd told, as even the incident with Gus might bring her reputation into question.

Merci felt her world surrender right out from under her. Everything that had sustained her up until that point finally collapsed, taken her with it. Any spark left, vanished in that violated trance. All she felt now was resignation. She had lost her trust in human nature and began to question God's purpose as well; wondering why he would allow her mother to give birth to her and not miscarry her as she had the others. Or why she hadn't also been aborted as she had her own child. Truth was, she felt like that fetus now, dead inside.

As her faith waned, and her diminishing world along with it, she grew hopeless. The glow that once filled her hazel-green eyes lost their glimmer, unable now to even put on a brave face.

Just then, there was an unexpected knock at the door.

Her first thought was Gus.

She grabbed a knife from the kitchen.

Though she didn't know what she would do with it.

But it felt right in her hand regardless.

With the stink of violation still dripping between her legs, she squeezed the knife so tightly, it began to hurt her knuckles.

A moment later there was a second knock on the door.

It seemed too gentle to be Gus.

Besides, didn't he have a key?

That thought never occurred to her.

But it made her grip on the knife tighten even more.

Then she realized she'd forgot to put the chain on when she came in.

She looked at it, dangling; swaying slightly from the vibration now.

It couldn't be Gus.

She was sure she could still hear his moans five floors down.

"Hello?"

It was a familiar voice, though she couldn't place it.

It couldn't possibly be her old roommates. They'd moved to LA.

And Bruce had no idea where she had moved to either.

It might be Bryan, she thought.

Wanting to apologize and explain what happened.

Though two syllables were too few to grasp its identity.

She had to be sure before opening the door.

But it had no peephole, so there was no way of knowing.

The knife painfully in hand, her fingers frozen around it, she waited.

"Miss Kay?"

The voice questioned her very existence.

Only then did she recognize it. She could almost see the face.

It felt safe.

Though she knew she had to keep her violations buried, however much she hoped to one day fill the void they had exposed.

"Merci?"

Her first name.

"Yes?" she answered, her voice brittle, cracking the air. But she needed further confirmation. "Who is it?"

"It's Officer Tyler."

Merci was still afraid to open the door even to the most welcoming of faces or soothing tones. It was what she'd come away with after all she'd been through; her trust in people nearly extinct now.

To her surprise the door opened, but she didn't recall crossing the room to open it.

"Are you okay?" he asked in a concerned voice.

She stared silently at the uniform. Then the face.

It held a last promise of hope, however dubious. But that hope perished when her body collapsed from under her without even a dream to hold onto.

The last thing she heard was her body hit the floor before everything went dark. For all she knew, she might be dead.

Merci woke in another unfamiliar room, one with strange sounds.

It was also too well-lit for public housing.

"Good, you're coming to," the voice said.

"Where am I?" she asked, disoriented.

"You're in the hospital."

"I thought I died," she confessed, still in a slight state of panic.

"You fainted. But the doctor checked you out. You're going to be fine. But they discovered several things we should probably discuss. First, do you remember what happened?"

Merci tried to focus. It was the same officer who came to the house in Oakland. And the same one at the door at the public housing unit.

"Officer…?"

"Tyler," he said.

"Right," she whispered in affirmation under her breath.

"Do you remember what happened?" he asked again.

"It'll be impossible to forget," she admitted truthfully.

"Can I run some things by you?"

Her response was weak. "Okay."

"You have a bruised knee. Do you recall how you got that?"

"Gus' groin," she said, attempting a failed smile.

"I assumed as much when I found him crawling on the lobby floor."

"That's just how I left him," she said with a firmer expression now.

"That's why I stopped by. We've had reports about him. Unfortunately, it was the only housing unit available at the time. When I saw him like that, I thought to check on you."

"I appreciate that."

"We should also talk about your medical report. Do you mind if I ask some personal questions?"

Merci braced herself.

"Okay."

"The tests show you had sex with multiple persons, Miss Kay."

"You can tell that?"

"I suspect it wasn't by choice."

"I was raped," she admitted, though she hadn't planned on sharing that information. But saying it now helped relieve some of the pressure.

"I suspected as much. So, I had the doctor run a rape kit just in case. Can you identify them?"

"I only have their first names."

She said them in a whisper as the images nearly made her cry again.

He wrote them down in his notebook.

"And do you remember where the rape took place?"

"At Jerry's house."

"Do you have an address?"

"Yes."

He wrote that down as well.

"I'll send a car to retrieve any evidence, as well as the suspects."

"I'm sure it's too late." She was nearly in tears.

"The rape kit revealed three different seminal samples."

Merci started to cry.

He gave her a moment.

"We're almost done."

"Sorry," she said, pulling herself together.

"I wanted to let you know that I had your car towed."

"That wasn't my car, or my drugs," she said out of reflex.

"Not that car," he said attempting to calm her down. "Your Honda. We towed it from the house in East Oakland and had it repaired."

"You have no idea how much that means to me."

Merci couldn't hide her emotions or the tears that ran down her cheeks. She felt those, and she welcomed them.

"There are a couple of other things, if you're up to it."

"Of course," she said, wiping her eyes.

She appeared reenergized. Freedom tends to do that.

"Do you know a Bruce Hawkins?"

"He's the reason I moved here," she said, curious why he'd mentioned Bruce. "Did you contact him?"

"Not about your situation here. He was arrested for passing bad checks, and your name came up in the investigation. We also arrested a transsexual named Darla."

"Really?" She couldn't help but smile.

"Do you know her? We arrested her for prostitution."

"We met briefly when I first arrived."

She was sure Bruce had no idea what he'd gotten into. Literally.

"That's everything. Do you have any questions? Is there anything I can do to help put you at ease? Anything at all?"

It was him smiling now.

Merci hadn't noticed just how good-looking he was.

But she noticed now.

From Carlton To Carton

Friday

With the recent smoking law in effect, a larger number of people than usual stood outside the bar, a tribe that wouldn't have necessarily engaged with one another inside, or otherwise for that matter; who were now equally ostracized in solidarity, sharing more than just the harsh elements and a few smokes.

It was in that mix that she first spotted Jasper, who, always with a ready and willing smile, attempted to blend in with the crowd as he usually did on a Friday night.

Allie noticed him immediately.

"I'd love a cigarette!" she said, in a flirtatious tone as she put a tender hand on his arm.

Jasper had just bummed one, but he obviously couldn't resist her terms. So, he handed her the one he'd just lit.

"You're a doll," Allie said putting her glossy red lips around the filter.

"I haven't seen you around before."

"I'm here for an anesthesiologist's convention," she said in a noticeably sexy exhale as she handed the cigarette back to him. "I know, I know, I shouldn't smoke," she added. "But there are a lot of things I shouldn't do."

"You're a doctor?" Jasper responded, clearly impressed.

"Thank you. Many don't acknowledge that fact," she said, pleased that he had. "Yes, a doctor, and not just a drug dealer."

Her words caught the attention of some of the others huddled close by.

"Who doesn't like drugs?" Jasper said.

"Maybe we should go back to my hotel then," she offered.

It was in Jasper's nature to jump at the slightest invitation.

They slowly worked their way through the crowded street to her car.

Saturday

"He says he's got a suite at The Marriott. Is that even possible?" Robert asked doubtfully.

Trevor was barely able to mouth the words.

He slurred, "If he says he does, then he probably does."

Trevor was sprawled out in the backseat of his convertible Bug, fading in and out of consciousness. He was in no condition to drive, especially since he lived thirty miles north of the city.

Robert tried nursing him with a cool towel and some water. He was also trying to figure out what to do next.

"A bit early to be in that condition, isn't it?" a familiar voice joked as he headed into the bar that Trevor and Robert had recently left.

"Someone put something in his drink," Robert affirmed.

The words spun around in Trevor's head as he tried to put a face to the voice.

Jasper came back to the car.

"You ready, man? There's even a space for his car. Then you can grab a taxi back."

"You sure you have a suite at The Marriott?" Robert asked, doubting the validity of the offer. He couldn't reconfirm with Trevor now, as he was out cold again.

Jasper seemed excited by his own proposal.

"Absolutely. No problem, man," he said trying to be magnanimous.

Jasper jumped into the car to ride shotgun before Robert even opened the door on his side. He still didn't have a good feeling about it.

Trevor opened his eyes slightly as he felt his feet stumble beneath him as they unloaded him from the car and carried him through the hotel lobby.

Jasper caught a look of discomfort on Robert's face.

"Don't worry man, they'll think he's just another drunk rock star."

Trevor looked the part with his black leather jacket and shoulder length hair, which covered most of his face. Robert was sure the ensemble added to the mystery guest, as well as the vintage Volkswagen, which was in cherry condition. Trevor briefly caught a glimpse of the patterned marble floor as they glided him toward the elevator. The last thing he remembered was the feel of the high thread count on his face as his head hit the pillow, before surrendering to the blackness and comfort of sleep.

"He'll be fine," Jasper reaffirmed.

They had known Jasper for several years, though not well. But Robert couldn't deny the surroundings. The suite was impressive. Two bedrooms, a bar, and a large screen television. Not to mention, an expansive view of the city.

"You sure this is okay?" Robert asked still having doubts.

"Sure man, no problem," Jasper said. "He'll be fine."

"I guess I'll catch that cab back to the bar then," he said.

"I can order room service, or have drinks sent up," Jasper generously offered; words Robert never expected to hear Jasper say.

Robert still felt that it was a dubious situation, perhaps even dangerous. Nonetheless, he needed to get back to the bar. And regardless of his instincts and whatever he thought of Jasper, he knew Trevor was at least safe for the night. After all, it was The Marriott, and not a fleabag hotel on Sixth Street.

"I should get back. We were supposed to meet friends for dinner. And I should let them know Trevor's okay. He will be okay, right?"

"He'll be fine man," Jasper said. "No worries."

The doorman blew his whistle for a cab. Robert tipped him and settled into the back seat. He lowered the window to let some air in. But even with a clear head, he still had his doubts.

Trevor woke shortly after midnight, feeling better than he should have under the circumstances. He washed his face with cold water and went out into the suite.

"Oh, hey man," Jasper said. "How you are feeling?"

He could tell Jasper was loaded and had made the best of the last few hours.

"I'm still not feeling great," Trevor said.

It took him a moment before he noticed the nearly naked woman sitting across the room in the bay window, posing like a failed model with the city beautifully draped behind her as she attempted to look seductive. But on her it seemed more a stolen persona, which made Trevor laugh, because he was sure she was rarely who she said she was anyway. The woman looked to be in her mid-thirties. Her bleached hair was pulled tightly back from her face. But there were strands that hung loose and disheveled as if someone had run their hands through it. It was only then that he noticed the frayed threading dangling from her brassiere, which was stretched tightly across her inflated chest. It certainly wasn't the image The Marriott would choose to advertise in Conte Nast Traveler, he thought.

With an excited bounce to his gimpy step, Jasper came over to Trevor and whispered, "Hey man, do you have sixty bucks I can get from you?"

The strong smell of alcohol on Jasper's breath made Trevor's stomach start to turn again.

"I'm not sure what I have," Trevor said. "Why?"

"I went down to the front desk and asked if they could give me sixty bucks and charge it to the room. But I guess it's against hotel policy or some shit like that. Some bullshit rule. Then I asked if they could charge her to the credit card like room service, but they couldn't do that either."

Trevor tried not to laugh, because the room didn't seem equipped for levity in that moment, not with Jasper all hyped-up. But even at high-end hotels, Trevor knew the night concierge was more accustomed to that kind of thing, as they were certainly more street savvy than those who worked the front desk during the day. But he'd be surprised if even they had ever been asked to charge a working girl to a room before.

"I think Visa specifically states they don't cover hookers," Trevor said.

"Well, they don't. And I'm in a jam," he said, bouncing around as if in need of a fix. But Trevor knew whatever was broken had already been fixed, and that was the reason why he was bouncing about like an ex-con on crack. "I need sixty bucks, man," Jasper repeated, but this time urgently nodding in the direction of the woman sitting in the window seat. "I mean, I helped you out, right?"

"And I appreciate it," Trevor said.

He was about to suggest that he bargain her down, but he suspected that she had only asked for forty bucks and that Jasper had planned on pocketing the other twenty.

Then with the skilled enthusiasm and slick demeanor of an experienced salesmen, Jasper added, "She said she'd also do you," as if were a salacious consolation.

"What?" Trevor was put off by even the idea of it.

"Yeah, she looked in on you earlier and I guess she liked what she saw. In fact, she said she'd do you for free."

"She liked what she saw? What the fuck. I was passed out cold. What do you mean, she looked in on me?" Trevor was not quite heated, but he didn't like the temperature he was feeling either. He was still trying to figure out how he ended up in this situation in the first place. So, getting his head around this was a bit of a challenge as well.

"I guess she wanted to make sure you weren't dead. Apparently, she's had a problem with that kind of thing before."

"With dead guys in hotel rooms?"

"I guess," he said nonchalantly, as if it were standard procedure.

Trevor took a better look at the woman now, wondering if he was going to get his money's worth; or rather, if Jasper would. It was only then that he realized she wasn't quite as young as he'd first thought, as she appeared to be closer to fifty, if not older now. She smiled at him as if to reaffirm the tempting offer she made earlier. That's when he noticed that she was nearly toothless. But he chose for his own sake and time not to attempt to calculate how many cocks it had taken to knock out that many teeth, as it was obvious her gums couldn't take the blows.

Trevor took out his wallet, surprised to see there was still money in it, not to mention his credit cards. "Here," he said, pulling out three twenties.

"Thanks, man!"

Jasper bounced back to the woman on the couch.

"I'm going back to sleep," Trevor said. "I'm still not feeling that great. And I don't want anybody looking in on me, you understand?"

"No problem, man."

Trevor headed toward the bedroom. But then he turned and said, hiding a sarcastic smile, "Thank your friend for the offer. Maybe next time."

"Sure thing, man," Jasper said as he excitedly finalized the transaction.

Sunday

When Trevor woke the next morning, he was still a bit lightheaded from the drug someone slipped into his drink. But he was even more curious now, how Jasper had commandeered a two-bedroom suite at The Marriott. He had his suspicions. So, Trevor decided to meet him outside and let Jasper check-out on his own. He was sure the front desk had their suspicions as well. Especially after he tried to charge a hooker to the room.

Even after twelve solid hours of sleep, he still found the early morning sunshine painfully bright.

He paid the valet and tipped him well.

Then he waited with the car running, as he expected things to get ugly. Trevor had never thought getaway car when he purchased the Beetle. But then he never anticipated being in a situation like this either.

A few moments later, Jasper bounced out of the lobby door, as happy go lucky as usual.

"Okay, what's the story," Trevor asked as he pulled out of the parking lot. "How'd you end up with a suite at The Marriott?"

"I met a woman outside the bar Friday night. A doctor. We got some drugs and went back to her hotel. Saturday morning, she got a call and had to go home early because of some emergency. But she said I could have the suite until Sunday if I wanted, as she'd already paid for it."

"Who did she think you were?"

"She never asked."

It was an unlikely tale that took his head for an unexpected whirl.

Then he noticed that Jasper was wearing new sneakers and jacket.

"Did your doctor also buy those for you?" he asked nodding at Jasper's fresh footwear.

"No man, I got these downtown."

Trevor recognized them as the same pair he'd seen in the shop window in the lobby on his way out of the hotel.

"And the jacket?"

"I don't know, man. I've had this for a while."

Trevor made a few more turns, and then pulled into the same spot in the alley next to the bar where he'd parked in the day before.

Jasper got out and started to walk away.

"Thanks again," Trevor said sticking his head out the window.

"Any time, man," Jasper shouted back as he headed down the alley.

Then Trevor watched as Jasper pushed a Safeway cart to the curb, as if parking a vehicle. A moment later, he crawled into a cardboard box, pulling the carton closed behind him as he curled himself up into it out of the near noon sun.

Trevor once joked that they'd all end up on the median in the center of the road one day with a sign and their hand out. He realized now that if you were clever enough, or just plain lucky, you got to step off it occasionally.

As Trevor drove off, he recalled a conversation that he had with Jasper earlier that summer. He'd mentioned having an alley in Miami he stayed in, as if proudly talking about a vacation home he had down there. He also said that he took the Greyhound to Florida in the late fall and came back in the early spring, as the winters in the city were much too cold for him. He also boasted, as a wealthy man might, 'I have a Public's cart down there as well.' A two-cart family, Trevor remembered thinking at the time.

As he rolled up the window of the convertible against the coming chill, Trevor knew that Jasper would be heading south soon. The funny thing is, whenever he disappeared for a period of time, everyone had assumed that Jasper was a guest at the county jail. Little did they know he was mooching in Miami and playing the streets while working on his winter tan.

Routine Questioning

Detective: It's called matricide.

Suspect: What are you saying?

Detective: It means killing your mother.

Suspect: I know what it means.

Detective: Did you? Did you kill your mother?

Suspect: No, that's crazy.

Detective: Well, that's pretty much what you've told me.

Suspect: That's not what I said at all.

Detective: You said that you argued with your mother at lunch. Then after a short walk back down the pier she was dead. It sounds suspicious to me.

Suspect: Yes, but---

Detective: Sounds like you caused of her death. Tell me, was it a long walk down a short pier? Never mind. (He laughed to himself) So, you said you argued. What'd you argue about?

(He watches it all play out in his mind again)

Detective: Did you hear what I said?

Suspect: Huh?

Detective: I asked, what you argued about?

Suspect: Thurgood Marshall. Though it wasn't an argument as much as a strained conversation.

Detective: Who?

Suspect: Thurgood Marshall.

Detective: Do I know him?

(His stupidity brings him out of it)

Suspect: He was the first black man to sit on the Supreme Court!

Detective: You think this--- uh, this black man killed her?

Suspect: What?

Detective: Never mind. (He pauses to rethink his questioning) So what was the argument about? Excuse me. The strained conversation.

Suspect: He had just died.

Detective: Did you kill him too?

Suspect: Now you're just showing how much of an idiot you are.

Detective: (He lifts himself up from the table and postures defensively) You want to take me out too?

Suspect: Sit down. Nobody's taking anybody out.

Detective: It would seem you give people little choice. You either like them or kill them.

Suspect: What?

Detective: What did this Marshall guy do?

Suspect: I told you, he'd recently died.

Detective: And you didn't kill him either, right?

Suspect: I haven't killed anyone, you moron. I never even met the man.

Detective: No need to get angry.

Suspect: No need to get stupid.

Detective: Be careful kid. (He pauses to compose himself) Okay, so tell me what the conversation with your mother was about exactly.

Suspect: Like I said, we were having lunch on the pier. I mentioned that Thurgood Marshall had just died. I wanted to get her views about that and how the balance of the Supreme Court might go. But she got upset. It was as if she knew him.

Detective: So, she knew this Marshall guy?

Suspect: No. (He pauses) You work for the government, right?

Detective: Of course.

Suspect: You wouldn't know it.

Detective: Don't question me, kid.

Suspect: Let me finish. My mother brought me up not to discriminate. Blacks, Jews, it didn't matter. We were all the same; fighting for the same thing. Especially back then.

Detective: Where are you from?

Suspect: Down the street. Why?

Detective: I haven't seen you around the neighborhood before.

Suspect: I moved. I'm just visiting.

Detective: Family?

Suspect: And the neighborhood.

Detective: Has it changed much?

Suspect: Apparently. Now can I go? I was going to confession.

Detective: You don't seem to be confessing much.

Suspect: What?

Detective: Nothing.

Suspect: If you were listening, I said that I was going to confession, at the church. Not confessing to you.

Detective: Denying would be more like it.

Suspect: I should just leave.

Detective: Wait. Continue.

Suspect: My mother was upset about Marshall. More because he was black, than anything else, I think. Which was odd, since she'd never taught me to think that way.

Detective: So, you argued about Marshall.

Suspect: About his being black. Because she'd been raped by a black man a few years after I left the city.

Detective: Did this Marshall guy, do it?

Suspect: No. (Resigning now to his stupidity)

Detective: You seem calmer. Good. So, you ready to confess?

Suspect: Yes.

Detective: So, you killed all these people. What'd you use?

Suspect: My wits.

Detective: They're not that sharp, kid.

Suspect: As if you could tell.

Detective: Funny guy. You know you're going down, right?

Suspect: I've been down before, it isn't so bad.

Detective: Welcome back then. (He paused) So, if you didn't kill your mother, who did then?

Suspect: Probably the rapist.

Detective: The therapist?

Suspect: I didn't say therapist. She didn't have a therapist.

Detective: Who then?

Suspect: You have a bad habit of hearing what you want to hear.

Detective: I have a lot of bad habits but that's not one of them.

Suspect: I said the rapist.

Detective: So, the rapist killed her.

Suspect: No. But having been raped no doubt played a part in it.

Detective: How's that?

Suspect: The rapist was black.

Detective: So, a black man killed your mother?

Suspect: No.

Detective: You trying to run me in circles?

Suspect: You're running in circles well enough without my help.

Detective: You trying to be funny?

Suspect: No, but thankfully, I'm easily entertained.

Detective: Okay, so what about this rape?

Suspect: It happened years ago.

Detective: How does it tie in with your mother's death then?

Suspect: It lowered her opinion of black men. It created a prejudice.

Detective: Wasn't that Marshall guy black?

Suspect: What a memory! What was that, five minutes ago?

Detective: But didn't you say that Marshall guy didn't kill her?

Suspect: Right, but the conversation about him may have.

Detective: A conversation killed her?

Suspect: Sadly, that may well have been the case.

Detective: Words don't kill. Conversations don't kill. I should know, I hear a lot of them in this business.

Suspect: This one might be killing me right now.

Detective: Don't be smart.

Suspect: One of us should be, don't you think?

Detective: Get back to the conversation with your mother.

Suspect: That was it. There's nothing else to tell. I told you everything I know. But I doubt you'll get it right. So, I'm leaving now.

Detective: Don't leave town.

Suspect: Wouldn't think of it.

Detective: Hey, one last thing.

Suspect: What's that?

Detective: Do you have an address for that Marshall guy?

Suspect: Check Arlington.

Detective: Okay. But leave your number with the desk sergeant. I'll be in touch.

Suspect: Just what I need, another prank call.

Detective: What's that? Wait, hang on. Come back here. What you do know about prank calls?

Suspect: Nothing. I was joking.

Detective: There's something you're not telling me.

Suspect: Only that every kid makes them.

Detective: You made prank calls?

Suspect: Of course. But it was years ago.

Detective: Who'd you call?

Suspect: Some woman.

Detective: What was her name?

Suspect: Lipschitz.

(Coming out of his chair now)

Detective: Did you say Lipschitz?

Suspect: How could I forget a name like that?

Detective: Did you know her?

Suspect: She was just a name in the phone book.

Detective: This is serious, kid. You may want to call a lawyer.

Suspect: What?

Detective: We may not get you for the killings, but we will for this.

Suspect: For what?

Detective: For those prank calls.

Suspect: They were just prank calls. Every kid makes them. Thousands of kids did the same thing back then.

Detective: But we have you. And we've been looking for you for a long time. The Lipschitz Prank Call Case. It's one of the oldest cold cases on the books.

Suspect: That's crazy.

Detective: What's crazy is, you may be right after all. Words can kill. You admitted your words might have killed your mother and that Marshall guy. I may not be able to prove that in court, but we got you for this.

Suspect: It was years ago. There must be a statute of limitations?

Detective: There's no statute of limitations for bad behavior, kid. And it would seem your behavior hasn't changed.

Suspect: What about those kids that make prank calls today? Are you arresting them?

Detective: Of course. We get those little buggers before they even hang up their precious cell phones. We have Caller-ID now. If we'd had it in your day you wouldn't be out there killing people today. You'd still be in jail.

Suspect: How are you getting this all wrong?

Detective: I doubt I'm getting anything wrong. Tell me, how'd your little prank go? What did you say to the old woman?

Suspect: It was the same every time.

Detective: Multiple times? Good, multiple charges.

Suspect: What?

Detective: Let's hear it. Tell me what you said to the old gal.

Suspect: I said, 'Hello, Mrs. Lipschitz?' 'Yes?' she'd answer sweetly, as if she'd been waiting for someone special to call, like the guy on that old Millionaire television show. Then I'd say, 'Mrs. Lipschitz, if your lip shits, then my ass talks.'

Detective: You think that's funny?

Suspect: We were kids, it seemed funny at the time.

Detective: You still think it's funny?

Suspect: You must admit it's still sort of funny.

Detective: You're the one doing the admitting, kid. I'm going to charge you for making those prank calls and whatever affect they may have had on that poor old woman. I'll look into everything; hospital bills, broken heart, whatever pain you may have caused her. Maybe even financial restitution since she may have also missed a call from that Millionaire show because of you. She might have been a rich woman if it wasn't for your prank calls. I might not get you for those other killings, but I'll get you for those calls and maybe even for killing the old lady. Then I can finally close the case.

Suspect: Did someone kill the old woman? And since when did prank calls become a crime anyway?

Detective: Your words may have killed her. Like you said, words can kill, right? Isn't that what you said?

Suspect: That's absurd!

Detective: No kid, that's retribution. It catches up with you in the end. That's how justice works.

Beyond Destination

Every Tuesday, Clara helped Shirley with her shopping. Shirley had recently turned ninety. One Tuesday, as they were slowly walking down the street, Shirley caught a glimpse of a young man as he approached at the crosswalk. She whispered to Clara, who held her tightly by the arm, "I went to college with that young man."

Clara smiled, and said, "Of course you did Shirley."

"And I had sex with him."

Shirley blushed as the memory came back to her.

Humoring her, Clara said, "And maybe you will again."

As she watched her footing Shirley said excitedly, "That would be nice, very nice indeed."

Clara held her. "Careful Shirley, you don't want another fall."

The young man grew closer. His wild and wavy auburn hair undulated in the breeze above his youthful face. His cadence was confident and strong, as was his sinewy stature.

"That's him all right," Shirley said matter-of-factly.

Clara smiled politely at the young man. And as he passed, he smiled at Shirley.

"He's looking remarkably well," she added.

Later that night Hayden called home.

"How is San Francisco?" Tom asked. "Has it changed in the three years you've been gone?"

"Some of its beauty has survived," he said. "I also ran into an old friend from college this morning."

"You make it sound as if it were a lifetime ago," Tom remarked.

"I guess it just feels that way," he said, smiling to himself.

It was rare that Hayden would return to a city he'd lived in so soon. As a rule, he'd wait at least a lifetime as it could get awkward, if not dangerous; just as running into Shirley almost proved to be. It had been seventy years since he'd last seen her, and it broke his heart to leave her again. That was always the most difficult and painful part for Hayden. That and the lying, as he was often forced to leave friends and lovers so as not to raise suspicion.

* * *

From Hayden's Journal

What am I? I'm not entirely sure. I just am, like everyone else. And just like everyone else, I continue to search for the truth, hoping to answer that question, among others. Though I wonder why I bother, since I'm right here. But when I look at my reflection it never seems to change. And I accept that as I do everything in life. We all have specific characteristics; height, eye and hair color, the way we talk and walk. We're all individuals with our own special qualities, and I'm happy with mine as I've been for several centuries. The difference is, instead of losing track of time, it would seem time has lost track of me.

My life is complicated, which is not surprising, as I'm sure most lives are. What does surprise me though, is when people say if they lived another hundred years, they'd finally be able to comprehend life. I haven't found that to be true, and I've been given that opportunity. Time doesn't always reveal the qualities of life. More often, it offers more of it to enjoy; or not, as is sometimes the case. For it's the soul that absorbs and identifies with life if you allow it the chance. Life's an intrinsic experience and time alone can't ensure its happiness. In fact, it can just as easily add to its misery as I've found more than once. Because if the soul doesn't connect with that essence, that core of life, then it's little more than a waste of time since everything else is irrelevant.

And just like time, there comes a time I need to move on, as familiar faces start to question my being. It's a drawback to my extended existence, as I'm repeatedly displaced from the people and places I love and hold dear. It's especially heartbreaking to leave those relationships that have been long established. And of course, there are the homes and rooms I've grown fond of, which I'm forced to abandon as well. And when I do eventually relocate and reinvent my life again, I'm consoled by little more than the memories I've taken with me. Since every fingertip, every touch, every lip I've kissed, is individual. Even the fists I've felt hard across my face are distinguishable, as it's not always the power of the hit, but the person behind it that causes the most pain. But even that blurs as we tend to forgive and forget in time. Thankfully, I occasionally succeed at doing just that. At least I try.

Though it's those few and sacred loves in life that are the most difficult and agonizing to abandon. It's often worse than death since I know they're out there living life without me. That's a lasting pain. There've also been times I've returned years later to sit with an old love before they died. Sometimes they recognize me, though often they don't as I'm sure I'm nothing more than a dream; hopefully a comforting one. But after one such visit, I heard a dying flame insist to a visiting relative that I'd been there a moment earlier. Of course, logic prevails, as the past is usually cast in reflection as one gets closer to the end, or so they say. But I find it interesting just how often that experience occurs, which makes me question if I'm alone in this extended sojourn. Perhaps what the dying sometimes see is as real as I am.

On a lighter note, I'm humored when I hear an older person explain to someone younger how times have changed. Times indeed change, but those times have a strange and mysterious way of slipping back into the present; as time goes in and out of history. Or rather, as history goes in and out of time on its cherished wave of existence; one I continue to experience. Just as I'm often amused when someone tells me I'm too young to remember The Sixties. With restraint I bite my tongue, wanting to ask, 'Which Sixties?'

Once I understood the journey I was on, I grew concerned with whom I slept with since I couldn't be certain I haven't fathered a child; as a doula, somewhere might have caught a progeny of mine without my knowledge, as several relationships ended unexpectedly or under dubious conditions. That thought haunted me two-fold. To think I may have missed the opportunity to have reared a child, would have broken my heart. Just as it would have if I'd unknowingly embraced an offspring sexually. Thankfully, science freed me of that uncertainty. Deoxyribonucleic acid is the clock inside us, the pulse of living time. But I'd be lying if I didn't admit that on more than one occasion I'd been overwhelmed by passion and had failed to collect that detail. But DNA wasn't the only thing on my mind at the time. I am human after all. Did I fail to mention that? I'm not an alien from another galaxy. Though I'm sure some would welcome that more than the truth. You see, I don't have an undetectable spaceship hovering above in the clouded sky, or one buried beneath the deep sea for that matter. What I have is an unexplained physical make-up, one which apparently doesn't age. At least not since I was twenty-four. Life seemed rather normal until then. Truth is, I failed to notice until people told me I looked exceptionally good for my age; and a decade later, unrealistically so. I even recall joking at the time, saying, 'I heard growing old wasn't much fun. So, why do it then?' But as time went on it seemed to startle some. I soon became mindful of the fact that people weren't bothered by change, if you changed along with them, that is. I'll confess, it frightened me too at first, though perhaps concerned would be a better word. Because it wasn't as if the image each morning in the mirror as I shaved terrified me. It wasn't a horror story. But I wasn't one for mirrors anyway, or for searching out my own likeness. Of course, there were times when my reflection was unavoidable. Though there were far more interesting faces to appreciate and adhere to than my own, and I found comfort in those. But I'll admit, if it had been something serious, like a cyst or cancer, I'd have gone to see a doctor. In fact, I eventually went to see one early on anyway.

I sat in his office filling out the needed forms.

Name: Hayden Kean

Age: I had to think for a moment. It wasn't that I didn't know. I just wasn't sure how truthful I wanted to be with the dear doctor. Especially, so early on. So, I decided to subtract several years from my actual age and put that down instead. I didn't want to be diagnosed for an ailment that wasn't there or dissected for some scientific experiment. I preferred the doctor not be distracted by disbelief. I wanted a basic physical; say ah, and all that. If he found something serious, or questionable; then we could talk about that, and then maybe the other. I'd seen enough movies to know I didn't want the government treating me like a freak or an alien. I drive a Bug, not a starship.

The doctor came back into the room shortly after I finished dressing. Surprisingly, I couldn't read the prognosis on his face, and I'd been reading faces for quite some time. I studied his eyes, but it was obvious the good doctor had been well-trained at hiding his emotions in such matters. I hoped he'd be more comforting and sympathetic in his bedside manner if that time ever came.

Finally, the doctor broke his silence.

"Young man, you're in perfect health." Then he added with a fatherly hand firmly placed on my shoulder, "You'll probably live to be a hundred."

That was unsettling news. It seemed I only had six months to live. So, I thought to make the best of the time I had left.

* * *

When Hayden returned home, Tom was working at the computer. He could see faint traces of the building he was designing from the doorway as he hung up his coat.

"Looks like that's coming along nicely," Hayden said as he drew closer to the light of the screen.

"You think so?" Tom said leaning back in his chair.

"Absolutely."

"You don't think I've taken on too much?"

"Nonsense."

"And you don't think the design is too progressive?"

"It's a progressive city," Hayden offered.

"But most of its beauty is anchored in history."

"I'm sure your design will complement it, and not spoil the waterfront as they have in San Francisco."

Hayden reflected on the wide vistas the city once offered.

"Boston has a notable reputation for being a visionary city. There have been countless architects who were convinced they'd accomplished just that, only to have their designs regarded years later as out of touch with the spirit of it. I want mine to be one for the ages. It needs to be timeless. Something that'll be considered a landmark in a hundred years, and not an eyesore to be torn down. And truthfully, I'm not so sure I can accomplish that."

"I'm certain it'll be emblematic and cherished in a hundred years. I can see it now." Hayden smiled to himself.

"You're no doubt biased," Tom said, fondly touching Hayden's hand as it rested on his shoulder.

"If I recall correctly, Gustave Eiffel didn't quite have the reception he'd hoped for either when he first proposed the design for his tower in 1889," Hayden said knowingly. "In fact, it nearly caused a second revolution. Now look at it. It wouldn't be Paris without it."

"I doubt this will be equally endeared."

"Have faith," Hayden said, giving him a light kiss on the cheek.

Tom changed the subject.

"So, who was this old college friend that you ran into in San Francisco? Some old beau I imagine," Tom teased, turning in his chair to face him now.

"It was an old girlfriend named Shirley, in fact," he truthfully admitted. Hayden tried to avoid as many lies as possible since he was forced to live so many others.

"A rare one. What are the odds of that considering you dated more men than women in college?"

"Women live longer," Hayden offered humorously. But he knew Tom wouldn't get the truer anecdote of his words.

"Don't remind my father of that fact. He's paid alimony to three wives for more years than he can remember."

Hayden had been forced to consider those same consequences during his long life. He'd never be able to commit to that institution without raising suspicions. The legalities of marriage could easily jeopardize his existence, as would divorce. And for that matter, death certificates, or lack thereof. All of which made it obligatory for Hayden to keep out of the system as much as possible, especially since every transaction and legal document could be easily traced now. For that reason, the house was in Tom's name. It was also why Hayden kept most of his fortune in cash in safe deposit boxes across the country. But even with cash, Hayden had to remember to rotate the bank notes when new ones were put into circulation. He once attempted to spend an exceptionally old bill, until someone kindly pointed out that it was worth a hundred times its face value.

Sadly, in the end, Tom's design wasn't received as he had hoped, but more as he had feared. Of course, there was a well-attended ribbon cutting, and a ceremonial cornerstone dedication. But most of the reviews had called it an architectural failure. One critic even referred to it as, 'an eyesore that even a blind man would find offensive.' Public opinion sided mostly with the critics; and like most things, changing public opinion took a long time. Unfortunately, Tom failed to have the patience or the heart to hold out that long.

From Hayden's Journal

There are times I think I see someone I know, someone out of my past. But I'm forced to consider the odds. Still, on occasion it feels as if a shadow follows me, despite the constant pace I keep. And not the one that naturally strides confidently alongside me. This one is different, as it tends to keep the same timeless cadence. And it's not like I'm being watched. I'm not haunted by it. It feels complimentary, in fact. Like coming out of a blue sea together into the sun. But it's an enigma I can't quite focus on, as it's just as elusive as I am. So, I'm left to wonder then, if it could possibly be someone like me, taking a similar journey parallel to mine; a timeless soul going through a life adjacent to mine. And if that soul existed, could I deny it anything? Would we even be compatible or attracted to one another? Life has taught me that even under the best of circumstances relationships are challenging, if not impossible. And what if that soul were cruel? Or worse, evil? Could I allow it to continue living? Or more importantly, could I kill it if necessary?

I'm also forced to consider the immeasurable pain I'd undoubtedly feel if I lost that perfection, that timeless love, as I had so many before. It would be a loss I'd be unable to endure, as it would certainly prove more tragic than the ones I previously prepared for; those loves I'd lived with and lived for. But each love holds its own intrinsic value, its own degree of affection; each unique to itself. And I'm sure I'd eventually be forced to question my own character as well, wondering if I would be able to sacrifice true love for the selfish hope and promise of being in a relationship with equal longevity, if only to avoid the repetitive loss and pain that I have felt over the years.

* * *

As Hayden moved on, he found it impossible to love again after losing Tom. He was incapable of dedicating himself to someone else, at least for several years, if not decades. In fact, he purposely declined the promise of love on numerous occasions.

So, the years that followed were spent in meaningless relationships, as they demanded less of him. They also helped ease the pain that continued to echo through his shattered psyche after Tom's unfortunate death. There are some things that time can't heal, and as life went on, he had a head full of them.

Hayden was born on the island of Manhattan. At one point, he even considered moving back again, especially since it was a vast and densely-populated metropolis. It even offered the distractions he sought, if not the promise of anonymity. But it was during a short visit there that he realized it was still a small town, only with bigger circles, and those circles tended to overlap, which would make his residence there certainly problematic. For that reason, Hayden remained unsettled, both physically and emotionally. He moved from place to place, more than usual, not knowing exactly what he was looking for.

From Hayden's Journal

I often find the dimensions of time surreal. For example, I'm forced to acknowledge the fact that the parents of future friends, if not lovers, have yet to be conceived. As a younger man, I was told to keep a tempting carrot in front of me, just out of reach, to help sustain life's indisputable energy. In a way, it's rather similar. Absorb that unique concept for a moment but try to avoid the awkward images that might blemish your perspective. Perhaps now you have a better idea how time projects itself for me. You see, I tend to lean more toward the future than I do the past. But both seem just as dependable. Because I know the past will always be there, unchanged, if not painfully so. Just as I also keep a measure of optimism close, hoping that the next offering of love will not only comfort, but help console the many losses that will forever dominate my considerable history. That's not to say, former loves don't continue to shine. They do, as I hold each in my heart as close as the day I embraced them. Though death on the other hand, is an enigma that holds a tighter grip on time, as I've seen it strangle the life out of so many.

Perhaps, I should explain. You see, I'm not immortal. An airplane crash can kill me just as easily as a bullet to the head. I'm not immune to death; just impervious to confronting it through age, or so it would seem thus far. And as you would expect, the journey has widened my perspective, if not my dreams. But with it also comes a long dark shadow that trails behind me; a path to keep one eye on as I reach forward as far as I can.

* * *

The years had passed since Hayden's time with Tom in Boston. In fact, nearly those hundred he'd spoken so distantly of.

He stared up at the magnificence of the building, even prouder now of how it graced the city skyline. It took decades, but it finally become praised as an icon, a landmark in fact. And it looked just as awe-inspiring and regal as it had when it first went up.

Hayden recalled that tragic day, and even if it'd been possible, he still wouldn't have returned to Boston sooner than he had. It took most of that long century for him to recover to be there in that moment to assimilate once again the artistry of Tom's building and its amazing and splendorous design. It remained a tribute to his undisputed talent, and not just the catalyst that ended his life. But Hayden refused to focus on those tragic images. He was finally able to bury them deep in his mind. He no longer saw Tom's distant and fragile figure perched on its grand façade. Or that final moment when he let his body freely spiral toward the pavement in the quiet of night, devoid of the spectators he had hoped would cherish it. In the end, Tom lacked the temperament to cope with that disappointment. The crowds he'd anticipated failed to show for more than a generation. But when they eventually did, it proved his design avant-garde, and ahead of its time.

Hayden proudly watched now as the dedicated line religiously circled the monument, snapping photographs as they went in hopes of capturing a piece of Tom's prowess and vision. Though Hayden would forever wonder if Tom hadn't in fact designed his fate in order to preserve the fate of his design; dying for his art, if you will, as many do.

It was then that Hayden noticed a familiar face in the queue, one just as out of place and out of time as his. Or rather, just as in time and in place as his, since Hayden easily adapted to his extended existence, having lived in a continuous flow with time from the start, never once feeling out of sorts with his surroundings. But he chose to existentially mark time by witnessing the changes in those around him, as his own changes were more progressive by nature, more a florisshen of his inner evolution, and not actually physical. But seeing that familiar face again was like a spark he hadn't felt in years. It was a face he'd caught a glimpse of somewhere in time, and it was just as fresh and youthful and full of life now as it had been then.

Kelsey Cooper had turquoise eyes that had successfully adjusted to the distance behind them.

"I knew I'd see you again," she said in a poetic whisper.

"I hoped we would. But I wasn't sure if you were still out there."

"I was more confident." There was a sweet cadence to her voice. "Even with forty-billion people, I could still feel you out there," she added.

It seemed an unrealistic statistic.

"Forty-billion?" Hayden looked perplexed. "Somehow I lost track."

"Where have you been?" she asked lightheartedly.

"In another world, I guess." He feigned an innocent smile.

"Doing what?" She was curious now how his spent his time.

"Writing and remembering. Though occasionally trying to forget."

"That sort of focus does tend to block out the peripherals."

"I did notice that places seemed a bit more crowded."

"Lost some elbow room, did you?" she said jokingly.

"I've learned to acclimate."

"I won't admonish you your distractions or your creativity."

"But can we even sustain forty-billion?" he asked seriously now.

"No." Her response was direct and to the point.

"You make it sound as if the end were inevitable."

"It's just gotten too far ahead of us."

Kelsey had come to accept the inevitable apocalypse, being aware of it for quite a while now. But she remained defiant regardless.

He couldn't deny that her words forced him to face a finality he'd never considered before. Not truly. At least, not his own. Hayden had gracefully guided countless others to their predictable end but had never actually faced those terms himself. But it would seem the future was now paved with his own mortality. And for the first-time Hayden caught a glimpse of his own possible expiration. However vague the writing on the wall, it had been written nonetheless.

Hayden chose not to dwell on the final chapter of his existence. Instead, he lamented the planet's inevitable demise, as it would undoubtedly be long and painful, and one that he might even witness. Perhaps they'd even die in each other's arms in a last romantic embrace, he thought. As they watched the annihilation of a once vibrant and lush planet as it crumbled beneath their feet. As he held onto that disturbing image, he wondered if it would be the cold that took it down or the fire below.

For the moment though, he had Kelsey, a sympathetic soul.

Hayden sensed her presence on numerous occasions as if in a distant courtship. He had felt her essence, and thought he'd even caught a glimpse of her soul. Not unlike a bride before her wedding. Just as he was equally sure that he'd witnessed her illustrious red hair caught in the wind. Hayden vividly recalled a vision of her now in the sun. It was on a beautiful day, in a city somewhere; on a street, standing out from the crowd, but still hidden amongst it.

If he had thought time passed quickly before, it only accelerated now with Kelsey in his life. They wisely agreed to allow their passion to ferment and grow at a gradual pace before giving in to their mutual desire. Because when they finally did surrender to that intrinsic love, they knew it could very possibly be forever, and they wanted to respect that, and not test it. They were equally cautious about bringing a child into a world faced with an indisputable fate. So, after considering the inevitable consequences of procreation, they decided not to conceive, agreeing it would be kinder not to bring a child into a world whose unfortunate destiny was predetermined. That chosen and well-thought out bit of wisdom proved futile though as it was immediately apparent their chemistry was unmistakably magnetic. And regardless of having used multiple prophylactics, their seed proved defiant, if not equally dedicated to one another. In proper time, they were blessed with a beautiful daughter named Corrine.

They both anxiously watched as she grew, uncertain of the outcome. Of course, no parent wants to inhibit the development of their child, but by the time Corrine reached her early twenties, they wished for just that.

Kids grow up so fast.

It was only then that they chose to share that part of their past with each other. Odd it hadn't come up earlier, he remembered thinking at the time.

Hayden readily disclosed his own stats, telling Kelsey that he'd stopped aging just short of a quarter century. But Kelsey wasn't as forthcoming. She hesitated as women are famously known to when asked their age, regardless of her youthful appearance. Or in this case, her extended longevity. Because Kelsey was just as reluctant to share that bit of information. All this time, Hayden had assumed that their experiences had been similar.

"I was forty," she finally confessed in barely a whisper. "So, it could be another decade or two before we know."

His first instinct was to tell her how great she looked for her age, but he stopped just short of making a fool of himself.

They carefully speculated on the consequences and uncertainly of their young daughter's future. The fact that she had never been sick was at least promising. But that wasn't necessarily a deciding factor.

"The thought of Corrine dying before us, would kill me," Kelsey said. "Parents aren't meant to outlive their children. It's not natural. In fact, it's a wound I know I wouldn't survive."

"The thought of it even now is killing me," he agreed.

Hayden had been blissfully content with Kelsey and the family life they created together, and he certainly had no reason to seek relations elsewhere. Besides, why would he risk losing her? She was one of a kind. But with the harsh and haunting possibility of his daughter's mortality looming over him like a dark and ominous cloud, and the undeniable dilemma that came along with it, confused and misguided, Hayden did in fact stray.

Men or women, it had never mattered for him. It had always been about the bond between souls, regardless of the body that came with it. He found that the various dimensions of life and the intrinsic nature of its very essence nearly demanded that one indulge in an equal taste of the human experience. He ascertained early on, that varying physical relations brought a solidarity, if not a better understanding to his own existence. In fact, Kelsey had taken a similar path until she met Hayden. It proved a fundamental wisdom, one that came with their shared journey through time. But with circumstances as they were, Hayden sought male companionship in hopes of connecting with his core again. But he obviously also wanted to avoid similar complications with another woman. In the end though, the exchange proved less satisfying than Hayden had hoped. The truth was, he knew exactly where he belonged, and he soon realized that it wasn't where he was looking.

Kelsey failed to comprehend his reasons for drifting from her and their love, especially now when they needed each other more than ever. They had everything a couple could possibly desire. Not to mention, the likelihood of multiple lifetimes together; if not an eternity. So, Kelsey felt emotionally abandoned. But she also felt a part of her soul had been shattered as well.

It was on one of those reckless and negligent mornings that Hayden returned to find both Kelsey and Corrine gone. He wasn't surprised. But he was certain they'd be back within a reasonable amount of time. There was the family core to consider. And their love. Of course, he should have been more cognitive of that fact himself before seeking solace elsewhere.

But Kelsey and Corrine failed to return, and Hayden had no idea where to search for them. There was no history to retrace, or family to reach out to. So, Hayden patiently waited where they left him, hoping they'd eventually return.

There were times when he even thought he'd caught a glimpse of them in the peripherals, just as he had sensed Kelsey years earlier. But the images moved too quickly for him to grasp. He began to lose focus. He had lost his wife and child, and there was no way now of knowing how many years his daughter had left to live, or if her body would challenge the aging process.

Time passed as it often does while deep in thought, while concentrating on something close at hand. A singular fixation such as that can easily cause one to marginalize their perspective. Only to realize when you look up that hours have passed and that time itself has disappeared.

At least that's how it felt to Hayden.

Ten years passed.

Twenty years passed.

Thirty years passed, and then some, as if it were a clock ticking away in ten-minute intervals. Hayden measured time by an alternate equation. And he lost himself in that alternate universe until he stopped counting entirely, mostly because it was just too painful.

Hayden refused to allow the years to tally up in his head. Especially since he had no idea if his daughter's life had expired without him there to comfort her. His ravaged inner being resigned to the very essence of time itself, letting the importance of any mathematical calculation dissipate along with it. And in doing so Hayden forgot his prime objective; the one rule that was sacred to his existence; the one that had kept him safe from suspicious eyes; he forgot to move on. And as he waited in the old Boston brownstone apartment where they left him nearly a half century earlier, he failed to be cognizant of the fact that more than forty years had slipped by. Just as he had failed to acknowledge the countless and curious, and certainly confused stares around him, as he had also neglected to be attentive to the changes in them as well; those changes that had always marked time for him.

Hayden existed in a limbo of timeless thought while remaining dormant in one city, on one street, in one apartment; buying groceries from the same corner store, and drinking at the same bar for over forty years. And now it was going to come crashing down around him.

Word quickly spread. Inquiries were made. Officials were called. When Hayden finally came to his senses, it was nearly too late.

"I don't think he's human," one neighbor started.

And that was all it took.

No talk of face creams or face-lifts could save him now.

From Hayden's Journal

That was bad. Foolish in fact. If not dangerous. It was undeniably one of the biggest mistakes I've made. The biggest of course, was betraying Kelsey in the first place. But it was the unbearable pain surrounding Corrine that had caused me to drift. But it was idiotic of me to attempt to seek comfort elsewhere. I should add, I found little consolation in that distraction. It's not easy to heal the haunted, and I was certainly haunted. In fact, I still am. And as mistakes go, a close second had to be living forty years in the exact same place, around the same people. Who does that?

It was no doubt a challenging situation to strategically escape. But with a bit of quick thinking I had the neighborhood convinced that I was in fact my own grandson, taking care of the old man, who was weak and bedridden in the apartment on the fifth floor where he lived.

Thankfully, I was his namesake. Or so I said.

One neighbor even kindly consoled me.

"I can see the resemblance. Especially in the eyes."

That blatant revelation made me question just how observant and astute people actually were. Or weren't, in this case. It made me wonder if my fears had been in vain for all these years. Regardless of that arguable point though, I'd plainly overstayed my residence in Boston. It would seem now that it was an unlucky city for me.

I was soon faced with yet another dilemma. It would seem my curious, heartfelt neighbors wanted to pay their respects to my ailing grandfather. I was compelled to inform them that he was in fact adamant about not having visitors, and that he didn't want people thinking he was on his deathbed.

Their response was: 'You tell that lovable old fool he's in our prayers.'

When the time finally came, getting the body out proved to be an even greater obstacle as nearly the entire neighborhood, not to mention three of the local funeral directors, had offered to pay for not only his wake, but his burial as well.

Unbeknownst to me, it was now apparent the neighborhood had truly loved him. In fact, I found myself envious of the reception he received at his passing. Though I suspect it had more to do with making amends for having caused an awkward, if not, embarrassing situation in the first place. Cause in the end, it had been a 'horrible misunderstanding.' I had little choice but to inform those concerned that I'd promised to take grandfather's remains back to his family in Florida, as they had planned on having a private service for him down there. I had to do some fast-talking. But we eventually got out of there alive. At least I did. And to be certain it stayed that way, I promised myself that I wouldn't return to Boston for several hundred years if I was lucky enough to have that time. I could no longer take anything for granted, and never would again.

I took some parting photos of Tom's building before leaving the city.

When I finally departed, with an empty coffin in my care, I was jealous of my late grandfather and the attention accorded him by his neighbors, as I was certain I'd never receive the same consideration at my own passing. But in an odd way it had been for me, and I was glad to have been there for it. In fact, I was strangely consoled and even endeared by the love extended me, regardless of the necessary lies I'd scattered.

After leaving Boston, I realized that my love for Kelsey had diminished considerably, if not surprisingly. Perhaps it was the change in environment. But it was enough for me to question its authenticity; wondering if it might have been the promise of its longevity and the idea of what we had that I'd fallen in love with in the beginning. Though maybe it was just the distance now, and the passing of all those years that made the feeling I had for her fade. Regardless, I continued to hold on, though more for Corrine than anything else.

* * *

Hayden first heard it on the news.

'A woman known as Corrine Cooper is wanted in San Francisco for the murder of her daughter Kelsey.'

He listened closely to every detail as the reality of the situation, as well as the horror of it, worked its way into his pained psyche.

Hayden hoped Corrine was still in the city regardless of her notoriety.

He remembered his last visit to San Francisco nearly two hundred years earlier. He knew he wouldn't run into Shirley this time. But it would have been nice to have been able to spend some time with her, he thought. He'd love to have those moments again, if only to say goodbye one last time.

Hayden was initially offended that Corrine had taken Kelsey's maiden name. But he empathized with her situation. He also knew she was justified in doing so, especially since her mother had been more of a parent than he had; sharing nearly every event in her life, good or bad, during the last half century. But by changing her surname, Corrine had also helped to keep his name out of the whole sorted affair. So, he was thankful not to be brought into a murder investigation as it would have no doubt complicated matters. Perhaps Corrine had anticipated that fact and wanted to protect him. Though that would have meant that killing her mother had been premeditated, and he couldn't accept that. The news nearly took the life out of him as it was. But that would have undoubtedly killed him. Hayden feared something poignant, something intrinsically painful and hurtful as this, would one day take him down.

They didn't show a photograph of Corrine, or of the crime scene on the news. But Hayden was certain now she had aged, and that they'd probably switched roles to explain their relationship as time went on. It must have been oddly painful for Corrine to watch those years slowly pass as she stood face to face with her ageless mother. And that short-lived moment when they looked almost identical as sisters sometimes do. Until that day, not long after, when one remained frozen in time for what seemed an eternity, while the other aged, and not so gracefully, and they were forced to reverse roles. He couldn't imagine how traumatic that must have been for their daughter.

Hayden recalled the day when they were no longer able to justify their youthful appearance to her with fabricated tales or innocent lies and were involuntarily forced to tell her the truth. From that moment on, Corrine anticipated inheriting that attribute, just as she had her mother's turquoise eyes and rich red hair. But when that hope eventually failed her, he was convinced her world changed as well, and that it was the catalyst, if not the primary motivation, for killing Kelsey.

If Hayden had learned anything: it was that you can't offer the promise of that kind of a future and not expect the outcome to be anything less than catastrophic when it's denied in the end. And that was obvious now. Just as it was equally clear Corrine didn't fancy the idea of dying before her parents either. But the thought of fathering a killer and consigning that killer onto an unsuspecting world devastated Hayden. Just as the horrific image of his daughter cutting Kelsey's face like sliced baloney, as they mentioned on the news, had. He imagined Corrine impatiently waiting in front of a mirror for that moment when she would finally hold onto her youth forever. Year after maturing year, she refused to give up hope. Until the day finally came when she was forced to resign to the face in front of her, as age inevitably took its toll. And in that vanishing, if not vanquished moment, Corrine had no doubt snapped, unable to be a spectator any longer to her mother's eternal youth. It saddened Hayden to think that vanity could be so maddening, so cruel and controlling. But just as the dream had died in the mirror for Corrine that day, so did her mother's life.

From Hayden's Journal

James and Joanne Kean died shortly after I was born. They were both twenty-four. At least that's what the records show. But I could never verify the truth of that information. My parents could have been older, like me, and have had numerous lifetimes together. I'd like to think that was the case. Of course, losing them at such an early age, denied me countless years of their love. It also denied me the opportunity to understand my curious condition. Though they may not have had the answer either, just as I failed to have one for Corrine. But unlike me, thankfully they didn't have to endure endless years of not knowing if their child would inherit their special gene. At least they'd been spared that disappointment. And I'd like to think I'd have been less vain. But a distance that great is undeniably out of focus to truly know now. But I'd also neglected to recognize my daughter's flawed and failed personality. In those brief years together, the girl I knew was sweet-natured. I never sensed a nefarious disposition. Though things were different then. And she was undoubtedly different then too.

My major objective now is to find Corrine. And when I do, I hope to at least find a remnant of that sweet-natured girl that I knew. And as much as I'm determined to stop her and her violent behavior, I'm also determined to love her as well. Because the thought of her having to spend the rest of her life in prison is far too painful. I've avoided the criminal justice system my entire life, as incarceration would have been nothing less than catastrophic. Twenty years would have no doubt raised questions. Just as a life sentence would've been not only endless, but curiously costly to the taxpayer. But I fear the verdict for Corrine in the end will be a death sentence. And if so, I would have lost them both. And for what? Time? I would have gladly given her mine.

I've lived my life as a devout, if not knowledgeable atheist. But that doesn't necessarily mean I haven't been equally curious about death or what comes after. I wonder as many do, what is written on the last page of that tome of time. The one someone foolishly tore from the binding. Though perhaps now I'm ready to read it, as I've grown tired of speculating.

* * *

The idea of Corrine killing anyone, no less her mother, made his heart feel like it was going to expire. It was an odd feeling, one that Hayden had never experienced before. Of course, the countless deaths which trailed his past were painful. But losing Kelsey now destroyed him to his core. Because he never truly anticipated that loss.

His long search for Corrine proved futile. Hayden left San Francisco, accepting the fact that it would probably be the last time he'd see it's golden light, as it would always be the place where the mother of his child had died at the hand of his daughter.

Each city Hayden resided in had its own history. Its own feel. Its own vibe. And he especially felt it when he returned to New York, the city where he was born. Though with each visit, he felt an underlying fear, a haunting in fact, not unlike a salmon swimming upstream against the current, fighting its way back to a foreseen and inevitable fate.

With an immeasurable quantity, if not quality, of life behind him now, Hayden felt his destiny growing closer.

He stood on the corner at the crosswalk waiting for the light to change.

If Hayden had learned anything in his extended existence; he knew that crossing a street in any city was probably the most dangerous thing he did in life. Even more so than driving on it.

It was while idling on that corner that Hayden thought he recognized a woman coming toward him. He was reminded of that day in San Francisco when he saw Shirley at a similar intersection. The woman even smiled like Shirley. Or so he thought. But he knew it couldn't be Shirley. Not unless she had kept the same secret; however, one long and cruelly delayed. But unlike Corrine, he knew Shirley would have been saintly patient and far less vain about it. He even whispered her name, but it quickly faded from his lips.

In that reflective moment, Hayden's mind blurred as it tried to scan the loves and endless friendships that filled his long life. But still, he couldn't place the face. It was lost in time, like so much of his life. He even thought to stop and ask the woman. But it would have not only been inappropriate, but dangerous. Best just to let it go, he thought. Besides, he wasn't curious by nature. But he did feel disoriented.

As he crossed the street, the sun caught Hayden fully in the face as it slipped between the tall narrow skyscrapers. He tilted his head to it, his eyes squinting as he accepted the warmth of it.

A perfect day for a crosswalk in Manhattan, he thought.

The long slender blade cut simultaneously through both cloth and flesh right to his core as if wanting to abort the life out of him. In fact, the blade went so deep she could feel her hand against the warmth of his moist red skin. She cut with skilled precision, as if attempting to remove a child from him.

Corrine had feared her father was immortal, unassailable in fact, but he went down as easily and quickly as her mother had. She was apprehensive at first to face him head-on, because he had always been the stronger figure in her mind. In fact, more a mystery, having been absent for most all her adult life. It was for that reason she decided to confront her father differently than she had her mother. But regardless of the anxiety and fear that raced through her narrowing veins and clogged arteries, Corrine decided to approach him directly, without hesitation, hoping her disguise would allow her the access she needed.

Hayden attempted to focus on the face as he slowly lost consciousness. But even close-up, he failed to recognize his daughter through the heavy layers of scar tissue and the comical wig that was now askew on her head. Though when he finally did, it was only because he'd caught a glimpse of her turquoise eyes through her heavily drooped and wrinkled eyelids. But even then, he thought it was Kelsey. He wanted to hold her close again. In fact, he pulled her to his chest as he went down. But once he saw past the reparative vanity and theatrical costuming, it was obvious that Corrine had unsuccessfully attempted to hold onto her youth. Though even in that horror, images of her as a child came back to him as he caught a faint glimpse of the open sky behind her, bringing forth the dark and light in fading contrast.

Hayden voluntarily resigned to the hand dealt him, if not literally. As he couldn't help but wonder if he hadn't walked into it knowingly as well. If he hadn't in fact helped press the steel deeper into his own flesh, wishing to die before his daughter as nature intended, as he subconsciously closed his eyes as he would to the sun.

For most of his life, Hayden had felt he'd traveled with time and not through it, as he assumed the dead probably did. With that thought in mind, he prepared for that next journey. Even blithely welcoming the path to it.

As his world gradually diminished, Hayden's life began to flash before his eyes. But as you'd expect, that took a while. Quite a while in fact, as you can imagine.

From Hayden's Journal

(There are no entries at this time)

Hardy Hughes Makes His Move
(It Was Nearly Dawn)

As winter settled into windowpane frost, Hardy Hughes found himself as he often had the last few years, sleeping in the spare bedroom downstairs at The Collins House, having reached that inevitable age when bunking with his best friend Russ proved inappropriate due to their budding and maturing bodies. For that long-awaited awkward day finally arrived when they woke, respectively, with substantial morning wood. But as you'd expect they were equally proud of the occasion as any young man would to be. Though it was embarrassing nonetheless.

At seventeen, they were a year younger than Russ' sister, Dawn, who recently had a cast plastered on her leg clear up to the top of her thigh; right up to her business in fact. Though technically speaking it hadn't quite opened for business. At least not yet. That would apparently be Hardy's opportune task that night when Dawn quietly came down to the guest room where he slept. In all the years he'd been staying downstairs, he wondered how long she'd waited until finally making her move, as she did that night.

Without saying a word, Dawn let her clothes fall to the floor. Then she approached the bed with a feigned, if not rehearsed seduction. Her prepared and practiced theatrics immediately aroused him. How could they not? But when their young flesh finally met she was surprised to find that his touch was so gentle. Perhaps too sensitive and endearing in fact for what she had planned. Because the exchange proved more intimate and loving than she'd prepared for, as she had designed an entirely different scenario in her head.

So, under the circumstances, she instinctively resisted his adventurous nature, as Hardy attempted things she hadn't considered, no less anticipated. Wanting to remain in control, she skillfully maneuvered him to follow her lead, if not her preferred position; one that was not only predictable, but also religious in nature. Though Hardy suspected it had less to do with faith and more with coordinating the act efficiently. But obviously with things as they were, it proved the better choice as her cast remained a stubborn, if not resistant, obstacle. Regardless of the situation, she remained resolute that he access her inner core. He worked tirelessly; youthfully determined to prevail as he fought to gain entry. All the while, his body and cadence continued in a thoughtful and tender motion as he gently touched against her.

He questioned why she'd chosen that night of all nights while wearing a cast on her leg to initiate sex, knowing it would not only make it difficult, but perhaps even impossible to penetrate her. Though he was determined to push on. He continued his attempt to insert himself into her as she lifted the cumbersome cast as best she could to allow him access. But even under such resistance, he found a measure of solace in knowing that it wasn't for his lack of prowess or firmness, or even size; as his erection had been constant the entire time. In fact, it felt nearly as hard as the plaster he fought against, which was more than determined to defend her female region from intruders at all costs. They were rivals going head to head. And as he fought to get the upper hand, he wondered if perhaps her father hadn't purposely instructed the doctor to go especially high with the cast, which he considered a worthy, if not steadfast opponent now, as a precautionary measure; a prophylactic of sorts, to protect her virginity against invaders such as he. He couldn't help but laugh at the idea as her father was a quiet and easygoing man who rarely remarked on the questionable conduct that usually went on under his roof. As a northeastern college professor, he was a liberal man, and open to most changes taking place at the time. But as a father, Hardy was certain he wasn't prepared for the changes taking place in his young daughter, and her naturally curious desires. Or for that matter, the carnal pursuits of the young men who would eventually appear. But it shouldn't have come as much of a surprise, for as a teenager, he'd been equally guilty of those same conquests. For that reason, he was confident that her father understood the possibilities and the consequences, as they had been a decisive factor in his reluctantly marrying Dawn's mother.

As they continued their attempt, trying multiple angles and positions, it occasionally got awkward. But regardless of his patient persistence, Hardy couldn't break her hymen. It was like banging up against a brick wall, one that refused to give an inch; though possibly a fraction of an inch, as he was allowed, almost teasingly, to feel a slight sensation from the moist warmth of her labia on the tip of him. He thought to suggest that she ride the banister down from the upper landing in the hallway to help tear the membrane, as it had been capably accused of having done so through history. But it was a recently well-established fact that the staircase was the nemesis and reason her leg was plastered as tightly and as high as it was, having tumbled down them while testing out her new holiday skis. The fall was apparently enough to break her leg, solid bone as it were, but it proved far less effective in breaking her hymen, as it remained securely intact and defiant against their efforts.

Hardy could see the disappointment on Dawn's face as her body failed to respond as she had hoped. But they persisted in their effort for well over an hour; patiently, and even playfully, until they inevitably accepted defeat. Hardy was proud of the fact that he hadn't been premature or softened under circumstances, and had remained an honorable, if not enduring and strong, seventeen-year-old rod; firm and resolute, ready and willing to conquer the moment, or the hour as it were. Though regardless of their dedication, by the end, they were beat and exhausted, at which time they offered a casual smile to one another, knowing they'd given it their best shot, as it certainly wasn't for lack of trying.

As a faint glimmer of morning light crested the horizon, they clothed and had coffee together as if the idea had never come up for consideration. They sat quietly across from one another without a trace of the passion that had previously flowed through their veins. At least it had for Hardy. They'd barely kissed. But it wasn't for his lack of trying, as every attempt he made was met with resistance. In fact, they seemed more of an intrusion. Which forced Hardy to acknowledge the true nature of her quest; that the encounter had been arranged for one reason alone; for her to lose her virginity, and little else. It was clear now, after the fact, that it had never been intended to be a romantic convergence, as Dawn hadn't bothered to even set the mood by turning out the light or close the door. It was as if she expected the entire affair to be embarrassingly quick, having heard that seventeen-year-old boys were likely to be just that. The reality was, he'd simply been chosen for the task because he was available when the time seemed right. Though it could well have been because he was moving to the West Coast within a couple of days. Whatever the reason, he knew it had been conveniently and purposely calculated on her part.

The sun continued to graze the horizon as he left that chilly morning. Hardy went quietly, without regret or remorse, or even the promise of a rain check. Or for that matter, a reason to return to The Collins House again, as he'd said his goodbyes the evening before. And for as close and intimate as they had been that early morning, the two never spoke again.

Hardy did keep in touch with her mother over the years. But when they spoke, she never mentioned her daughter. Which didn't surprise Hardy since she blatantly flirted with him that last year of high school. Something Dawn never considered. Of course, her affection for Hardy didn't go unnoticed by her husband. Though he probably would have preferred that Hardy have sex with his wife rather than his daughter anyway, if for no other reason than to preserve her virtue; something Hardy reluctantly left intact nonetheless. But the truth was, Dawn's father had lost interest in his wife long ago.

Looking back years later as the once familiar house faded to little more than a distant memory, Hardy was grateful of the reprieve offered that night; grateful they'd avoided the complications that are often associated with sex. Or in this case, attempting to have it, at least, as Dawn hadn't allowed it to be misconstrued. And for that reason, it lacked the intimacy he had hoped. And without that intimacy, Hardy would always remember it less for it, and more for the comical interlude it was, as he was convinced Dawn had failed to anticipate the consequences of having sex with such a cumbersome, if not stubborn cast on her leg. She'd undoubtedly wanted it without the traditional fanfare or the emotion that usually went with it, hoping to put it behind her as quickly as possible.

Of course, Hardy would never know the truth. Though he suspected the urgency to lose her virginity was either a need to present herself to someone she liked as sexually experienced; or that she'd lied about her virginity and felt compelled to cover that lie before she was forced to face it again in a moment of undisputed consummation, unlike their night together. But he'd always wonder if she'd be a stranger to intimacy and remain emotionally celibate regardless of the exchange and be forced to feign her feelings. But he hoped once the cast was off and the ice broken, that she'd discover the passion buried inside her.

In the end though, Hardy was consoled, if not content, knowing he'd soon be on a plane on his way to his next adventure. Hopefully one truer to heart.

Loving Daughter

Jules stared at the enigmatic envelope in his hand for several minutes before opening it, curious who had sent it. The sizable typeface was vague and broken in places, which in effect made his name appear shattered, not unlike some of his memories, he thought. But he couldn't help but consider it a preemptive warning since there was no return address or any indication of its origin, as even the postal stamp was faint, offset, and blurred. Even after opening it and reading the letter, it still took Jules several moments to recall that part of his past. Though he was eventually forced to revisit the man he was in those early years, as he had certainly gone through numerous transformations since then; far too many in fact to even calculate. But that man eventually came back to him in pieces, though they'd been pieces even when he lived them. And those pieces were even smaller after the nearly three decades since he had last seen her, or even thought about her, for that matter.

Her words were direct, specific, and without a trace of kindness. They were undeniably pointed and to the point; brief and brutal; unforgiving, and certainly unforgivable.

He read the letter over again, even though his stomach remained tight and uneasy from reading it the first time.

Before I die, and by the time you read this I can assure you I will be dead, I felt I should tell you that you have a daughter. Her name is Lisa. I probably should have told you years ago, but what we had wasn't really a relationship. Would you consider two nights a relationship? I wouldn't. And as you see, I didn't. So as far as I'm concerned, the matter never warranted notifying you. If you disagree, forgive me for failing to think of you in your absence. But you were merely a memory, a moment lost in time. But if I recall they were fun moments; not fabulous, but fun nonetheless. Though perhaps I remember the wine we shared better, as it remained my favorite for years. But here's the cruel if not difficult part; and I should probably apologize first, as you should expect the worst. You see in all these years, I haven't spoken kindly of you to Lisa. In fact, to secure my relationship with her, I blemished anything that might have made our history together the slightest bit memorable. I must confess, (isn't death the time for this sort of thing?) I invented more horrors about you than could possibly be true about any one person. So, believe me when I say that I created a monster of you, and that she seemed to find comfort in that creation. My life was about comforting her, not you. You weren't there. I confess (yet again), I haven't been fair about any of this; and possibly telling you now is even less fair, especially since I know she'll never have you in her life. The fact is, with all the hate she has for you, I can't imagine there'd be room for the person you are even today. You'll always remain an absence; a void that will never be filled in her.

I should keep this short. There's no reason it should go on any longer or have any more thought put into it than you did our time together. Though I should also mention that if you think of showing her this letter, which as you see I have typed and not signed, I assure you she'll never believe a word you say, because the walls she's built around her are impenetrable.

Lastly, if you choose to see her, I suggest you do it from a distance, or as a stranger; as she'll certainly take to a stranger better than she will to you. Believe me in this.

I'd say goodbye, but we did that years ago.

As mentioned, there was no signature or name on the letter, just cruelly typed and equally broken words across a thin white page. It took Jules quite some time to remember Joan, but that single moment in his life eventually came back to him. He could see her face clearly now as it gently rested on an oversized pillow smiling up at him. But the truth was, he too remembered the wine better, and it was no doubt the wine that helped him remember her; the same wine that had helped him forget, along with much of his life.

Jules braced himself for the worst, just as Joan had warned. He thought hard and long about how he would approach Lisa. At the age of forty-eight he would gladly welcome a child into his life now. He had wanted children for some time. In fact, since the death of his mother nearly a decade earlier. But now that blessing was cursed, as any relationship he could hope to have with Lisa had been sabotaged. Still, even as Joan's words ate away at him, Jules knew he had no choice but to seek out his daughter, regardless of the consequences. Or so he thought. Because when Jules first saw her, the blood that ran through his body seemed to change course. In fact, it felt as if it ran out of him and into the universe, as it flowed toward a never-ending future. The world he saw now appeared more expansive to him, and he felt himself expand with it.

When they met, as Jules had casually planned, Lisa felt an immediate attraction toward him. Especially after realizing that he wasn't like most of the men she knew who were struggling with their early careers; and who were usually too dedicated and focused on staying ahead of the game in the corporate arena than on building a relationship. Because Jules was already well-established, though he still retained a youthful passion. He also hadn't lost himself or his joy for life. In fact, he seemed captivated by life, and by her especially. When she thought about it, he actually wasn't much older than her, not in the scheme of things. He wasn't quite fifty yet, and he still had a full head of hair and a ready smile; one that easily allowed others to offer one in return. And if Lisa needed anything after recently losing her mother, it was a ready smile.

She felt an immediate, if not intrinsic closeness to Jules, enough that she felt the need to confide in him.

"I don't know why, but I feel I should share something personal with you. Something I never told anyone before. And when I'm finished I never want to speak of it again."

Jules listened as he watched the girl, the woman, the daughter he never knew existed until recently, describe in harsh detail the monster that he had been; the one her mother had created for her. Of course, he didn't recognize himself in her horrific portrayal because it wasn't him, and never had been. Though with genuine compassion he absorbed every word she spoke, which eventually brought him to tears. And it was that show of empathy that drew her even closer to him.

"I wanted to share that painful and important part of my life with you, so you could understand me better. But now with it said, I need to leave it behind again, and hopefully forever."

The topic was closed. Jules knew that if he tried to approach the subject again she would abandon him just as she'd thought her father had her. It was a survival tactic that she prepared as a defense, one she was ready to engage when necessary. But she was surprised that she'd shared that part of her life with him since it had been buried inside for so long. Maybe it was the recent passing her mother that forced it to resurface again. But more likely, it was because she had found something special in Jules that made her want to disclose that part of her past to him. Perhaps now she'd be able to bury it, and never let it be an issue again, she thought.

With that said and done, Lisa made her intentions known, which proved overwhelming, if not disorienting for Jules. The last thing he expected was a romantic relationship. He had come with the simple hope of being friends. But she denied him that option, giving him an ultimatum; take all of her, or nothing at all. Lisa offered him her heart, and her friendship, but she wouldn't allow him to take one without the other. She needed more than a friend in her life. She had friends. Many in fact. What she needed more than anything, was love. But before Jules could argue the matter, Lisa pulled him close and kissed him so deeply, so intrinsically in fact, that it felt nearly spiritual. And when she finally leaned back and stared intently into his eyes, she misunderstood his responsive look as emotional consummation. But in that startling moment, Jules not only felt a part of himself die, he also felt what once resembled his soul expire as her lips pressed against his. But he was forced to resign to her proposal, and eventually her offer of sex, which he would one day learn to observe from a distance; one he'd only gradually be able to fathom. Jules would have done anything to keep Lisa in his life, and it would seem he had done just that, however morally wrong.

Lisa quickly adhered to Jules physically and emotionally, which caused him to feel simultaneously elated and confused. She insisted he take her love or nothing, and he knew he couldn't live with nothing; not again. He'd done that for far too long. Jules also knew his heart, and he witnessed it break into brittle pieces. But still he saw no escape but forward. Of course, he'd prefer loving Lisa on his terms and not those dictated by Joan, or the situation she presented or forced upon him. Regardless, in that instant he realized he was falling in love with her. It was in her smile and the passion she had for life. It was right there in front of him; in her face and eyes, and the shine of her auburn hair; and specifically, in the way she spoke. It certainly would have been easier if she were a different woman and he a different man. But that obviously wasn't the case. Though in some strange way she was a different woman, because there were no past images of her in his mind. At least no truthful ones. Just those Joan hatefully instilled. There were no photographs or memories captured in time of birthdays or holidays. In fact, there was no paternal history at all. No advice had ever been given, or embrace offered, to help comfort her. Jules had never been called upon to protect her from the world or the adolescent boys he was sure populated her young life. The truth was, Lisa was a stranger to him. Certainly, more that, than a daughter. And Jules knew if they had met accidentally, just as Lisa had thought, there'd be no difference. Not really. Because there was always that possibility they might have met and married without ever knowing the truth. At least that's how Jules started to rationalize the horror in his head.

In the beginning though, it was nearly impossible for Jules to embrace Lisa without his body convulsing and collapsing inside. But he was sure she never noticed. And he hoped the feeling would eventually subside. But there was no reason why it should. Because each time he pressed his body against hers, he lost a piece of his sanity. And in order not to go completely mad, or numb inside, Jules eventually imagined it was Joan he made love to every night; a younger Joan of course. Though not as young as the woman he had slept with decades earlier. Instead, Jules made love to the woman that he missed in those years in between; the years they might have had if they stayed together. His was thankful that their features were similar enough for him to create the illusion in his mind. Enough so, that the contours of her face in the dark could have easily been mistaken for Joan's. But even with the continued hatred he had for her, he now found a love for Joan through Lisa. He had never loved Joan. But he loved her now, only because he was forced to. He knew that hadn't been her intention. Strangely enough though, it was Joan in his arms now when he held Lisa. It was Joan that he kissed when he kissed Lisa. And it was Joan's legs that he tenderly held in his arms as he entered Lisa, as he pressed deeper and deeper into her. It was the only way he could possibly endure the truth in front of him. Regardless though, it nearly killed him on more than one occasion when that image momentarily broke apart, as he wasn't always clever enough to hold it together. But he knew the illusion had to succeed in order for him to survive.

When Lisa looked up at him from her pillow, he saw Joan now. Not the Joan who pulled his heart from his chest in a letter, and by doing so, killing everything he held right and precious. No, this was a new and untarnished and reimagined Joan. Not the one that destroyed his relationship with his daughter, as a daughter, which forced him to sacrifice his very being to be with her. No, that Joan had left him one option, which continued to tear him apart regardless of his overworked imagination.

Eventually though, Jules found it easier to alter that reality. Especially when his fingers discovered those secret places in that secret darkness. He had sacrificed everything for that love; a love which had forced him to turn a blind eye to the fact that he was sleeping with his own daughter. But Jules knew without that dubious design, Lisa wouldn't be in his life. Of course, he could have walked-away. But he had nothing, and he knew he couldn't live with nothing again. He'd never been in love before. Not truly. Loving Lisa was the closest he ever came to love, and he couldn't lose that love now. He couldn't deny the love he had for her or live with its absence. He sacrificed his very being just to keep her and that love in his life. Surprisingly, he was still capable of finding an occasional smile regardless of how cruel the world had been to him.

Of course, Lisa failed to perceive or even sense the struggle Jules was going through. It wasn't just the complicated and fragile facade he chose to hide behind. Lisa also hadn't known him long enough to recognize a change in him. She only saw the man she fell in love with. So, the conflict he fought against went unnoticed. But still, she helped balance his life, but only while his eyes were open. Because in the dark, when he was forced to close those same eyes, it was Joan; the woman who had denied him his daughter, who offered that same balance. Lisa was the adhesive that enabled him to keep it together, however artificial. And he knew if Joan weren't already dead, this certainly would have killed her, just as it was killing him still.

Being unable to throw Joan's cruel and caustic letter away, Jules chose to reseal it and hide it in his desk draw. He even thought to redact its hateful words to make it seem less shattering, hoping that one day it might bring a measure of salvation or at least a degree of reparation. Failing that, he hoped it would read differently one day.

Two years passed in what seemed a fortnight. But Jules knew it was his love for Lisa that made time disappear. That, and the virtual image of Joan in a shadowed corner of their bedroom, waiting patiently.

Jules became skilled at balancing that image to keep his sanity. He had what he thought was a healthy grasp of an unhealthy situation. In fact, he learned to deny the truth in one hemisphere of his brain by day and rely on a solid illusion of Joan in the other hemisphere while making love to Lisa at night. Though regardless of that practiced adjustment, deep down Jules was still a shattered man; one who would never truly escape that fact.

In celebration of their anniversary, he bought a special bottle of wine, which Lisa immediately recognized as the wine her mother used to drink. An uneasy sensation came over her as he filled her glass. Maybe it was the smile on his changed face, which seemed oddly uncharacteristic. Or maybe it was just the wine. But in that moment, she was forced to relive the loss of her mother again. In fact, she could almost feel her presence in the room. She'd been told that it took two years to assimilate a major loss like that, but it was apparent now that two years wasn't quite enough.

By the second glass, Lisa noticed a change in Jules, as the wine began to alter his personality. And the more he drank, the more he reflected on the past, something he rarely did. But the familiar bouquet overtook his senses just enough to cause him to confuse the illusion he created with the reality around him. And that new persona frightened Lisa.

As the evening went on, the multiple images he saw continued to blur. For a moment, Jules even thought he was sharing the wine with Joan again, just as they had years earlier. He didn't call her by name, but he mistakenly mentioned something about their time together. As he continued to babble, incoherently, Lisa became concerned since she could no longer make sense of what he was saying. Of course, she blamed the wine. At least at first. But she suspected that something else haunted him, something deeper. Perhaps a secret he'd been suppressing was eating away at him. She braced herself for that eventual revelation, praying they'd get through it together, whatever it was.

Later that night as they began to make love, Lisa tightly held onto that hope, just as she had him, even as it seemed to quickly unravel around her.

Jules instinctively embraced the obligatory mindset that he'd created in order to make love with Lisa, putting the ready, and well-rehearsed illusion in place, which provided his mental escape from the truth. As practiced, he saw Joan, but then he'd been seeing her most of the evening as it was. But with her head now gently resting on the pillow beneath him, that image was now fully recognized, and the wine only helped to reinforce the illusion. But from the moment he entered her, Lisa knew she'd be unable to simulate his passion or reciprocate his embrace. It was as if her body had abandoned her because she began to question his touch and his kisses. She couldn't explain it. Nonetheless, she felt the urge to fight against his very being as a sequence of unexplained feelings echoed through her; however vague and out of focus they were. It was as if she'd caught a subtle wisp of a fragrance she couldn't identify. Her senses instinctively went into high alert as she surrendered to them and their defense.

Though in the end, it was a single defining and unsettling whisper that would trigger the unmistakable truth, as it attempted to lovingly reverberate into her ear. A sound that was not only deceptive, but devastating, because that lone syllable would shatter her life forever. In fact, it was the very same one which had kept her safe and sane for most of it. It was also inarguably the same syllable that kept it together for Jules as well. But in that solitary moment, its juxtaposition to the present caused her world to come crashing down in the darkness around her.

Lisa had never mentioned her mother, or her name for that matter. Not even when she told Jules about her father. She wanted her mother to remain pure and unsoiled, and not part of that horrific history she had shared with him. So, when he mistakenly whispered it passionately into her ear, Lisa felt her entire being collapse inside.

"What did you say?" she shouted as she frantically pushed him away.

His thoughts immediately ricocheted against the beat of his heart when he realized his error. In that moment, Jules knew nothing would ever be the same again.

"Lisa!" he said trying to imitate the sound. But instead his world closed in on him as the images seemed to conflict in his head.

"That's not what you said!" Lisa screamed. "That's not what you said!" With a thin blanket pulled tightly around her naked body, her back against the wall now, she screamed again, "That's not what you said!"

The room suddenly stopped in time as the darkness appeared to wrinkle the shadows cast across it. In fact, every created image was shattered in that moment. That once frail, though promising illusion dissolved into a tangled nothingness, along with her touch. All he could feel now was the emptiness between them, and he knew that abyss would only grow. There was nothing he could say, or do now that could justify or remedy the situation since he knew there was nothing left to salvage. Whatever they shared had vanished in that one moment, with that one word, that single syllable; and his very existence seemed to dissipate with it.

Lisa remained with her back against the wall looking petrified, as if she were caught in an inescapable trap. Captured now by her worse nightmare; caged by an unspeakable crime.

"You're a monster," she said, barely able to utter the words as her mind and body were equally defeated. She looked at him now as if he'd crawled out of the dark from under her bed and into her sheets. "You're even more of a monster than she said you were. God, how could you have done this?"

Tears streamed down her innocent cheeks.

Jules remained speechless. There was obviously nothing left to say. All he could possibly do, was close his eyes now and wish it was Joan standing there instead. But it wasn't Joan. The voice and face were unmistakably that of the daughter he wished he could have loved as a child. The daughter he would have done anything not to lose, and inevitably chose to do just that, and lost her just the same. Because she was as far from him now as physically and emotionally possible, and he knew that he'd never be able to change that. He would never feel her skin or touch again or hear her sweet voice. Sadly, Jules couldn't even recall her last touch because it was Joan's touch he'd felt, so even that was lost to him now. It was true; in his choice, he had become even more of a monster than Joan had fabricated. He became that lie and turned that lie into a painful and inescapable truth, just as Joan had written in her letter.

Lisa remained with her back against the wall in the darkness, frail and broken, wrapped tightly in a blanket. But she soon resigned to that darkness, and quietly disappeared into its shadows, until the shadows disappeared, as shadows eventually do. In the next moment she was gone, and the image of Joan was gone with her.

In that final second before she vanished, Jules thought to show her the letter from Joan, hoping it would help to justify his actions, and explain why he did what he did; because he loved her, and not the insipid and immoral love that they had shared, but something more decent, more palatable. Jules needed her to understand, he did what he did because he was afraid of losing her forever. He wanted to profess his love now, as a father would, but Jules knew that opportunity was lost as well.

Lisa was right; he was a monster as charged, and there was no escaping that prophetic fact now. In the end, Joan was right as well, even if she didn't know it at the time.

Jules thought to throw himself down a well, but killing himself would prove redundant, for he was already dead inside. And he knew if one day, tomorrow, or next year, if Lisa had decided to take her own life, or attempt to find happiness again, he'd never know that either. Because she no longer existed now, just like before. Just as he no longer existed now either.

Winners and Losers

Jimmy was a loser who always felt lucky. But then losers always feel lucky, especially when they hit rock bottom and think the only way back is up again, as they wait for their next big break.

Jimmy's break would come, he was sure of that.

Jimmy was sprawled out on the couch on a Saturday afternoon in front of his television set watching the game. He shouted to his girlfriend Betty as she went out the door to go shopping that afternoon.

"Don't forget the lottery ticket before you come home, babe." Then he added mindfully, "Play the same numbers we always do!"

"Don't I always?" she shouted back, irritated at his low opinion of her.

He whispered under his breath, "She'll forget. And watch, the numbers will come up." But Jimmy was too lazy to go out and buy the ticket himself.

Jimmy's kids chose to live with their mother after their messy divorce. But he knew they still loved him regardless, even if they never came to visit. He knew being down on his luck depressed them, just as it did him. All he needed was a lucky break to bounce back. He deserved a break, he thought. It was long overdue.

Betty was still a good-looking woman, in her early thirties and certainly more than he deserved. She was respectable, but perhaps not too bright. In fact, whenever someone told a blonde joke, the first thing Jimmy thought of was Betty. Poor Betty.

Somewhere along the way Jimmy lost sight of the important things. But his dreams remained unchanged, not unlike his life.

Betty pushed her way through at least four crowded department stores that afternoon before heading home to fix dinner. As the sun set, the busses ran less often. At least she missed the heavy traffic, she thought.

When she got to her stop, she walked a block down to the corner grocer to buy a few things for dinner. When she finally got home, Jimmy excitedly called to her from the living room.

"Where have you been?" he shouted, still on the couch.

"Hold your horses. Let me at least put the food away first."

"Just get in here!" he yelled.

Betty brushed her blonde hair away from her face with the back of her hand, straightened her skirt, and walked down the narrow hallway.

"What's so important that I can't even put the groceries away first?"

"Did you buy the lottery ticket?" Jimmy asked excitedly.

Betty had to stop and think.

It'd been a long and tiring day. She slowly went through her checklist in her head again.

Finally, she said, "Of course. It's in the bag."

"Quick, get it!" he shouted.

As she went back into the kitchen her voice echoed behind her, "I'm not a moron, you know. Have I ever forgotten anything?"

Jimmy was too distracted to recount the numerous times.

"I know it's here somewhere," she said from the kitchen.

Then there was a long impatient silence.

"Well?" he shouted, still on the couch. "Don't tell me you forgot!"

"No, here it is."

"Quick, get your ass in here. I think we won!" he said excitedly.

"We won?" Betty said with equal enthusiasm now.

He hurriedly checked the numbers hoping that she'd put down the right ones. "Jesus Christ!" he shouted, nearly losing his voice.

He grabbed Betty and squeezed her even tighter than he had that first night when she foolishly mistook his strong embrace for love.

"Quick, give me the phone. I have to call the kids!"

Jimmy was eager for them to know he wasn't the loser, and that he was someone. That he could be someone.

His fingers fumbled as he dialed.

"Whatever you kids want," he said trying to compose his voice now to impress them, as if he'd been a winner all his life. But when his ex-wife got on the line he changed his tone. He would never forgive her for leaving him, and not even for another man, but for a woman.

"Yes, they both get a car," he said listening as well now as he had when they were married. "Two are enough. You can drive theirs." He delighted in hearing her grabble.

"Listen, I have to go," he said. "We're going out to celebrate. No, not at Murphy's. We eat there all the time," he lied. "Somewhere special." He was barely listening now. "Have them call me on Monday."

He hung up without even saying goodbye.

He wished he'd practiced his tone before he telephoned. But his mind was racing every which way and back again trying to get his head around his newfound wealth.

Later that night he dropped a hundred bucks at Murphy's and left less than the minimum tip.

"I wonder how long it takes to get the check?" he said to Betty on the drive home. But all he could think of was how life was going to change now that he could buy anything he wanted, do anything he wanted. But more importantly, he could be anyone he wanted.

Jimmy had trouble sleeping that night. In fact, he wasn't sure he'd slept at all.

Betty set the table on Sunday morning

"Do you want some breakfast?" she asked.

"I'm not that hungry."

Jimmy was already looking past their relationship. He knew he could do better. Much better.

He made a list of what to do with the money.

Of course, cars for the kids, and a new house.

Jimmy thought to buy a bar, but the idea of working seemed contrary to being a winner. He wrote out a list of friends to help financially. But after reading the list again he crossed most of them out. No reason to overdo it. No one had ever been generous to him. He made it this far on his own; he'd spend it on his own, he thought.

Later when they went to bed, Betty noticed a change in Jimmy.

He turned off the light and said, avoiding her eyes, "You know, maybe you should move back in with your mother for a while. I imagine the kids will want to stay here now, and there isn't room for all of us. At least until I buy a bigger place. We can figure all that out later."

When he woke the next morning, Betty was gone.

She'd planned for this day.

And it was as good as any, she thought, if not better.

Regardless of the money, she knew he would never change. At least not into the man she'd hoped. Because for some time now, she felt his embrace more a strangulation, and she was glad to be free of it. Besides, the money made it easier for her to leave. It comforted her to know he'd at least have that, and his children now.

Betty had always been a giver, and in her own way she was giving even now. She left feeling like a winner.

Jimmy hoped to get to the lottery office when it opened, but he first had to call his boss before his shift started to give him a piece of his mind.

"That's right, I won the lottery," Jimmy beamed.

"I guess this is where you tell me to shove the job up my ass."

"Don't make this any less sweet. But yeah, shove it up your ass until it hurts, and then shove it up some more!" He was still laughing when he hung up.

Jimmy was too excited to shower or even shave. He just threw on the same clothes that he wore the day before and called a taxi.

"You know where this is?" he asked showing the driver the address on the back of the play-slip.

"I drove someone there just last week," the driver lied. "Nice guy too. He tipped me a hundred bucks."

"Well, I don't have a hundred bucks. Not yet anyway."

As they drove he watched his world as it passed by, knowing the drive back would look different. Richer in fact.

The driver pulled over.

"This is it, buddy. That'll be nineteen bucks."

He handed him a twenty. "Keep the change. Sorry it's not more. But I'll make it up to you next time."

Jimmy nearly tripped on the steps to the entrance of the building.

The lottery office was surprisingly unassuming. He expected something more appropriate for the occasion. Like marble with gold trim. Perhaps even a symphony playing his favorite tune. He was sure they'd at least have a red carpet and balloons.

"I have the winning ticket!" he shouted, into the quiet room.

"For which drawing, sir?" the woman behind the counter asked.

"Last Saturday."

"Not last Saturday, sir. There was no winner last Saturday."

"It's right here, you see?" he said waving the ticket in the air.

The woman reached for it, but Jimmy pulled it away. He wasn't going to hand it over to just anyone.

The woman said, "Sir, I have to look at the ticket."

Jimmy started to hand it to her but pulled it away again.

"Do you have a pen?"

"Of course, sir," she said handing him one.

Jimmy signed the back of the ticket, which made him feel better about handing it over.

"May I please see the ticket now, sir?" she said reaching for it again.

He gave it to the woman, but as he did, it felt as if a chest of gold had been lifted from his hand when it slipped from his fingers.

The woman put on her glasses, which hung by a chain around her neck. She looked at it, then at the watch around her wrinkled and spotted wrist. Then she looked at the ticket again.

"I'm sorry sir, but this ticket is for next Saturday's drawing."

"That can't be!" he said, feeling his throat and chest tighten. "That can't be right, she bought it on Saturday!"

"That's correct. But it was purchased after the drawing on Saturday."

Jimmy frantically grabbed the ticket from the woman's hand. He looked at it, but he could barely focus, so he went over to the window.

"That can't be right!"

"I'm very sorry, sir. They are the winning numbers. But that ticket is for next Saturday. It's a remarkable coincidence, if not a bit of bad luck. But the fact remains, there was no winner for last Saturday's drawing."

"You don't understand, this is my entire life. It's everything!" His knees gave out from under him. He leaned against the counter dramatically pulling at the collar of his shirt. "It's everything," he echoed.

"I'm so sorry, sir."

168

When he emerged from the lottery office, his world seemed more brutal than he remembered. Certainly, more than he predicted it would. It appeared broken and even lonelier now.

Betty's mother said she'd moved to Atlanta to live with her sister.

Jimmy's ex-wife left endless messages when she heard the news.

His kids never called.

His boss was anally freed and unforgiving.

Jimmy remained a loser.

Raising the Bar

Din was working the door.

There was a small crowd gathered outside smoking.

"You got an extra one of those," someone asked.

"Sorry man, this is my last one."

Xaco came out from inside the club and lit one up.

"Everything all right out here?"

"Just the usual moochers."

Xaco pulled a card out of his jacket pocket.

"Here are the updated iTat codes for tonight."

Din took the card and scanned it.

"I did have a crazy old guy out here a while ago who told me the planet had nearly been destroyed years ago by aliens."

"That explains a lot," Xaco said, keeping an eye out for trouble. "Though I suggest you believe what you see and not what you hear, especially around this place."

Just then a couple approached.

"Better scan them. They look young."

"Evening guys. I'll need to see your iTats."

They offered a generous measure of attitude as they reluctantly extended their forearms. The entryway lit up green when Din scanned the state issued iTats.

"Thanks guys. Have a good time tonight."

"What's with the attitude," Xaco said after they went inside.

"Like the guy said, we were nearly destroyed by aliens. It would seem they're still around."

"Very funny." Xaco laughed.

Just then he noticed a red truck slowdown in front of the bar. The guy riding shotgun yelled out, "Fucking fags!"

Xaco offered a mischievous grin as he shook his head.

"I haven't heard that in a while."

Then he pulled a weapon out from behind his waistband and shot the perp with the skill of an expert gamer.

Din was dumbfounded.

"What the fuck was that?"

"I modified an old tranq-gun. It's harmless. But it should amplify his sexual desire."

"No shit?" Din said feeling a sense of redemption.

"It'll either make him a team player if he isn't already. Or he'll hate himself as he does us for an hour or so. Either way, it should be interesting. He might even discover his true nature."

"And his friend?" Din asked.

"I imagine he'll have his hands full. It'll give a new meaning to riding shotgun."

"That's cool as fuck, man."

"Less violent than straight bashing," Xaco said humorously.

"I should try and catch up to him while he's on it. He wasn't bad looking."

"Go for it. Make your mark. Fall in love. Do what you can, while you can. But when he comes out of it and the stars are no longer in his eyes, be warned that his rage might return. And if it does, make sure you have your iFlyers on, and a good head start."

"No problem. He'll be too sore anyway," Din said with a smile.

Xaco pushed his smoke out into the ash can hanging at the door. "Make a run for it. I'll get someone to cover for you."

Din prepared himself for the run. A moment later, he was off.

Xaco watched as his iFlyers made their way down the street.

"Good luck!" he shouted.

Xaco went inside and found Dooney doing a security tour.

"Cover the door for a while. Din's on a run."

Jimmy sat quietly at the corner of the bar as he did most nights, his antenna extended, patiently waiting for the latest transmission. He once told Xaco that the human mind was incapable of thinking on its own and that the brain was merely an organic conduit that accepted inter-galactic radio waves from out in deep space. Xaco didn't feel quite so connected, but he wouldn't argue that his was probably not in working order and likely in need of repair. He also thought it a cool looking accessory.

Diododi was a stately, prominent and well-proportioned figure, not to mention the tallest person in the bar. Even seated, he towered above the rest. So much so, that his stature was usually the first topic of conversation when people met him.

"So, where do you hale from stranger?" Meruela asked, her heart beating faster than usual.

"Colora," Diododi said. "In the next solar system."

"You're kidding, right?" She tried pushing a pretty smile to the front of her face. He could tell she was nervous. In fact, he could hear her heart begin to slightly fibrillate.

Meruela continued her inquisition.

172

"I hadn't heard about visitors from Colora."

"We've been here for a while now."

He offered a welcoming smile.

"It would seem I missed yet another invasion," she said. "There was a time when I'd be out there with all the other girls to welcome you guys." He imagined her waving her panties as if they were rock stars caught in a new music mania. She added, "But I don't get out as much as I should."

He continued his smile.

"Tell me, how do you find our little rock?"

"I find the temperature change rather interesting."

"You must have a sun on Colora? You couldn't possibly survive without one. Besides, guys like you don't grow without sunlight."

"In fact, we have a double sun. So, it never gets dark."

"I guess that's what bars are for," Meruela said taking a slow sip of her drink. "But that's cool."

"Actually, it never gets cool. The temperature is consistent."

"It was just a figure of speech."

A quizzical look came over Diododi face.

"Speech has a figure? Is it like a man or a woman?"

Meruela took a longer sip of her drink.

"Never mind," she said. "Why did you come to Earth?"

"I came for the women but stayed for the men."

"I had a similar experience. So, we're not that different then."

Meruela nodded with a smile.

"I too have found many similarities," Diododi said.

"We go through a period of sexual discovery here on Earth," she added. "It's called adolescence. It can be an awkward journey."

Diododi offered a wider smile.

"You weren't being serious, were you?"

Meruela was embarrassed now.

"I do appreciate your valued insight into the sexual maturation of your species. It was enlightening."

"It's more interesting when you live through it," she confessed. "So, I'm guessing this was your attempt at levity."

"I apologize. Allow me to buy you a drink. It's the least I can do," he said sincerely.

"Damn right it is. And it'll cost you a double."

"Bartender?"

On the other side of the room.

"Then show me!" Alus said excitedly.

Lude gently touched the side of his temple with two fingers and projected the image from his mind. An animated hologram appeared balanced in the air between them.

"It looks like quite a night," Alus said as he watched his memory of the event.

The projection was unable to transfer lies or false images, but it did allow for a small degree of personal influence as the grey matter encircled, nursed, and digested the memory.

Lude ended the transmission just as another image appeared; one too personal to share. Besides, he didn't trust leaving the portal open for long periods of time. Like a computer, his thoughts could easily be hacked, causing major damage to his brain, if not his memory.

"Who was the woman on the couch? The cute one in the multi-muul sweater?" Alus asked with youthful curiosity. "I wouldn't mind having another look at her."

Lude tried to envisage again, but the image started to flicker.

"I'm run down right now, and I won't get anything solid again for a while," he said. "I had to show my mutha extensive images of last semester earlier. She wanted to see how I was spending my time, tuition being what it is. She wanted to be sure that it wasn't slacking off. She even had to take a second job."

"My dad's the same. Do you remember her name by chance?"

"I think it's Anuga."

"There's got to be a couple hundred women named Anuga in the city," Alus said obviously discouraged. He was forced to resign to the fact that he'd probably never get another glimpse of her since the image in Lude's mind would eventually become little more than an obscure blur, not being a cerebral priority. Not to mention, it had been medically affirmed that projecting the same image repeatedly, proved harmful to the brain's delicate grey matter. With that scientific fact established, the high court ruled unanimously that no individual could be forced to involuntarily diminish their own mental capacity. It was alarming then to discover that the current deputy minister opposed the decision and relentlessly tried to have the ruling overturned, causing the electorate to be suspicious of the political party, as it was apparent they had a vested interest in interrogating and torturing individuals in order to protect their agenda.

"What's new with you?" Lude asked. "Anything worth seeing?"

"If I had anything interesting to share, you know I would."

Alus was notorious for projecting images that would either boost his reputation or offer a good laugh.

"I meant to ask, what happened with Bainer."

"Fuck Bainer," Alus said. "He's repeatedly asked to see the same image. I finally told him I needed the space and deleted it. He flipped out."

"What was the image?"

"I can't remember. But I'm glad to be rid of it."

Lude nodded in agreement.

"I just hope it wasn't important," Alus added. "I'd hate to think it was something I could have prevented."

"I wouldn't worry too much. Besides, there's nothing you can do about it now anyway."

Alus resigned to that truth.

Twila came around from behind the bar.

"There's another drawback to her leaving," she said.

"There's more?" Jondi asked. "More than just the heartbreak?"

"Isn't there always?"

Twila knew he wouldn't remember the conversation later, if for no other reason than the vast amount of alcohol he'd consumed. But she had to tell somebody. She had to get it off her chest.

"I know you won't believe this," Twila said lowering her voice, "but everything around us is an illusion. It's all coming from inside Trin's head. She created it all. You should've seen it before we fell in love; the place was a total wreck. But while there's still a trace of that love, it'll continue to stay like this. That's how these things work. The very foundation of the bar is built on that love. But when the last trace of her presence diminishes, it'll revert to the dump it was before, and I can't imagine going back to that again. Funny thing is, I can't even remember it."

"I love illusions like that," he said. "Love's an illusion too, you know."

Then he downed half his drink.

"That's obvious now," she agreed, "especially after having lived it. But it also means it will take a lot of work to make this place look like this again. In fact, if you look closely, you'll see some of the wall fading over there in the corner near the floor."

"You need to find someone with the same qualities," he offered innocently.

"Finding an alien to love isn't easy. Though I do have a better understanding of it now. But finding love in general is difficult. There are countless variables that can challenge its very existence. I'll never understand how people can go from one relationship to the next in a matter of weeks or even months. They must compromise a lot. But I couldn't do it. And then you go and throw an alien into the mix, and you're faced with an entirely different assortment of obstacles, as you can imagine."

Twila recalled the first time she saw Trin, and even the memory of it now made her body twitch and moisten a little.

"Let's just say that I've been spoiled, because no one can probe a woman as properly as an alien."

Just then Xaco came up to the bar.

"It seems we have a problem, Twila."

"There's always a problem, sweetie. But why aren't they ever an illusion?"

"Sorry?"

"Never mind. Let's see what's up."

Then she turned back to Jondi.

"Remember what I said?"

"No, what?" he looked at her quizzically.

"Good."

At the door.

"What exactly does it do again?" Dooney asked as he twirled the gun around playfully on his forefinger.

"Be careful, who knows what it'll do if you hit the wrong person with it," Din said.

"I thought you said it was harmless."

"You'll have to confirm that with Xaco."

"Guns are never harmless," Kadi added.

"You said he hit some guy with it, right?"

"Yeah, but I don't know what effect it had on him."

Just then Xaco appeared in the doorway.

"Guys, we have a problem."

The security team followed him back inside.

"I'm sure you can handle this," Twila said, shaking her head as she walked off laughing. "If you can't, I'll have to get new staff."

"Isn't that the guy I tranqed earlier?" Xaco asked, getting a better look at him now. "I'm guessing you didn't catch up to him. But how did he even get in here?"

"I don't know. But the truck was doing forty before I even got my footing," Din said in his defense. "And when I did finally get up to speed, they were long gone."

"Well, he's our problem now."

"Do you think the tranq is still working?"

"Who knows, he could still go nuclear."

Pointing to the naked man on stage with the large, and now fully erect member, Din asked, "Is that one of the side effects?"

"I'll be sure to shoot myself later, if it is," he said. "But for right now, we have to get him down."

"I can give it another go," Din eagerly offered.

"Are you sure you're up to it?"

"I know when to swallow my pride."

"And his too, I'm sure. Just catch him this time."

In the alley, next to the bar.

"He either forgot or he deleted it," Bainer said. "Either way, the image is gone."

"Do you believe him?" the voice on the telephone asked.

"He seems like an honest kid."

"So, we have no proof then?"

"None."

"What about you? What do you remember?"

"Nothing. Whenever I try, I lose it. I even had the kid show it to me again, but I couldn't keep the image locked in. It just evaporated."

"They still have a few tricks up their sleeve. I'm sure of it. And that's probably one of them. I need more information."

"They're probably just benign creatures," Bainer suggested.

"Don't be a fool, they're up to something."

Bainer closed his eyes to focus better. For a second, he'd felt his unsavory disposition replaced with an unsettling pureness. He didn't know what was happening to him.

"Of course, you're right," he said finding himself again.

"I know I'm right. They're playing a waiting game," the voice added assuredly. "We need to stop them before it goes too far."

"I guess." There it is again, he thought. He tried to shake it.

"There's no room for guessing, Bainer!" the voice shouted. "We need to know what they're up to, and that bar's a part of it somehow."

"Okay. I'll hang around and see what I can find. But just so you know, it's not my scene."

"Adapt Bainer! We all have to make sacrifices for The State."

The phone went dead.

Bainer hated The State as much as the next guy, but he loathed that bar even more. He also detested betraying his basic nature as he had on the phone. Bainer didn't know why he involuntarily exposed a weaker and more sympathetic side of himself. It was out of character. Perhaps he damaged some grey matter when he attempted to capture that imagery from Alus, he thought. Or worse, had caught a contagion that seeped into his brain like a fatal virus since he felt as if he were losing his mind. That may be the case, but he wasn't going to lose out on the money they offered him to do the job.

He pulled a pill from his pocket and swallowed it dry. Then he turned into the shadows and unzipped his pants.

"Was that woman bothering you earlier?" Xaco asked.

"Actually, I found her rather amusing." Diododi smiled.

"She can be that. But she can also be a handful."

"She was okay. She was sweet in fact."

"She practically lives here now."

"She alluded to something like that. But I think she's had a tough time of it."

"She dated Kadi for a while. Though Kadi doesn't seem to mind her hanging around. I guess it helps remind her of the kind of women to avoid."

"It must be a nuisance having lovers hanging around."

"You have no idea."

Diododi smiled again.

"I see you had a show tonight."

"It wasn't planned. Some rogue guy needed to get something out of his system. But he had nothing on you."

"Just so you know, I'm considered a regular guy where I come from. Some even blame me for lowering the planetary average."

"You know I don't believe anything you say, right?"

"Really?"

"Seeing is believing. I only believe what I see."

Diododi pulled him close and kissed him gently.

"That's what I love about you, your innocence."

"You think I'm innocent?" Xaco said in a defensive tone.

"I do." Diododi widened his smile.

"Really?"

"Okay, what if I told you that everything around us is an illusion. Would you believe me?"

"You and me?"

"Not you and me. This," he nodded his head at the room.

"I'd need to see the illusion first."

"What if this is the illusion and you just didn't realize it?"

Xaco looked around.

"I'd say, you could do better than this."

"I'm sure I could. But it's not my illusion."

"You know that Twila designed this place, right? So, if you have a problem with it you should take it up with her. But be warned, she's sensitive about it. Especially these days. She thinks it's falling apart."

"The place isn't falling apart. But the love holding it together is."

"Twila loves this place, probably more than anything else."

"That might be the problem. In fact, I'm sure it is. Because the one thing that's not an illusion, is love."

"I'm not sure I understand."

Din came over.

"Twila needs you. The guy you tranqed finally returned to Earth. She thinks you should talk to him."

"Interesting choice of words," Diododi said.

Xaco reluctantly pulled himself out of his arms.

"Reality calls. I should deal with this."

"The illusion will still be here when you get back."

"Just be sure it is."

Xaco joined the others at the table.

"You look better. How do you feel?"

"Naked, and out of sorts. Other than that, I feel fine."

Din wanted credit for that, but nobody offered him any.

"Let's start with your name."

"He doesn't seem to remember that," Din confirmed.

"We'll call you Tranq for now then."

"Suits me. I don't even remember what happened."

"I wouldn't mind it happening again," Din said smiling.

Tranq leaned against him affectionately.

"That probably means that you don't know where you live, or if you even have a job," Twila said.

"Or where my clothes are." He shrugged his shoulders.

"We'll get you more than a bar towel to wear," Xaco said.

Tranq adjusted the bar rag delicately balanced on his lap, which proved barely adequate to the task.

"I'm sure we can take care of the rest. What do you think? Can we give him a job Twila?" Xaco asked.

Praying the illusion would last that long, she said, "For now. But we'll have to see how it goes."

"And you can stay with me," Din offered, playfully pressing his shoulder against Tranq. The bar rag appeared to react before he could vocally affirm his appreciation. Din slipped his hand under the table.

"It's all set then," Xaco affirmed.

They started to get up.

"One last thing. I want to apologize for shooting you."

Tranq smiled.

"It was a liberating sensation. In fact, you did me a favor."

"I'm glad it worked out, and that it didn't fuck with your head. But if it had, you would have deserved what you got."

"Sorry for being such an asshole."

"I have one question. Will he snap out of it and bash my head in while I'm sleeping tonight?" Din asked.

"Probably not. But I can't be certain." Xaco smiled.

"It'll have been worth it." Din tightened his grip under the table. Twila smiled at the lack of illusion.

"What do you want, Bainer? What are you even doing in here?" Alus nervously asked.

Bainer pulled a chair up to the table.

"I thought I'd shake it up a bit."

"What, my head?"

"No. But that's only because there's nothing in there. I checked."

"I told you, I deleted it. I wish I could remember now, because it might have been important. Apparently, important enough for you to come in here. Because this isn't your kind of place."

"I've heard a lot about this place. I thought I'd check it out. I've never been in a bar like this before."

"And what kind of bar is that?"

"The kind that accommodates perverts."

"So, you thought you'd fit right in?"

Bainer offered a twisted smile.

Alus said, "I know you Bainer. You wouldn't take your dick out to even piss in a place like this."

"That's why I took a nice long leak against the wall in the alley. I thought to wash off some of the stink."

"You brought the stink with you. Why are you even here?"

"Careful asshole, or I'll crack your head wide-open and project your shit on that piss-soaked wall outside for everyone to see."

Bainer felt good in his skin again as his old disposition returned.

But just then a deep, thick voice from above asked, "Everything all right here, Alus?"

Bainer nearly fell off his chair when he turned around to find his face barely at the man's knees.

"Whoa, what the fuck!"

"I think you should go. In fact, I recommend it, as I'm sure your doctor would as well. He'd also prescribe not coming back again."

Bainer disappeared. Alus couldn't be certain if it was voluntary. For all he knew he might have been vaporized.

"Thanks, Diododi. I wasn't sure how I was going to get out of that one."

"I feel an overload of darkness on this planet," he said.

When Diododi left, Alus called Lude.

"That fucker Bainer came into the bar looking for me. Luckily Diododi came over and scared him off. At least, I think he scared him off. What? No, it's just I'm not exactly sure what happened. What? I don't know. He may have disintegrated the fucker for all I know. Or maybe he just peeled out of here, though I doubt he had the footing to move that fast. What? I don't know. No. I called to tell you, I think I remember what I deleted. You know, the thing Bainer wanted. What? Of course, it's possible. I don't know, maybe it was the surge of fear that came over me. Or maybe being at the bar again made me flash on it. Because it has something to do with the bar. What? I'm not entirely sure. Come and help me figure it out. All right, see you when you get here. And hurry!"

Diododi returned to the table.

Putting his hand gently on Alus' shoulder, he said, "I just wanted to see how you were before I left."

"I'm fine, thanks" he said confused. "Why wouldn't I be?"

"No reason. Have a good evening."

Shortly after, Lude came running in.

"I'm here! Now project! I want to see if Bainer was vaporized!"

"What are you talking about? And why are you even here?" Alus asked in voice calm.

"You called and told me to come down. Is this a joke? Did you run out of money again and need me to cover your tab?"

"I have money," Alus said. "In fact, let me buy you a drink now that you're here."

"So, you have nothing to project?"

"Nothing in particular. In fact, it feels strangely empty in there. It's like an echo. I probably need another drink."

Lude leaned back in his seat and looked around. Nothing seemed out of the ordinary.

Alus couldn't recall anything, and there was nothing in his head now to prove otherwise.

With her second drink firmly in hand, Jono playfully allowed the barstool she sat on to slowly spin around, until it surprisingly settled in the opposite direction. Only then did she realize that the room was slightly askew. She also noticed a faint light coming in through the wall in the corner near the floor. It hadn't occurred to her that she'd been sitting in an illusion all this time; a near perfect projection, one almost undetectable but for a single crack at the seams, making her curious why the structure had become so fragile. Had the alien recently died and left the illusion to slowly die along with it?

It was then that Jondi came in.

When he finally settled in with a drink, Jono asked to no one in particular, "Can you feel the room coming apart?"

"Pardon me?" Jondi said obviously confused.

"The room? Does it seem as if it's coming apart to you?" Jono asked again, though this time to him directly. "I have a feeling the walls won't be capable of holding the place up much longer. It would seem that the metaphysics are evaporating."

Jondi didn't have a clue what the woman was going on about but having had similar hallucinations he offered a helpful solution.

"I think it's the drinks. They're just that good here."

"I agree they're good. But not so good as to make me think I'm seeing things; unless they're laced with something else."

"I find alcohol can explain pretty much anything," Jondi said. "It makes dealing with reality that much easier. Or in this case, the lack of it, it would seem."

Just then, Twila came in from the back.

"I was just telling this fine woman how wonderful the drinks are here," Jondi said.

"Kadi does make an impressive cocktail," Twila agreed.

From the far end of the bar, Kadi accepted the compliment with a slight nod of her head.

"The drinks are excellent, I won't argue that. But I also said that I thought the place was falling apart."

Twila came to the bar's defense.

"The bar's been around a very long time."

"I could help. It really wouldn't be much trouble."

Twila turned to the woman. The attraction was undeniable.

"What it would take is a magic touch."

"I've been known to have one." Jono said offering a warm smile.

Twila suddenly felt drawn to the woman, both emotionally and physically. Though she didn't recall making a move in her direction. In fact, it was as if the air between them became adhesive. Twila had felt the same sensation when she first met Trin. Both experiences were equally enigmatic and instantaneous, without regard for caution, or even hesitation. It wasn't love at first sight, but something more.

Colorians had an inherent ability to recognize their attraction to others and seize their destiny once identified. Twila felt that energy now, though she didn't feel controlled by it, or by her. Instead, she felt pulled toward a destiny she couldn't deny. And in that moment, it was revealed to her once again that loving an alien was easier and far less complicated than loving one of her own kind. It lacked doubt and indecision. It was set in time like a flawless jewel in stone; one that presented itself as honest, without disguise or the possibility of deceit. It was pure and nothing less than love.

In the next moment, the entire place began to slowly come apart in stages and reconstruct itself at the exact same time. As one wall came down, another immediately went up from under it. The chairs, the tables, the shelves behind the bar, even the paint took on a fresh design. In fact, it was so instantaneous that no one even noticed the bottles momentarily floating in mid-air as they patiently waited for the new structure to secure their place once again on the shelf. Twila didn't witness it happening as much as she felt it happen, because her eyes were lovingly locked on Jono.

Jondi's barstool was lowered and brought magically up again in one fluid motion, with him still balanced on it.

Once the room finally settled, and was level again, he ordered a double. Kadi, who rarely drank, poured herself one as well.

Shortly after everything was in its place, Xaco came into the bar.

"You renovated without my help? But how did you get it done so quickly?" he asked.

"Change happens regardless of time," Jono said.

"What does that even mean?" he asked.

"It means, sit down, relax, and have a drink," Twila said.

"It means what you're looking for is just around the corner. So, don't cross the street," Jondi said taking a sip of his cocktail.

"Love is irrational," Kadi said feeling a bit tipsy.

"Love is the only thing that is rational," Jono corrected her.

Xaco didn't understand any of it.

He resigned to asking, "Is there anything left I can do?"

"It's done," Twila said in full glow now.

"Except for proper introductions," Jono said.

She embraced each of them individually.

Twila took a bottle of her best champagne from the fridge.

"What's the occasion?" Xaco asked.

"Do we need an occasion?" Twila said hiding a smile.

She popped the cork.

"I just noticed how great the place looks," Kadi said.

"It does, doesn't it?" Xaco agreed.

"And the drinks are also great," Jondi added.

"Well, cheers everyone!"

"Few remember," Jono explained when they were finally alone, "when we arrived, the planet was little more than a heap of ashes. More a dumping ground; a baron wasteland that had been destroyed by an earlier invasion."

"I don't recall an invasion," Twila said.

"You weren't meant to. It would've been too devastating on your psyche. It wasn't a very peaceful time. In fact, it was a long, hard, and painful period. And after many years of being ravaged, the planet was abandoned and left for dead, which it nearly was."

Jono allowed her a moment.

Twila felt a surge of energy surround her. The room seemed to breath along with her. Then she felt a twinge through her body.

"I expected to have to start over in brick and mortar," Twila said. "There's an old foundation from a previous owner named Badger. I was going to build on that if I had to."

"You won't have to worry about that now," Jono said.

Twila kissed her.

"I have to ask. How much of the planet is still an illusion? I can only sense this one."

"That's because your love is part of it. There are major areas of the planet that need to be restructured, some almost to the core. The devastation was horrific. Much of what you see is still an illusion."

A moment later the room began to flicker, as if interrupted by an exterior force. Twila looked shaken by the unexpected effect.

"What the hell was that?" Xaco asked as he and Diododi came into the room.

The illusion flickered again.

Twila could feel the ions tingle on her skin. The sensation wasn't completely unfamiliar since she'd experienced a similar phenomenon whenever she had sex with Trin. But then another surge occurred, this time stronger. So intense that an entire wall momentarily vanished. Twila was certain it wasn't an orgasm.

A negative energy filled the room.

"What's happening?" Xaco shouted, holding onto the bar to keep his balance. But then the bar began to fade in and out as well, causing him to fall to the floor.

A moment later the entire illusion disappeared, leaving nothing but the old brick foundation beneath them.

"Did you see that?" Xaco shouted as he picked himself up.

Other than the random structure, they were surrounded by mostly baron and smoldering terrain. An unbearable stench filled the air.

"Jono!" Twila cried loudly as she witnessed the world in its true state for the first time.

"Remain calm," Jono insisted as she attempted to mentally brace against the intruding force.

In the same moment, Diododi cast a multi-dimensional sphere of solid space around them; a transparent illumination that empowered him against the protonic energy pressing down on the planet.

"The Repulmians have returned," he defiantly affirmed.

The Interviews

Cal placed an ad online looking for a roommate. In it, he stated that he wanted to meet applicants off-site as a cautionary measure before showing the place since there'd been numerous reports of robberies and assaults from meeting people on the internet. His landlord was equally concerned and asked specifically that he be given the name and telephone number of his new roommate when he found one.

Cal replied to only a few of the more than thirty emails he'd received. After filtering through them he scheduled a meeting with a guy named Isaac at a nearby coffee house. He was punctual, but to his surprise he felt as if he were the one being interviewed.

"So, tell me about the other responses to your ad," Isaac said.

Cal thought it strange, but he figured the guy was probably just curious by nature. He never suspected he had an ulterior motive. In fact, it seemed as if he were just inquiring about his competition.

"The first response I got was from a woman who said her daughter flew rescue helicopters somewhere in the mountains and that she would need to drop off her things on a Thursday and return the following Thursday to sort out payment and other details."

"Sounds suspicious," Isaac said.

"I thought so too." Cal added a smile to his response. "It was as if she needed a place to store her stuff for the week."

"I'm guessing you didn't reply to that one."

"I didn't reply to most of them. I saw no need for unnecessary dialogue if I had no interest in sharing with them."

"And the others?"

"There was another woman with a rather unusual name. So, I Googled her. It turned out she'd recently been arrested in Mississippi for something called simple battery."

"What's simple battery, I wonder?"

"Not sure. Though I imagine simple battery in Mississippi is probably a felony here in California."

They laughed in unison.

"I received several responses from mature women who were into yoga and spirituality. That's fine, but I wouldn't necessarily lead with it if I were replying to an ad."

"It sounds as if a nearby Ashram might have closed down," Isaac said.

"Right? One even added that she liked long walks on the beach."

"Is this beachfront property?" Isaac asked.

"No, but there is a creek nearby." Cal smiled.

"Did you mistakenly place your ad in the personals? It sounds as if she was looking for a relationship."

"Some of the women were definitely looking for more than just a room to rent."

"That's pretty clever."

"I thought it rather desperate."

"You're probably right."

"Another woman responded with a four-year-old son, even though the ad specifically said that I was looking for one person to share."

"She probably needed a babysitter as well."

"So, she could go out and get pregnant again."

"Or just leave the kid in your lap and take off."

"Just what I need, an abandoned child."

"I'm guessing you're not the parental type."

"Not right now."

"And the others?"

"Another woman insisted that I couldn't help but fall in love with her dog Norton. Though I do like the name."

"But the ad said no pets."

"It just shows the nature of people these days."

"So, you responded only to the men."

"Because the women were probably looking for husbands, which meant there'd be strangers sleeping over. It also meant sacrificing bathroom time without getting any. You know what I mean."

Cal attempted another smile.

"So, you're not looking to 'get any'?"

"I don't know what I'm looking for," Cal said evasively.

"Tell me about the men who responded."

Cal was relaxed enough that he didn't realize he was being deposed.

"Actually, I didn't interview any."

"Why is that?"

"Because I'd checked out their profile online first."

Isaac leans in almost sympathetically.

"And I'm sure you didn't like what you saw. I know how that can be."

"Exactly."

Isaac settled back into his chair.

"Can I say something? Can I tell you what I think?"

Cal felt they'd established a bond of sorts, so he said, "Of course."

"I think you're looking for a boyfriend as well as a roommate."

Cal felt his blood pressure rise.

"That's crazy."

"You should have been honest and mentioned you were gay in the ad. That way you might have gotten the response you were looking for."

Cal sat motionless, staring off into a distance that appeared closer than he realized. "That wasn't it. At least not entirely."

"It would have been the right thing to do," Isaac added.

"You make me sound like one of those women."

"At least they were being honest."

Cal searched for firmer ground.

"It's wasn't really like that. I am looking for a roommate, albeit, one easy on the eyes. And maybe one who might even find me attractive, if only as a friend."

"Still, there are similarities, don't you think?"

"Does this mean you're no longer interested in the room?"

"I don't know. It might be too complicated. You may be looking for too much. I'll call and let you know, if that's all right?"

"Sure."

After meeting with Isaac, Cal answered a few other responses.

The first was from a tall thin somewhat disheveled guy who constantly checked his cell-phone as if it was his leash on life.

"Do you own any books?" Cal asked.

"Dude, I haven't read a book since high school. Even then, I used cliff notes. All I read are texts from my girlfriend." Then added with a grin, "She also sends pix, if you catch my drift."

The second was from a man named Kent, who sat rigidly with his back firmly against the chair.

"I work all night and sleep all day," he said directly.

His pasty skin was pale and translucent. Almost lifeless. Cal suspected that he probably slept in a coffin.

Kent was a nurse who was especially fond of the letters that came after his name. "I insisted that the DMV put them on my driver's license. It took a call from my attorney, but they finally conceded."

He showed Cal the license to prove his point.

It read: 'RN, BSN, CCRN, CNRN.'

He expected the address to say Alphabet City, because the letters didn't stop there. During the interview, Kent also mentioned he had ADD, as well as OCD. He brought it up several times, which made Cal realize that he was even obsessed about having it.

Kent was undoubtedly intelligent. But he was also conceited about his accomplishments. He also repeated what he'd said several times, and even seemed a bit confused and out of sorts. In fact, Cal found himself watching Kent rather than listening to him, as it proved a more visual experience. But Cal knew he couldn't room with him. If for no other reason, then he wore Axe cologne, which made him smell like a serial killer.

"I'll let you know," Cal said.

After several disappointing encounters, he reconsidered rooming with a woman, regardless of the fact that it might reopen doors to a once familiar though distant passion. So, Cal approached each response with caution. But when a remarkable woman named Wendy inquired about the room, he was instantly enamored, and not just by her beauty, which was flawless, but her demeanor as well. He was also equally drawn to her genuine and unpretentious nature; a quality he seldom found in people.

Not wanting to complicate matters, at least at the start, he mentioned he was gay, thinking that it would put her at ease. He also hoped she'd find it a challenge, as some women did. But the truth was, he'd always been sexually ambiguous; he just hadn't acted on that abandoned desire for quite some time, as it took an exceptional woman for him to cross that line. And Wendy was likely that woman.

While in line at the market some years earlier, an attractive guy queued up behind Cal, who immediately noticed the woman in front of them in the tight skirt and busty top. When he caught Cal's eye he nodded his head and whispered, "Nice, huh?" Cal was fascinated by that sort of camaraderie, as if it were expected they be hormonally aligned while eying a shared prey. But he also knew it was that same hormonal impulse that could just as easily have them beating one another to a brutal death. If the guy hadn't also been equally attractive, Cal would have returned the nod in agreement and let it go at that, as he had on previous occasions. But instead, he replied with an engaging, if not flirtatious smile, "It's not usually my first choice." It was obvious the guy didn't understand what he'd meant. At least not at first. But a moment later, Cal watched as the guy's face morphed out of shape when he eventually realized the intention of his words.

Sadly, Wendy decided against taking the room. But Cal was pleasantly surprised when she telephoned the next day and invited him to dinner. He excitedly accepted, anticipating, if not a romantic evening, then perhaps the possibility of developing a friendship; one where he'd be able to confess his attraction to her, and his ambiguous nature. But instead, when Cal arrived at the restaurant, Wendy introduced him to her overly animated and effeminate gay friend, Frank. Who seemed like a nice enough guy, but it proved more an awkward moment than anything else. It made him realize that he should have told Wendy the truth in the beginning. Because if he had, things would probably have turned out differently.

Even years later, he regretted the choice he'd made that day.

They were an attractive looking couple.

"I like it," Heather said as she continued to look around. "I think it'll suit our needs. I especially like the deck."

188

The ad Cal placed had specified that he was looking to rent to a single person. But after meeting the couple he considered making an exception.

The woman's boyfriend sat quietly on the couch. Cal could tell he was apprehensive about taking the place. But he knew he'd follow her lead since she obviously made all the decisions.

"I really wasn't looking to share with a couple. But you seem like nice people," Cal confessed.

"Oh, I didn't realize that," she said. "I'm sorry." Cal suspected that she was bending the truth some. But then she added, "We've looked at so many places, I must have somehow overlooked that."

"Like I said, you seem like nice people. So, it might work. That is, if you want it."

"Allen works a regular schedule. Monday thru Friday. But I'm home a bit more often," she said.

"That won't be a problem. I work from home. But mostly in my room."

Allen remained quiet, failing to offer an opinion.

"Do you mind if I use the bathroom?" she asked.

"You know where it is," Cal said, adding a smile.

As Heather started to leave, she stopped and added in a flirtatious tone, "I especially love the tub. It's so big."

The moment she left Allen came to life.

"To tell you the truth, I don't think I'd be comfortable living here. It's a great place and all. But I don't think it's right for us."

"Why is that?"

"Honestly, I don't think I'd feel comfortable living with a gay man," he said getting right to the point. His tone wasn't discriminating. In fact, it was gentle, but obviously filled with concern.

"Can I say something? I think you'd feel better knowing the other guy in the house wasn't after your girlfriend. That I wasn't always checking her out. Especially in the morning when she's running around in her underwear. I'm sure you'd feel better knowing I didn't want to screw your girlfriend? Just as I'm sure you know yourself enough not to be tempted to cross that line with me. I can see you're straight and madly in love with Heather."

"You could right," Allen said after thinking it over. "Guys are always hitting on her."

"I'm sure they are."

"Like you said, I know myself. So, there's no problem there," he added less convincingly, as if subconsciously exposing a side of himself he hadn't yet discovered. Or perhaps he was recalling an earlier time in college when he went through an experimental phase.

When Heather returned from the bathroom she sat closer to Allen than she previously had. He remained just as silent as he had before. But this time his composure was more relaxed. It was obvious she was a stabling factor in his unbalanced world.

"I guess we'll take the room," she said to Allen as she brushed her hand along his muscular thigh.

"If you think it'll work," he said in a resigned whisper.

Heather shook his leg with her hand in a motherly fashion.

"He's shy at first. But you'll see, he'll come around."

She seemed more like a parent enrolling her child in a new school. And just like a parent, she failed to fully understand the true nature of her child. In fact, Cal wondered if he might eventually come around just as she said. But he accepted their relationship as it was. And he had no intention of interfering with it.

Allen mustered a dubious smile.

It didn't take very long for Allen's fears to come to fruition, as things eventually turned out just as he had suspected. Though not exactly how he'd anticipated. Because Allen soon found himself resigning to a long-denied desire as he watched Cal move about the kitchen each morning in his boxer shorts. Heather seemed unaware of her boyfriend's nurturing obsession as she went about her daily routine. Cal was no doubt flattered. What gay man wouldn't be? But rather than respond to his overtures, Cal found himself paying more attention to Heather. Something that Allen failed to notice.

Allen had conceded to the move not fully realizing his attraction to Cal. Perhaps it was living so closely to that once distant taboo now that drew him closer to it, as the flat allowed him access to something that had otherwise been out of reach. Cal was undoubtedly a reminder now of that attraction, if not a past that Allen hadn't quite put entirely behind him. It also didn't take long for Heather to prove Cal's theory about some women wanting to turn gay men with their sexual prowess. Which sadly reminded Cal of how much he'd wished that Wendy had made that same attempt. But Allen's obsession with Cal led to his neglecting Heather. Which in turn dampened their puppy-love romance.

One evening, after Heather turned her back on Allen when he crawled into bed reeking of alcohol, he drunkenly stumbled into Cal's bedroom.

Allen whispered to the figure sleeping in the dark.

"Wendy doesn't want me. And to tell you the truth, I'm not sure what I want any more. Or maybe I do now," he confessed.

Unaware that Cal had spent the afternoon with Heather while he was at work, Allen pressed his body closer. Cal hoped Allen was too drunk to catch her scent, or her sex for that matter, which he was certain still lingered in the room. If not, he was sure that Allen would discover it once his head hit the pillow. But Allen proved too inebriated not to think that he hadn't brought it in with him.

It was then that he heard Heather's voice from the other room. "Get it out of your system, Allen!" But Cal knew the system didn't work that way.

And rarely was it reversible.

Unfortunately, the sex that he had with Allen was less than memorable. Later that evening while alone in bed, he had to admit the sex with Heather had been better in fact. Of course, Allen was intoxicated and out of sorts. But his hands had lost any familiarity they might have once had when it came to a men's body. In comparison, Heather opened and blossomed beneath him like a sweet and fragrant flower. But he wasn't surprised when he woke the next morning to find their room empty. In fact, he'd expected it. He also knew vacating the flat couldn't have taken them more than ten minutes since they'd barely moved anything in. Just a couple of boxes and suitcases.

On the kitchen table, Cal found a check for the next month's rent. At least that's what he suspected it was for, though he couldn't help but laugh thinking it might be compensation for his matinee performance with Heather the previous afternoon. Or even for his labored tryst with Allen later that night; however less spectacular that proved to be. But he knew it was likely a token of appreciation from Heather for rescuing her from what would have certainly been a miserable life with Allen. It was obvious now that Heather had questioned Allen's sexual proclivities from the beginning. Perhaps there was something in his touch that eventually revealed his dormant tendencies to her. But there was no question in her mind now. Just as it was clear to Cal that she took the room for that very reason; as a test for Allen. One he would eventually fail, proving her intuition correct.

Only then did Cal take a closer look at the check.

Written in the memo line next to her signature she wrote, 'Thank You!' Of course, he could only speculate what she meant. But deep down he knew.

Cal placed another ad online. It read: 'Singles only. No Exceptions.'

A few days later the phone rang.

"Hi Cal, how are you?"

"Who's this?"

"It's Isaac."

"Isaac? I didn't think I'd hear from you again."

"I told you I'd probably get in touch."

"But I never expected you would."

"I see you're renting the room again."

"I am."

"Is it still available?"

"It is."

"Can I come by and see it?"

"It hasn't changed much."

"I imagine it hasn't. But have you?" Isaac asked.

"Perhaps," he said with a measure of resignation.

"Did you find someone to take the room or did you just not list it for a while?" Isaac asked when he came by the apartment.

"I ended up renting it for a couple of months."

"Only a couple?"

"It was short term."

"So, about the room. I thought we could come to an arrangement."

"What kind of arrangement?"

"I'll move in, and we can see how it goes."

"Isn't that usually the arrangement?"

"You know what I mean. We can see how we get on. I'll admit I was attracted to you. But you seemed somewhat messed up at the time."

"I think I got it out of my system," Cal said, a measure of guilt still in his voice.

"I was hoping you would. So, what do you think?"

"I think that'll work. See how it goes. See how we get on."

"Good."

They smiled at one another.

It was a good start.

Cal called his landlord.

"I have the name and number of my new roommate for you."

"What happened to that cute couple?"

"It got complicated."

"Again?"

"I also have his license plate number as well. In case I get abducted and you have to issue an Amber Alert."

"You know they only issue those for missing children, right?"

"I'm sure I'll scream like a little girl if I'm abducted," he said jokingly.

"Like the one I recently heard?"

"Like that, but probably with less passion."

"That would depend on who abducts you, I would think."

"I guess."

"Well, good luck with that."

"I'm sure I'll need more than luck," Cal confessed.

Making the Cut

Howard spent well over two years working on his second book, rewriting draft after draft. Though as hard and long as he worked on it, Howard still wasn't truly content with the result. His new publisher, Mr. Barry, kept pressuring him. So, he rewrote it until he was satisfied with the final product. Only then, did he present it to Mr. Barry, who accepted it with great anticipation.

A few days later Howard was called into Mr. Barry's office.

"I like it, son. I really do," Mr. Barry said. "It's good work. Maybe even your best yet. That said, it could be a bit shorter. I'm sure you know what I mean."

It wasn't the response Howard had expected. Disheartened, he went home and worked on it again.

About a week later Howard returned to Mr. Barry's office, where he scanned it right then and there.

"Good. Better." Then looking over his glasses he added, "But it still needs a bit more. Thin it out a bit. You know what I mean?"

Howard didn't quite know what he meant. But nonetheless he took it home and went through it again. He thinned out what he thought might be considered excess, though he wasn't happy doing it. But apparently, it had to be done.

He returned a week later.

Mr. Barry took even less time evaluating the work.

"It's still a bit heavy, my boy. It needs to be lighter. You know what I mean?" he said again over his glasses. Howard thought his eyes seemed smaller, even narrower than they had before.

Howard nodded, but said nothing. He had spent weeks cutting the weight out of the piece. What had started out as two hundred-fifty pages had been trimmed to less than two hundred. Now he was told to take out even more and make it even lighter. Whatever that meant.

A week later Howard returned to Mr. Barry's office, his manuscript barely a hundred and twenty-five pages now. Half of what his heart had originally put into it.

"Ah, that looks much better," Mr. Barry said, as if evaluating the piece by its actual weight, than by the weight of the piece. He scanned the pages, though even quicker than he had the last time. Mr. Barry glanced over his glasses again with a look that seemed to justify the briefness of his editing.

"You've almost got it, my boy," he said offering a smile. "Almost. Just comb through it again and take off just a little more. You know what I mean? Just a little."

The truth was he understood less and less of what Mr. Barry meant with each visit. Howard nodded again, but this time he added a grunt to accompany it.

"Remember, just a little!" Mr. Barry echoed with encouragement as Howard closed the door behind him.

Howard took what remained of the story and cut it down by more than half just to be sure. He returned to his office the next day with fifty pages of what he'd originally written. More a synopsis of the piece. He was now left with what he would have been expected to submit to an editor in hopes of expanding on his work; basically, a general idea for the book. Howard had trimmed nearly everything. One more edit, and they'd be nothing left than what was written between the lines. Howard wondered if that was in fact exactly what Mr. Barry wanted.

"Now that looks much better, my boy!" Mr. Barry exclaimed with excitement, without even turning a page.

Howard was now prepared to stand his ground, as he braced for yet another critical response.

Mr. Barry quickly thumbed from page to page.

"Well?" Howard finally asked. "Is that what you meant?"

Mr. Barry looked him squarely in the eye and said, "That's it. That's exactly what it needed, my boy. It's nearly perfect. You hear me? Nearly perfect!"

"Nearly?" Howard questioned.

"Perhaps it needs a just little tease in the middle. You know what I mean? To help elevate the character. And dust it a bit."

"Dust it?" he asked, even more confused than before. "At this point, it hasn't had time to collect dust."

"You know what I mean. Just trim it a little." Then Mr. Barry added with a degree of trepidation, "To tell you the truth, my boy, it could use a bit more color as well. Some parts seem a bit lackluster. Try and add an international flair to it. You know what I mean? Something continental."

Back at his apartment, defeated and deflated, Howard slumped deep into his couch. He stared at the work in front of him, and then again at the discarded, though reassembled pages on his desk. Then he reluctantly went to his typewriter.

The next day at Mr. Barry's office, Howard handed him a single sheet of paper, without even a cover attached. But that was because the piece no longer had a title, or perhaps even an author.

Mr. Barry carefully took the single sheet of paper as if it were a fragile and priceless work of art.

"Hmm, what do we have here?" he said glowing. "This might just be it, my boy."

Mr. Barry looked up at Howard with a wide grin across his face as if he'd struck gold. He excitedly pushed his glasses up his nose and stared at the two short sentences written across the center of the page.

After a long and seemingly tense moment, Mr. Barry nodded with affirmation, as he read them again.

'Not to split hairs Mr. Barry, but I think you have mistaken me for your barber. Va te faire foutre!'

The room remained silent.

Satisfied, Howard opened the door to leave. But just then he heard a loud roar behind him, which made him shutter.

"Brilliant! Absolutely brilliant!" Mr. Barry bellowed. "My boy, it's got everything! Thought. Conflict. Style. True character. Not to mention a flare for the international, however off-color. But it also has the perfect protagonist. You understood exactly what I meant!"

Dubious he'd ever understand, Howard cautiously agreed.

"It would seem we're on the same page then, Mr. Barry."

"Absolutely, my boy. Absolutely!"

Scenes from The Island

Chapter One

When Evan picked up the phone, the familiar voice on the other end hysterically broke through the wire before he could even say hello.

"I've hurt my back on this damn island. You need to come down. I need your help." There was an undeniable urgency in his voice.

"You know I'm working, right? London doesn't shut down like Italy in August. We actually work year around here."

"And I thought you Brits were civilized," Elliot said.

There was no response.

"It's 34 degrees here," Elliot offered.

The telephone remained quiet on the other end.

"Did I forget to mention there's a ticket waiting for you at Gatwick?" Elliot tried again.

The silence broke.

"What time's the flight?" Evan asked.

"Seven tomorrow morning. And bring Vicodin!"

Evan arrived on schedule.

"Yasu agapi mou!" Elliot greeted him with a big hug and kiss on each cheek.

Evan gave him a suspicious look.

"You haven't actually injured your back, have you?"

"I couldn't let you miss a season on the island."

"Does this mean we're going on that scooter of yours?" he asked with a distinct fear in his voice.

"Yes, as a matter-of-fact," Elliot confirmed with a widening grin.

"And what am I supposed to do with these drugs?"

"You actually brought them? We'll figure that out later."

"And where am I staying?"

"With me, of course. I've rented the old house again."

"If I'd known that I may have come willingly," he offered.

"I couldn't risk it. It wouldn't be the same without you here."

Elliot took his arm and the lighter of Evan's two bags.

"Who else is here, and did they come of their own accord, or were they also recruited as drug mules?"

"Everyone's here," Elliot said with a smile as he straddled the scooter. "And most came voluntarily."

Evan climbed on the back of the beat-up machine with hesitation.

"You know I hate these things, right? I'd prefer not to end up plastered to the crotch while on holiday."

"Just hang on!" Elliot said as he balanced Evan's bag between his legs. He could feel his grip tighten as he sped off. It was pleasantly familiar. He shouted back into the wind, "Relax we're nearly there."

"Where? Heaven?" Evan shouted nervously.

"We're already in Heaven!" Elliot shouted, turning his head slightly to offer a welcoming, if not convincing smile, which nearly caused the scooter to weave into oncoming traffic; and Greek traffic at that.

"Watch the road!" Evan cried nervously as he gripped his waist even tighter. "If this is Heaven, I'd hate to think what Hell is like!"

The house was just as Evan had remembered it.

"I thought Stravulla gave the house to her daughter as part of her dowry when she married?"

"They have another house, which is bigger. She was gracious enough to rent this one to me. After all these years, I'm like an uncle to her."

Elliot sat and watched as Evan unpacked.

"So, what did you tell them at work to get away?"

"The truth is, they were glad to be rid of me. I'm sure I wasn't pleasant to be around anyway."

"Did you tell them you had a sultry woman waiting for you on a toasty beach?" Elliot teased.

"I tell them as little as possible."

"You're so mysterious."

"I'm not mysterious. If anyone knows that, it's you."

"I'm sure there are a few things I still don't know."

"You'd be disappointed."

"I doubt that."

Evan closed the empty suitcase.

"Do you want to rest before we go down to the harbor?"

"It was a short flight. But I will shower first."

Evan's access to the island was more convenient than Elliot's. It was as simple as catching an early train from London to Gatwick. Then a brief and usually festive flight on the charter to the island. In comparison, Elliot was forced to endure a brutal journey from California. One he often dreamt to shorten by diving into one pool at home and coming up into a similar one on the island; a sensation that was only truly realized once he resurfaced from his initial plunge after he arrived. If nothing else, it helped to therapeutically heal the experience.

"Then I'll leave you to it."

Elliot closed the door behind him as he left.

After enduring a tepid Greek shower, which was dubious at best, Evan spread his naked body across the length of the short mattress. It was nearly as familiar as his own back in London. In truth, it had seen more action and held more memories than the one at home.

Evan was pleased to see little had changed in the old house, as many on the island had been recently renovated, causing them to lose much of their charm. He watched the morning light through the transparent white linen curtain as it gently billowed against the open window over the built-in stone settee.

Evan felt at home again.

Chapter Two

It was late August on the Aegean, and a more peaceful place now that the Italians had left. Each season Elliot watched their exodus, and every year they seemed more like conquerors leaving a bloodied battlefield, as the only reported incidents of violence on the island usually occurred during their occupation. It was humorously and accurately suggested that if you wished to visit Italy in August, you should travel to a Greek Island.

They were the first to arrive at The Blue Chairs; the cafe on the harbor where they gathered before heading off to the beach, or dinner most nights. And not unlike the Champs-Elysées in Paris, everyone eventually passed by.

The late morning sun reflected against the aqua-blue water.

The anchored fishing boats bounced colorfully on the undulating sea.

The bank queues congested the newly white-washed stone streets.

The ferries docked across the circular bay rocked against the pier, their loud horns and chains rattling and echoing against the quiet hillside.

Sophia made her way to the table.

"Kalimera sas!" she said warmly.

"Kalimera, Sophia. Ti kanis? Kala?" Elliot asked.

"Ne kala. Esi?" Sophia smiled.

"Kala, efharisto," Elliot smiled back.

"Yasu Evan," she said. "Welcome back."

"Thank you, Sophia. You look well."

"The season finishes soon. I feel young again."

They ordered two coffees.

"It was the worse year on the island," Elliot continued. "My friend Hugh was sick for quite some time before we arrived, but he was still determined to come regardless. It proved to be a scary couple of months, and it only got worse toward the end of the trip."

"How sick was he?"

"Sick enough that he probably shouldn't have come in the first place."

"I ask because there's really no hospital to speak of on the island. They can plaster a leg brilliantly if you get into a scooter accident. But little more than that."

"I mentioned that to him before we came away. It only made the island that much more attractive since he'd been in and out of hospitals for months. I doubt he thought much past that."

"You said he got worse?"

"He had some bad days. I'm sure the constant wind here didn't help his lungs either."

"Getting sick on this island is one of my biggest fears," Evan said, "And I'm in good health."

"I'm glad to hear it."

"So, how sick did he eventually get?"

"He woke late one night in extreme pain. He couldn't move, or even sit up. In fact, he could barely breathe. I'd never seen him that uncomfortable. I immediately went for the doctor. When I got to his house I knocked several times, but there was no answer. I knocked again, even harder, but there was still no answer. From the top of his stairs I quietly watched the early light begin to break through what seemed like eternal darkness, until the doctor eventually came to the door with an unmistakably erect, and what appeared to be a recently pleasured penis. Which I should mention, was still sticking out of his unzipped trousers. But he wasn't embarrassed. In fact, he seemed proud of it as he attempted to put it back in its proper place again. Oddly, he wasn't so much concerned, as he was annoyed by the interruption. I told him my friend was seriously ill and that he needed to see him right away. As he reluctantly continued to sort out his impressive bits, which was obviously against his basic nature, he asked what I thought might be wrong with my friend. I told him that Hugh was in pain and couldn't breathe. But the doctor remained distracted, clearly more concerned with the woman waiting behind the door who repeatedly moaned, no doubt still sexually unsatisfied, 'Ella moro,' than he was with my friend's well-being. He even whispered to her over his shoulder, 'Endaxi nostimoula, endaxi.' Then he told me to go see if my friend was still in pain. And if so, come and get him. It was obvious his passion took precedent over any oath he'd taken."

"This is Greece, after all," Evan said. "Then what happened?"

"He repeated his instructions again before closing the door. 'Go. And return if your friend is still in pain.' What else could I do?"

"It would seem his penis took priority."

"And that his marriage vow was more sacred than the one he took to Hippocrates."

"If that was even his wife."

"Good point."

"What happened when you got back to the house?"

"Hugh was sitting up in bed and breathing comfortably again. The pain had subsided. Whatever he took had apparently kicked in. It was only later we discovered that his lung had collapsed."

"Nothing worse than getting sick on this island."

"I thought so too, but it got worse."

Evan leaned forward in his chair.

"Don't tell me you had to ship his body home."

"Even worse than that."

Just then Turi and Doreen came along. Doreen was hobbling.

"What happened to you?" Evan asked.

"I need a drink first," she said, in noticeable pain.

Sophia came to the table.

"A Metaxas please, Sophia," she said smiling through her discomfort at the attractive waitress.

"I'm not privy to what you girls get up to in bed, but it sure looks like something went terribly wrong," Elliot said jokingly.

"Don't make me laugh. It hurts too much."

"What happened?"

"I fell off one of those bloody bikes, that's what happened. I told Turi we shouldn't have rented one."

"It's not as bad as it looks. She's just being dramatic," Turi said.

"I'm not being dramatic. I cut my elbow," she said trying to locate the scrape. "And I bruised my bum. But I'm not showing you that. I also broke two nails that I recently had done."

"We were just talking about scooter accidents," Elliot said.

"This is exactly what I mean," Evan reaffirmed.

"She's just making a fuss. Don't listen to her. She doesn't deserve your sympathy. It's not as if she's plastered up to her business. She's fine."

"I was fine before I got on that bloody beast."

"It's just a scooter, babe. It can barely make it up the hill to the room."

"I'll never put one of those monsters between my legs again."

"What exactly happened?" Elliot asked.

"Do you want to tell them, or should I?"

"What's to tell? I'm a banged-up dyke who needs sympathy."

Turi ignored her.

"She fell off the back of the bike while we were parked in the lot above the beach. We weren't even moving."

"It doesn't matter. They're still dangerous," Doreen pleaded.

"And it was even up on the kickstand," Turi added. "The truth is, she was fussing with her hair."

"You don't appreciate the risks I take to be beautiful for you."

The boys couldn't help but laugh.

"It's not funny," Doreen said, trying not to laugh herself.

Sophia arrived with the Metaxas.

Doreen slammed it down in one fluid motion.

"Another palikalo!" she said to Sophia.

"Remember Lucy's scooter accident a few years ago? She was coming back from the beach with Stavros, when he quickly swerved to avoid a bus going around a turn, and she flew off the back," Elliot said.

"And she barely had a scratch, if I remember," Turi added.

"She said it was because she was drunk. And her body was relaxed."

"I wasn't entirely sober either," Doreen confessed.

"Just think, it might've been much worse if you were," Turi said.

The second Metaxas arrived.

"Oriste," Sophia said setting the glass on the table.

"Thank you, Sophia. You're the only one who seems to care."

"Endaxi na pume," Sophia said, her hands on her hips. "Alla' prosehe, Doreen. Prosehe."

As Sophia walked away she nodded her head upwards and clicked her tongue, as Greeks do to emphasize the negative.

"Was she flirting with me?"

"She said be careful. I suggest you take her advice," her girlfriend said.

Chapter Three

Elliot came upon Colin quite by accident several years earlier as a bombastic but cheerful British rant behind him at a club above the square as the music roared across the crowded bar.

"Six thousand drachmas a night for a room that's barely the size of my WC at home," Elliot had heard him say to the person he was with. "I can't afford to drink on this bloody rock. Not to mention I'm a mile out of town!"

When Elliot first arrived on the island nearly two decades earlier after a long grueling night on the ferry from Piraeus, he was greeted by a mob of Greeks, mostly women, frantically waving placards as he came off the boat. At first, he thought he'd walked into the middle of a general strike, picketing for higher wages. But on closer inspection, he soon realized that their signs promised scenic and affordable rooms for rent. Of course, first time visitors, especially those weary from traveling, eagerly accepted their offer. If for no other reason than the convenience of settling in as quickly as possible after a long journey. That day, Elliot found himself hustled along with the crowd of college-aged backpackers. Until a slight woman persuasively abducted him, and hurriedly guided him through town until they finally came to a door just off what was obviously the main street. At first, Elliot thought it a coup to have found something right in the center of town. That is, until he saw it was little more than a twin mattress curtained off behind a buzzing refrigerator in the back of the woman's kitchen. Not to mention, the shower and toilet were only accessible through an adjacent door on the street, which meant that Elliot would have to scurry from one to the other in a towel as people passed on their way to the beach or dinner, depending on the time of day. A scenario that certainly looked as if he'd been caught in a compromising situation. One with a knife welding husband in frenzied pursuit. But being exhausted after the long trip from California, Elliot took the room till he could find more suitable accommodations.

Being sympathetic to the Brit's dilemma, Elliot turned around to find a tall broad-shouldered fellow wearing a tightly fit Manchester United jersey.

"If you're interested, I have a room in town just off the square that you can have for a thousand drachmas a night."

"You'll have a friend for life if you're serious."

"I'm cautiously serious," Elliot said with light-hearted hesitation.

"Don't be," he said, adding an attractive smile.

With impressive strength, Colin hugged Elliot, and then held him out at arm's length with pride, as if holding a trophy or a newborn baby.

"Let me buy you a drink. Now that I can afford it!"

The next day Colin moved into one of the bedrooms upstairs, where he continued to stay during his subsequent visits.

With everyone finally settled in, Elliot planned a dinner party.

Doreen was preparing the salad.

"Most people come to the island for the sun and the beach."

"And the sex," Alec added.

"Yes, and the sex. But I come for the tomatoes," she said.

"You mean the women?" Alec added as he wrapped a dolma.

"Of course." She laughed. "No really, the tomatoes. I love them here."

"I come for the eggs. I'd like to know what they feed the hens on this island to make them actually taste like eggs."

"The same thing I feed mine," she said, offering an informative smile.

"Don't put me off eggs. I wouldn't know where to spend my holiday."

"The fish is nearly ready," Elliot said sticking his head in the doorway. "How's that salad coming?"

"We're nearly done."

"It looks great. I can almost taste the love in it."

"You want love? Look at this cucumber!" Doreen said as she waved it teasingly at him. It was nearly a meter long.

Elliot smiled and disappeared. Then he stuck his head in again.

"Is that from upstairs?"

"Upstairs? Why would you keep cucumbers in the bedroom?"

"Never mind," he said disappearing again.

"Should I not use this cucumber?" she shouted.

Doreen was frightened of it now as if it would come to life in her hand.

"It's fine," he yelled back. "We always use protection!"

They dined outside on a long marble table under a trellis draped in deep red bougainvillea, which swayed gently in the warm island breeze.

"We didn't actually meet that first year," Elliot explained. "I was sitting at the bar above the square having drinks with friends one evening, when Martin passed-by on the street below with his fiancé. It was rather romantic. Like a French film that didn't need subtitles since it was obvious she was browsing the gold store windows intent on finding just the right ring. While Martin was eying the boys above on the balcony. He smiled when he saw me. I smiled back, shaking my head dubiously."

"It was divine intervention," Martin said. "A sign from above."

"We met the following year/ But only because he'd left his wallet on the bar. I ran after him to return it."

"Do you still have sex with women?" Turi asked.

"It hasn't been an easy habit to break," he said jokingly.

"I know, right?" Doreen agreed.

"No, the truth is, I don't," Martin confessed.

"I think bisexuality is a temporary state of confusion; fence-sitters who always seem to fall onto the gay side," Turi said.

"As opposed to what, the dark side?" Colin added.

"Seriously, I'm always tripping over their splintered asses."

"I totally agree," Warren said from the far end of the table.

Turi gave the Greek sideward nod of affirmation.

Evan felt a need to challenge that.

"If a straight man sleeps with another man he must be gay. But if a gay man sleeps with a woman he's never thought to be straight. I don't see the difference. That's a flawed double standard."

"If someone tells me they're bisexual, it's the same as an atheist saying they're agnostic," Warren said sternly. "It's meant to appease the situation so that everyone feels comfortable."

Evan continued his defense.

"I disagree. Whoever I'm with in that moment is where I want to be in that moment. If I'm with a woman, I never wish I'm with a man. And when I'm with a man, I never wish I'm with a woman."

"So, when you're with a woman, and you're running your fingers along the inside of her thigh in the dark, you never once wished you came across something entirely different when you finally found your way, you know, *there*?" Turi asked.

"Not once."

"Is one more familiar than the other? Or more desired than the other?"

"They're equally desirable. And I never confuse the two. I never expect something from a woman that only a man can give me. And I never expect anything else when I'm with a woman."

"Then a night with me would confuse you." Turi smiled.

"I'm sure it would," he said, with a slight grin.

"And the women you sleep with don't mind?" Colin asked.

"Not usually. It's the men who tend to have a problem with it."

"So, you fuck women and men fuck you?" Colin said.

"Yes, but I wouldn't put it so crassly."

"Enough talk of cross-pollination," Alec said finally joining in.

Warren gave him a suspicious look. One Alec expected.

"What I find offensive, is when gay men joke about switching for a hot female celebrity," Elliot said. "It damages our credibility and only reinforces the belief that we actually have a choice in our sexuality. You never hear a straight guy say he'd switch for some hunky actor."

"Isn't there an extraordinary woman you'd switch for?" Alec asked.

"Give it up," Warren said, his voice bordering on anger.

"I see no one's touched the salad," Elliot said, changing the subject.

"There's just too much food," Turi said.

Nearly everyone agreed.

"I know it's the cucumber. I should explain. I bought two the other day. Each about a meter in length."

"They were impressive," Colin confirmed.

"I suggested Colin put one under his bed upstairs and pull it out in the dark when he brought someone home. But just to be clear, it's not the same cucumber."

"We can find a use for it if you don't," Doreen suggested.

"I'll never eat another cucumber," Warren said, put-off by the image.

Alec took some salad and passed it around.

"Getting back to Martin. I should probably share another story."

"I thought you might," Martin said, leaning back reluctantly from the table as if hoping to disappear.

"Martin called me over the winter about a trip to Florida."

"Which I ended up taking."

"To meet an online connection," Elliot continued.

The table moaned in unison.

"I told him I wouldn't be able to pick him up if it didn't work out. That it wasn't like driving down to Brighton from London."

"Who'd you meet online?" Alec asked.

"A twenty-year old surfer dude who said he owned a bed and breakfast on the beach," Elliot added before Martin could respond.

"It did sound dreamy," Martin reaffirmed with the same enthusiasm he had on the telephone with Elliot that winter.

"I told him it was unlikely a young surfer had that kind of money, and not to be surprised if he turned out to be older than he expected."

"You have to love the Internet," Warren said. "If nothing else, then for its comic offerings."

"That was the last I heard. Until he called me from Florida."

"In a thunderstorm," Martin added.

"It turned out even worse than I anticipated. The guy was over seventy and rather round. And I'm certain he'd never been on a surf board."

"How embarrassing," Martin said as he hid his face in his hands.

"Then Martin called and asked if he could fly out and see me."

"We had a nice dinner," Martin said with enthusiasm.

"He was like a puppy with his tail between his legs when I picked him up at the airport. I could have fed him dog food."

"I'd have been satisfied with a bone," Martin admitted.

"And now we come full circle," Elliot said with a smile.

"How long did you stay in San Francisco?" Alec asked.

"Just the weekend."

"He was eager to get back online," Elliot added.

"Thankfully, there's no internet on the island," Turi said.

"Not yet," someone added.

"It's nearly one. We should head down to the square," Colin suggested.

"Kala. Pame!"

Chapter Four

When he woke, Alec shared a dream that he had with Warren.

"This will sound crazy, but I dreamt I kissed a princess."

"Really?"

"The thing is, she never woke up."

"You're gay, Alec. Why would she? And don't you think it strange that you're dreaming about kissing a princess?"

"It was just a dream. Dreams aren't reality."

"But they usually have a meaning."

"Not always."

"Then there must be something out of balance in your life which needs to be resolved."

"You're reading too much into it," Alec said.

"Am I?"

"Images find their way into our subconscious and our dreams all the time, especially after we watch a film or something on television. It doesn't mean we're living it."

"Okay, let's leave that for now. So, she doesn't wake up, right?"

"Right. Why doesn't she wake up?"

"It's simple. Because you're gay. There's no reason to wake up."

"She does move though. Rather she stirs."

"At least you know she's not dead."

"Funny. But like I said, she stirs."

"She's probably waiting for a straight guy to kiss her."

"I think I'd wake up if a straight guy kissed me while I was sleeping."

"Now you're dreaming," Warren challenged.

"What's she doing then?" Alec asked, ignoring his jab.

"You said she was sleeping?"

"But she stirs."

"What do you mean she stirs? Is she restless? Or turning over? Maybe she's turning away from you."

"Oh, that's nice. No, she seems uncomfortable."

"No offense, but even I'd be uncomfortable if you tried to kiss me while I was sleeping."

"But I have."

"What?"

Alec could tell Warren wasn't pleased. Mostly because he needed to be in control of every situation.

"I kiss you occasionally when you're asleep," Alec admitted.

"How do I respond?"

He could see the idea disturbed him.

"Sometimes you wake up. Sometimes you don't."

"What do you do if I don't? Wait, I don't think I want to know."

"You're not the princess you think you are," Alec teasingly said.

"I don't know what that even means. But I'm not surprised that I don't wake up. It would seem even when you're not dreaming your kisses aren't that effective."

It wasn't going exactly how Alec anticipated. They hadn't spoken of dreams in sometime, and he wondered if they might have abandoned them entirely now.

"Regardless, she usually stirs when I kiss her."

"How many times do you kiss her?"

Alec could see he was losing focus.

Warren added, "Maybe you're dreaming about some woman in your life."

"There aren't many women in my life. At least not straight women."

Warren didn't hesitate. He got right to the point.

"Maybe it's your friend Candida."

It was a conversation he'd wanted to have for some time.

Alec wasn't surprised to hear her name though.

"She hasn't been on the island for years."

"But you fucked her. Maybe she's your princess."

"I told you I never had sex with Candida. That was Evan."

"Who was she then?" Warren demanded.

"I don't remember *his* name," Alec said.

"Oh, that's nice!"

"Do you remember the name of every trick you slept with?"

"Maybe not. But I'd sure as hell remember the name of a woman that I slept with. In fact, I wouldn't forget it! Tell me, when was it? The year we met? The year after?"

"It wasn't a woman. Besides, it was before we met."

"Look me in the eye and say that again. Look me straight in the eye and say it."

Alec turned toward Warren and looked him in the eye, but he didn't say anything. He just stared at him.

"You can't, can you?"

Alec continued to look Warren in the eye. Finally, Alec said, "It was a guy. And it was the year before we met."

Warren watched every pore on his face, patiently waiting for his sweat to bleed through, and for the truth to seep out along with it. He waited for his body to physically react to his lie and reject it as it would a toxin.

"You're lying. Then why does she send you a card every Christmas?"

"Everyone sends cards at Christmas."

"She'd have a different reason to send one though, wouldn't she?"

"Why do you continue to insist that I slept with Candida?"

"We're way past that. Where was it? Here where we said we loved one another? In this bed, that we shared every summer for the last five years?"

"I told you it was a guy, and it wasn't here. We didn't have this place. We weren't even together then."

"You know why she sends you a card every year?"

"I told you, she sends everyone a card."

"She sends you a card to be sure that you haven't died of some fucking disease! That's why she sends you one. She needs to know you haven't died of fucking AIDS!"

"That's ridiculous."

"I'm sure the one you send her every Christmas is the only one that really matters, as I expect it gives her a bit of hope that she won't die from something you may have given her."

"But why would it matter? I'm negative anyway."

"But she doesn't know that, does she?"

There was no point arguing. Alec also knew that he wouldn't be kissing Warren while he slept that evening since he already decided he was going to sleep alone.

Chapter Five

Elliot had first met Edmonton in Sloane Square while on a stopover in London one year on his way to the island. The weather was tepid enough to take an outside table for lunch that afternoon.

Shortly after settling in and placing his order, a large, plump gentleman in a bright colored ascot and tweed suit took the adjoining table next to him. At first, Elliot failed to notice the Corgi pup tucked warmly under his great coat. Though he was sure the choice of pedigree was influenced by Royal preference.

The gentleman chatted Elliot up straight away, offering a well-polished, if not exceedingly flamboyant biography of his current life; finishing with his recent excommunication from Buckingham Palace, and the reason for his fated, if not forced departure from the Queen's service. With an overly exaggerated and manicured flair, Edmonton explained it in vivid detail.

"That particular afternoon, I'd come directly from an early pub session to my employ at Her Majesty's Palace. After struggling into what had only recently become a somewhat ill-fitted, though still deserved uniform, I took what I thought to be a well-rehearsed, if not an awarding-winning portrayal of sobriety, from the Royal Tearoom down the long ornate corridor to the elevated lift. It was there I performed my last official duty for the crown, as I carefully, if not instinctively, placed one of The Queen's priceless tea-sets into the dumbwaiter to send it down. It was only when it left my trembling, unsteady hand that I realized the dumbwaiter had been just as absent as I'd been absent-minded." He paused for dramatic effect. Then colorfully, if not theatrically added, "I remember a determining draught coming up from the vacant shaft; a welcoming breeze if you will, against my flushed and ruddy face, which no doubt helped me acknowledge the error of my action." Then in an equally exaggerated tone, Edmonton said, "My dear, I was out the palace gate before it even hit bottom." He paused, allowing Elliot to picture his predetermined fate, but this time he offered a thin smile. "But in my own wicked way I'm sure I'd beaten it there anyway," he added. He ended by saying, "When I was decidedly accosted and brutally stripped of my official garment, it was as if God were taking the skin off my poor, brittle bones."

Sometime after that, with Elliot's reluctant recommendation, Edmonton made the occasional appearance on the island, coming and going, as his now unaccredited and dubious work schedule would allow. Some suspected he'd commuted from London on the charter twice a week, as he seemed to appear as you'd expect a butler might from time to time.

It was during one of his brief sojourns that Edmonton insisted on taking Elliot for drinks at a bar above Taxi Square.

As they came to the top of the marble staircase, Edmonton recognized a woman and her companion sitting at a table on the balcony.

"There's that awful Turi woman," he said to Elliot.

Elliot knew from their first meeting not to put much faith in Edmonton's prissy comments, as it was his nature to criticize even the best of people.

Then under his breath Edmonton added, "She used to go with my friend Emily, before she malevolently dumped her for the woman she's with now."

Elliot chose to take in the view of the harbor instead.

"Well, hello!" Edmonton said in his falsely overacted vibrato.

"Edmonton?" the woman said, surprised to see him. It was as if the life had gone out of her. He was obviously the last person she'd expected to see on the island.

"Do you mind if we join you?" he asked, as he quickly pulled up a chair without waiting for a response.

Elliot witnessed an immediate discomfort on the woman's face.

"I'm sorry. We were just about to leave. But you can have the table."

The women quickly said their goodbyes and departed, their wine glasses still nearly full, insisting they had to meet friends for dinner.

Elliot found his aggressive behavior crass and highly inappropriate, and more fitting for the wounded party than an outsider like himself. He knew in that moment their association in the future would be limited.

The next day while out, Elliot ran into the woman.

"Well, hello," she said.

"Hi!" he was genuinely pleased to see her again.

"I think we have a casual...acquaintance," she said with hesitation.

"That'd be nice if it were actually true. I'm sure we can both agree he's more a casualty than an acquaintance."

"I'm sure the Queen would agree."

If Edmonton was famous for one thing, it was for being tossed out of Buckingham Palace.

"I'm off to meet my girlfriend," she said. "Care to join us?"

Elliot was always looking to add the right people to the mix.

Chapter Six

Warren grudgingly dragged the twin mattress from the extra bed into the narrow exterior entranceway. Then he curled up on it keeping his face to the wall in case Alec went out again. The tension that remained between them could easily heat the cool night island air.

Warren remained dormant, feigning sleep. Though he occasionally fell in and out of it as Alec moved about the room inside. With every sound, he could feel himself drifting further from him.

Alec slipped into bed with his back to the door, his eyes firmly closed to the darkness, unable to sleep. He waited patiently, as he had on numerous nights, hoping Warren would apologetically and passionately crawl in next to him, physically aroused and ready to lessen the distance between them. Regardless of how he felt, Alec still wished that Warren would hold him and whisper he was sorry; however short-lived that sentiment usually proved to be. At least that's what he needed in the moment.

He heard him enter the room. Alec could feel his presence at the foot of the bed as he stood there anxiously contemplating his next move. He even thought to turn and face him, but instead he waited for Warren to utter those words of endearment that he hoped to hear through the silence. Alec listened as he opened the dresser drawer and began rustling through it as if looking for something. Alec knew the night air had no doubt brought a chill with it. So, he assumed he was getting a pullover. But he also suspected he might be packing. Alec was about to turn and look, when he heard a long, steady stream of urine hit the toilet. He could picture Warren standing over it, as he usually did, leaning into the wall with one arm outstretched, drunk or sober; playfully rupturing the waterline and the surfacing bubbles as a small boy might. When the stream finally faded, he heard the toilet flush. He listened as he came back into the room. Alec changed his breathing so that Warren would think he was sleeping peacefully and not troubled by their recent disagreement. But Alec also knew that he was trying to imitate noises only a lover would know. So, he changed his breathing yet again. But with each questionable, and rehearsed breath, Alec could hear his step hesitate as if contemplating crawling in with him, until Alec heard him leave the room and the quiet return once again. The same quiet that his acute hearing had waited to break moments ago. But all he heard now was the sound of his heart in his ear as it pounded repeatedly through the pillow beneath his head. Shortly after, he heard Warren restlessly adjust himself on the mattress in the doorway again.

Warren remained quiet and still in the late August night breeze with just a thin sheet to cover him; though only barely, as he hoped to keep his sex ready and teasingly available to Alec as he fussed about inside. The familiar sounds were unmistakably those of a five-year relationship. He also knew Alec could be unpredictable, as he'd learned through the years as they held each other in the night.

Warren listened to every move he made as he went about the room; even acutely listening as he used the toilet. But in his strained and solitary concentration, Warren finally drifted off into a deep sleep just as he might while watching television.

The room remained still. Only the wind whirled gently across the island as the morning sun started to challenge the dark sky. And with it came the harsh and unmistakable reality, one that would force them to reluctantly lean into one another again. But even under the circumstances, they were no less angry than they'd been the night before. In fact, the distance between them now would only widen with time. But as with any loss, not unlike death, in that moment they needed one another. Regardless though, they still held the other responsible.

"The bastard took everything we had: our passports, credit cards, cash; even my fucking cigarettes. He pissed on us, and I listened while he did it. I listened to every drop. I even waited for him to shake it off, picturing it was you."

"I'm touched." But Alec could see by the look on Warren's face that his words had been misconstrued as sarcasm. The truth was, Alec could still taste the resentment in his own mouth from the previous day, so he couldn't be exactly sure how he'd meant it himself now.

He let it go.

Warren was too distracted by their situation in that moment to bother to respond. He was more concerned with their being left with nothing; not even airline tickets, which meant an inevitable ferry ride to Piraeus, and the brutal inconvenience of returning to Athens, which they both found insufferable.

Chapter Seven

There's something to be said about a place that name's its wind as if it were a time-honored saint or cherished lover caught in the historic depths of mythology, as it blows the antediluvian dust through the veins of its narrow streets, stirring up time; time and time again.

Later that morning Alec met Evan at the café on the harbor.

"Kalimera."

Evan still felt the previous evening lingering in his throat. And he kept his eyes hidden behind his sunglasses hoping they'd defend him against the harshness of the bright sun.

"Nothing good about this morning," Alec said.

"Is it Warren again?"

"Yes, and usually. But it's worse than that. We got burgled last night."

"What'd they get?"

"Everything. Including what was left of our relationship."

Evan suspected that there wasn't much of it to salvage. So, he decided against saying anything.

"Was it broken into when you got home last night?"

"It happened while we slept. I knew this trip to the island was doomed from the start, without being burgled in our sleep. Or in our stubbornness, as we both lay there unable to sleep."

"Quiet buggers. They expect us to be passed out at that hour."

"Aren't we usually?"

Evan ignored the change in his demeanor.

"I feel as if I've been dragged back to the scene of a crime."

"I don't understand."

"I wasn't sure I wanted to come this season, especially with how things are at home," he said, though perhaps more rehearsed than true.

Evan listened.

"I don't even recognize myself. I'm lost in this bloody relationship, and not in a good way. At least not in the way you're supposed to be. Before we came away Warren said he wanted to recapture the magic we had here. But this island is not the place for that, and how we got away with it for this long is surprising. I love the island, but when you fall-out with someone you can just as easily fall-out with the place that tied you together. Otherwise, you're bound beyond reason."

"What are you saying?"

"I'm saying the burglary might have been a blessing."

"This island was yours long before you met Warren."

"But I'm not so sure I can come back again without him now. It's been a big part of us. It'll take time before I think about coming back again."

"You have a life here. It's how we spend our summers."

"But there comes a time when you have to change your routine."

Alec's words seemed final.

Evan witnessed numerous breakups on the island over the years, but he never expected he'd lose a friendship over one.

"Here they come," Evan said, giving Alec a heads-up.

It was noticeably awkward when Warren chose to sit across from Alec, and not next to him as he usually would. Then without even acknowledging him, Warren said, "I guess he told you what happened?"

"He did. The island's not always the paradise we think it is."

"Was it ever?" Warren said, with a trace of disgust in his voice.

Alec listened as his life seemed to collapse in front of him.

"These guys come from war-torn countries," Elliot interjected. "They think nothing of taking what we have. And even someone as tough as you probably wouldn't be a match for some of these characters."

"There was just the one," Warren affirmed matter-of-factly. "And given the opportunity, I assure you the outcome would have been different."

"It would seem they've imported a desperate, if not impoverished lot, to do their dirty work this season," Evan added. "The Greeks insist on hiring cheap labor, but they never consider the consequences. And I'd be surprised if the guy didn't have a weapon on him."

They were fit men, and coincidentally, both had been rowers in college. Warren was especially impressive with his shirt stretched tightly across his large, muscular chest. Alec was only slighter in comparison.

"I'm not saying that you couldn't have turned things around on the guy. But if put on the spot, I'm certain he'd have thought nothing of killing you. That's why he was so bold."

Evan's words caused a chill to run through Alec.

Warren remained defiant.

"He had balls, I'll give him that. To step over me on his way in and out, took guts."

The others knew, given the opportunity, Warren would step over Alec whenever possible. So, the irony of the situation didn't escape them. In fact, they'd have considered it karma if Alec hadn't been involved. But they also knew that holiday friendships lacked the same resilience as those at home, so rather than complicate things, they decided against saying anything.

Instead Evan asked, "Were you both asleep?"

"I was out like a light," Warren lied, without looking at Alec.

Alec knew if he challenged him, it would only create more problems.

"They have nothing to lose," Elliot said. "They're without conscience."

"I can be without conscience too," Warren said angrily.

"It certainly gives a bit insight into the hardship of other cultures," Alec offered, reflecting on Elliot's earlier words about foreign labor.

"It has nothing to do with being impoverished. It's just the nature of their culture," Warren said in bitter resolve. "They're gypsies."

His comment brought an awkward silence to the table.

Evan got up.

"I'm going to buy gifts for Alec's family. Will you be here?"

Elliot caught Evan's eye, agreeing it would be best to separate the two. "You guys go. We'll catch up with you later."

Alec left without as much as a wave.

When they were gone, Warren stated with indifference, "That chair's as empty now as it was when he was sitting in it."

"You'll work it out. You always do." Though Elliot knew there wasn't much truth in his words.

"We barely made it past our first fight here. How can two people be so intimate and still feel nothing for each other? Alec is a different person now. You have to admit he's different."

"Alec is Alec," Elliot insisted. "I don't see that he's changed."

"You don't know him as I do. The person I knew has changed."

Elliot decided to let it go. But Warren still needed to vent.

"I should have expected he'd let something like this happen."

"You were both there," Elliot said in Alec's defense.

"It was an inside job. He should've been aware of what was going on in the room."

Elliot wanted to point out that he'd let the guy walk over him, not once, but twice. But he decided to let that go. Just as he decided not to attempt to salvage Alec's relationship for him again.

The morning wind began to pick up. Elliot held onto his frappé.

"You'll need new passports," Elliot said changing the subject.

"We're taking the last ferry on Sunday."

"It'll be packed with Athenians going back after the weekend."

Warren ran the itinerary through his head again.

"After we get our passports and some money, I also need to change our flight."

"You're not coming back?" Elliot said feigning surprise.

"I'm not. I don't think Alec will be either."

"You still have a couple of weeks left."

"It wouldn't be much of a holiday."

"What about next year?"

"We won't be here next year," he said.

His words had a curious finality to them.

Chapter Eight

Colin and Martin were sitting alone on the rooftop lounge over-looking the square, taking in the full view of the harbor.

"This is one of my favorite spots on the island," Martin said. "It's also the best place to watch meteor showers."

It was a moonless night and the stars were in full bloom.

"I'm surprised it's not more crowded up here," Colin said regarding the empty tables.

"It's too removed from the action. But that's also why I like it."

The lights in town began to flicker and dim. A moment later some went out completely, which made the stars shine even brighter.

"That's the fourth brownout this season," Colin said.

"It's election year. They know their demands will be taken seriously."

"I like it better with the lights out and without the music."

"I especially like the wind up here," Martin said.

"That's probably another reason why it's empty."

"They complain about the wind until it stops. Then when the humidity returns, they pray for it."

"Like so many things in life."

They could only hear the wind now.

"Do you think Alec and Warren will return after they sort things out in Athens?" Martin asked into the quiet darkness.

"I doubt Warren will. But I hope Alec does."

"I wouldn't want to travel with Warren under the circumstances."

"I wouldn't want to travel with Warren, period."

Their words were lifted into the wind.

A moment later, Turi stuck her head in thru the rooftop doorway.

"Are you coming down? The show's about to start."

"But there's no electricity. No music."

"Honey, they did drag centuries before electricity. Clitty's going to sing a cappella by candle-light," Turi said.

Martin stole a glance at the stars.

"Hurry!" she said, as she disappeared back thru the portal.

"I think I'll stay up here. I'm enjoying the quiet," Martin said.

"If you don't mind, I'll keep you company."

They leaned into one another.

Chapter Nine

The next morning, they waited at the Blue Chairs for the others.

"Your problem is, you're too considerate."

"Is that even possible?"

"Absolutely."

"Maybe I'm too sensitive. But I doubt one can be too considerate."

"You sacrifice too much of yourself being considerate."

"Isn't that the point, to surrender a part of yourself?"

Warren gave him a cold stare.

"Like saying please," Alec continued.

"I only say please if I'm asking someone to pleasure me."

"You can't possibly live like that?"

"Of course, I can."

"Please is asking something from someone; not a demand to fulfill your wishes."

"It would seem we live different lives."

"And thank you?"

"I never use it. It goes against my nature."

"Excuse me?"

"I might use that if I accidentally run into someone."

"I think you missed my point."

"Probably not."

Alec no longer recognized the man sitting across from him.

"How did I miss this flaw in you?" he asked, though he didn't expect an answer. He knew his physical attraction had played a big part in it.

The others appeared from out of the narrow street behind them.

Alec saw no reason to change the topic of conversation. In fact, he felt a need now to share this recent development in his five-year relationship.

"We were just arguing about when to say please and thank you," Alec said, when they finally settled in.

"We weren't arguing. We were discussing."

They all knew the consequences of conversing with Warren.

Elliot took a different angle on the topic.

"I always found it interesting that the only words most Americans learn in a foreign language when they travel abroad are the same ones they forget to use at home. Like thank you, please, and you're welcome. Then they beat them to death."

"Then they think they're fluent," Evan added.

"That's because they have no respect for each other back home," Alec said. "They're forced to use basic considerations again on the island."

"Respect is mandatory," Evan agreed. "We're guests here."

"No wonder it's a battlefield back home," Colin said.

"That has more to do with poverty," Warren added.

They ignored his opinion.

"You've allowed our language to deteriorate." Evan joked to Elliot.

"Not one person said thank you while I was in Florida," Martin added. "It's not much better in London, either, to tell you the truth."

"You only say thank you if someone saves your life," Warren said.

They quietly digested that, but no one could get it down properly.

"Poverty isn't the cause of your crassness," Elliot finally said.

Warren didn't respond. But Elliot knew that his words weren't received well nonetheless. He also knew that something else had caused Warren to be so cynical.

"People feel humiliated when forced to be considerate, as if doing so was emasculating," Alec said.

"You're just too sensitive," Warren said.

"I'll get by, thank you," Alec said sharply. His tone surprised everyone. It was obvious it didn't sit well with Warren either.

Elliot felt the need to rescue the conversation.

"I should probably mention that there are drugs amongst us. And a drug dealer," he said lightheartedly.

"Really?" someone whispered.

They looked at one another.

"What drugs?" someone asked.

"Not good," Warren said sternly. "Not on this island."

"Who is it? And how'd they get them here?" Colin whispered again.

"I always wondered how Candida got X onto the island," Alec said.

"Candida? Really?" Warren's tone was even angrier now.

"That was ten years ago. Besides, I was a younger man then."

Warren just stared at him.

"We did X in London. But it was always nice to get away from it here," Evan said.

"It's been here for a long time," Alec added.

"So, who's the drug dealer, and what drugs?" Warren asked.

"I guess that would be me," Evan confessed.

"Yes, it would." Elliot smiled.

"What did you bring?" Warren asked.

"Vicodin, for Elliot. He's an addict. He's been in and out of rehab like everyone else in California."

Elliot smiled.

"The question is, what to do with them? Should I just toss them?"

"I could use them," Warren said. "In case I get another migraine."

"You haven't had a migraine in years," Alec challenged.

"I think I'm getting one right now."

"I'll get them to you later," Elliot said. But he wasn't happy with the idea. Then he jokingly added, "The usual price."

Warren attempted a smile, but his mind was already elsewhere.

Chapter Ten

"When did this beach get so crowded," Turi asked as they fought their way through the overpopulated sand.

"I forgot it was Saturday. We shouldn't have come to this one," Doreen said. "The Athenians invade this beach every weekend."

"Who keeps track of what day it is while on holiday?" Colin asked as he tagged along behind.

"Women do," Turi affirmed.

Colin looked confused.

"It would have been quieter on the other side of the island," Doreen offered.

"We're here now, so we might as well find a spot and settle in," her girlfriend said.

"I think there's one over there." Evan pointed.

He spread his towel out in the light breeze.

"Do you think it was a good idea to give those drugs to Warren?"

"Probably not," Elliot confessed. "In fact, the more I think about it, the more I think it was a mistake."

"Maybe he'll take one or two and change his disposition."

"It'll take more than that," Turi said.

Elliot was barely able to squeeze his towel between Turi and a guy with a rich tan who was sleeping.

"Candida would never find a spot for her king-size sheet here," Elliot said, slipping out of his shorts.

"But she was always the first to arrive," Turi said assuredly.

"The girl never slept," Doreen said closing her eyes to the sun.

"I'm sure she's doing just fine in Ibiza then," Turi added.

"Does my back still look British?" Evan asked.

Doreen blindly brushed her hand against it.

"You just need to find a nice woman and get off it more."

The guy sleeping next to Elliot started to breathe deeply as a thin smile came over his handsome face. Just then, his penis slowly became erect until it towered like a sundial.

"That must be one hell of a dream," Turi whispered to Elliot, nodding her head toward the phallus.

"I wouldn't mind being in that dream," Colin quietly added.

Elliot was inspired by the strength of it. But he was more curious about the image that had aroused him so fully.

"We need to talk about Alec," Doreen insisted, her eyes still closed to the sun, unaware of the activity a couple of towels over. "We can't allow him to just leave."

"The whole thing's insane," Evan said, his back still to them and the sun. "Especially being burgled like that."

No one responded.

"Hello?" Doreen said. "We should talk about rescuing Alec. The island won't be the same without him."

There was still no response.

The bronzed god also had Evan's attention now.

"Is anyone listening?" she asked, her eyes still closed. When she finally did sit up and turn around, Doreen immediately screamed "Turi!" when she caught sight of the monolith sticking up firmly from out of the sand.

"It's not me, babe," her girlfriend replied. "Though it does look like my doppelgänger."

The erection slowly made its way back to earth, bouncing gently with each rhythmic pulse as the blood drained from it. Until it finally rested on the side of his muscular thigh, his pubic hair glistening like gold thread in the sunlight.

"Now look what you've done," Colin said.

"Me?" Doreen blushed.

"I'm still hard," her girlfriend teased as she reclined on her towel again.

The disco music blasted loudly.

"This is not the same place that I scattered my mother's ashes ten years ago," Elliot said looking around at the crowded sand.

"It was so peaceful then," Evan confirmed.

"And undiscovered," Doreen added, having recovered from her case of mistaken identity.

"I never expected it to change so drastically."

Elliot wore the disappointment on face now as he recalled that last day on the island years earlier when he'd scattered his mother's ashes.

He'd driven up the steep summit with his friend Riki, who ran a small, intimate tavern in town. Elliot feared for his life as the open jeep made the dubious climb, bouncing about on the dusty broken dirt road as they rode dangerously close to the edge of the cliff. Though once at the top, it seemed almost spiritual as the view spread out before them across the clear horizon.

"I bought you something to say thank you for doing this with me."

Riki opened the box to find a thin gold necklace with a dancer in flight attached to it.

"It's beautiful," she said. "Thank you."

"I'm sorry you never got to meet her. You would have liked her."

"I'm sure I would have."

Then he braced himself as he cautiously opened the porcelain container with his mother's ashes. Elliot expected to find pieces of black broken bone. Instead, he discovered tiny white crystals that blended with the cliff he stood on, as if destined for that very spot on Earth. Then he gently tilted the ashes toward the edge and slowly sprinkled them into the air. Just then the wind picked up, and unexpectedly blew them onto Riki's face.

"Your mother has a sense of humor," she said, gently wiping her eyes and mouth.

"I forgot to mention that."

"I hope your mother likes euro-disco," Colin said.

What had once been a serene and pristine stretch of white sand, was now lined with umbrellas, sun beds, and piped-in music.

"I pray the Gods took her to a quieter place," Elliot said as he stared at the blue water stretching toward Paros and Naxos.

"It might be time to discover a new island," Evan offered.

"But this one is so familiar," Colin said.

"That too will change eventually," Elliot said, a sadness in his voice.

The slender tan figure beside Elliot began to slowly come to life. As he stretched his arms out with a yawn, he accidentally struck Elliot.

"Sorry," he said, surprised to find someone sitting so close. "There was no one here when I arrived." Then looking around, he added, "Now it looks like Jones Beach."

"You're from The States?" Elliot asked.

"Unless you're the tax man. Then I'm Canadian."

"So, you're also working here?"

"Just to get me through the summer."

Elliot introduced himself and the others.

Jeremy had a natural glow to his smile.

"Have you been here the whole summer?"

"Only about a month. I'd hoped to get to Greece a few years ago. But I got unexpectedly involved in Rome, which altered any plans that I had."

"Love's an acceptable diversion," Elliot said. "Assuming it was love."

"It's all about letting the diversions take you where they will."

"I was about to have lunch. Would you like to join me?"

"Absolutely."

"Are you hungry?" he asked the others as he and Jeremy dressed.

"You guys go. We'll catch up," Turi said.

"I don't think that'll work out," Evan offered after they left.

"Shame too. Such nice equipment," Colin added.

They took a table by the water.

"Has it changed as much as you said? It would seem I missed the best of the island."

"I thought you were sleeping?"

"I woke when you mentioned your mother."

"No wonder you lost your erection."

"I thought I dreamt that part."

Jeremy showed no sign of embarrassment.

224

"The island is ripe for interesting dreams," Elliot offered.

"It must be the mythology."

"Something like that."

"So, what's good here?"

"Besides mythology? The horiatiki, and the skordalia, which used to be difficult to find. In fact, until recently, I had to go all the way to Tinos for it. It's more a peasant dish. Which I'm sure didn't appeal to the jet-set crowd. And of course, the calamari, which they knock out fresh daily."

They pointed to the dishes they wanted from the display case.

"Tell me more about the island."

"It's certainly not your typical island. And along with Delos, its history runs deep. It's also notorious for its drastic, if not unusual changes. I don't just mean new roads and buildings. Though they did recently construct a new town. In fact, an entire side of the island that was once dark and invisible at night, is lit up like a cruise ship now. But there are also seasonal changes as well, which are usually the result of the gambling that goes on here during the winter when nearly everything is closed and boarded up; when it's more like a ghost town. That's when money and property unexpectedly change hands. For example, when I first arrived, there was an outdoor cinema in town. Which was great for catching the occasional film al fresco. But then the following year, they turned it into a swimming pool. That was nice as well. Especially when you're too hungover to get to the beach. But then it got real Greek. Shortly after arriving one year, we went to the pool and discovered it was an antique store. But instead of covering the pool, it was drained and filled with furniture. It's now a restaurant."

"In the pool?"

"Nothing that creative. They built a bridge over it and put tables on it. But the blue water at night is a nice effect."

"Can you still swim in it?"

"It's never that logical."

"That seems a waste."

"This is Greece. You never know what to expect."

"Except the bearing of gifts, which I hear they're famous for."

"Even that can get comical. At the end of each season, I usually receive several gifts. One from the woman whose house I rent for two months. One from the woman where I rent my scooter. And one from the proprietor of the café that we inhabit during our stay. One year, I received the same gift from all three women."

"What a strange coincidence. What was it?"

"Windmills. I'm sure you've seen them. They're large and fragile, with delicate white sheets. To make it even more problematic, I received all three the morning of my flight. So, I had no time to ship them. Not that I'd be able to anyway. I suspect few make it off the island, as it's impossible to travel with them. Of course, they make a wonderful gift if you live here. But I'm guessing most end up back on the shelves in Matyianni Street."

"What did you end up doing with them?"

"I stored them in a friend's attic who lived here year around. Sadly, he passed away that winter. So, who knows what happened to them."

"They'd be nice in a window back home."

"It would probably be easier to bring the home here instead, though."

"It sounds like you've made this your home."

"During the summer, at least."

He instinctively knew that Jeremy wasn't gay. Regardless, Elliot leaned in anyway, for the attraction he felt was undeniable. In fact, it was as if he'd been pulled into an alternate universe, Though one strangely familiar. And it wasn't just the impressive erection that had lured him, but something more intrinsic, more visceral. Besides, he was still curious what caused Jeremy to swell so nicely on the beach. Elliot was surprised then, when he volunteered that very image.

"Adelia continues to tempt me in my dreams. And even more so in the summer heat."

"Like a succubus?"

"Time demonizes even the best of us." He offered a smile. "Sometimes I even see smoke and hear bells."

"That's quite the effect. I'm sure there's a literary or religious reference buried in there somewhere."

"I was living in Rome when the pope died. We woke that morning with every church bell in the city echoing the news. It was non-stop. Until the white smoke finally appeared three days later."

"I find sex trumps religion. Or I should say, love does."

"Sex is a close second. We stayed in bed those three days."

Jeremy leaned over and kissed Elliot lightly and briefly on the lips.

"I had to do. I'm sure you understand."

Elliot understood. Just as he knew that words would have ruined it. He also knew it didn't change his sexual orientation, because it had been more than that.

Just then the others came up from the beach.

"I've always loved this spot," Doreen said pulling a chair into the shade next to them.

"But it's too crowded," Turi reaffirmed.

"Elliot was just telling me how the island has changed."

"Ruined is more like it," Turi said.

"She has a few good years left in her," Doreen added with optimism, as if talking about a woman holding onto her beauty.

"We should venture out and discover another island," Evan said.

"For now, let's have some wine instead," Elliot insisted.

226

Chapter Eleven

"Remember to get rid of those pills. It would be unfortunate if you tried to get on a plane with them," Elliot said.

"I already took care of it. It wasn't difficult to find an interested party on this island."

Elliot didn't like the idea of having helped facilitate the spread of drugs on the island. He wished now that he'd just thrown them away.

"In fact, it helped with the boat tickets. So, I owe you."

"That's drug money. I wipe my hands of it."

Elliot offered a failed smile.

Just then, Alec rejoined them.

"That's everything. I double checked."

"It couldn't have been difficult. We have less than when we arrived."

"It didn't seem like it."

"You bring too much shit anyway," Warren said.

"We should get this stuff to the car," Elliot insisted.

The ride down the hill was quiet. Even the port seemed strangely silent when it finally came into view.

The turquoise water glistened in the distance.

At the waterfront, engine smoke filled the late afternoon air. The sound of heavy chains shattered its tranquility as two men secured the ferry to the cleats imbedded in the stone wall.

When the stern, which doubled as a vehicle ramp was finally lowered, a steady stream of cars and motorcycles slowly boarded. Once loaded, a cast of backpackers ascended.

"Have a good trip," Elliot said with dubious encouragement. Though he doubted they'd survive the six-hour journey without killing one another.

"I intend to sleep the entire way to Piraeus," Warren stated. "Then after we sort things out, it's straight to the airport. I have no desire to hang around Athens."

Alec refrained from commenting on the itinerary, knowing once he got his passport and some money he'd be free to do whatever he wanted.

"Goodbye Elliot," Warren said without even offering his hand. "I doubt we'll see each other again."

Elliot welcomed the sentiment, and hoped his words held true. The two had never been close. In fact, they usually found themselves at odds. Warren had been little more than an unfortunate consequence of what Elliot had considered an erroneous relationship. But he'd always be curious what kept them together for nearly five years. He hoped it wasn't just his superficial good looks. He wanted to give Alec more credit than that.

Elliot failed to see the change in Alec that Warren mentioned earlier, but what he did see in that moment was an obvious pain in his eyes.

Warren grabbed his bags and headed toward the ferry. Without turning around, he shouted, "Say goodbye."

Alec hugged Elliot.

"I'll miss you. I'll call you when you get home."

"It won't be the same without you here. You know that, right?"

"Thanks."

Alec squeezed him tightly.

"You better come back next year."

"We'll see."

"And be sure to come alone," Elliot whispered in his ear.

"I promise," he said pulling away.

Warren shouted, "Don't miss the boat, Alec!"

"If only that were possible," he said grabbing his bags. But then he put them down again and gave Elliot another hug.

"I may be back in a couple of days without him. We'll see."

Then he ran toward the ferry with tears in his eyes.

The ramp closed with a loud bang, and the cleats were cleared.

Elliot watched the ferry fade into the distant horizon, wondering if he'd ever see Alec again.

Chapter Twelve

Alec considered his limited options as he patiently waited for Warren to finish his business at the American Express Office.

"I have enough cash for both of us. There's no need to get any."

His generous offer took Alec by surprise. For a moment, he thought he recognized the man he'd fallen in love with. But he questioned his motives since he never knew Warren to be magnanimous. He suspected it had more to do with being in control again.

"I'd still like some pocket money."

"Hurry. We don't want to miss our flight. We changed it once already. And it wasn't cheap."

Now that was the Warren he knew, Alec thought.

There remained a heavy military presence at the airport. Armored tanks were anchored at every entrance. Soldiers patrolled the perimeter even years after the TWA hijacking.

Alec was immediately pulled aside at customs.

"Did you pack your own bags, sir?" the woman asked.

"Yes," he replied casually.

"Has anyone given you anything to carry for them?"

"No."

The woman looked at him closely.

Alec's natural response was to smile. But he knew better than to expose that emotion to unfamiliar Greeks.

"Are you traveling alone, sir?"

"No, I'm traveling with...." But when Alec turned around Warren was gone. Perhaps he chose to abandon him there after all, he thought.

"You look nervous, sir," the woman said, her voice thick and deep with that tonal quality some Greek women have when they speak English.

"I'm confused. I'm traveling with my boyfriend. But he seems to have disappeared. Did someone pull him aside as well?"

"Not that I know of, sir," the woman said, without showing concern or prejudice. "There was no one behind you," she added.

"But he was right here," he said looking around again.

"Please open your bags, sir,"

Alec had been pulled aside several times while traveling to Greece. So, he was no stranger to this exchange. He opened his carry-on first. Then with tight rubber gloves, the woman worked her way through it thoroughly. Once she was satisfied, she closed it.

"And the other, sir?"

Alec lifted the larger bag onto the table.

"It's mostly dirty laundry," he said apologetically.

Customs was nearly empty, and there was still no sign of Warren.

The woman tossed his tank tops, shorts, and swimwear, into a stirred heap as her arm dug into his bag. A pair of briefs fell to the floor, which he quickly retrieved.

"What are these, sir?" she asked.

He immediately recognized the bottle, which he'd meant to put it in his carry-on.

"It's a prescription for Valium. I take them to fly."

The woman shook the bottle as she held it to the florescent light. Then opened it to check them.

"So then, you are nervous," she said.

"Of flying, yes," he replied.

She continued searching his suitcase.

"And these, sir?"

He was startled to see her holding up a plastic bag.

"I'm not sure what that is," Alec said nearly losing his breath. "I didn't put that in my suitcase."

"But you said you packed your own bag, sir," she reminded him.

"Yes, but I didn't put that in my bag!" His voice desperate now.

"Do you have a prescription for these as well, sir?"

"I'm not sure what they are," he lied, instantly recognizing them as the Vicodin Elliot had given Warren.

"Come with me, sir," she said. "This way, please."

She took him by the arm and escorted him. A uniformed man came up from behind and closed the bag and followed her lead. Two others appeared at her side.

As Alec was being led away, he recalled Warren asking while he was shaving that morning if he had room in his bag.

"Put whatever you need in the large suitcase," he recalled saying now, thinking even then that the exchange had been surprisingly lighthearted.

Warren smiled through his reflection in the mirror.

"I always seem to leave with more than I bring," he said.

As Alec was led away he caught a brief glimpse of Warren on the other side, having no doubt passed through customs without incident. But now he was shaking his head with what was obviously a fated smile on his face.

"Why would you do this?" Alec cried out.

But Warren quickly disappeared into the crowd.

As the door closed behind him, the sound echoed with chilling finality; one that reaffirmed what he had feared, that he'd gone beyond his intended destination.

Island Aftertones

Chapter Thirteen

Caught in a Corridor

Still the devout, adolescent altar boy at heart, Leo caught Elliot just as he was heading out the door.

"Where you're going?" he asked catching him fully by the sleeve of his jacket.

"I shouldn't be here," Elliot insisted, as if he were losing a battle inside his head. "I have to go."

"Are you kidding? Everyone's waiting for you."

"I can't put a face on for this," he said slipping out of Leo's grip.

"Death doesn't always demand a face," his friend solemnly said. "But it does need for you to be here."

He respectfully lowered his voice.

"I can't do this, Leo. My being here will only cause even more damage than my absence will. Believe me. Besides, no one wants me here."

"Are you kidding? What do you think they're going on about in there? They're all asking, 'Where's Elliot?' 'Isn't Elliot coming?' You're part of the family. You're needed here. The room would feel vacant without you."

"I doubt they're saying anything favorable. And I'm sure they created their own scenarios about what happened, and why I'm not in there."

"No one's saying anything bad. Especially in church," Leo said.

"I'm sure they're thinking it."

"I doubt that as well."

Leo put a comforting arm over Elliot's shoulder.

"How's Ryan?" Elliot asked. "Is he inside?"

"He has a friend visiting from Buffalo."

"Must be important for him not to be here."

"The living can be just as demanding as the dead. Besides, Ryan didn't know Hugh as well as we did. But right now, this is where you need to be."

"I thought to slip in the back without anyone noticing. But now I think it's just better that I leave."

"You can't do that, Elliot."

"You don't understand," he said.

"I understand that Rose is upset and feels you abandoned Hugh at the end. She said it was as if you dumped him back in The States after your trip to Greece, and just walked away."

"That's exactly what I did."

"Regardless, she'll be glad to see you even if she doesn't understand why you weren't with Hugh at the end."

Elliot watched the words come at him. They hurt. But they should hurt, he thought. He deserved every bit of their pain.

"I walked him most of the way there. I just couldn't be there when the end came. Hugh knew that. I doubt he expected me to be there either."

"I thought it strange that he never asked why you didn't visit him in the hospital. But I think he hoped you'd be there all the same. We all did."

Elliot had often imagined that day. In fact, he still had a vivid image of Hugh laying there as he balanced between life and death. He could see the light and the shadows of the room. He even pictured the bright sun through the hospital window casting a last glow on his face as he finally let go; his brow calm, his lips at peace, while his closed eyes were focused on eternity.

"At least talk to Rose. She needs some closure."

"I know," he said, shaking his head. "But I can't." Elliot felt every bone in his body tighten and twist, ready to break. "She'd never understand."

"You need to give her something. She has nothing now. She needs you. She needs you to help her heal. She needs you to tell her whatever it is she doesn't understand."

"There's nothing I can say that will make it better. What I'd say would only make it worse."

"Tell me, then. I'm at a loss here too. Help me understand."

"It's about loss, isn't it? Especially today." Elliot closed his eyes as he pinched his fingers at the bridge of his nose. Then he brought his hand over his mouth, cupping it, as if to capture the words before they involuntarily escaped. "It wasn't by choice," Elliot finally said. "You have to understand, it was a mess at the end. A lot died before Hugh did." He paused. Then in an emotional burst he said, "I can't do this here!"

"What could possibly have torn you two apart? You were so close. You were like brothers."

Setting his eyes on Leo, he nodded. Then he said, "We were brothers. I was closer to him than I'd ever been to anyone. But on that last trip it fell apart. It started even before that, while we were in Montreal the previous summer. But in Greece it completely fell apart."

"He told me you guys had a great time in Montreal. And an even better time in Greece."

"We did. In the beginning. In New York. And on the way to Montreal. The drive was fine. The stops were great. But Hugh crossed-over on the first night we got to Canada."

"What do you mean he crossed-over?"

"I told you how he tried to jump from the car while I was driving over the bridge one night when we were coming back from the city."

"I remember you saying you had to tie him into the seat after you left a party because he was acting crazy. Did he really try to jump out of the car?"

"I'd never seen anything like it. He was out of his mind. It was as if he were fighting his way out of his own head to escape himself. If I hadn't tied him in he'd have been road kill. In fact, his face was so red and distorted that you'd have thought it already took some ground."

"And what happened in Montreal?"

"He was even crazier when we got to Montreal. He crossed-over again. Though this time his anger wasn't just self-destructive, he also focused it on me. He became viciously hateful. I thought for sure he was going to hit me. It's not like me to want to take anyone out. But I readied myself for just that. I was even ready to bust a hand if I had to."

"I'm sure a single shot would have done it. I can't imagine it would've been a problem."

"But I'm not sure how many hits I'd have taken before I had the heart to give him one back."

"You loved the guy."

"Like nothing I'd ever experienced. It was everything but physical. Not that I didn't want that as well in the beginning. But eventually it turned into something stronger, more a brotherly love. So, I knew I'd take his punches. And probably as many as he had before I'd land one on him."

Elliot brought his words back to a whisper as he found his voice getting louder in the quiet church corridor.

"What do you think made him cross-over like that?"

"I wasn't sure at first. Looking back now, it should have been obvious. It wasn't until we got to Greece that it occurred to me that when he stopped taking his meds he seemed more balanced. Like his old self. But then of course, he'd get sick again. One thing you don't want, is to get sick on that island. All they can do there is plaster a broken leg if you have a scooter accident. They're artists in that respect. Anything more serious and they have to airlift you to Athens by helicopter."

"He went off his meds in Greece?"

"After he met a boy named Stathis, he decided to trade his health in for a proper hard-on."

"Did he also go off his meds in Montreal?"

"Not as much. But that's because he didn't plan on using his dick while we were there. After the first night, he decided that he wasn't attracted to French-Canadians. So, it didn't matter. He found them rude and pompous. He also didn't speak French. At least in Greece they speak English."

"So, he turned violent in Montreal?"

"He came close. When we got back to the hotel after our first night out, he was drunk and shouting all kinds of shit at me. I was sure he was going to take a swing at me. But he never got a chance."

"What'd you do?"

"I didn't do anything. I turned to get a cigarette off the night stand and the next thing I knew he was passed out on the floor."

"It must have been a bitch getting him into bed."

"I imagine it would've if I'd bothered."

"You left him there?"

"He was being such a bastard I let him sleep on the floor."

"You're kidding?"

"He went down on his own and I left him there, undeclared."

Leo tried not to smile.

"Like you said, you never hit him."

"I knew it would piss him off. Because after we checked in, he told me how incredible the sheets on the bed were, and how he couldn't wait to get into them when we got back later that night. He even buried his face into the pillow like a little kid hugging a security blanket."

"They were that nice?"

"The room cost a dollar per thread count. It was one of the best sleeps I've ever had. And I really didn't mind spending the money."

"Why'd you book something so expensive?"

"I originally booked a hotel across town. But he thought it was too far from St. Catherine's Street. But I got a more reasonable hotel the next day."

"So, he never got to sleep in those sheets? I imagine he was furious."

"He accused me of leaving him there on the floor when I knew he was looking forward to sleeping in that bed. I told him I fell asleep while he was still in the bathroom."

"And he bought that?"

"I knew he wouldn't remember. That was the one good thing about his crossing-over. He never remembered it. If he did, I'm sure it would've killed him."

"I've never heard of anyone going crazy like that on meds."

"I guess people react differently. Especially when mixed with alcohol. Because it obviously caused a chemical imbalance."

"It's better he didn't remember. How bad did it get in Greece?"

"It was worse on the island. We were there two months. And if you do anything there, it's drink. But when he went off his meds, he got sick. It was bad."

"What happened?"

"We weren't sure at first. He'd been off his meds for a couple of days. One night instead of going out, he decided to stay in bed, so he must have felt something coming on. But everyone gets sick for a day or two there. It's the wind. It eventually gets to you. So, I didn't think too much of it at first. I came back early that night and found him sound asleep. He was out cold like he was on the floor in Montreal, but in bed this time. Sadly, thread count on Greek sheets is in the double digits, though the price doesn't reflect it. At least not on that island. Anyway, I thought he'd feel better after a good night sleep. But sometime in the early morning, Hugh woke up screaming in pain. He couldn't breathe or move. It was scary. He could barely swallow an Ibuprofen."

"Did you get him to the hospital?"

"I immediately went for the doctor since the hospital was closed at that hour. I knocked and waited. I could hear him rustling about on the other side of the door, undoubtedly hoping I'd go away. I knocked again. He eventually opened the door with an erect and recently occupied boner. Because it was still slightly moist. Trying not to stare, I told him my friend was ill, and that he needed to come immediately. But then he said in perfect English, though with an accent as thick as his mustache, 'How sick is your friend?' I told him it was very serious, but his dedication was somewhere else entirely. Because then he said, 'Go see if your friend is still sick. And if so, come back.' Then he closed the door. It was obvious that his priority was to finish whatever I'd interrupted. It was unprofessional, to say the least."

"You didn't kick the door down?"

"I wanted the doctor, not the dick," Elliot said trying to offer a measure of humor in what was otherwise a tragic tale. "Anyway, when I got back to the room Hugh was sitting up and feeling better. Apparently, the Ibuprofen kicked in. He said his side was still sore but that the pain was mostly gone."

"Did you ever find out what it was?"

"When he got back home the doctor said his lung had collapsed."

Elliot listened to the quiet of the corridor. He could smell incense in the air now.

"Whatever came between you must have been serious."

Elliot checked the corridor to make sure it was clear.

The light beveled down through the religiously stained-glass in strong contrast to the shadows below.

"It got bad. Hateful in fact. I never expected him to do what he did, and then lie about it."

"I'm listening," Leo said, preparing himself for a view of the fall.

"Hugh spent the last few weeks of the trip with Stathis, that Greek boy. He was nineteen, and of course cute. But shortly after, he got sick again. Not as bad as that night. It was like the flu. I'm sure he was also congested from not taking his meds."

"I can't believe he'd go off them for that long a period."

"I guess he wanted that boner as much as the doctor. And if you'd seen Stathis, you might have made the same sacrifice."

"It was his choice. You can't blame yourself for that."

"I was responsible for his care, which I was prepared to do. But I wasn't prepared for him to get sick voluntarily."

"I guess going off his meds was like committing suicide."

"It probably was."

"Was that it then? Was that what ended it for you guys?"

"No, it was the look on the boy's face," Elliot said.

"But you said it was beautiful."

"It was that. But it was also scared."

"Why?"

"When Stathis questioned Hugh's health, he told him it was just the flu. Of course, he believed him. At least at first. But I insisted he tell Stathis the truth as it was more likely bronchitis, bordering on pneumonia. He agreed to tell Stathis that he was HIV positive, and that his symptoms were likely a result of that, and probably not the flu. Hugh's intent was to leave his illness back home where he felt it belonged; in that waiting room at his doctor's office. I wouldn't deny him that freedom. In fact, I wanted that for him more than anything. The trip was meant to be liberating. It was the reason he went to the island, to try to escape his diagnoses. If just for a short time. But when he brought that innocent boy into it, the dream began to crack. Until it was no longer a dream, but a nightmare. Several days later Stathis repeated his concern about Hugh's health. It was then I realized he hadn't told Stathis as he'd promised. The boy was still frightened. He'd lived his entire life on that island; one that barely had telephone service at the time. He knew nothing of Hugh's world, or his charts. Or more importantly, the untouched meds at the bottom of his suitcase. It was also his first sexual experience."

"What did you tell him?" Leo was nearly in tears.

Just then Elliot thought he heard someone crying. He expected to see a procession of mourners coming out the chapel. Or perhaps someone running late for the service, coming through the corridor. But the corridor remained empty. Elliot kept a close eye on the door to be certain they were alone.

"The service is probably starting," Leo said.

"I can't stay. I can't tell Rose that her son had unprotected sex with an innocent boy and that he'd purposely lied about it. How else do I explain the distance between us without telling her that? Without hurting her? I don't want hurt Rose. The pain of losing her son is killing her as it is."

"I don't know what to say," Leo whispered, his words drifting off as he felt his limbs go loose.

Elliot held him until his strength returned.

"I remember what Hugh told me when he was first diagnosed."

Leo listened.

"He told me he knew who infected him. That he remembered the night. I asked how he could be certain? He said he just knew, and I'd know too if I were infected. I said it was a cruel and unfounded allegation since he hadn't been previously tested, and there was no point of reference for him to make such a claim. But one thing's certain. If that boy gets infected, he'll know where he got it."

Leo leaned heavily on Elliot.

"I tried to tell him that two-people pulled the trigger the night he was infected. But Hugh refused to listen."

Elliot held Leo.

"Why are we gunning each other down?" Elliot asked, his words filling the empty corridor. "Why do we continue to hear the shots?"

The crying that Elliot heard earlier grew closer and louder now.

In a corner, off the corridor, in one of the shadows away from the light, Rose continued to bang her head violently against the stone wall, unaware of the blood that merged with the tears on her cheek. It was all she could do to help alleviate the pain.

"I'll be back in a minute," Elliot said. "Are you going to be okay?"

"I think so."

"Good. But I need you to stay here."

Elliot walked down the corridor toward the sound.

"Where're you going?"

"To try and rescue a memory. It's all I can do now."

Chapter Fourteen

Roses by The Window

Rose looked at the world through the large window of her living room just as she had a thousand times before. It once held a bright and hopeful, if not promising future.

She silently watched with amusement as the small children danced and played beneath the crystal snowflakes. Rose enviously watched as her friend Alice made a snow angel on the white ground. The other children laughed, as children are supposed to, innocent of the world around them.

Rose sat wrapped in a blanket on the couch in front of the window in her pajamas that day, the chicken soup her mother made her balanced on her lap. Alice waved playfully through the glass again. Rose waved back. She hated being sick when school was out. Especially during the holidays.

Alice made a snowball and attempted to throw it at the window. But she missed. Rose covered her hand over her mouth and giggled. Alice made another snowball, a larger one this time. So, large in fact, that it took both her small gloved hands to toss it, which caused her to lose her balance. Rose watched as the snowball hit the center of the large pane of glass. Then she excitedly jumped off the couch and ran to the window as it turned into slushy snowflakes. She traced its magical path with her delicate finger as it slowly dripped down to the windowsill below.

Then as if in a dream, the snow disappeared, along with Alice.

Rose looked out onto a warm promising spring day.

A handsome young boy on a shiny new bicycle appeared, one sneaker resting on the handlebar, the other on the driveway to keep his balance. Billy smiled up at Rose. And she smiled back, not sure if he could see her through the glare of the early morning sun.

Billy turned on his transistor radio.

'Imagine me and you, I do ...so happy together'.

Rose always loved that song.

A few days later, Billy gave Rose her very first kiss. His thin lips tasted like chocolate milk. And she remembered liking it even more because of it. He also tried putting a nervous hand up her sweater. But Rose was a good Catholic girl, one who didn't roll her pleated skirt up above her knees.

She watched now as his dark attractive bangs blew freely in the gentle wind. Which made her wish now that she'd broken a few more rules back then, and perhaps even sinned a little more. Life might have been different if she had, she thought.

Rose looked over her shoulder into the suffocating room behind her. It immediately took her smile away, as it had for so long now.

She turned to the window again. It had become an imaginary escape in that moment. But it had offered her a promising and optimistic world during those young years.

Rose had spent her entire life in that house, and in front of that window. It'd been in her family for decades. She knew it and that window and nearly everything that passed in front of it, as well as every hope that unexpectedly slipped away. Not to mention every dream that disappeared through it.

Rose looked out at the expansive and reflective view again.

Tommy's red Mustang convertible was parked out front under the high summer sun. Rose watched as he checked his hair in the rearview mirror and adjust his collar before excitedly honking his horn. She purposely made him wait. Perhaps a bit too long, she thought now. How foolish she was then.

Later that night, he kissed her.

She watched herself tease him, playfully resisting his unskilled moves, until she finally gave in to his boyish embrace. She could still feel that kiss on her lips even now. And it was just as sweet and promising as it was then. Though the taste of chocolate milk had dissipated with the years, replaced now with a trace of stale beer. She finally pushed him away and said good night. Rose watched as he excitedly jumped into the convertible, kicking his heels in the air as he went over the door into the driver's seat.

Rose glanced again into the room behind her, wondering what it would have been like if it had been filled with his laughter, and not smothered as it had been for years with disappointment and pain. If Tommy hadn't died in Vietnam, her life would have been different, she thought. Instead, she ended up marrying a man without his smile or good nature, or even his good looks. The man she married was far less romantic; one who failed to even carry her over the threshold or take her on a long-awaited honeymoon. The man she married made promises for years that he never kept. And those years trailed behind her now with little more than regret as witness. The fact was, Rose never ventured further than the kitchen. She lived a loveless life, journeying back and forth to the refrigerator to make lunch or dinner for him. Or to fetch him a beer as he watched whatever game was on television. It wasn't how she pictured her life through that window. The truth was, she couldn't even recall his image in it. Or even her wedding day, for that matter. Her life with him was a lost reflection; one she could barely make out now as she glanced around the quiet room, measuring the misery it had generously given her. Because the stench of the pain was unmistakable.

Rose turned back to the window again in search of another small piece of her past to free her from the present, hoping to find the world that she had wanted. The one promised her. The one she'd expected to live. The one little girls dream about. The one that she watched as it disappeared with time.

It was also through that window that she watched her son Hugh grow-up. Just as she remembered her own life through it, she saw his. He was the single joy that helped ease the pain in her world. She watched him play with his best friend Jimmy. They were more like brothers. Friends forever. Until Jimmy eventually fell in love with a girl named Debbie, which broke Hugh's heart. It had been puppy love. But love nonetheless.

Mother's usually know their children better than they know themselves. Particularly in those early years before they escape into adolescence. For that reason, Rose knew it had been painful for Hugh to lose Jimmy like that. But she knew that day would come. Because she also knew Jimmy, and he wasn't like her boy. Not in that way. But still she hated to see her son so sad. And even more so because he'd grown up watching her be sad as well.

Rose recalled him bravely waving to her through the window the night he took a pretty girl named Rachel to the senior prom. She watched as he took someone that he not only didn't love to a dance, but who felt falsely decorated on his arm, as it went against not only his nature, but his basic design. Rose witnessed the pain her son carried through his teenage years, and she even attempted to carry that pain with him, if not for him. She remembered the day his was born and came home with him nestled in her arms. Rose held him when she could. In fact, she held him until his weight proved too much for her small frame. She held him because she loved him. But also, because she hoped her husband wouldn't hit her with a baby in her arms.

Rose watched another early summer day appear in the window.

Hugh excitedly waved as he and Elliot loaded their luggage into a taxi as they set off for an extended trip to Greece. She tried to persuade him that it wouldn't be good for him to make that kind of a journey, given his current condition. But he insisted he needed it more than anything, regardless of his illness, or how sick he might become. In the end, she conceded with anxious sobs and joyful tears. All she could do was pray that the trip would do him good and offer him a measure of peace. The boys were good together. Elliot was like a brother. Even more than Jimmy had been. But still she cried when they waved goodbye.

Rose had only recently acknowledged that she'd lived with more tears than her fragile body was designed to endure, and it was unmistakably reflected in every line on her face.

As she looked out the view changed again. And sadly so. She attempted to close her eyes to the harsh reality of it, but it was as vivid as the day she'd witnessed it. And it remained so, as it had been the most intrinsic pain in her life.

She turned again to the broken room behind her.

How different it looked now, she thought, in comparison to the life she nearly lived; the one that she dreamt about through the window during those younger years. Strangely, it still seemed viable, certainly deserved. But it all faded as the truth found its way into focus again. Not even her closed eyes could hide that painful glimpse of the hearse outside the house. Rose knew she would never be able to justify or forgive her son for what he'd done, as Elliot's words continued to haunt her even now. Just as they had when they echoed through that church corridor.

It was her son's death though, that finally gave Rose the courage, if not the fortitude, to do what she did; what she'd wanted to do for many years. But she had nothing to lose now. She had lost Hugh, and he was everything. Even the emptiness she felt in that moment was lost in the abyss.

Rose had hoped the future through that window would prove kinder to her son, than the one she was forced to see through it. But that would never be the case with him gone now.

There was one image left to shatter. The one reflected in the window in front of her now.

She heard the approaching sirens, just as she had the day the ambulance came for her stricken mother. Though they failed to save her as well.

Rose remained calm as they came through the open door.

Of course, she'd have preferred an old memory walk through it instead. One that would rescue her from the unfortunate choices she'd made. But it was too late for that now.

"He's been dead for some time."

"Can you determine the cause of death?"

"There are no visible wounds. He probably choked. There's still half a sandwich here."

"He's a big man. I doubt she could give him the Heimlich Maneuver."

"She looks pretty beaten up over it."

One of the men came closer.

"Are you all right, ma'am? I'm Officer Weston."

Rose barely heard him. His words were more a distant whisper.

"Can you tell us how you got these bruises, ma'am?"

She instinctively looked at the marks on her arms.

"She has abrasions on her neck as well. And some bleeding."

"Ma'am, can you hear me?"

"She's in shock. Probably devastated that she couldn't save him."

"Or perhaps more devastated if she had," his partner said.

"You think she…"

"I might think it. But I'm not writing it up that way."

They stood in front of the large window and watched as the paramedics carefully helped Rose into the back of the ambulance.

"I wouldn't give the bastard the satisfaction," he added.

Rose looked up at the window from the back of the ambulance. The sky and clouds reflected in it now as if it had all been a dream. But Rose knew the dream had died long ago while looking out the other side of it.

Chapter Fifteen

Candida in A Closed Café

Distracted by the sounds coming from the next apartment, Alec found it difficult to concentrate. In fact, it became a considerable challenge to fight off the imagery in his head.

"I received a Christmas card from her every year," he said. "Which was odd, since I hadn't seen her in over a decade. In fact, the last time I did, she was distant and somewhat removed. You can imagine how surprised I was then when the cards continued to arrive every year. But I was even more curious why they eventually stopped coming, than why she'd initially sent them."

"Did you stop sending her a card as well?"

"I continued to send them. I mean, who doesn't scramble to send out a card after receiving one, even at the last minute. I receive Christmas cards from people I've sent them to well into January sometimes. But I stopped getting cards from her a couple of years ago."

"Were you close?" Gus asked.

"We were for a while. But the mix of friends constantly changed on the island. Every year the group would be different. One determining factor was when someone arrived with friends, or a new romance. But they'd usually spend their time together. At least for the first week, which is wise. Because that island is a dangerous place to bring someone you love. Especially in the first year of a relationship."

The unmistakable sounds of a leggy woman walking up and down the hardwood floor in the next apartment interrupted their conversation. The thin walls only amplified her styled cadence as she paced back and forth like a gazelle in stilettos. At least that's how Alec pictured her; giving her the benefit of the doubt, if not the benefit of beauty. Though her rhythm seemed somewhat comical, as he envisioned her wobbling. Perhaps even using the wall for balance, as if practicing being a fashion model wearing unfamiliar footwear. But it was nearly three in the morning, so Alec knew that she was probably drunk as well.

Gus lightly stroked his fingers against the side of his forehead.

"Tell me more about Candida. You suggested there was a reason she'd sent you a card every year."

"I realized the cards were her way of knowing that I was still alive."

"As any friend would," Gus said.

"But I suspect it was more than that."

"How so?"

"I'm sure she was more concerned about my health. Rather our health. If you understand what I mean."

"I think I do," he said, taken by surprise. "So, you and Candida...?"

"Yes," Alec finally confessed.

Gus was justifiably humored by the news.

"Did she know you were gay?"

"Most of the men around her were. She liked the company of gay men. Besides, this was Greece."

"I'll assume to know what that means," he said, as he offered a curious smile. "But that's clever of her. Though imagine how shattered she'd have been if one of the cards she sent had been mistakenly returned to sender."

Alec laughed. "I'm sure that would have been unpleasant."

"Does she send many cards for that reason?"

"I'd like to think I'm the only one."

"I would imagine so. But why did she stop sending them?"

"She's alive, so it's not that." Alec smiled. "But it's been over a decade and the incubation period has undoubtedly passed. But there's also the possibility she fell in love and just decided to move on." Alec paused. Then added. "I'm negative anyway."

"You could have just told her that."

"I doubt she would have believed me. Besides, I like getting cards."

"Tell me," Gus asked, leaning forward. "How it is a gay man nailed a woman named Candida on a Greek Island?"

The stilettos made another dubious turn down the neighboring runway. They seemed even more challenged now than before.

"You would think someone would've bedded that broad by now," Alec said jokingly, hoping to avoid the question.

"She'll probably go down once the booze runs out," he said. Though he couldn't help but wonder what pain drove a woman to empty nearly every bottle within reach. He was sure she was also weighing her options. Perhaps even considering other men in other rooms. Though it would seem the idea of calling a taxi never occurred to her. But Gus wasn't easily distracted. And he was even more determined now to hear the rest of the story.

"I'm not leaving till you tell me more about Candida."

He knew he meant it, so Alec continued where he'd left off.

"We were a large group, as we were most nights. After dinner, we went for drinks down in the square. It was a normal evening on the island. And at the end of it, we headed back to our respective accommodations. And since our rooms were close, Candida and I usually walked back together along the harbor. That evening as we casually staggered past the closed and canopied cafes along the waterfront, she pulled me into the darkness of one of them and kissed me passionately. The kiss soon got deeper. And before I knew it, we were fully locked into it. Our bodies no doubt took over from there."

"No doubt."

"I remember the table I'd perched her on creaked so violently that I was sure it was going to collapse beneath us."

"Such sexual prowess. I'm impressed. A natural reflex, I imagine."

"More an instinctive one."

"Did you draw a crowd."

"A few stopped to watch for a moment as they passed-by. I've done it myself on occasion there. But I'm sure they didn't think much of it. That island can be a labyrinth of sexual activity at that hour of the night; both gay and straight."

"Did it get awkward afterwards?"

"She could barely keep her balance."

"Is that a testament?"

"Not necessarily. But she wasn't quite that way before."

Alec could barely hide a smile. Mostly because he hadn't been allowed to before. At least not openly.

"Kudos to you then. But was she okay afterwards?"

"She seemed a little put-off when she realized that her panties were still dangling from her finger."

"I guess she would be. What did she say?"

"She innocently asked what she was supposed to do with them."

"And what did she do with them?"

"I took her red thong and gently tucked it deep into her cleavage until it disappeared."

"Was she okay with that?"

"She seemed pleased enough."

"Anything else?" Gus obviously wanted more.

"She said, I guess that'll do."

"And that, was it?"

"That was it. We never spoke about it. Or did it again. It was as if it had never happened."

"Right," Gus said slapping is thighs as he got up. "I guess that'll do."

"That's all it took to get you revved and ready?"

"I only needed a boost. Though I never expected to get it from you."

"I'm happy to oblige." Alec smiled.

"Besides, I should get my ass next door before the girl kicks her heels off for some gay guy." Gus laughed.

"We're not all easily swayed," Alec said.

"Maybe so. But I won't chance it."

Gus was still laughing when he closed the door behind him.

Chapter Sixteen

Smart Alec

They sat up in bed talking afterwards…
  …one more breathless than the other.

"That was nice," Eric said.

"Nice?"

"You know what I mean."

"Sounds suspiciously vague," Alec said.

"Do you want me to say it was great?"

"Only if it was."

"Like I said, it was nice. Very nice, in fact."

"I've found sleeping with men different then sleeping with women."

"Having never slept with one, I wouldn't know. I assume it would be."

"It's harder to satisfy a woman. There are more dimensions to it."

"We all need to be satisfied."

"You know what I mean. It takes some maneuvering."

"As I said, I never slept with a woman. But it seems like a lot of work."

"They say you should like what you do."

"I thought that applied to what you did for a living?"

"Work is work." Alec offered a slight grin.

"But it still seems like a lot of trouble to me."

"Not if you enjoy it."

"Did you?"

"I wouldn't have done it if I didn't. Besides, it wasn't that often."

"That's good to hear."

"I have a friend who makes exceptions for exceptional women."

"Is that what you did?"

"I was usually less discriminating."

"Were you good at it?"

"I've been told I was," Alec said modestly.

"More than once?"

"One time in particular."

"What did she say?"

"That I was the best lover she'd ever had."

"She actually told you that?"

"Not exactly. She told a friend that."

"And this friend told you?"

"Apparently, they were sitting around one afternoon talking about sex, as women sometimes do. And the subject came up."

"It would seem men do too. So, you were the best lover she ever had."

"You find that hard to believe?"

"We just had sex. So maybe."

"All right, so it wasn't great for you. But was it okay?"

Eric didn't respond.

"It wasn't even okay?"

"It was fine." Eric smiled. "But it was just sex."

"Did you expect something more?"

"No. Not yet at least."

"You have to understand, sex for women goes to a deeper level."

"I imagine they're more emotional."

"They are."

"So, is it more of an accomplishment?"

"It's definitely more of a challenge."

"Perhaps."

"And it obviously meant something to her."

"How was it for you though?"

"Truthfully, I don't really remember," Alec confessed.

"Would you tell her that?"

"Why would I?"

"Keep your kudos close, I always say. I completely understand. But if you don't recall, then maybe it wasn't all that great after all." Eric laughed.

"Apparently, it was for her."

"Maybe she met someone who's made more of an impression on her."

"I doubt it."

"Why?"

"She was married at the time she said it. And she's still married."

"And there's no chance her husband improved his technique?"

"Doesn't the opposite happen the longer you're married?"

"Remind me not to propose."

Alec rested his head lightly on his shoulder.

"You don't think that she's cheated with someone? Someone better, perhaps? Or did she recently reaffirm your sexual prowess?"

"I told you, I don't go there anymore."

"That's right. You no longer know the way."

Alec lifted his head and looked at him.

"Exactly. But why are you spoiling this for me?"

"I'm just curious why you find it so important."

"It's nice to know I could do that for someone."

"Perhaps whoever she compared you to were just awful in bed."

"That never crossed my mind." Alec pushed into his shoulder.

"Why would it?"

"Exactly."

"Tell me. Have you done the same things to me that you did to her?"

"That's not entirely possible."

"I guess not. But what I mean is, as far as you could?"

"You don't feel I gave it my best, do you?"

"I know you'd like to add to your kudos. Should I huddle with the boys and sing your praises?"

"Only if it's true. But you need to understand, I do different things with different people, with different equipment."

"Were there limitations with me that you didn't have with her?"

"The equipment is different. What goes on in our heads, not to mention what goes into them, is different. I do things with you I didn't with her."

"I'm sure she never said, suck my dick."

Alec laughed.

"As a matter of fact, she did once. When she was angry."

"That's a rather odd thing for a woman to say, don't you think? But old habits are hard to break, I imagine. It would seem removing the dick doesn't necessarily remove one's intrinsic reference to it. I'm sure it's like having your leg amputated, and that phantom feeling that makes you think it's still there. No surprise then, that it was on the tip of her tongue."

"She wasn't transitioning." Alec playfully pushed into him again.

"The newly transitioned are not usually as demanding when it comes to sex. Not in the beginning, at least. I'm guessing that she'd be appreciative of even the worst of it. Until she learns the game, that is. If you sleep with her again, I suggest that you hang on, as I'm sure she's more experienced now. No wonder she was impressed with your sexual prowess."

"She wasn't transitioning," he said again. Though it made him think for a moment.

"How do you know?"

"She mentioned having had a miscarriage," Alec recalled.

"Easily said. But not as easy as actually having one."

"Why are you fighting me on this?"

"I'm just teasing. Though I can't help but question your cockiness."

"Very funny. But you still don't think I put my heart into it, do you?"

"I can't help but compare the experiences. That's all."

"That was years ago. I doubt I'd even know what to do now."

"Are you saying you lost your technique?"

"Of course not."

"Maybe I'm just not getting what that younger man had to offer."

"I thought it got better with age?"

"You're thinking of wine and cheese."

"Speaking of food. Are you hungry?"

"What?"

"Suddenly, I have an appetite."

"I couldn't eat right now."

"Are you upset?"

"No, I just don't like sleeping on a full stomach."

Alec pulled him closer.

"Then let me have another go at it. I promise I'll do better."

"Give it your best shot," Eric said. But that'd been his motive all along.

Alec was certain it would be better the second time. Just as he was sure if he'd had the same conversation with Warren it would have gotten ugly. Even physical. And not in a good way either. His life was better now, and less chaotic without Warren in it. Especially after having narrowly escaped being set up by him at the Athens airport, where Alec was hauled off by customs' agents after Warren had cleverly slipped drugs into his suitcase the morning they left the island. It was a cruel and vindictive thing to do, even for him. Thankfully, Alec had a second prescription; however questionable its legitimacy since it wasn't specifically for Vicodin. Though in the end, he skillfully fabricated an excuse, explaining the other bottle broke and that he forgot he'd put them in a plastic bag. Regardless, he still missed his flight. Though it was probably for the best as there would've undoubtedly been a scene if he'd caught up with Warren, resulting in both being kicked off the plane, and left in yet another dubious situation together.

In the end though, Alec was detained for only a short period of time, as they were more concerned with confiscating hard drugs than in the few pain pills that he had with him. But Alec paid a harsh price nonetheless, as it was enough of a questionable offense to ban him from entering the country in the future, which also meant the island.

The conversation he had with Eric went better than anticipated. Though he purposely didn't mention that night with Candida on the island. It would have only complicated matters and given Eric a reason to doubt him in the future. It would have also exposed his spontaneous, if not vulnerable side. A quality; however impromptu, he considered a part of his character, one he'd never deny himself. He also knew that Eric would have found the scenario in the café just as comical as Gus had, though, probably not as stimulating. But he couldn't risk telling him. Besides, he'd shared too much information as it was about his sexual escapades with women. Alec also hoped to leave that part of his life behind. But he had to admit that it felt good being honest about some of it at least.

It took several years before Alec missed the island routine. But he also knew that it was a dangerous place to bring a relationship. Especially if you wanted to spend the rest of your life together since few survived there, as he'd witnessed on numerous occasions. The truth was, a thousand tan, naked men can challenge even the most trusted and dedicated relationship; just as one woman had.

Alec was aware of how unforgiving the island could be. And it was for that reason he insisted he and Warren go back that summer. He would let the island do his dirty work for him, without the stability of house and home to persuade them to salvage the little that was left of their relationship, as it had before. In fact, Alec counted on Warren to revisit his suspicions concerning Candida. He had even helped to nurture and facilitate those suspicions by fabricating a dream about kissing a sleeping princess. The truth was, he was confident in the effectiveness of his kiss if ever called upon to awaken either a prince or princess.

Having dealt with Warren's jealous nature on numerous occasions, he depended on that jealousy to break them apart. But he hadn't anticipated Warren being so vengeful. Though perhaps he should have since he knew he was capable of almost anything. Nor could he have predicted their being so boldly burgled while they slept. Or for that matter, the consequences that resulted from it, which led to his being banned from the island. But he knew it was for the best if he ever hoped to hold onto a lasting relationship.

Alec had always thought of the island as a beautiful and never-ending dream; one filled with over two decades of cherished memories. But it was a dream he knew he'd eventually need to wake from; however reluctantly if he was ever going to have a loving and promising future.

* * *

As a self-published author who is destined to make roughly ten cents an hour in writing this book, which undoubtedly makes minimum wage seem a cherished fortune; if you enjoyed reading it, then perhaps you could suggest it to a friend, or blog about it. Or post a review wherever possible.

If you didn't, well, then never mind.

Available on: www.lulu.com

www.ingramcontent.com/pod-product-compliance
Lightning Source LLC
Chambersburg PA
CBHW031216020726
47499CB00002B/606